Praise for the Et

On Yesteri

[Danielle Ackley-McPhail] certainly seems to ......
— Piers Anthony, bestselling author of the *Xanth* series

Yesterday's Dreams and Danielle's writing style is like a warm blanket you wrap
yourself in to keep off the chill — comforting, deep, and welcoming.
— Tee Morris, co-author of *Phoenix Rising*

A powerful, poignant tale...a writer of talent, imagination, and
superb storytelling ability. — The Midwest Book Review

"Yesterday's Dreams is an interesting mix of Celtic myth, women's empowerment
literature, and urban fantasy...The story, though set in a modern period, is imbued
with all the details and richness that readers expect from Celtic lore."
— John Ottinger III, Grasping For The Wind Reviews

"This novel will appeal to fans of Charles DeLint with its urban approach
to Irish mythology. At times I was mesmerized while at other times...
I had to get up and turn the lights on..." — Bitten By Books Reviews

"Yesterday's Dreams is an engaging book...As a reader, you don't want to miss a
word. ...Yes, the roller coaster eventually stops. Yes, you are much disoriented as
you look up from the pages of the novel. Yes, as a child would, you want to ride
the roller coaster again." — Urban Fire Book

On Tomorrow's Memories

"The artist in me itches to have a crack at some of the vivid images that are
filling my brain after reading this book. I am eagerly awaiting another installment.
Please make it soon!" — Helen Fleischer, artist

"Danielle Ackley-McPhail seems to get better with every book...I didn't want
(Tomorrow's Memories) to end, and I'm looking forward to reading the third
novel of the trilogy." — Douglas Cobb, BookspotCentral

Dark Quest Books
With Danielle Ackley-McPhail

The Eternal Cycle Series
Tomorrow's Memories
Today's Promise

The Bad-Ass Faerie Tale Series
The Halfling's Court
The Redcap's Queen

The Defending the Future Series
Breach the Hull
So It Begins
By Other Means
No Man's Land
Best Laid Plans
Dogs of War

The Legends of A New Age Series
Dragon's Lure
Eternal Flame

In An Iron Cage: the Magic of Steampunk

A Legacy of Stars

The Literary Handyman:
Tips on Writing From Someone Who's Been There

LaToya,

Dream Big!

[signature]

Danielle Ackley-McPhail

Yesterday's Dreams

Book One in the Eternal Cycle Series

Dark Quest, LLC

Howell, New Jersey

PUBLISHED BY
Dark Quest, LLC
Neal Levin, Publisher
23 Alec Drive,
Howell, New Jersey 07731
www.darkquestbooks.com

ISBN (trade paper): 978-1-937051-07-5

Originally published in different versions by
Vivisphere Publishing and Mundania Press.

Interior Design: Danielle McPhail
Sidhe na Daire
www.sidhenadaire.com

Interior Art: Musical Notes ©Soleilc http://www.dreamstime.com/

Cover Art: L.W. Perkins and Christina Yoder
Cover Design: Christina Yoder

Copyediting: Elektra Hammond
www.untilmidnight.com

DEDICATION

To Peter Cooper.

Thanks for seeing the potential all those many years ago.

To Neal Levin.

Thanks for resurrecting and perfecting it.

PRELUDE

The two men walked the crowded Manhattan streets with guarded care. One led, his dull brown eyes averted, darting everywhere, but they always slid away before another's gaze could capture him. Beneath a torn and crusted flannel jacket—one that had long ago ceased to be useful—his shoulders hunched and tensed. His careworn face was haunted as he clutched his companion's hand. Suddenly, as if nirvana were in sight, he dashed for a night-shrouded alley, dragging the other man behind. As they scurried away, billowing steam rose from out of nowhere to cut the alley off from view of the street.

Dropping into a crouch in the shadow of a dumpster, the vagrant ran trembling hands through his lank hair, the color indeterminate beneath years of grime. "They're following us, they are...hurts, the burning hurts, the eyes sting...they can't help it you know...nope, they can't help it, in their nature...no one sees them but Angus and Angus says to run, he says 'Gerry'—that's me, buddy—'Gerry, just run, because they're *right* behind you.' They have to do it, but we can't let them see us...have to hide, buddy, have to hide." Gerry continued to babble, forgetting for a moment that he was trying to avoid attention. He punctuated his words by wildly slashing his hands through the air. One clanged against the battered and rusted side of the trash bin. Beside him, his friend sat placidly, unmoving save for the occasional sluggish blink, until finally the vacant-eyed unfortunate rolled his head to stare with vague interest at the sound. Gerry just kept muttering.

"Come on, can't stay here, he'll sniff us out...yeah regular bloodhound, gotta move, buddy, can't let them get us...Sell our body parts to the voodoo guy down on Christopher Street he will...I betcha he will...or something like that."

Gerry had to haul his friend up, grunting and cursing as the simpleton slowly came to his feet, his watery blue eyes showing nothing as he moved through the world in a dream state. Nothing Gerry tried could draw him into a more hurried pace. They went up the fire escape and then in, climbing through a gap offered by a once-boarded window three stories up. Looking back only once, Gerry trembled as the alley continued to fill with an unnatural fog.

"...Long time ago, this used to be a brothel, you know, doesn't look like much now, but the best five bucks I ever spent...ain't no more 'birds' here...hehehe...but maybe we can find a pigeon...pigeon would go real nice right now.... Naw, gotta keep moving, can't let him see us...no, that wouldn't be good, no way. Come on, buddy, have to hide, for Chrissake!" Gerry ended his fractured diatribe and began to sing to himself. Song had always been a comfort to him, no matter what his situation. He sang softly all the way up twenty-five flights of stairs. His companion only hummed, very low and disjointed, as he rubbed the empty ring finger on his left hand. He did not even look up when they burst through the door leading to the rooftop.

Dark, ominous clouds hung low on the horizon, thrown into stark relief by the glow of distant lightning. In the immediate area, the static built to an uncomfortable charge, making the air crackle like an angry insect swarm. Gasping and jerking his hand out of Gerry's grip, the silent one huddled in a crumbling corner of the rooftop, transfixed by the flashes. Frantically, he continued to stroke his finger, bobbing back and forth with growing agitation. His battered soul had climbed out of limbo only to perch on the edge of insanity, unaware of the tingle across his scalp and the way every unhindered hair on his body rose. A shock of matted black hair set off his pale, stark face like a mask and faded blue eyes glowed like a beacon in the darkness. His shackled potential was more than tempting. What it drew down upon him was beyond anything his fractured mind could take. Insanity claimed the man completely.

Beside him, Gerry yipped like a startled dog, ending with a gurgle and a gaping mouth. His eyes grew wild and his blue-tinged tongue swelled until it protruded from his lips. Slowly, as if lifted at the end of an invisible and powerful arm, Gerry rose in the air until he dangled above a large pile of rubble. It felt as if something crushed his chest until he felt bones break and flesh rip. His brown eyes darkened with despair and tried to plead eloquently with the thin air, for his arrested voice could not.

In moments it was over. A sharp shake, like a rat in a terrier's jaws, and Gerry's neck snapped. His body fell from the air, his lifeblood streaming over the pile of masonry as if it were an ancient altar and he the sacrifice; the only thing missing was the chanting.

Drifting from above the corpse to hover instead over the supine form of the now-mad man was a cold, dark shadow—a density that made the patch of night around it darker than could be accounted for by the clouds, a swath of blackness that was not lightened by the periodic flickers in the sky. A menacing presence added to the weight of the humidity and a feeling of waiting filled the night.

Heralded by an explosive clap of thunder, a truly amazing display of lightning crackled across the evening sky, lighting up everything below it with a cold, harsh glare. In that energized flash a homeless man whose name had long ago been forgotten completed an act of slow death that had begun with his life on the streets—and Lucien Blank was born. Both wore the same face.

Unnoticed by the world, a gaunt figure rose, as if compelled, from the corner of a crumbling roof and raised its eyes to the universe. With trance-like motions, it ripped away the filthy, tattered clothes it wore, dropping them carelessly from numb fingers. A startling transformation took place when it closed its eyes and raised its arms to the sky. The pure electrical power dancing through the heavens rushed toward the naked embrace, sending streams of raw current through the emaciated form, scorching the very air as the man twitched and screamed with the awesome energy. Ruthlessly, he was remolded by the pure, burning power, held upright as his very shape was sculpted by the demanding, brutal force.

As if this were a signal, the clouds let loose a flood of freezing rain to drench the skyline. The new creation merely stood beneath the violent downpour and shed the final remnants of its former self as completely as it had discarded its clothing just moments before. The thunderstorm rinsed away the thick, encrusted dirt from twitching limbs that grew less skeletal with each passing second. Black, matted hair fell away in clumps, leaving only smooth, silvery stubble. When the last strands floated away toward the gutter, the transformed creature collapsed with the same abruptness as a marionette whose strings had been cut, banging the back of its head on the broken masonry.

The hovering power swelled with malevolent anticipation, a growing darkness against the clouds of the city sky. All was in order; now to complete the picture. Materializing in the corner where earlier the man had huddled, positioned as if it had been franticly hidden beneath the rubble, was a monogrammed wallet filled with identification. Quickly, more items appeared, setting the stage with appropriate props. In the stairwell, expensive but commonplace clothes were artfully scattered, as if dropped in a panic by startled thieves. In the alley, a briefcase full of documents waited to be found. Among the contents was a newly signed lease for a building in Chinatown. The name on the lease was Lucien Blank.

The victim's memories—what was left of them—were wiped clean, disrupted by the immense force that had been released this night, leaving its mind ready for the power to shape. Enough clues and identification had been scattered to ensure that even without a memory, this new creation would be positioned well enough to be effective.

The timing was perfect; just as the last dregs of energy were used, a helicopter passed overhead. In a flash of lightning, an illusion of movement fluttered by the door to the stairwell, drawing the pilot's eye. The plan was well begun as the police helicopter engaged its spotlight, discovering the "crime scene."

The power known as Olcas faded into the background to bide its time. While it rebuilt its strength, it would use its leisure to sculpt this new tool, as well as to gather its resources. As Lucien Blank was taken away on a stretcher, one last burst of lightning lit the scene brilliantly. There was time—plenty of time.

Chapter I

Tossing restlessly as the grey, pre-dawn light crept into her room, Kara
smoothed back her damp, tangled bangs. As she lay strung out from yet another
troubled night, her mind circled again to the growing pile of collection notices
on her desk. Any day now, she feared a foreclosure notice would join them. Each
time the mailman turned up their front walk, Kara held her breath, and each
night she stared at the ceiling, wondering what would come with the next day.

Her parents were already stressed over her father's health. Once he'd grown
too ill to work, keeping their financial head above water had gotten harder and
harder. It didn't help that each time they turned around, some household crisis
complicated matters. Last week it was the death of the refrigerator; the week
before that it was burst pipes. Now there was a balloon payment due on the
mortgage, and they did not have it.

Kara did the best she could. Moving back home and getting a job helped, but
she had been foolish to think it would be enough. She'd tried hiring out with
Quicksilver for parties and events, but there wasn't enough demand for a solo
violinist to make the effort lucrative. Busking in the subway hadn't been much
better; way too erratic, no matter how good she was. Finally, she had been
fortunate. An instructor left the school where Kara had learned her craft, and the
Director offered her the position.

Her entire salary, minus her own small expenses, went toward her father's
medical bills just so Mathair could put her wages toward everything else. But
Kara didn't make all that much as a music teacher, and her schedule made it
difficult to hold down a second job. She had had four since she'd left...since
she'd come home. Always, she juggled her obligations, shorting herself on sleep
and a personal life, quiting the sword training she'd used for exercise and enjoyment, anything to make a complicate job schedule work, until something gave
and she found herself without a part-time job once more.

It had happened again last night. The scene replayed itself in her mind.

The store was really busy. Kara tried to scurry past the front counter while Mr. Amed was helping Mrs. Kopeki. Maybe he wouldn't notice her; maybe he didn't know she wasn't already here. Maybe she would wake up tomorrow and Papa would be magically as healthy as a twenty-year-old again. Yeah, right!

"Kara...I would like a word with you in my office once you've clocked in." Mr. Amed's voice was calm and pleasant, but Kara was in no doubt that that was only because of all the customers.

"Yes, Mr. Amed." She could feel the blood drain from her face. She had tried so hard to be on time...she would have made it too, if Amy Perkins' mother hadn't cornered her outside the Music Center to hint that Precious Amy should definitely have her own solo in the next recital. Kara squelched her anger. She didn't have the energy for it right now; besides, it wouldn't make any difference. Throwing her purse into one of the battered lockers lined up along the far wall, Kara yanked her smock over her head and punched her time card. She couldn't hold back her dejected sigh as she left the locker room and headed for Mr. Amed's office.

"Kara, what are we doing here, yet again?"

How did he always manage to sound so unruffled? "I'm sorry, Mr. Amed. It w..."

"Don't say it! Don't even say it! We both know it is not true." *Okay...unruffled until she opened her mouth and said the wrong thing.* Gone was the pleasantness; her boss's words were biting. "Am I not a reasonable man, Kara? Have I not given you a job you desperately need? All I ask in return is that you actually be here to do it!

"Do you realize that in the month you've worked here you have called out no less than three times? And that you have been late six times? We are not just talking about a few minutes here or a few there, you are half-an-hour late today, Kara. What more do you want of me?"

Kara didn't even attempt to respond; it would only infuriate him more. By will alone she kept herself calm and composed, standing there silently as he went on and on. The only way she could even hope to come out of this still holding her job was if she didn't antagonize him any more.

"You receive more preferential treatment than any other girl who works for me because I respect your family and I understand what you are all going through, but I have a business to run here. I need to know that my staff is reliable, dependable. What am I to do?"

He went on for another fifteen minutes; she called out too often at the last minute...she couldn't work the schedules he gave her...she was consistently late or having to leave early... Kara had to admit how bad it sounded. She was ashamed to be seen in such a light, regardless of the legitimate reasons, but what choice did she have? Papa came first.

Determined to give Mr. Amed no further cause to be dissatisfied with her, Kara threw herself into her tasks that night. Fronting the aisles with efficiency and speed, restocking the soft drink cooler without being reminded, putting away the returns in record time. By the time she punched her time card she was exhausted. And yet it was for nothing. She was chatting with Susie, the other cashier working that night, as they both started down the stairs to leave.

"A moment, Kara," Mr. Amed's neutral voice rang out from his office, startling both of them. "Susie, we will meet you down by the door."

"Yes, sir?" Kara stopped at the threshold.

Mr. Amed held something out to her and she felt dread settle heavily upon her chest. When he finally spoke, she could clearly hear his regret. "I'm sorry, Kara, truly, but I must let you go."

She just stared at him, and the check in his hand, without even the energy to try and mask the bleakness of her expression. *What would she tell her parents? They would understand, there was no doubt of that, but it was going to add to their already considerable worries.*

"Take it." He stood and came closer, the envelope before him.

Kara could hear the hint of compassion beneath his unyielding tone, though it would not do her much good. Friendships aside, this was business, and no matter how bad Mr. Amed felt, or how much of a family friend he was, he was a businessman first. With numb fingers, she took the check from him, only half noticing that it was a full week's pay, even though the pay period had just begun.

"But..."

"Just take it and go, my dear. I may have to let you go, but that does not mean I do not understand what you are going through. It is the least I can do."

It didn't feel right, just taking the extra money. They might be having difficulties, but the O'Keefes had their pride. "I will work out the rest of the week."

"No. Do not even bother to say so; something else will only come up." His tone was not cruel, but it hurt Kara just the same, knowing he was likely right. "Now go on, before Susie gets tired of waiting."

Guilt pricked Kara as the memory played through her thoughts. She sighed, feeling yet another tension headache coming on. Despite her best intentions, this continued to happen, even when Papa was feeling well. Her unconventional schedule at the Music Center always complicated any part-time job she tried to hold. She supposed it was selfish, really, refusing to give up her teaching position. What she made in a week didn't come close to what her father used to bring home with overtime from the docks. It would make much more sense to quit and get two full-time jobs somewhere else. Even at minimum wage, an arrangement like that would bring in more money than teaching did. *But could she bring herself to sacrifice her music right along with everything else?* It was such an important part of her—vital, even.

The thought alone made her ill. Kara pushed aside the matter and threw off the tangled blankets. Her eyes wandered the room in desperate hope for some inspiration she might have overlooked before. The dense shadows lessened as the morning light grew, but even in the pitch darkness of a mere hour ago, Kara knew what lay in each corner of her room. In the past few weeks, everything she owned had been measured with a critical eye that revealed nothing of much worth. She knew the lack of potential in her short life's assorted landmarks. She was surrounded by childhood toys that bore the scars of youthful affection, the high school mementos that held meaning only for her, her battered practice swords, and a jewelry box containing nothing of intrinsic value. There was nothing...nothing at all that could be translated into financial resources. Unless...unless she bowed beneath her earlier admission and gave up her music.

A gracefully curved silhouette by the window captured Kara's eye and wouldn't let it go. Her heart clenched and she felt icy tingles run across her shoulder. Could that be the only answer? Had she reached the point where she could not dismiss the traitorous idea that had first come to her two weeks ago? It had been impossible then, but if she gave notice at the center, there would be nothing to prevent her.

Kara swallowed against surging nausea and climbed from her cold bed to run a hand across the leather case containing Quicksilver. The violin was her only legacy from her grandfather, handed over to her by her father when she had learned enough to do it justice. It was one of Papa's few comforts in these trying times. She looked toward the growing pile of papers on her desk. They stood out in stark whiteness against the thinning dark, pushing her to make the hardest decision she had yet to face in her twenty-three years.

Dressing quickly, she spared a glance at the alarm clock. It was barely 6 a.m. For a moment, Kara nearly lost her resolve. Nothing would be open at this time of day, but if she didn't leave now she risked discovery and her plans would end before they'd even begun. Choking back a sob, Kara grabbed the case in one hand, her jacket in the other, and hurried out her bedroom door. Papa would never forgive her, but Quicksilver was the only thing she possessed of any value, besides her family. To Kara, there was no contest between the two.

As she made her way through the near-deserted streets of Richmond Hill, Cliodna moved with purpose, her muscles taut and her gaze intent. Tension swirled about her like a gathering storm. She was so wound up, in fact, that she hadn't stopped to wonder at how long it had been since she had thought of herself by that name; the name that belonged to another life, the name of her oath. It made no matter how dusty it was with disuse: she was a hunter today, and the name went along with those primal skills. Her ancient birthright threatened to show through her glamor's thinning veil, glorious and terrifying.

"Come on, catling! Must I wait all day?" she muttered, her voice lovelier than an angel's, though her raw nerves gave it an edge. "Busy are we, then? Never mind...I'll just find out for myself, shall I? What are a few less hours to make a difference?"

The woman struggled to rein in her frustration. The tension was taking its toll. It wasn't the cat's fault. All Cliodna knew was that she was driven and anxious...had been for some time now, years even, though it had gotten worse over the last week. There was nothing so distinct as a vision or an omen to blame. That would be easier to bear; a nice clear mental image to reveal the precise threat to her charges.

But no, that would be too easy, make too much sense.

Tossing her fiery tresses, she stalked the sleeping neighborhood, hunting threats. Her attempts to control her agitation were abandoned. If she'd had a tail, it would be twitching.

She made a final circuit of the block before stopping in front of a house intimately familiar to her, though that knowledge would have shocked those living there. The green trim was faded, the white siding was dingy with the passage of time, but the place was clean and tidy despite its obvious age. Everything about it, from the green plaque and its brass street numbers, to the neat flowerbeds, marked this place as more a home than simply a house. True, one that had seen a touch too much strife, but a home nonetheless.

With an ease born of centuries of practice, Cliodna reached out her esoteric skills, caressing the magical tripwires that laced the structure. In seconds, the protections were revitalized, mage energy making them glitter as the sun brightened the morning sky. She doubted any beyond herself could see her handiwork, but then, she was the one needing reassurance right now. Perhaps with the wards at full force, she would shed some of her anxiety. Perhaps...

Cliodna sighed. Her eyes scanned the façade, coming to settle on the second floor. There, in an upper window, a frantic little marmalade cat pawed at the glass. And here she had been thinking such uncharitable thoughts about the creature. It calmed immediately as she caught its eye, going from clawing at the pane to rubbing against it.

"No fret, catling," she murmured reassuringly. "There's no help for it. Soon enough..."

The cat went wild, mewing pitifully as Cliodna turned away, until she could hear the ruckus even from the street. She swore and tensed once more. The distance might be too great to convey particulars, but something was definitely wrong.

Caught up in the second-story antics, Cliodna barely fell back in time, hiding herself across the street in plain sight, cloaked by the *Fe-Feida*, supernatural mists older than time itself. She swore yet again, much more creatively this time, as a young girl slipped out the front door, clearly taking great efforts to close it quietly. With a trained eye, Cliodna took in every detail. There were no tears streaming down the youthful cheeks, but the amber eyes were feverishly bright and the jaw clenched. Her too-pale face glowed beneath waves of tousled, dark brown hair.

For a long moment, the girl stood on the stoop, her expression haunted. Cliodna experienced a disquieting thrill. Cradled in the girl's arms was an item that radiated both age and power. An object more familiar to Cliodna than it was to the girl herself.

Damn! What was going on? Cliodna could sense the lass's turmoil from here, nearly tangible upon swirling currents of raw power. Knowing something of her troubles, Cliodna could well understand the strain, the burden on those slight shoulders, hunched and taut. Yet something more was wrong here. This was not an early start to the day, not with the fatalistic tension charging the air.

"What merry chase do we begin now, child?" She murmured to herself as she waited for the girl put some distance between them before falling in behind.

Energy pulsed, flowing through the rooftop greenhouse in ever-diminishing waves. Fear and pain and hunger flavored the air as Lucien drew one final rune on the naked belly of his slave, careful to exactly duplicate the lines prescribed in his newest tome. It was done.

Normally, he wouldn't bother performing the cleansing rite to protect the slave against the demon he'd summoned. But she still held some use for him. Were she left unprotected, the creature would feed on her indiscriminately through the link she'd been instrumental in forging.

Wiping her blood from his fingertip, he motioned for her to rise and turned back to gather up the newest gem of his secret library. The book had been quite a find. Well worth the outrageous sum he paid for the auction lot of items that were useless to him, bid upon for just this treasure. Closer examination revealed it to be a grimoire on summoning lesser demons.

A cold smile lit his face as he looked in the shadowy corner of the greenhouse, where his very first demon slowly absorbed the bowl of blood Lucien had tapped from the slave. *Yes, precious, drain it dry,* Lucien thought smugly, *just a little more and you will be bound to me completely.*

Lucien turned away as the last drop of crimson faded from the bowl. The ritual was complete. He need waste no more of his morning on it. With the demon secured against rebellion, there was nothing more to do here; now Lucien would please himself.

"Return to the room, girl, and wait for me as you have been taught."

Without even looking, he picked up her robe and tossed it toward her, magnanimously allowing her to dress before she crossed the long expanse of roof to reenter the building. Yes, he was very pleased with the morning's results. Besides, it amused him to be gracious; it unsettled her so.

Power thrummed through him, glorious and addictive; there could never be enough. Lucien sauntered to the parapet wall edging the roof and stopped to scan the city spread before him. His black satin robe fluttered in the autumn breeze revealing bare flesh beneath, as smooth and perfect as polished marble. Irreverently, the wind ruffled his white-blonde hair, but nothing could dispel the intensity of his expression. There were thousands upon thousands of energy sources hidden away in this modern warren of society, waiting for him to claim them. He couldn't see them, but he knew they were there. From those that pulsed most gently, to others that pounded like a drum beat. The knowledge taunted him.

And then there was the city itself. It had taken his life, his identity, his well being, and only by extreme determination had he reclaimed any of it. His teeth clenched and the muscles of his jaw worked silently. Ten years had passed since he'd lost his memory, and he had barely scratched the surface of the man he had been. Much had been taken from him and little reclaimed, but it would not be thus much longer. With each passing day, he grew stronger, more powerful, and soon he would unleash his simmering retribution. Let the creature that was New York City think he had been cowed...when he discovered the key to the dark, cryptic knowledge in his collection, Lucien would possess every bit of power within his reach. Only then would he be finished with this place. With that power he would be reborn and the city's arrogant skyscrapers would be nothing more than rubble beneath his feet.

Contemptuously turning his back on the skyline, Lucien descended into his lair.

He did not stop on the top floor, though that was where the girl waited for him. She was but a slave and he the master. Whenever he chose to join her in their playroom, he would find her naked, on her knees, her back to the door and her forehead planted firmly on the ground. There would be an array of implements beside her—carefully arranged by her own hand—all ready for his use. He knew she would remain that way until he arrived, not moving for anything, lest he come in to find her not ready for him. That had happened once. It would not happen again.... Today, it amused him to picture her trembling with the strain throughout the long hours, not knowing when he would enter.

For now he went past, taking the stairs down two flights to his office on the second floor. He had a business to consider, after all, aside from his private goals. Perhaps today was the day for some hunting? He had not circulated much lately. Time to put in an appearance at Sotherby's, or better yet, Swann's Galleries, closer to the Village. Not that he expected to find much. The general auctions were an indulgence. As an estate broker, his official work was tied into the daily obituaries. But the offerings were rather sparse recently. Of course, he didn't really expect much before the holidays; that was when despair and excitement churned things up nicely. In the meantime, he made a token appearance now and then, and worked on expanding his private collection.

Taking a moment to clean up in the attached bathroom, a naked Lucien returned to his office and opened the Victorian wardrobe by the door. Inside was the outfit he'd left there before going up to the roof this morning, a black silk shirt and pressed slacks that would be perfect for his planned excursion. Dressing quickly, Lucien pulled on a charcoal grey blazer to finish the ensemble and considered his reflection in the antique mirror angled in the corner. Quite respectable, as devastating as ever, but then, he had expected nothing less than perfection.

Lucien wasted no more time on appearance. He settled down at his desk and flipped open the classifieds. One or two promising auctions caught his eye, but most singularly lacked any potential to forward his professional or personal interests. He would take himself to a few, throw out a couple of bids, and then return to the Village to browse through the pawnshops. Maybe he could find something there to salvage the day; much of his private library came from such ventures.

Unfolding himself gracefully from his chair, Lucien tore the page from the paper and placed it folded in the pocket of his blazer. It had taken him years to expand his resources and rebuild the life he had nearly lost on a rain-drenched rooftop a decade ago. There had been plenty of time to plan his vengeance when he was learning to walk again. The hour of retribution was nearly here.

Running aching fingers through his curly, silver-shot red hair, Patrick O'Keefe shifted himself carefully on the paper-covered exam table. He was merely here for a check-up and test results, but just sitting there fully clothed gave him flashbacks to his months of cancer treatments. The sensation was unsettling.

"Where the hell are ye, Arn?"

Each second he sat there, he expected the jab of a needle or some other discomfort. He hated the feel of his sweat-moistened palms sticking to the paper. Each time he moved, the protective cover crackled with a noise that grated on his nerves. It would be quite some time before he could sit on an examination table without experiencing extreme anxiety—if ever.

The truth was he didn't really want to know if he was out of remission. Patrick was tired of cancer and medication running his life. If the cancer was going to win anyway, he wanted to enjoy the time he had left, not spend it fighting until he didn't know which made him feel worse: the treatment or the disease. He'd only shown up because he'd promised Arn. With anyone else, Patrick would have probably broken that promise; all of this unsettled him that much. But it wasn't anyone else. Arn Barnert was his best friend.

When Kate, the physician's assistant, brought Patrick to this room to wait, she had told him Arn would be with him in just a moment. After an hour, Patrick was beyond ready to give up. The nurse hadn't even been in yet to take care of the normal stuff she did before the doctor saw him. He was anxious enough as it was, without that break in routine.

Gripped by an overwhelming desire to be elsewhere, Patrick stepped off the exam table and reached for the jacket he'd draped over the chair. It was time to go home now, to the comfort of his wife and daughter. Besides, the longer he waited, the more certain he was that he didn't want to hear the results.

He had intended to invite Arn to lunch when this was over, but the way he felt right now food probably wasn't such a good idea. Before he could reach for the handle, the door opened, as if on cue.

"And where do you think you're going?" Dr. Arnold Barnert stood with one hand still on the knob and the other one planted on his hip. "Didn't Katie tell you I'd be right in? I would have been in sooner but Mrs. Taylor called," Arn looked like he was caught between amusement and annoyance. "Apparently she found wherever her husband hid her copy of *The Physician's Desk Reference*.

"Why is it the woman has enough intelligence to figure out most of what's in there, but lacks the common sense to finish reading the description before letting herself get worked up?"

Just standing there, self-consciously shifting his weight from one foot to the other like a guilty child, trying to figure out which direction held his best chance at escape, Patrick chuckled dutifully.

"I swear that woman can be a nuisance. She kept me on the phone for half-an-hour this time. I'm going to have to call her husband and tell him to come up with a better hiding place." Then, without even a pause, Arn reached for the chart on the door with one hand and pushed Patrick back toward the table with the other. "So, back to you. Have a seat, my friend, you know the drill."

With a sigh, Patrick settled himself back on the table and watched as Arn turned toward his equipment. He'd almost gotten away. Resigned, he started rolling up his sleeve. They went through this every time he came in. Arn didn't even need to prompt him anymore. Perhaps that was why mental alarms began to go off when, instead of pulling out the cuff Patrick expected, Arn turned around with a rubber tourniquet in his hands. There was a syringe ready on the counter behind him. Normally Arn didn't draw the blood samples, but this was obviously an ambush. Patrick's panic must have written itself clearly across his face.

"Now, Pat, just relax," Arn said, as he reached for the arm Patrick had conveniently exposed for him, "there is nothing to worry about. I just need a little more blood. There was a mix-up at the lab and they need to redo some of the tests."

"An' is that supposed to reassure me, then?" Patrick asked, trying to keep the fear out of his voice. "'Do'na worry, sir, there's nothin' wrong with yer tests, savin' the people runnin' them are incompetent.' 'Tis na much o' a sellin' point, Arn."

The doctor chuckled deeply and finished what he was doing, shutting Patrick up by simply filling his mouth with a thermometer. "That's enough of that, Mr. O'Keefe. Now be good and keep your mouth shut long enough for me to take your temperature. Once we finish the rest of the routine I'm treating you to lunch." Patrick was too distracted by his thoughts to refuse the invitation or even notice his friend's efforts to shake him of his mood. He sat with the thermometer clenched between his teeth, and wondered if it was just coincidence that the tests that would tell him he had a clean bill of health had to be redone.

CHAPTER 2

Halfway through his second fruitless auction of the day, his eyes expressionless and his mind wandering, Lucien rose abruptly and indiscreetly in the middle of the bidding on an ornate vase attributed to the Ming period. He had wasted his time; there was absolutely nothing here he considered of value—economic or otherwise—and his own final bid had just been topped on an antique, but otherwise unremarkable desk he sensed held some mildly interesting secrets in a trick drawer. Nothing else in the lots even vaguely interested him, and he had made enough of a token appearance today.

As he made his way to the exit, those directly around him glared at his departure from auction etiquette. The man at the door moved toward him, obviously intent on ending the disturbance.

"Excuse me, sir..." the man got no further. Caught beneath the withering, contemptuous gaze that Lucien had perfected in the last decade, the poor attendant turned gray and unconsciously stepped back to his post. The man scrambled to open the door with the anxious air of a servant who is fearful he hasn't moved quickly enough.

Determined he would get some enjoyment out of the afternoon, Lucien strolled obtrusively down the aisle, taking perverse pleasure in the commotion he was causing.

"Thank you, my kind man." Lucien projected his voice throughout the room with the skill of a trained thespian. The entire auction buzzed with varying degrees of annoyance, anger, and even a bit of amusement here and there.

Unable to ignore the commotion in the house, the auctioneer slammed his gavel down on the podium, completely missing its stand.

"Sir," he enunciated very carefully into the microphone, "if it is your intention to leave, kindly do so...quietly and immediately! We would like to get back to the business at hand."

Stopping just inside the doorway, Lucien half-turned toward the man. A ghost of smugness settled across his features and he inclined his head slightly to the auctioneer with the type of self-important conceit one would expect from thirteenth-century nobility. Lucien could sense the official go rigid behind his podium as the door slammed behind him with a reverberating thud. A malevolent smile wreathed about his face and his exit from the room was accompanied by the priceless sound of shattering china, followed by the most gratifying uproar.

With just a parting thought and the smallest expenditure of power, Lucien blurred the memories of those in the auction room. They would remember everything that had just taken place, and most likely would be agitated over it for weeks, but from this second on they would never connect the dignified and always correct Lucien Blank with the crass individual who had disrupted this afternoon's proceedings and caused the destruction of the ancient vase. After all, while it was mildly amusing to work up the rabble like that, he still needed to maintain his respectable public image; it wouldn't do to alienate those he needed to deal with in his business. Still, that had been extremely satisfying!

The sign above the quaint storefront read simply: Yesterday's Dreams. If not for the universal triple-globe symbol on the sign—a declaration of pawnshops everywhere since the time of the Medicis—she would never have noticed the place. As Kara hesitantly opened the door, there was no out-of-place whine of a motion sensor, just the musical tinkling of a bell.

"Hello?" she called out quietly. Clutching the polished leather case to her chest, she very nearly hoped there was no answer. "Is anyone there?" This time it came out almost a whisper. With an odd, sinking relief she turned to leave.

It wasn't as if she wanted to have to do this anyway. She had been wandering the city since early morning. It was now late afternoon. Her feet were worn raw and worry had her stomach clenched tighter than a miser's fist…and all for nothing if she walked out now. Kara stopped and fought with her conscience.

"Be right there, dearie!" a woman called from the back.

A faint whimper slipped past Kara's lips as she looked over her shoulder, clutching her burden even closer. As she waited, Kara could hear the woman singing as she finished whatever occupied her in the back. The voice was soft and lilting, very pleasant to the ear. Somehow it soothed Kara and made her feel safe among all this cared-for age. As she looked around, it occurred to her that every item was like a slice from another time, with each piece painstakingly preserved. Even the building showed its advanced age in the tiny details, from the rich, warm glow of the wainscoting to the intricately carved crown molding, which was clearly a custom job. Modern builders just didn't spend time or money on that kind of rich detail anymore.

In no way did this place resemble any of the smoky and ill-lit shops she had tried to force herself to enter throughout the day. At all of them it had been clear, through the dirty plate-glass windows and the various depths of dust blanketing every surface inside, that the items left there meant nothing but a fee to the shop owners. She had turned away from them all, unable to bear the thought of carrying Quicksilver through those doors, let alone leaving her behind.

More than once Kara had been ready to give up and go home. That was, until something drew her down this quiet street, as she made her way to the subway. Once there, she loitered in the pocket haven, not quite ready to brave the bustle and frenetic activity waiting for her on Canal Street. Between the shops packed with industrial goods, the Chinatown merchants with their wall-niche stores, and all those eager consumers looking for a bargain, the crush of pedestrians was more than Kara had been able to face.

But here, here was a sanctuary. Surrounded by peaceful brownstones, on this tree-lined street, Kara felt she could breathe deep for the first time that day. More at ease, she followed her impulse and ended up in front of this shop; now that she was inside, she didn't know whether to be glad, or rue the fact.

She drew her mind away from that uncomfortable thought and began to look at the old photographs hanging behind the orderly counter. At first she thought they all contained the same woman, but that just wasn't possible; they obviously spanned a period of at least seventy years. Each one featured the shop, a woman, and various others.

Kara's favorite photograph was one of the more recent ones. Judging by the style of the clothes, it was most likely from the early sixties. In it was one of the women, looking ageless, her head a mass of red gold curls and braids and her bright green eyes sparkling. There was a mischievous smile on her lips and beside her stood a young man in a green cardigan. He looked disturbingly familiar. In the picture, he stared at the woman with a look of adoration that bordered on worship. The two of them were posed in the middle of some kind of dance. Both the man and the woman were tall and gracefully slender; she could almost picture the fluid motions that would have followed the captured image. Such a pleasant moment caught for all time, with hazy, warm colors and sunshine. The picture held a promise of hope.

"Hallo, love, can I help ye?" the melodious voice called out through the velvet curtain. Startled, Kara stepped back, feeling guilty.

As the curtain moved aside, a shiver ran down her spine. If she didn't know better, she would have sworn this was the woman from the picture...looking no older than she had then, at least thirty years ago. Two sets of identically merry green eyes waited patiently for her response, as the woman stood with the photograph visible just beyond her shoulder. Shaking off her shock, Kara admitted how silly she was being; plenty of people looked like a younger version of their relatives. It was uncanny though—the only obvious difference was the hairstyle and clothes.

The pawnbroker interrupted her reverie.

"Can I help ye?" she repeated with a smile and just a bit of concern.

"Uh, yes. Please...." Kara hesitated even more; surely there was some other way. But no, she had exhausted all the possibilities. "How much will you give me for this?"

"Well then, give it here an' let's have a look at it." The woman held out her hands but did not reach for the case. Rather, she waited for Kara to relinquish it, as if knowing how hard this was for her. With extreme reluctance, at least on Kara's part, the instrument case exchanged hands.

"They call me Maggie, Maggie McCormick." The woman's soothing voice, combined with the care she took in handling the instrument, did much to put Kara at ease. "But please, just call me Maggie."

In her preoccupation, Kara didn't offer her name in return. She watched intently as Maggie fingered the strings of her precious violin. The woman seemed particularly interested in the brass nameplates on the case. Kara dared not hope that would stop her from buying it, although the thought was tempting.

"Well, 'tis no Stradivarius," Maggie continued, as if she hadn't even noticed the lack of exchange, "but ye've taken good care o' it."

"Thank you." The compliment was a kick in the gut to Kara. She could already feel a piece of her heart grow sick, even before they agreed upon a price.

"Are ye sure ye want to give it up, dear?"

Kara could feel the weight of Maggie's stare as she waited for an answer. Her own eyes could not leave Quicksilver's mahogany finish. It had been her Grandda's fiddle, and it meant more to Papa than the entire world. He had, in turn, passed it to her on the day her instructors at the Music Center declared her skill had surpassed anything they could teach her.

She could still picture Papa that day. That was the last time she had seen him in reasonably good health, on the evening of her final student recital. The image was engraved on her memory.

There he stood, a tall burly man more at home on a dock than in a concert hall. Kara hadn't been sure if he would be able to make it to her last performance. He'd been sick recently and he'd told her he might have some problems getting off of work because of it.

Kara rushed down the hall to meet him. She hadn't wanted to let on how disappointed she'd been that he couldn't be there. Even with Mathair inside, it just wouldn't have been the same without him. Papa had always been the one there to push her when she'd gotten lazy, or was frustrated with a difficult piece. She wouldn't be here today without him.

As she got closer, his expression made her heart sing. It had been some time since she'd seen such joy on his face. He'd been so tired and worried lately. Now his eyes sparkled with satisfaction and he nearly vibrated with suppressed energy. Papa was clearly excited and proud, and it was all because of her.

It was then that she noticed what he held: Quicksilver, in a new leather case. Mounted on the lid were two engraved brass nameplates; the first was the name of the violin, the second was her own: Kara O'Keefe.

She knew how Papa felt about that fiddle; she didn't feel she was worthy to call it her own. Besides, it was Papa's, left to him by his father. How could she accept it? There were tears in her eyes as Kara hid her hands behind her.

Letting loose a great belly laugh, her father held out the instrument insistently.

"Come now, lass," he said. "There are but two things o' this world I love more than my fiddle here, an' only one o' them can play!" He gently tugged her hands forward and laid upon them the violin.

"Take Quicksilver an' play her well, Kara," he continued, "for each time ye do, ye'll be playin' her for me." He hugged both her and the violin as she cried. She didn't know if her tears were because she was happy or sad.

"Dear, are ye sure ye want to give her up?" the woman repeated patiently, snapping Kara back to the present.

No. Of course, she didn't want to give up the fiddle, but she would for Papa. That long-ago day, she put aside her old violin and had never played upon any other since she'd taken up Quicksilver. The instrument meant that much to her. Well, it was only fitting; Papa's greatest gift to her would be the one to save them all.

"Yes," Kara answered after just a moment of thought. "I think I must." She couldn't quite read the expression on Maggie's face. Uncomfortable, she looked away.

"Well, she looks as well used as she does cared for," Maggie responded. "Why do'na ye make her sing for me? Just so I can hear her tone, o' course." It was more of a demand than a request, though a well-meaning one. Kara reached apprehensively for the violin. Carefully tuning the strings, she took this time for her own farewell. *How many times had Quicksilver sung for her, soothing sorrows and celebrating joys? And how many times had the two of them removed the grimace of pain from Papa's face, if only for a moment? Too many to count.* Kara clung to the hope that this last duet would pay for the peace Papa needed to truly heal, leaving him to enjoy his life.

She began softly, barely drawing the bow across the strings. With each full-bodied, heartfelt note, Kara and Quicksilver gave voice to their joint suffering—the agony of watching Papa waste away, the weight of the bills and collection notices stacking up at home, and the sorrow of helplessly watching both parents suffer, powerless to help. As she continued, the rising, haunting tune unfolded with no predetermined path to restrict it. Mingled with the sorrow was Kara's own exuberance for life, which even her heartache could not quell. The music took on its own life, filling the shop and carrying the two women along, leaving them in a kind of shock as it ended of its own accord.

Silence....

"Goodness, my dear!" Though deeply moved, Maggie recovered first. "How can ye bear to be parted? That fiddle there's o' a piece with yer soul."

Still in the thrall of the performance, Kara couldn't respond. Lowering the violin from its perch beneath her chin, she let the dark brown curtain of her hair fall forward to shadow her bleak amber eyes. She could not stand to let this woman know how her heart was dying. She had played the music her father loved to hear and only now did she understand why he'd given her Quicksilver in the first place. Some things weren't about skill or learning, they were about resonance, and if nothing else, she and Quicksilver resonated. This was how the instrument deserved to be played. But there was no other choice. Drawing resolve around her, Kara quickly handed back the violin.

"How much?" she asked when she was able to speak, her voice carefully neutral. She didn't let herself entertain the thought of leaving with the violin, not when the money it brought would solve at least their most pressing financial problems.

"Well now, love," the thoughtful look on Maggie's face left a feeling of sinking dread in Kara's stomach. "I'll have to take a look at my records in the back.... Do ye have somewhere ye have to be?"

Confused, Kara shook her head just slightly. "Umm, no...why?"

"Nothin' to worry ye," Maggie smiled. "'Tis just...well I'm ashamed to say it, but my records an' back room are nowhere near as organized as my shop. This may take a little while."

Once more Kara was tempted to make some kind of excuse; she could always tell the woman that she had a pupil waiting for her. The very thought made her cringe, though, as it forced her to wonder what was she going to tell Mr. Cohen, the director of the Music Center, if she went through with this.

Maggie may have given her the perfect opening, but Kara could not take advantage of it. This sacrifice was necessary or she never would have come in the first place.

"I can wait." It seemed to her that Maggie's disorganized records were only a pretense, but she could see no reason behind it. Not that it mattered; it was late in the day, and highly unlikely Kara would seek out another shop if she were unsuccessful here.

"Good!" It was impossible not to return the smile that accompanied the response. "Ye're welcome to browse while I'm diggin' in the back." Maggie disappeared through the curtain without a further word.

Breathing deep for the first time, Kara lost herself in the scent of citrus oil and cedar, threaded with a whiff of peppermint. This was like another world, a haven from the harsh, acrid odors of the city, an island of peace and beauty that even time did not seem to invade.

Everywhere light glowed off of polished wood and rich, vibrant colors. From the Chippendale end tables to the Wedgwood china in its graceful, glass-fronted armoire, the place brimmed with treasures. In a corner she spied a sword in a detailed scabbard that made her palm itch for the feel of the swept hilt in her grip. There were even some clothes that would make her friends drool, or at least those who were involved with costuming and period pieces. Kara looked around her, noticing that not one thing in the shop was anything less than an antique.

In the window was Kara's favorite item: an old lapboard with a polished cherry finish. It was well crafted, with a tapestry bottom padded for the comfort of the writer, a built-in space for an inkwell (filled), and a rest for the quill (occupied). Around the writing surface was an etching of what looked like forget-me-nots and shamrocks, a small touch that gave the lapboard a simple charm. It had all been carefully maintained, looking as if someone had just set it down. She almost expected a Victorian lady to come sweeping through to finish a passionate letter to her intended. Kara carefully lifted the top and fingered the textured ivory parchment inside. It told its own tales, without the aid of a writer with a pen. Caressing the sides of the desk, she could almost picture herself beneath its elegance, sitting in a window seat with a quiet countryside to distract her eyes or inspire them. She grinned at her own fancy.

Any one item in this room was most likely worth a fortune. Kara thought most of it must have been there for years. She couldn't imagine anyone selling this stuff recently when just about all of it would bring quite a price from a collector, or even a museum. Of course, she also saw the sense in it; those options were permanent. Even though it wouldn't bring as much money, at least a pawnshop offered the slim hope of someday recovering the treasure left behind. If Quicksilver went into a collection somewhere Kara would never see her again.

Not even wanting to think about it, Kara once again wandered over to look at the photograph behind the counter. Something bothered her about the picture; the man seemed so familiar. She wondered who he was. The picture wasn't that clear, but she felt she should know him. Not much else had changed from then to now: the shop, the street, and even the woman, looked the same. The only real differences were the items in the window and the absence of the man. Looking closer, Kara realized what else bothered her about the snapshot: in the very spot the lapboard now sat, there was a violin that looked hauntingly like Quicksilver. Well, at least that meant that Maggie bought them from time to time—and sold them. That thought did not hearten Kara at all, even if it did get her mind off the man.

On a side street in the Village, Lucien Blank, with a look in his eyes that bordered on obsession, did his best to remain unnoticed. He had come searching for items of power. It had been his plan to spend the afternoon leisurely combing a few pawnshops without too much expectation of finding anything, but hoping to be surprised. At this moment, he wasn't merely surprised, but downright astounded; his eyes fairly burned with covetous desire. With extreme restraint, he held his place and considered what to do next.

"It seems this day will not be such a waste as I thought." Menace was heavy in his voice as Lucien carefully scrutinized the quiet street. In the midst of his usual rounds, something drew him to this block with a strength he could not resist—any more than he could defy gravity or the need to breathe. He was unfamiliar with this particular pawnshop. Hunger rippled through him. Whatever led him here was far more powerful than any item he had ever encountered. *He must have it! The question was, how?* Mundane signs of residual power trails hung in the air like heat waves—trails that were already dispersing. When they were gone there would be nothing to trace. The item hadn't been in the shop for long. Perhaps the pawnbroker would turn it away. He had no idea what the object was, but he was determined that it would end up in his possession.

Lucien moved casually down the dusky street toward the store in question. In his thoughts was the rudimentary plan to enter and "browse" until he could get a look at the treasure he coveted. Perhaps he could manage to buy it himself, if the owner didn't intend to come back for it. Of course, that was assuming both that the item itself was being offered for pawn, rather than something else, and that the transaction hadn't yet been completed. There were too many variables. Lucien had the feeling this would be no conventional acquisition.

Unnoticed, Lucien leaned close enough to peer in the window, only to have a series of disturbing shocks ripple across his personal shields. The occurrence itself was unsettling enough, but each time the shields received a jolt it was like an electric flash going off before his eyes. Nothing had ever caused such a reaction before; something wasn't right.

It was a small thing and caused no pain. Lucien saw no reason to believe it could harm him. Discounting it as an annoyance, he brought his attention back to the pawnshop, eyes riveted on those inside. Through the window he could see the usual clutter of mismatched items, but he wasn't interested in the bartered dreams of desperate people. His eyes focused on the two women standing directly opposite the window he was peering in, one facing his direction, the other with her back to him. He couldn't make out much else. That was when he put his finger on what was wrong: He could sense absolutely nothing from the other side of the glass. It was like looking at something on the television, or in a photograph; he could see what was there, but it was missing some of its dimensions.

As he watched, the pawnbroker walked into the back room, leaving the young woman alone. Now was the perfect time to approach her. Trying to disregard his uneasy feelings, Lucien reached for the door handle. Before his hand connected he realized two things: the immense power trail that had drawn him here seemed to end abruptly at the door, and so did his attempt to enter. Like one who had once grabbed a red-hot poker, Lucien Blank was warned now by the tingling of every nerve ending in his palm that it wasn't a good idea to grasp that knob.

Whoever owned this store had more in common with Lucien than earning a livelihood from things no longer wanted; the shields on the shop spoke of more than a passing knowledge of magic. If he tried to even touch this door, not only would he experience extreme unpleasantness on several mental and physical levels, but he would set off an unknown number of alarms. That definitely did not suit his intentions.

Lucien nearly trembled with anger and frustration. Power possessed by someone other than himself both drew him and taunted him. He must have it all! How to go about securing this little morsel, Lucien couldn't say. Somehow he must enter this place without giving away his own nature. If one power item had passed through this door, without him being able to sense it beyond the threshold, then there was no telling what else might be within. He had to have that item. If it was powerful enough to leave such a residue, imagine what its full strength must be! Lucien hurried on as if he'd changed his mind about entering, pulling out his cell phone as he went. He had cultivated tools for just such events as this; it was time to use one of them.

"How are ye doin', dearie?" Kara jumped as the woman poked her head through the curtain. She had practically forgotten Maggie was back there. "Sorry about that, just thought ye might like a bit o' tea while ye're waitin'...."

"Yes," Kara nervously nodded. She felt like the woman had caught her snooping. "That would be nice."

"Good, come on back an' fix it up the way ye like," Maggie held back the curtain for her, "then ye can either brin' it out there, or sit in the back an' relax while I continue my hunt."

At that suggestion, Kara stopped. It was one thing to accept the offer of a cup of tea, but to intrude in the shopkeeper's private space...she wasn't sure.

"Come now," Maggie smiled kindly, "I do'na mind either way, but why should ye stand here waitin' when the comfortable chairs are in the back?

"Unless, o' course, ye want to look around some more?"

Kara shook her head, growing extremely uncertain about the situation.

"Is it takin' too long, dearie? Is there someone waitin' on ye?"

"No, it's fine," Kara answered. "I guess this place just feels so personal; it's like I'm intruding."

Maggie's laughter flowed like music. "Do'na be ridiculous, love! No need to be uncomfortable. Most o' the memories here are'na even mine. They all belong to other people. Besides, I have to do the paperwork in the back, anyway. Please, come an' relax." She gently pulled Kara forward. "It will'na be much longer, an' to be truthful, ye look ready to drop."

Kara followed her into another world. Surprisingly, it seemed newer than the one she had just left. In carefully locked, wire-mesh bins were all the items

Kara would have expected to find outside in the store. Each piece was carefully tagged and just as well cared for as anything in the front. In this back room were guitars (electric and acoustic), paintings, and beautiful quilts carefully folded in blanket bags. There were even some books tucked away in a corner, well dusted even back here. If this was disorderly, she was curious to see what orderly was like. She did have to admit the corner of the desk, just visible in the next room, groaned beneath mounds of papers. On top was a buyer's guide for classical instruments. Next to that was Quicksilver. Kara looked hurriedly away.

"Over here, love," Maggie led the way. "I do'na have a true kitchen down here, but the electric kettle does me fine. If I need anythin' else, why I just run upstairs." The woman seemed to be trying to reassure Kara that she was not impinging on private space. Maggie rinsed out a mug in the utility sink and handed it to her. "The fixin's are right over there; just help yerself."

Leaving her to her tea, Maggie returned to the desk in the back office, seemingly checking what she found in the buyer's guide against other sources.

"I do'na mean to make ye wait so long," Maggie apologized, "but I must admit, I firmly believe in givin' a person what an item is worth. It canna hurt me, an' most definitely helps them.

"If ye do'na mind my askin', why are ye givin' her up?"

Kara took her time fixing the tea, all the while trying to think of an answer she would feel comfortable giving. Her tongue betrayed her while she was thinking.

"My father has cancer. He has insurance to help with the doctor bills, but it doesn't cover them completely." Bitterness dominated her face and she kept her eyes riveted on her cup. It was a safe place to look. "That means there isn't enough money for the rest of the bills, let alone the emergencies that keep popping up. No one is sympathetic with a cancer victim...they all want their money today, because after all, you might not be there tomorrow, right?"

"Oh, lass...."

"No!" It came out nearly a growl. Her breath came in quick huffs and the overwhelming urge to escape swept through her. Ashamed, Kara looked up with a stricken expression on her face. "Please, don't call me that...it's painful to me."

"I'm so sorry," Maggie left her desk and stood in the doorway.

"No, I'm sorry. Perhaps I better go; I've taken up enough of your time." Kara looked for a place to set down her cup so that she could leave.

"Please wait, we have'na even discussed a price." The pawnbroker turned and reached for a scrap of paper on the desk. "Do ye think this would be acceptable?"

Taking the paper, Kara looked down and nearly dropped the mug she was holding. She couldn't believe the sum.

"There's no need to worry 'tis charity," Maggie began kindly. "As ye can see, I'd written it down before ye'd said a word. Truly, 'tis what the fiddle's worth."

"I had no idea!" It stunned her to think she'd been playing on something with so much value.

"Well, love," Maggie answered. "I said she was no Stradivarius, but that does'na mean she is'na valuable."

Kara was numb with disbelief. As she sat down in a chair, face pale and eyes dazed, the paper fluttered unnoticed to her lap. Maggie carefully removed the teacup from her fingers and managed to place it on top of the mesh bin before the doorbell interrupted her.

"Damn!" she swore, and her gaze darted between Kara and the shop, out of sight on the other side of the velvet curtain. Maggie called out to the unknown in the outer room. "I'll be right there."

Turning to Kara, she said, "Love, this will take but a moment. I'll deal with this person an' lock up so we can discuss all o' this."

Kara didn't notice her reassuring smile but she nodded in agreement. She was too stunned to leave now anyway.

"Can I help ye?" Kara could hear Maggie clearly from the back, and something struck her as odd. With difficulty she climbed out of her daze and began to pay attention to the conversation in the front room.

"Yeah, what'll ya give me for this?" answered a hard, masculine voice.

There was a brief silence as Kara supposed Maggie looked over whatever item he handed to her. "Na a thing at'all." There was an ice in Maggie's voice the girl never would have supposed possible.

"What do ya mean nothing?!"

"I mean, take yer garbage elsewhere, if ye must, but do'na try an' peddle it with me!" Kara was taken back by the anger in Maggie's voice. "I know what yer up to, an 'tis none o' it I'll be havin'. Ye keep yer distance from me an' mine."

"Ya got a problem, lady?" There was no question that the faceless voice meant that in the Brooklyn sense.

Kara was afraid. Why was Maggie provoking the man this way? What purpose was there in inviting violence? For surely, the challenge in her words and attitude would drive the punk to it. If Kara didn't know better, she would have sworn it wasn't Maggie out front. Gone were the warmth and patience that had greeted a reluctant girl; now the shopkeeper acted distant and abrupt. It didn't make sense. Could she trust someone with such a radically changing personality? Doubts began to grow, fed both by Kara's confusion at the change in Maggie and her own underlying reluctance to sell. The quoted sum was very tempting and more than enough to help her parents for at least a little while, but what would the hidden costs be? She had to wonder as she listened to Maggie's reply.

"No problem, as long as ye turn around an' remove yer taint from my store." There was steel in Maggie's voice.

The man's voice was filled with challenge as he answered. "Well, maybe ya should make it worth my while to leave, huh?"

Kara cringed. No good could come of this. In fact, she had the sinking feeling that doing business with Ms. McCormick would be a moot point when this guy was done. She was tempted to look for a way to escape out the back, but only for a moment. Then she thought of the money, and Maggie's kindness and willingness to help, and instead, Kara searched for something that might serve as a weapon.

Grabbing a wrench she found by an ancient boiler, just in case, Kara crept closer to the curtain, needing to know what was happening. On the other side of the counter, she saw a tall, wiry young man, his body radiating threat and his posture poised to deliver it. She couldn't see his face clearly through the thin gap, but by what she could see, he wasn't a pleasant man. She couldn't believe Maggie was staring him down. *Could she find it in herself to leave the relative safety of the back room and stand beside a woman who was nearly a stranger?*

The decision was taken from her. Leaning too close, Kara just barely brushed the curtains. *ClinkClinkClink.* Damn! The decorative brass rings from which the velvet divider was suspended jostled each other on the metal pole. So much for going unnoticed. She drew back sharply as his attention moved in her direction.

I can do this, Kara told herself, *Maggie needs me.* But the fear was too much; she merely stood her ground, trying to find the courage to step forward.

All at once, something streaked by her from the office, swishing the curtains as it went. Beyond the barrier, she could hear the man's oddly high-pitched scream and the frantic jingling of the bell as he slammed the door behind him. She hurried forward to peek through the drapes just as he fled, leaving behind both the television he'd been trying to sell and a wicked knife on the floor.

"Sorry ye had to witness that, love." Maggie, once again the sweet person Kara met earlier, seemed to be searching the shop intently. For what, Kara couldn't tell. She watched warily as the woman made her way to the front of the store, locking the door and pulling the blinds. Curiously, she avoided the items left behind on her way back to the counter.

In an oddly detached way, Kara noticed how the woman's crimson-flushed cheeks merely emphasized the milky glow of her skin. Even in the aftermath of anger, Maggie possessed an ethereal beauty.

"I'll just ring the police an' then we can discuss our exchange," Maggie commented, rigid with control. She picked up the phone behind the counter, one of the few objects in evidence that was modern—complete with built-in answering machine and speed-dial—and hit a single button. "Hallo? 'Tis Maggie McCormick, down at Yesterday's Dreams...."

Kara listened as she went on to describe the punk and what had happened. It shocked her to hear Maggie tell the person on the other end of the line that the television set was stolen.

"I appreciate it, officer; just tell them to knock. I've locked up for the day but I'll be in the back."

As she hung up the phone, Kara had to ask. "How did you know?"

"Oh, 'tis simple, love," Maggie answered. "I've a friend who's a detective on the force an' he gives me the descriptions o' stolen items. After all, 'tis a pawnshop, makes sense to check here." She smiled and moved toward the back. "Shall we?"

Kara was confused, she felt like the woman had hesitated ever so slightly before answering but she couldn't be sure. And her answer...was that how things were done? It wasn't like Kara had a lot of experience with pawnshops *or* stolen goods. It was still unsettling how Maggie had antagonized him, though. That part would never make sense to her. *What had scared him away?* Kara knew something had passed her, but she hadn't even known there was anything in the back with her until then. Actually, she still didn't see whatever it was...where had it gone? Ill at ease, she followed Maggie into the back room.

It was time for business. Whatever had happened, if her family was to survive, they desperately needed the money the pawnbroker offered. The longer she waited, the harder it would be to go through with this, and the more chance it would be too late. Returning to the back room, Maggie now led her into the small office. Rather than look at Quicksilver on the desk, Kara let her eyes wander around the room. Maggie's office was little more than a closet. There was barely room for the desk, two straight-backed, kitchen-type chairs (one at the desk and one beside it), and a narrow filing cabinet. To make up for the lack of room, there were shelves everywhere. Each jumbled shelf was full of assorted references and computer paraphernalia. The entire office gave the impression of fraught activity. Just looking around her, it was apparent to Kara that Maggie had more than enough work for one person, but she seemed to handle it all alone. Or at least, there was no sign of an assistant.

"Well now," Maggie said as she waved Kara toward the chair beside the desk, "shall we begin the business end o' this deal?" At Kara's silence she continued. "Have ye ever pawned anythin' before, love?" Kara shook her head in response, reluctant to speak.

"I'll explain as we go, then." As she went on, Maggie settled herself at the computer, which took up half of the rather small desk. Punching a few keys, she continued. "First, ye've offered me an item for pawn an' we've agreed on a price; the next thin' we must do is take care o' the formalities." Taking a moment to call up her database program, Maggie looked up at Kara, a reassuring smile gracing her lips. "Do ye have two forms o' identification?"

Kara took out her wallet, extracting her driver's license and her work id from the Music Center.

"Good," the pawnbroker said, as she accepted them. "I am required by law to keep a copy o' yer identification on record, a description o' the item, an' the amount I'm givin' ye for it.

"This serves two purposes: 'tis used by the authorities if they discover that an item is stolen, an' it ensures that someone else canna claim yer property. If ye'd no identification, I could'na have continued." Maggie took a moment to type in the information, photograph the cards with a special camera that captured an image of both the id and Kara at the same time, and hand them back. "To be truthful, all o' this helps me keep track o' thin's as well."

Apparently noticing Kara's expression, Maggie paused. Compassion must have moved her to reach out. "Are ye sure ye're okay with this, dear?"

Uncomfortable with both the touch and the question, Kara flinched away. She looked up but avoided Maggie's eyes. The pawnbroker immediately let her hand fall. "I'm sorry, Kara; I just do'na want ye to do somethin' ye are'na sure o'."

"No, please don't apologize." Kara gave her a sad smile and swallowed hard. "I *don't* want to do this...but I also don't have a choice. Please continue."

"As long as ye're sure."

Maggie turned back to the computer and called up a different screen. "This is my standard agreement when an item is pawned. Basically, it says ye have six months to come back an' either pay off the loan, or pay a fee to continue the contract. If ye do'na do either, at that time I can offer the item for sale. Generally the time is less, but I believe in givin' a person a chance."

"So, does that suit ye?" Maggie looked up at Kara.

"Yes...I think that will be fine," Kara answered with quiet resignation.

"All right then." Humming to herself, Maggie printed up the information on the screen and held it out to Kara. "This is a pawn ticket; it outlines the terms o' the agreement: a description o' the item bein' pawned, yer description, the amount bein' paid, when 'tis due, an' the fee owed if the contract is to be carried over. Take yer time an' read it carefully. Let me know if anythin' is wrong. If 'tis all in order, sign right here on the bottom."

She felt as if a trap had closed around her the moment she accepted the carbonless-copy printout. It did her little good to see it, and reading it was out of the question. Her eyes flooded at the thought of signing Quicksilver away. Fumbling at a pen on the desk, she quickly added her signature to the form, not even trying to read it. It was done.

Kara finally met Maggie's eyes as she handed back the agreement. It made no sense but she thought she saw the ghost of a tear in the pawnbroker's eye. "Yer father's a very lucky man to be so loved. Ye do him an honor." The woman took down a ledger and wrote out the check. With a gentle smile she handed it to Kara along with a copy of the pawn ticket. Kara simply slipped the papers in her pocket. She wasn't ready to see the evidence of her betrayal.

"So, love," Maggie said casually, "would ye care for a new cup o' tea?"

The phone rang before Kara could answer, giving her the perfect excuse.

"No, I should be getting home," Kara replied as Maggie picked up the phone. Anxious to be away, Kara quickly got up to go; so quickly that her jacket slid to the floor. She blushed furiously as Maggie scooped it up and handed it back to her. "Thank you...for everything."

As Maggie stood to walk her to the door, the phone rang again. The pawnbroker just looked at it, as if trying to decide if she should answer it, or let the answering machine pick up so she could see Kara out.

Quickly assuring Maggie that if she didn't mind an unlocked door, she needn't walk her out, Kara fled the back room without even waiting for an answer. As she reached for the front door, she noticed on the back a sign she'd missed before. Across the top was the name of the store, YESTERDAY'S DREAMS, and below it read "...If it meant something once, you'll find it here." Her heart clenched as she hurried out into the autumn night and she struggled not to cry. Kara left with the promise of a healthier bank account, but her soul felt mortally wounded.

Guilt was her silent companion. So many people would be disappointed in her for what she had done today. Kara made her way home in relative quiet, mulling over what she would tell them, *how* she would tell them. Their faces drifted across her thoughts like fallen leaves on the wind, whirled about in a violent dance. Their eyes were haunting, accusing, hurt, dismayed, how could she let them down like this? Her students...Mr. Cohen...her mother...Papa...that was what had made this so hard, not the pain of giving up Quicksilver—which was agony in itself—but the fact that none of them, her father most of all, would ever understand.

All the others faded from her thoughts, leaving only the image of Papa's face, wounded and disapproving. Kara nearly lost her control; a single, strangled sob fought its way clear of her throat before she could suppress it. Those passing eyed her nervously. She didn't even notice. Thoughts of Papa dominated her awareness.

There was no hiding from him what she had done; he asked her to play for him nearly every night. She thought of the bills piled up on the desk at home and the worry lines etched into her mother's face. No, she had done what she must. She would learn to live with his disappointment. It was one thing holding on to something precious when there were other options, but the alternatives had reached an end. Without the money Kara had gotten for the violin, there would be no way to pay the mortgage.

Halfway home, Kara stopped to look at her watch; it was seven o'clock. Her bank was open until seven-thirty on Thursdays. She changed course and picked up her pace. She would be much more comfortable with the check in the bank. Arriving just in time, she joined the long line of last-minute people. For about the hundredth time since leaving Maggie's shop, Kara reached in her pocket, making sure the check was safe.

That was odd...nestled in the same pocket as the check was a small, crinkly bundle, a bundle she hadn't noticed until now. She didn't pull it out, especially not knowing what it was. Native New Yorkers learned at an early age that a sure way to "lose" anything valuable was to let strangers on the street know what pocket it was in. What could it be, though? Except for a silk scarf she always kept there, she'd thought her pockets had been empty, and the only things she recalled placing there since were the check and the pawn ticket.

Kara laughed bitterly to herself, diverted by the thought of that little slip of paper. She might as well use the ticket as a bookmark. She would never have enough to reclaim her precious violin...even if there was a chance it would still be there.

Quickly forcing her mind away from that thought, Kara shoved everything but the check deep into her pocket. She was next, and very glad of it. Her luck had been so amazing she didn't want to risk it changing now. As soon as the bank transferred the money, there would be one less worry for her. Her hand trembled as she slid the check through the gap under the inch-thick clear Lexan. Passing it to the clerk removed a proverbial weight from her shoulders. It wasn't that her concern had ended, but the problems no longer seemed insurmountable. She now had the means to take care of things for Papa, leaving him free to focus on getting well. She dared to let herself hope for the first time since he'd been ill, though it was a hope tinged with fear. Now she must tell her family what she had done...now she must answer to her father.

Still not sure how she was going to explain to Papa, Kara tried to put it from her mind and focus on getting home. Outside the fluorescent glare of the bank, the black chill of the autumn night waited to engulf her. She shivered in response as she walked through the door. Autumn was not her favorite time of year, particularly now when its progress seemed to mockingly mirror that of her father's. In the still-gentle warmth of the day all appeared well, through eyes dazzled by glorious color, as the leaves exchanged their verdant finery for a more vibrant one. Few people stopped to realize that those bright reds, oranges, and yellows were the equivalent of foliage death shrouds. Kara knew it all too well. In horrible mimicry she saw the flush of her father's fevered cheeks and the yellow-green tinge of his skin after a treatment. The night was even worse, when the world and her father both put on their ghostly pallor of moonlight and weariness. No, autumn held little favor in her eyes, only slightly more than winter and its skeletal trees...the season of death.

Well, if we aren't morbid today! Kara thought sternly to herself. She should be concentrating on what to tell Papa, rather than wallowing in melancholy and grisly metaphor. He wouldn't be happy with her. She could only hope he would understand her sacrifice. Looking around for the nearest subway, Kara resigned herself to a less than restful night, beginning with the fact that she must walk at least to West 4th Street to catch her train. With a sigh, she began the end of her day, all too certain that what was to follow would be the hardest part.

CHAPTER 3

Haunting...magical...inspired...that was the intention, anyway. The music drifted from the open windows of the seventh-story studio on the corner of 46th Street and 9th Avenue. On the fringes of the Theatre District, surrounded by the dignified glamour of Off-Broadway and the restaurants catering to that crowd, the studio blended seamlessly into the landscape. The curtains in the tall, leaded windows were nothing more than draped scarves, sheer and flowing in the grudging breeze coming off the Hudson. In contrast to the dark, mahogany furniture and matching woodwork, the soft white of the walls and the bright jewel tones of the window treatments and other accessories glowed richly.

"Damn it, Thomas, ye've all but got it an ye'd just concentrate a little more." Cian rose from where he lounged, on pillows of worn velvet and old satin, in a window seat tucked in the curved turret looking out onto the intersection below. Moving about a loft that somehow managed to look spacious despite its modest footage, he switched on the bright, industrial lights he'd only nominally masked with billowing yards of translucent white silk. The sudden light made his black hair shimmer with glints of violet and a faint gasp behind him brought a tension to the lines of his generous mouth. This was precisely why he avoided lighting the scattered candles he usually preferred at twilight. He definitely didn't want Thomas getting any more ideas.

Turning, he could not help but notice the hopeful, hungry look in his pupil's gaze, and his own grass-green eyes had darkened with annoyance he did not bother to hide. Enough was enough. "Cut it out, Thomas, save it for yer theatre crowd. Now come on, ye've half an hour left. Show us a bit o' that talent that got ye in the door."

"Honey, I'll show you talent, alright." Thomas's eyes glowed, eager and hopeful in his delicate face, and his glossed lips smirked with the cocky confidence that had first held Cian's attention.

The young man picked up the guitar he was using for accompaniment today and began to strum lightly, preparing to start the piece over, his face intent and serious from the moment he took up the instrument, all other thoughts banished.

"You want me to start from the beginning, or where we stopped?"

Cian was struck once again by the boy's intensity. When Thomas actually dedicated himself to his craft, all else fell away: reality, worry, affectation...everything but the music. The boy was a rare gem, possessing both talent and diligence in spades. He had nearly played his fingers bloody in the past, just to get a difficult piece right. That was the main reason he was here. Cian had no patience for those lacking in dedication. He did not accept just any students. No matter that time was the one thing he had in abundance; he would not waste it on spoiled dilettantes with the attention spans of bumblebees, flitting from one new interest to the next.

No, commitment was not the issue. He was afraid Thomas had developed a crush. Not unusual in a teacher-student relationship, but not something Cian would ever encourage, even had he shared Thomas's proclivities. He allowed a cool, neutral smile to grace his lips before moving to stand outside the young man's range of view. Maybe he should get Eri to come over before Thomas's next lesson and pretend to be his girlfriend. That might work. For now, he would try to remember that any informality between them would have to be sacrificed until he was able to discourage the crush or it died the death of youthful fickleness.

"From the beginning, please."

Much better. The gypsy lament rose to fill the silence. Its ancient sorrow and rich, layered notes wove together the threads of instrument and voice, until the soul could not help but ache. As the melody unfolded, Cian could nearly see the doomed gypsy girl draped over her lover's fresh-turned grave. To near perfection, Thomas's sustained and vibrant vocal tones painted the picture of the scheming villain as he crept forward. Defiance and suffering dueled from verse to verse as the spirit of the music refused to bow beneath despair, instead celebrating the human capacity to love life even in the face of loss. By the time the gypsy girl found her new love, her true love, in the final notes, Cian's mood was much improved.

"Better, but work on those fingerings in the second verse; you still have a tendency to overextend." Cian was grudging with his praise; Thomas was too likely to twist it into encouragement. "Now, we have time for one more short piece. Have another try at the reel we went over yester...."

Suddenly, the air grew taut and heavy, smothering the rest of Cian's instructions. A bitter tang teased the throat and the beginning of a sulfurous stench filled the room. Overhead, the bright white light took on a dull yellow tinge. His sanctuary was not invaded, but malice stood at the threshold, poised to enter. Behind him Thomas's music faltered and faded into silence.

Damn! Thomas.

As far as Cian knew, the young man was not a sensitive, but he could still be injured by this unseen threat. Not knowing what he faced, or from which direction the attack would come, Cian feared the safest place for his pupil was right where he was. Mercifully, the boy did not move or speak. Thomas simply watched him with a mixture of fear and faith glimmering in his eyes. Perhaps he was more aware than Cian suspected.

There was a shuddering crash and the entire building shook, as if a bus had collided with the ground floor, or an earthquake rattled the foundation. Thomas's caramel complexion paled and his eyes grew wide. Cian's obsession had always been the protection of innocents. Those impulses kicked in with force right now. Gone was the laid-back, distant façade he assumed to deal with the world; the warrior he had been in his long-ago youth surfaced in an instant. He stood poised and ready, his attention trained on the approaching danger. This was no probing of boundaries; it was a full assault. Without a word, Cian reached over and yanked the boy from his chair, shoving him down beneath the sturdy table.

"Do'na move, nor speak, until I tell ye." Cian's tone was not to be argued with; fortunately, Thomas had the sense to obey.

How their roles had reversed; now Cian's focus and dedication were to be tested and he could not give his student another thought if either of them were to survive. He was sure everyone had felt the building shake, but he was certain only he had experienced the malevolent surge moments before the tremor. Another impact and the sound of bricks hitting metal and concrete outside jarred him. This was not something they could wait out; people would be hurt, if they hadn't been already. Drawing on reservoirs of power that had not known exercise for decades, Cian wove a protective spell encasing the two of them in a shell of scintillating energy. Once the shield was in place, he probed the surrounding area.

This felt personal, but so far the foe had not declared himself. Cian cast his occult senses wide. His body may have stood still, but his awareness circled the loft, examining every edge of his long-standing protections. The attack came again and he gained a better sense of his enemy as another psyche brushed against his own. There was malice, yes, but also a drive to possess, to claim, a hunger for power that was unrelenting. After another strike against the exterior, faint cracks ran along the loft wall. Dust drifted on the air after the walls stopped shaking. Much more of this and the building would collapse and then none of his shields would make a bit of difference.

It was time to end the attack. Dividing the shield he'd just erected, he locked Thomas in a separate little shelter. Cian used his own as the foundation for a counterassault. He drew in every wisp of mage energy within his grasp, wrapping it about himself like a cocoon. Thicker and thicker it grew. In brilliance, it rivaled a small sun; in density, a black hole. Soon it would burn even him, but it would not reach that point, for he had intentions for the force he had gathered.

The space within the shield grew smaller and smaller until he felt encased in mage energy to the point of near-immobility. Only then did he sever the energy tendrils he'd used to build his offensive. Flexing ever so slightly, Cian got a feel for his creation. It was tensile and fluid, throbbing with a pulse his heart kept pace with.

It was ready. Alternately tensing and flexing, he braced against the inner surface of the shield surrounding him. Cian built up a rhythm that affected the construction like a spherical ripple. With each contraction he drew the power to him and each expansion sent it cascading a little further away. He would have to calculate this exactly. Too much force and he would mind-blast any sensitive within the radius. There were none in his building—he was certain of that—and he had to hope none were passing by.

The building shook again with growing force. Screams reached him from the surrounding floors despite the soundproofing. His face was set with determination and his hands clenched.

Now!

Pulsing, he sent the harnessed power billowing past the wavy glass of his loft's windows, right into the next assault. The shockwave of the collision was worse than any of the physical impacts on the building. It hit him hard, flooding his mind until he feared the energy would overload him. With grim determination, he held his balance and stabilized his construct until a shield solidified just beyond the surface of the building. Another impact and the shield trembled, but held. The attack was over.

Hovering just beyond the protections, he could see a roiling mass of darkness through his favorite window. It opened sulfurous yellow eyes and their gazes locked. He had heard of such demonics, but this was his first encounter with such a creature. Somewhere, out in the city, a master waited for the triumphant return of his slave. He would wait a while longer. This encounter was a draw.

Finally turning the bolt for the last time that night, Maggie watched through the shop window as the patrol car pulled away. In the back seat were the television and a sealed bag containing the young man's knife, both with his fingerprints intact.

She was very glad the police hadn't shown up while Kara was here. The girl was nervous enough without their presence. Maggie had helped her in the only way she could, for the girl's need had been very great—great enough that she had been willing to sell an item invested with a bit of her soul; not that she would have known that. If she'd been frightened away it might have gone to a darker sort, rather than sitting safe in Maggie's back room. Very few would have seen it for what it was, but many would have bought it cheaply, given the chance. That could have meant nothing to Kara, or it could have meant the death of her soul. At the very least, she would never realize her dreams without the instrument. Now, some day, she would have the chance to reclaim them.

Fearing the protections she needed to weave for the violin would be complex and problematic, Maggie steeled herself for a long night. Normally the items she accepted, while always special, didn't require the consideration she must take with this one. She wasn't quite sure what the difference was, for something was muddling the flavor that would have told her what magic she had before her. Yes, there was no doubting the importance of both Kara and her Quicksilver. Unfortunately, without a good deal of study, there was also no telling why. The only thing Maggie could be sure of was the Lightness of their music. This would take considerable thought.

Pulling the shade, she turned to view her little shop, lit only by the streetlight outside the window. Maggie didn't bother with a light; her eyes didn't need the assistance, even in the dark of night. Her intent gaze could not find where Beag Scath was hiding. The sprite was the same height as a mortal infant, but proportioned like a miniature adult: He could be just about anywhere. This was a favorite game of his, to hide in the front of the shop any chance he could get. Though there was little likelihood of someone with mage blood—even diluted—turning up here by chance, she dared not give him free run of the place.

Most mages were the product of cross-matings between humans and the Tuatha de Danaan—the Celtic elves also known as either Áes Sidhe, or just the sidhe. Very few mages came from pure human lineage. In any case, they usually ended up locked away as mad. It was very difficult to keep reality straight when one was born with a touch of the gifts but none of the knowledge to make sense of it. Those who hadn't been institutionalized generally lived the life of the recluse, far from the overwhelming presence of society.

Maggie didn't make the mistake of assuming that meant no care need be taken. The risk of someone seeing Beag Scath's true nature was too great. There had to be a few of mage blood wandering about who had either obtained training of a sort, or had figured out enough to realize they were quite sane. (Either way, they would know enough to conceal their own differences from others.) Anyone with the sight, trained or untrained, would know immediately that something was odd, even if they knew nothing of their gift. True, at night it was quite safe for Beag Scath to roam, but she couldn't allow it even then; his reasoning was too simple for him to understand that his freedom would not extend to the daytime. The only reason she didn't block him from the front completely was his usefulness at times like earlier this night. She felt safe in the life she had set up for herself, the full strength of her own mage magic was quite enough to shield her from unskilled detection. No, she didn't fear for herself, but if someone saw Beag Scath she couldn't be sure he'd be so careful. If he were not such a comfort to her, she would have left him across the ocean, though it would have torn her heart.

"Beag Scath?" Maggie scrutinized the room. "Beag Scath, ye ornery soul, show yerself before ye wake up in Eire." Something shifted behind her, in the far corner of the shop. Dutifully playing her part in this game, Maggie turned. It was no surprise to her when she heard the tinkling of the curtain rings, now behind her. With a loving smile on her face she followed the sprite into the back room.

Expectantly, Maggie glanced into her office. There—the epitome of innocence—was Beag Scath, guarding Quicksilver. He looked so endearing with his miniature arms wrapped around the belly of the instrument and his head resting against the neck. This had been her first clue to the nature of both the instrument and the girl. Power drew him; he couldn't resist its thrumming in his blood. If Maggie hadn't sung the sprite to sleep, a task complicated by the need to keep the magic contained in the back room, there would have been no keeping him from the two. She had been quite surprised to find the girl awake when she was finally free to go out front. Maggie knew some of the spell had gotten away from her; Kara should have been drowsy, if not completely out on the floor, as the sprite had been. That had been her second clue: the girl's natural protections. Yes, there was much to think over here, now that the violin was safely in her possession.

"Ah, my friend," Maggie ruffled his hair, "while ye're watchin' over that, who'll watch over ye?"

Stretching with an artful sleepiness, Beag Scath snuggled against her hand, as it remained resting on him. Picking up both the tiny sprite and the violin with one arm, Maggie turned off the light and made her way to the basement door. For the sake of appearance and possible need, the upper floors were arranged in the perfect image of a lived-in home. That wasn't where Maggie made her home, though. They were the building's only occupants, but she still couldn't shake the habit of living underground. Maggie was more comfortable living in the basement than above the shop. The depth allowed her some relief from the unrelenting mental noise of the city. She had even expanded downward, through the judicious use of a little magic. Her neighbors would be amazed at the complex that ran beneath their own basements. It almost reminded her of home, though the magic here had gone wild with disuse.

It was just as well that she had created such a safe haven below. She would need it now, while she tried to determine exactly what she'd taken into her keeping and how to protect it. Maggie had her suspicions, but couldn't be sure. The violin itself she knew from times past—the story of which she would someday pass on to Kara—but somewhere in the trek from then to now, the magic of it had transformed. When she'd seen it the very first time some forty years ago there had barely been a hum of magic left to echo in her blood. Now the power of this instrument, even when silent, was enough to make her blood sing.

As Maggie descended the stairs, Scath clambered to her shoulder, his tiny, perfectly formed hand slipping through her curls to gently grasp her ear.

"Ye be careful now, Little Shadow!" Maggie warned her small friend. "I do'na have a hand free to catch if ye fall." Tittering, he cowered beneath her hair in mock fear. She laughed heartily and long in response, needing the release it offered. Beag Scath joined in, pleased with his success in cheering her.

Revitalized, they continued their descent to the lowest depths of the *rath*. If Maggie were to work the stronger magics, best to do so there where the ripples would be less noticeable. Rather like the wise trout, swimming on the bottom of the pond where his movements leave the surface undisturbed. It would take someone with a powerful and trained talent to uncover what she'd attempt here tonight.

"Go ahead, my friend," she said, "tonight I must lock the way behind us." Obediently leaping from her shoulder, the sprite stretched and shimmered, continuing his downward journey wearing the form of a glossy black raven. So instinctive and natural was this for him that when Maggie closed her eyes she sensed only the barest of ripples in the flow of magic. "Show off!" Were she to assume the same form the ripples would continue for hours, and never would she accomplish it without much preparation. It exhausted her just to contemplate the attempt.

With an envious chuckle, Maggie turned to her own weaving. Her eyes still closed and the entrance above pictured clearly in her mind, Maggie reached for the individual currents in the magic flow. She pinched a bit here, gently tugged there, and in moments she'd hidden the doorway to all but those below. This was where she and her small friend differed, though the magic coursed through both their veins: he morphed with less than a thought, but he'd never achieve the greater magics. Maggie must carefully plan her transformations, but they were the least of the wonders she could achieve.

Continuing down the stairs, Maggie could hear Scath's lilting voice absent-mindedly wandering through a song from their homeland. He did this often when he was pleased. She didn't have the heart to tell him how it hurt to hear it...how it made her yearn to call the clouds to bear them back again. But no, her oath held her here, and her Shadow would never leave his Maggie.

She sighed deeply as she reached the bottom and Beag Scath, once again in his anthropomorphic seeming, came to her, a daisy in his outstretched hand. Sitting on the last step with the violin across her lap, she accepted his gift, exchanging it for a smile. She watched him closely, for she knew this game well and it often delighted her. The discontented frown on his face was barely perceptible as his large, burnt orange-colored eyes—a shade generally only seen in felines—briefly went unfocused. So great was his concentration that he trembled ever so slightly; something Maggie only realized because his thatch of unruly hair, tresses that were a mixed jumble of nearly every shade of brown and red, moved with each tremor. One would think it was the effort that made him shake...but then one would be wrong. Scath vibrated with the very flow of the feral magic. Within moments, his hand shimmered faintly and the whitest of lilies took shape.

She tucked the daisy behind her ear and accepted his second offering, kissing his tiny fingers in return. As he began to try once more to tempt her, she rose, scooping him up in the process. He wanted the violin, which she could never give him. They both knew it, though he would bury her in exotic flowers on the off chance she'd forget. Some days she allowed his attempts to continue, just to see what rare blossoms he would pluck from the air. This was not one of those days; they didn't have the time. Besides, she'd only let him continue if she was free to gift him with the item he desired.

Anyway, enough; there was work to do now. Given Beag Scath's reaction to the instrument, Maggie had no doubts that she needed to get the violin beneath some hefty protections; sprites were not the only creatures drawn by the craving of mage energy. The weaving would be tricky and convoluted, but not difficult.

To separate the sprite from Quicksilver, she moved him to her shoulder and placed the violin case on the pedestal of Connemara marble in front of her. She removed the instrument from its leather case and carefully considered them both. Though each vibrated with magic, in just those few moments since she'd taken out the violin, the magic surrounding the carry case began to recede. Maggie was relieved; she wouldn't have to guard them both. This considerably simplified her task. If she'd had to leave the two mated one in the other, the leather case would have hampered her efforts greatly. Because the magic of the case was that of contamination, having been soaked up from the violin itself, she wouldn't have been able to use it to anchor her protections and she didn't want to divide the energy to shield each of them separately. The violin was too important. Luckily, she could set the case aside to fade on its own while she focused her will on Quicksilver itself.

"Here, my friend," she handed the case to Beag Scath, "move this away so it does'na ripple my work." She knew he'd been eyeing the tiny streams of magic that were drifting away from it; she might as well let him absorb them. Besides, that would take them both out of the way. The sprite's low, sub-vocal moans would have been quite a distraction had she let him stay. It wasn't his fault; the flow of magic called to him. The stronger it was, the more he longed for it. As he scampered off, Maggie began to raise the protections she would work within. She closed her eyes in concentration and gently grasped the power streams flowing through the chamber. The threads drew taut as she wove their pattern as intricately as the knotwork of her beloved Eire. The sprite would fret at being outside but he would remain both safe and out of the way.

Within her shields, Maggie reached out her hand to caress the violin, trying to comprehend the nature of the magic there. She could sense many things rooted in its grain. With her eyes still closed, Maggie saw the differences in each, like fleeting reflections in the very flow of the magic. Most prevalent were the many loves involved; that of music, of family, and deep down, foundation to it all, the love of Ireland. She would build on what was already there.

Deep in her throat, Maggie sang an ancient Celtic verse, each note settling into a web of protection around the instrument. Adapting techniques she learned long ago, Maggie mingled her song with the hum of power flowing from Quicksilver. By mixing the magics, she hoped to camouflage the violin, blending it into the background.

But it wasn't working. Something was wrong. Her task should be done, but she could still feel the violin. In fact, it was even more visible to her mage sight, as if it had become a dark, flat rock absorbing the rays of the sun.

All that effort, all that energy, wasted! What had thwarted her? She could feel Kara's essence—wispy tendrils of the girl's soul were clearly evident—but that wasn't what stood in Maggie's way. As she delved deeper, she could sense a primordial power surge within the instrument, stirring as if awoken. Curious. *What was the truth of the treasure that lay before her?* It was as if some consciousness was seated in the very grain...some being that resented her meddling. Maggie could not afford a struggle against an ancient force she did not understand. Something struck out at her, reaching for her personal power, drawing it away as if to weaken her.

I don't think so! Maggie thought fiercely, blocking further drain and raising her defenses. Whatever she roused, she needed to send it back again into slumber long enough, at least, for the defenses to be set.

Taking up the threads of her magic yet again, she wove into the weft traces of the soothing spell she'd used against Beag Scath earlier. The entity resisted. Its awareness swirled around Maggie, plucking at her shields, probing for signs of weakness, analyzing her essence until she felt laid bare. Whatever it was, it was ruthless, but she could not afford to fail in this task. It was not Maggie alone who would suffer if the entity triumphed; what would happen to Kara, whose soul was linked to the instrument? That thought was enough to strip several centuries of Maggie's life, if she let herself dwell on it.

No. Maggie had a vow to honor. The girl would come to no harm when Maggie could prevent it. She held nothing back as she tried once more. If this did not work, she was lost; they were lost. Once the entity woke fully there would be no fighting it.

Frustrated and angry that such a simple task was proving so costly, Maggie ground her teeth and screamed aloud in the subterranean silence, reverting to her ancient tongue. "What the hell are ye, an' why do ye fight me so?"

A stillness filled the chamber, intense and looming. Bands of what could only be described as thought encircled her. *Was this it, then? Had she met her fate, alone and far from her people? Would she die on the wrong side of the ocean?* But there was no pain, no wrath, no final strike. Something reached out, despite Maggie's defenses, and gently caressed her thoughts. Right down to her soul, she was sampled and explored even deeper than before. She should have felt violated, but the invasion was so fleeting, so unassuming. With the absence of threat, she was left with only confusion. Whatever it was withdrew just as swiftly. Maggie felt bereft and drained...and she was not done. Was this a strategic retreat, or had the entity truly withdrawn? Whichever, Maggie was going to take advantage of the opening. With a quick chant, she called up the cloaking spell once more and again wove in the soothing sleep she'd perfected against Beag Scath. Quickly, Maggie anchored her spell to Quicksilver, relieved to see that *this* time it took. No one would be able to sense it by its humming, though it was visible to sight. Frowning, she ended her word-weaving. While it was beyond unlikely any mage would penetrate this far into her domain, she could take no chances. More disturbed than she had been at the beginning of the task, Maggie was certain of one thing: the violin must never fall into unsavory hands.

Shaking herself to loosen the stress of her efforts, Maggie considered the situation before her. She was beginning to curse whatever fate had placed the enchanted relic back in her hands in this charged state. The unexpected confrontation left her drained. *How was she to defend the instrument now?* There was one more precaution she must take, but it would leave her personal energy dangerously low. Lower, in fact, than it had ever been.

There was a possibility. With just a wisp of her own power, she might be able to harness the feral magics surrounding her to cast one more spell. It would take great effort, and a bit of help, but she must attempt it, and now, before she thought on it enough to change her mind, before something else interfered.

Maggie settled herself at the base of the pedestal and gathered her concentration, along with the last vestiges of her strength. She then extended her hand through the field to physically touch Beag Scath. By that connection she drew him inside the shield's bounds. This could only work through him.

"Come, my friend," Maggie said quietly. "If I am to finish, I shall most definitely need your help."

His attitude much subdued from earlier, the sprite crept into her lap, exactly like a child in need of reassurance. His tiny hand reached up to brush against the wilted daisy behind Maggie's ear. She was far from done and she already felt as faded as his earlier gift. Holding him close, she wove her consciousness through his. In such a drained state, the only way to handle the feral forces around her was to bond with her friend, whose very strength was in his instinctive use of the wild magics. It was a part of him. By combining her control and his affinity, her final task would take much less effort than if she attempted it alone.

Eyes closed, Maggie allowed her mind to follow the sprite through the surrounding currents. She had to be careful not to reach for the tantalizing streams of power. It was important to gather up only what flowed through Beag Scath if she wanted to survive.

Rapidly grasping the fluid strands, Maggie began her weaving. She felt her blood sing with renewed strength. Only the cool sweat that drenched her reminded her the feeling was dangerous. She dared not get lost in the reviving illusion. Each stream she took into herself sapped her own energy because of the effort it took to control it.

Her focus absolute, Maggie held in her mind the image of both the tablet that she rested against, and the violin that lay on top of it. She could see subtle connections between both of them. Nothing strong, but enough to serve as a foundation for the defenses she had in mind. She bound Quicksilver tightly to the Irish marble until her mental sight viewed the two as one. Maggie visualized the objects of her focus as fluid as the power she used to bind them, complete with the subtle swirls of counter-currents to mingle them together. It would take someone who had been present at this weaving to unravel the cords. She thought briefly of the stirring she'd subdued earlier but pushed the thought away. Concentration was of the utmost importance. Maggie shuddered with the final bind and let loose her tentative hold on the power streams only moments before she lost her grip on consciousness.

Beag Scath whimpered as he removed himself from Maggie's limp grasp and reached to touch her face. His slight frame trembled in response to the chill of her skin. With concern, he patted her cheek, willing her to awaken. Maggie moaned slightly and began to shake. She did not rouse. Scampering out of the room, the sprite came back dragging a folded blanket from a nearby storage room. Slowly, he tugged at it, drawing it across the room until it covered her. Once that was taken care of, the fading residue of scintillating magic above his head uncontrollably drew Scath. With the innocence of a child, the sprite scampered over Maggie to view where the violin had rested. He climbed atop the empty pedestal, utterly perplexed: to all the earthly senses, Quicksilver was gone. Hands running absently along the surface of the marble, Scath muttered in confusion before climbing down and settling himself in Maggie's lap to wait.

The sunlight streaming through Kara's window was obscenely beautiful the next morning. She lay tangled in her twisted sheets and could do no more than sigh. Staying where she was would only draw out the torment, and it would add to her parents' worry. Not that they would worry less once she confessed. Still she was tempted to roll over and bury her head beneath the pillow. She would resist temptation. With resolve, Kara climbed out of bed and dressed hurriedly. Grabbing the envelope she had prepared the night before, she headed down to breakfast.

"Good morning, sweetie," Mathair bustled from stove to fridge and back again, assembling the meal in their daily tradition. Papa wasn't at his seat, but the tea by his place was half empty. A steaming cup was already beside Kara's place. That simple, everyday kindness almost undid her. She stood in the entranceway of the kitchen and fought the urge to run.

Instead, she drew a steadying breath and remained where she stood. She didn't want to sit at that table, didn't feel she deserved to, though that was stupid, when she'd only given up Quicksilver to make sure they still *had* a kitchen next week.

"Well, go on, sit down. Your father ran to the corner for the paper." Kara would have bolted then and there if not for the sound of the front door closing. The rising lilt of one of Papa's favorite ditties reached her before the man himself walked out of the shadows still cloaking the foyer. As he came up behind her, Kara's fear faded. There was no running now.

"There's my lass," his voice was warm and contented, as any man would be, surrounded by his loved ones. The weight of Kara's guilt grew harder to bear. The fear may have lifted, but her nervousness had not. She put on a good face and leaned up to kiss Papa's cheek.

"Morning, Papa, sleep well?"

"Aye, like a wee babe." He looked at her more closely and she could see curiosity and concern slip into his gaze. It should have warmed her. Instead, it filled her with dread, particularly when he spoke further. "Somethin' wrong, lass?"

"No." Kara managed a smile as she quickly turned away and slipped into her chair at the table. The move was purely evasive; if he looked at her too closely, she was certain he would know everything that was going on. She had no idea how she would manage to eat, but she still hadn't figured out how to tell them what she'd done. Helping herself to a muffin, she dedicated her full concentration to applying butter and jam, intensely aware of her parents as they moved about the kitchen. She was glad of the time while their attention was elsewhere; it gave her a chance to think.

"Oh, Kara," Mathair's request was casual as she placed scrambled eggs and bacon on the table. "Could you pick up your father's prescription for me when you go in to work today?"

Kara's butter knife fell with a clatter from trembling fingers and she looked up in a panic, startled into meeting her mother's unsuspecting eyes. Kara hadn't told them! With everything that had happened, it had slipped her mind. It never occurred to her to lie. Her eyes dropped down to her plate as she spoke. "I won't be going in to the pharmacy today...Mr. Amed fired me."

Her head rose slowly as both parents gasped. Mathair still stood, with a white-knuckled grip on the back of her chair and a forgotten plate of cantaloupe tipping precariously in her other hand. Kara looked at Papa and caught a flicker of hopelessness in his eyes before he quickly closed them. They both remained silent, but she knew what was going through their thoughts, the very things that had concerned her in the thirty seconds after the ax had fallen: What would they do now? How would they survive? Where would the mortgage money come from?

Well, now was as good a time as any to set them at ease. She cleared her throat. His self-control reinstated, Papa looked up, his eyes wary. Mathair sat. There had been little peace in their lives—lots of love, but little peace. Kara was about to perpetuate that tradition. Her eyes went from one parent's face to the other before she took a deep, steadying breath and reached into her pocket. She drew forth the unsealed business-sized envelope with their bank's familiar logo preprinted in the upper left-hand corner, and the payment address in bold across the front, laying it on the table and pushing it toward Papa.

"Don't worry, the house is safe."

"Excuse me?" Papa's eyes narrowed and Kara had a hard time not flinching beneath his considering gaze. "What is this?"

"Open it, it's the balloon payment for the mortgage."

For several long minutes, the only sound in the kitchen was Mathair's gasp. Kara felt stretched taut by the strain of the moment. All she wanted to do was shake off the tension and curl up beneath Papa's arm. That wasn't going to happen, though, not when he found out what she had done. Watching her closely, Papa reached out and drew the envelope to him. He tapped the edge against the table without opening it.

"Supposin' ye start by tellin' us what's goin' on here?"

Kara took a deep breath and braced herself for the uproar. She blurted it out before she could think twice. "I've pawned Quicksilver."

CHAPTER 4

Standing in the shadow of the backyard staring into the green-tinged water, there was no escape for her this night, only self-exile. She couldn't even momentarily forget the pain on Papa's face. So Kara hid here in the dark, wishing to be as forgotten as this pool, too low on the list of priorities for anyone to bother with.

Swirling her hand in the clouded and stagnant pool, Kara took a perverse pleasure in the slime that coated her fingers from that casual touch. The gesture summed up how she felt about herself that night. She found it so difficult not to feel self-loathing when confronted with the constant replay of her confession to her parents.

"I had no choice!" She was startled by the bitter defensiveness in her hushed voice, but she could keep silent no longer, even if it was only herself she sought to convince. There was no doubt in her mind she'd done the right thing. But even so, she couldn't help but feel wretched.

What was a little green slime when she felt herself no better than pond scum? Not only had she put a price to her father's gift, she had betrayed him, and all the dreams he had for her future. Worst of all, she had sold away one of his few comforts. Maybe it was her imagination, but she swore she could see him crumble behind his proud expression this morning when she'd told them what she'd done.

Things had gone both better and worse than Kara had thought they would; Mama had cried with relief, but Papa's eyes had glittered with tears he would not shed. There had been great love and pride on his face as he held her against the shaking of her own sobs. He hadn't said a word of any kind. She almost wished he would, even if it was only to damn her for giving up his precious Quicksilver and her dreams. Somehow his gratitude and silent understanding were more painful to bear. Kara felt more guilt now than she had when she'd signed the agreement.

"An' are ye hidin' again, lass?" Kara jumped as Papa came up behind her. "Ye used to be better at it."

He knew her too well. "No, Papa, just thinking."

He reached across her to lift her hand from the algae-rich water. Without taking his eyes from her face, he pulled a towel from the backyard line, wiping away the slime with quick, gentle strokes. Not wishing to see his pain and unable to meet his gaze, Kara stared at the water in the moonlight. Both were silent as the ripples formed patterns in the scum on the surface of the pool.

"Come now, Kara, join us inside." He draped his arm across her shoulder and gently guided her toward the back door. "Mathair's made a bit o' cocoa for us." The love and concern in his voice undid her control.

With the barest of whimpers, Kara stopped where she was as he kept walking. "Papa, I am so s-sorry," her voice broke as she managed to force the words past the despair that weigh heavily on her chest. "I-I didn't know w-w-what else to do."

Papa stopped and stood silently with his back to her. Her heart clenched as the silence continued. Finally, stretching his neck so that his head was back and his eyes looked up to the stars, Papa sighed. Slowly he turned to her with a look of sorrow in his eyes that matched the tears running down her own cheeks. He looked so tired. So very tired...and old. Kara shook with the effort not to sob. She suddenly found it difficult to breathe, standing there snuffing to keep her nose from running. She dropped her eyes.

The silence was too much. With her head still down and a sob clawing its way from her throat, Kara stumbled past her father toward the back gate. She never made it. Within a dozen awkward steps, he intercepted her, his arms closing firmly around her. Feebly fighting against the startling strength of his grip, she tried to smother her sobs against his shoulder.

"Ye're twenty-three, not three! Act yer age, girl!" he reprimanded her. "Ye've no right to give yer Mathair more heartache." He shook his head and just held her closer. "I'm proud o' ye. Ye knew what ye were doin' yesterday, an' ye knew why; do'na start to question it now."

Hindered by the catch in her throat, Kara could only nod in response. She continued to avoid his gaze.

Holding her at arm's length, Papa gave her a little shake, forcing her to look at him. When he had her full attention he began, keeping his voice low so it wouldn't carry. "I canna say I'm happy ye've let go o' yer dreams, but it warms my heart that ye did it for me. Have ye any idea o' the hope ye've given yer Mathair? Do'na take that away from her by doubtin' it now.

"Right now ye're our strength, lass." Setting Kara down on the lawn chair, he picked up the towel and ran it under the outside spigot. "Now wipe yer face before Mathair comes lookin' for us. The cocoa should be ready by now."

Papa turned to splash water on his own face or he would have seen her rise to come behind him. "I love you, Papa." It came out hoarse and low but, as she hugged him, it was enough. She said nothing more as they turned to the kitchen door, arms still resting on one another.

Papa stopped just before they entered. "Promise me one thin', lass...go back for it as soon as ye can. Ye've a long life before ye, an' dreams are the difference between livin' an' existin'." That said he continued inside, not waiting for her response.

"I swear it, Papa," Kara whispered to the dark night—a promise as binding as if she'd said it to his face. Only then did she join her parents.

Entering the soft light of the kitchen just steps behind her father, Kara could still see the strength of his shoulders despite his slow, tired gait and the newly touches of silver hair mingled with the auburn. While his ordeal had aged him, it hadn't yet made him brittle. This, more than anything he'd said earlier, reassured her.

Patiently, Mathair waited for them in the living room, three mugs of marshmallow-frothed cocoa lined up on the table in front of her. She watched them enter with bleak determination. Kara took one look at Mathair's face and was certain she knew something had happened in the backyard. Poor Mathair. Papa had always been her strength, the one who shielded her from all life's worries. She was haggard with the need to finally do the same for him. She was a gentle, nurturing woman, but not strong.

This wouldn't be a pleasant evening. With Mathair thinking she must resolve whatever conflict she imagined between them, it would be uncomfortable at best. Not having the energy to dance around the truth, or discuss it, Kara excused herself. She kissed her parents good night and took her cocoa to her room.

Reality returned with a numbing chill that intensified the burning across Maggie's hips. Letting her head roll limply forward because she lacked the strength to hold it upright, she used every effort just to focus. She should not be so weary. *Why was she so tired...drained?* Something hovered on the edge of her thoughts, but she couldn't quite grasp it.

Looking to the sprite brought no enlightenment. Sitting in the hollow of her sprawled lap, Beag Scath watched her with anxious eyes. Held loosely in the sprite's hand was a wilted, lavender rose. Evidence of his previous efforts lay scattered around him. He had obviously attempted to entice her awake with their favorite game. From the sheer number of blossoms, it had been going on for quite some time.

Her attempt to call to him produced no more than a croak from her dry, tight throat. Still, it was enough. Perking up with the resilience of an innocent, Beag Scath climbed closer to Maggie. He wrapped his arms around her neck with care and crooned sweetly, his concerns dispelled by her return to consciousness.

Maggie was stiff from her hours on the cold stone floor and had to concentrate on loosening tight muscles. She tried once more to speak.

"Water, my friend," Maggie prompted gently, "an' food."

The sprite's reasoning did not flow precisely the way a person's did, but the concepts of food and water he had no trouble grasping. As he scampered off to another room in the rath, Maggie took a moment to reflect on her surroundings. She had never been so drained by a magical exercise and so hadn't been prepared for it. If the sprite hadn't been with her, she wouldn't have fared very well.

Waiting for Scath to return, she thought of the changes she would make for the next time, should there be one. Right now, the room was rough stone on all sides, with the pedestal of Connemara marble in the center. She didn't keep much else here, though at one time she'd intended to add carving similar to that which ringed the ceiling in the shop above; one or two triggers for emergencies, along with some meditation patterns. Of course, this was the first time she had a need for such things. Normally, she seldom needed anything but her voice and her will to work her magic. It had been all too easy to procrastinate. Maggie winced as she shifted from one uncomfortable position to another. Her own lack of forethought annoyed her. She realized now that while she needed little to work her craft, some concessions would have made swift her recovery from the night's efforts.

"What happened?" she whispered, her voice a coarse reflection of itself. Her thoughts spun drunkenly and her frustration grew. Vague memories tugged at her, but oblivion tugged harder, until she drifted off to sleep still wondering.

Not bothering to turn on the bedroom light, Kara made her way through the darkness and settled into the cushioned window seat with her mug warming her hands. She had been too upset earlier to appreciate the beauty of this evening's sky. More at peace now, though still stabbed by intermittent guilt, she could admire the crisp, cold light of the half moon and the occasional star, stronger even than the city's lights. Kara rested her head against the chilled glass of the window and let her mind loose to wander.

Thwap! Crackle. Thwap! The sounds of the cat playing with her latest conquest brought Kara away from her thoughts and back to her cooling cocoa. Taking a sip through the sweet froth, she closed her eyes and savored the rich chocolate. The melted marshmallow had capped it off and kept it pleasantly warm.

Twapthwap!

"What are you playing with, Pixie?!" Kara placed the mug on her night table and turned on the light. The marmalade cat froze just for a moment in the sudden brilliance. Once she saw it was only Kara, Pixie continued her vigorous swatting. When a wild swipe sent the object skidding toward Kara's perch, she quickly intercepted it. She sat back to examine what she'd rescued. Kara did not recognize the bundle, though she was unsettled by how familiar it seemed. It was a smallish, undistinguished package she was sure she'd never seen; only it kept tugging at her thoughts.

Looking around the room, her eyes caught on her tumbled jacket. She had draped it across her desk chair when she'd come home last night. Now it was a crumpled mound on the floor. Pulled halfway out of the pocket was her silk scarf. Apparently, Pixie had tugged on it to get at something else that was there. She remembered back to the bank two nights ago, and the mysterious item she'd felt in her pocket. Pixie had discovered it when the jacket slid from the chair.

Absently deflecting the cat's efforts to reclaim the prize, Kara folded back the layers of crinkly paper. There, nestled in ivory parchment, was a simple but exquisite brooch. Immediately entranced by the knotwork setting, she held it up to the light. It was so delicate...obviously old...a masterpiece. Set in the enameled bronze was a fine, clear crystal about the size of a quarter. Fascinated, Kara peered closely at the pressed wild flowers just beneath the surface. How had the craftsman managed that? The crystal wasn't glass, that she could tell; and there weren't two crystals back to back, with the flowers between them. More important, how had the brooch come to be in her pocket?

Apparently losing interest in her repossessed toy, Pixie lounged quietly beside Kara on the window seat. Casually stretching, the cat repositioned herself count-less times just in the few moments Kara examined the mysterious piece. Slowly, almost absently, the cat reached forth her paw, batting at the parchment. The paper crackled and slid to the ground. Predictably, she pounced.

"Oh no you don't!" Kara intercepted Pixie in mid-leap, rescuing the parch-ment from an almost definite shredding. Putting the cat down behind her, its tail twitching violently with the pulse of the thwarted hunt, Kara leaned forward to pick up the paper. She took it to her desk, spreading it carefully, trying to smooth out the wrinkles. This wasn't just a wrapping for the precious brooch; it was a letter, and at the top was Kara's name. What was more, it was on the same kind of paper she'd seen in the lapboard at the pawnshop.

Dear Kara,

It is hard to find in this world a soul as giving as your own. Selflessly, you gave up your dreams for your father—fear not that they have gone. You've entrusted me with something that is the key to your soul and, as I breathe, your Quicksilver shall come to no harm in my keeping. She will always wait here for you. I sell nothing while the one who holds it dear still lives.

Wrapped in these pages you have found a gift, a mere token compared to the gift of music you played for me today. Forever will I carry the memory of that performance, and treasure it and the story it told. The brooch holds a bit of shamrock and forget-me-nots, for luck and remembrance. Please wear it always and think of me.

Someday you will return for your yesterday's dream. Until you do, be well and safe. Remember, in me you have made a friend. Should you have any need, I am here.

Always,
Maggie McCormick

Kara sat there in stunned silence. She turned the brooch over and over in her hand, mesmerized by the shifting colors of electric light on clear, faceted crystal. Her world had narrowed to this bauble and the puzzling woman who had slipped it into her pocket. She was an odd person, Maggie. Almost as ever-changing as the patterns of light on the brooch, the woman left Kara feeling quite off-balance. The girl had the distinct impression that she had seen the barest surface of that complex personality.

With a shiver that had nothing to do with the October chill, she put down the pin. Kara wasn't comfortable with Maggie's easy ways. Excessive generosity to strangers was usually accompanied by ulterior motives. She was curious about Maggie's. One thing was clear; whatever the reason for the gift, this pin was too valuable to accept from a stranger. Tomorrow she'd return it.

Carefully wrapping it back in the parchment, she reached for her jacket. Tucking both the scarf and the bundle into the pocket, Kara hung the jacket carefully on its hook behind the door.

She sighed as she climbed into bed with her cocoa. Like her disturbed night, the chocolate was just something to finish quickly, rather than savor. She didn't bother. Leaving it on the table beside her bed, she turned off the lamp. Somewhere in the darkness, she could hear Pixie renew her efforts to claim some other unknown item from the dresser. She made no effort to chase the cat to the floor for, in a perverse way, the identifiable sound was comforting.

As tired as she was, her mind pursued random thoughts with a diligence that mirrored Pixie's. She hadn't even resolved today's problems and already there were more for tomorrow. She would simply have to plow through the demands. The first thing she must do was return the brooch to Maggie. Once she accomplished that, she would have to go have a talk with Mr. Cohen, her boss and the director of the Music Center. It was a toss-up as to which she dreaded more. Kara didn't care to think beyond that point. Curled up in the darkness, she wrapped the down comforter around her for warmth, willing herself to sleep. It did not work. Across the surface of her closed lids played haunting images of the past two days: Quicksilver left behind on the pawnbroker's desk; her parents in tears, Papa's from pain and Mathair's from relief; and the faceless, nameless man with the television and the knife. Lastly, and strangest of all considering she had seen no such thing, was an image of Maggie crumbled in a field of flowers, looking pale and cold.

As she drifted off into a restless slumber, she noticed the sounds of feline pursuit had stopped. Silently, Pixie joined Kara in her little nest, twined herself around the folds of the blanket, gently kneaded the spot behind Kara's shoulder, and protectively settled down with a sub-vocal purr. The cat was a comfort as the image of Maggie pursued Kara into sleep. Everything about the vision stayed tantalizingly beyond the reach of her dream sight; it was just the sight of Maggie unconscious on the floor. Kara had the frustrated feeling that there were many more details in the fogged portion of her dream. Occasionally, an image would come into painfully sharp focus, but only for a few seconds. There were flashes of Maggie dancing with the familiar man from the picture in her shop. In mid-leap he transformed into the thug with the television and smashed the glass window where the violin in the photograph sat, only to be chased away by Maggie, dressed like a Victorian lady brandishing a quill pen like a sword. Again came the image of Maggie sprawled on the ground, only it wasn't Maggie...it was Kara herself with Pixie huddled across her hips. An impression surfaced of Quicksilver looking oddly like she was carved from green marble instead of wood. The violin hung in midair over Kara/Maggie, who now was blue with cold.

It all ended abruptly. Kara lay panting in the predawn twilight, finally chased awake by a glimpse of dream-Pixie yipping and staring warily back at her through tiny human eyes. Shaking and coated by a thin film of sweat, Kara glanced at the angry red numbers of her alarm clock: 6:15 a.m. glared back at her. She briefly considered going back to sleep, but it was no use.

Kara climbed carefully from the bedclothes, making every effort to avoid disturbing Pixie. All she needed was for the cat to wake up and imperiously demand her breakfast in the middle of Kara's attempt to, once again, quietly leave the house. Dressing quickly in jeans and a sweatshirt, she laid out a cream-colored blouse and amber slacks for work. A glance at her daily planner reassured her there was no one scheduled for lessons until this afternoon. She ran a comb through her hair and promised herself a shower after she had returned the brooch to Maggie; hopefully the shop would be open by the time Kara got there. Something about the piece of jewelry left her deeply disturbed, like she was being stared at.

CHAPTER 5

Patrick O'Keefe stood in the doorway to his daughter's room. For a moment he was ready to rouse her, eager to shout out his betrayal. But he knew he couldn't. Instead, his body slumped against the frame, his head resting on the woodwork as if it were too heavy to hold up. The moment of self-righteous indignation passed.

He watched as Kara slept fitfully, clearly wound up by the events of recent days; he longed for even that much rest. Since his illness, he had never felt as tired as he did this night, yet he could not sleep. Any other night there would have been music after dinner, with Kara practically playing his pain away. Her soothing tunes seemed to unravel the illness-induced tension, forcing his body to relax in spite of itself.

He quickly slammed that thought away. It made no sense to further stoke his anger.

He would miss the way her fingers danced across Quicksilver's strings. It tore at his heart that she had given up the violin. Worse yet that it should be because of him. He never would have allowed it, if he'd known. That one small fact made it so difficult for him to reconcile his feelings. She hadn't even asked. On the surface of his heart, he was proud of the sacrifice she had made for him; deep in his private core, he was furious she had given up her dreams—whatever the reason. His teeth clenched with resurgent anger. He had worked so hard to give her the chance to develop her gift, and in one afternoon she not only rendered his efforts useless, but she also denied him the one pleasure he could still thoroughly enjoy. Patrick found himself trembling with the effort to hold back the furious words he again wished to hurl at his sleeping daughter. If she were awake, he would not have been able to restrain himself. He knew he wasn't being fair. Fairness took strength and he had none to spare while fighting the illness that tore him apart. No matter how much he loved his daughter, it would be some time before he was able to let go of the betrayal he felt. With effort, he unclenched his fingers from the doorframe.

Turning from Kara's room, he felt as if life itself sat heavily upon his chest, leaving no room for breath. He stifled a sigh and took himself downstairs. His muscles were so tense that he trembled with each step. He couldn't join Barbara in their room with such emotions battling across his face. She was a dear woman, but she would never understand why he felt the way he did. It was better to keep his baser side to himself. His wife had enough of a burden with his illness and the debt it had caused them.

Patrick crossed the darkened living room in silence, carefully avoiding the furniture as he snatched up an afghan from the couch in passing. He had no desire to be comforted right now and if Bobbi were to join him that was exactly what she would try to do. His face settled into a resentful glare at the truth of his thoughts. Sometimes a person didn't want to reconcile his pain; if he did he might drift away with no anchor to hold him. No, all he needed was some quiet time to harness his temper. Stopping in the kitchen for a Guinness, Patrick took his beer and blanket into the backyard, unthinkingly mirroring his daughter's earlier actions. It took a conscious effort to keep his movements quiet when his temper wanted to stomp and slam and roar about with its illusionary energy. Wrapping the blanket around him, he settled into the lawn chair to contemplate the sky through the dark glow of his beer. Maybe the solitude would relax him enough to sleep.

Watching the clouds, silver-lined as they passed across the moon, Patrick was reminded of the tales his Mathair and Da used to tell him of the faerie folk. Long ago, the Áes Sidhe, the fair ones, left their homes in Falias, Gorias, Finias, and Murias, riding upon the clouds. They arrived in Ireland and loved the land and its people enough that they made it their home, settling in to become the Gentry. Oh, to be able to ride away on the clouds to a better place.... Finishing his beer, Patrick set the bottle on the ground and burrowed deeper into his blanket, still staring at the sky as he drifted into tentative slumber.

Hours later, Barbara woke, wondering where her husband was. She found him asleep in the lawn chair, huddled and faintly pouting, like a child who had exhausted himself with anger that he was too stubborn to release. She knelt beside him and lovingly caressed his exposed cheek. His lips curled in an untroubled smile at her touch. This being the first restful night Patrick had had in almost a week, she would not disturb him. He was neither feverish, nor chilled, and the autumn was still young enough that the nights were only slightly cool. He would be fine for the few hours left before dawn. She tucked the blanket more firmly around her husband's shoulders and crossed the yard to check the lock on the gate. Only then did she return alone to their bed, assured that Patrick was comfortable and secure.

As he awoke in the chilled glow of the autumn morn, Patrick ran a casual hand through his dew-sprinkled hair. Cursing himself for a fool, he stretched thoroughly, watching for the aching signs that he should regret his open-air bower. There were none. He found himself stiff, but well rested and content this morning as he glanced toward the kitchen, knowing it was his wife's quiet bustling that had woken him. A deep, satisfying sniff in the direction of the back door told him there were fresh honey cakes and orange marmalade for his breakfast. Between the tempting smells and the nippy morning breeze that had found its way through the twisted folds of the blanket, Patrick knew it was time to leave his unorthodox bed.

It wasn't until he saw the scum-stained towel by the spigot that he remembered why he'd spent the night outside in a lawn chair. Shrugging the memories off, he strolled through the door as if taking his rest in the yard was a common thing.

First glancing to be sure he wouldn't ruin the wonderful breakfast that had enticed him to wake; Patrick swept his wife into his arms. "Barbara, ye hard woman; whatever possessed ye to leave me out in the cold? Do ye love me no more?" The carefree mischief beneath his pitiful tone—returning with a vengeance like the prodigal it was—forestalled her instant bristling at the accusation. Instead, with as sly a glance as his, she mock-swooned against his chest.

"'Twere the devil himself, claimin' yer Irish heart had gone cold!" she gave a throaty chuckle as she imitated her husband's brogue. "Seems he was wrong." Only five foot four inches tall to his six feet, she went up on tiptoe to pull him close enough to place a kiss on his nose. He gave it no conscious thought to bow his head to accommodate her. She giggled and he attempted a fierce scowl.

"Give it up, Patrick Kyle O'Keefe! Kiss your Bobbi the way she deserves or you'll get none of the honey cakes she's been slaving over while you slept as pleasant as you please!"

With a put-upon sigh deeply at odds with the loving look in his eyes, he kissed her every bit the way she deserved, which was twice as well as she expected. Laughing, he set her on the kitchen chair, her honey-brown hair rumpled and blue eyes dazed, and escaped upstairs to wash up. She could not chase him, weak-kneed as she was.

At the top of the stairs, Patrick hurried past his daughter's room; not quite sure if it was her actions he was avoiding, or his own shameful reaction. Eager for a taste of the ambrosia-scented honey cakes waiting for him downstairs, Patrick ignored his inner darkness with single-minded determination and went to the master bath to clean up.

After a final splash of icy water to complete his morning ritual, the familiar face that met his gaze in the mirror seemed more at ease. The deep brown eyes were still weary and the wrinkles were of equal parts laughter and strain, but there was a tentative peace staring back at him that he hadn't seen in a long time. He grimaced at the threads of silver-white running through his reddish-brown locks, but they weren't much, really. If not for the pinched look about his eyes, one would think he was fine.

It just went to prove how deceptive appearances could be, Patrick thought wryly.

Drying himself with a vigorous rub of the towel, he pushed away the traitorous thoughts and walked into the bedroom to change his clothes. There were no demands on him today; no trip to the doctor, uncomfortable treatments, or endless waiting at the pharmacy for medication that seemed to do no good. And so he found himself standing before his closet, searching for what he would wear, with only comfort in mind. He pushed aside binding sweaters and cotton work shirts with choking collars and burrowed toward the back, searching for the second half of his father's legacy. There, carefully wrapped and hung on a cedar hanger were the soft folds of his father's cardigan. Even as he reached for it, he stopped short. A battered shoebox on the shelf above the sweater caught Patrick's eye. With one shaky hand he reached up and brought it down. These were his parents' memories. With the box cradled in his arms he reached for the almost-forgotten sweater. Perhaps today was a day for remembering.

He laid the box of memories on the bed and returned his attention to the sweater draped over his arm. He had never seen his Da without its comforting knit across his shoulders. Mathair had made it for him herself just before they emigrated. She had often joked that if anyone told her she'd be burying Da in that cardigan, she'd have made it of a more appropriate color than emerald green. His father had always just laughed, rubbed his cheek against the sweater's velvety warmth, and quickly disappeared whenever she threatened to take it away for washing. He claimed it was his last bit of Eire and he would not give up the comfort of home.

Patrick chuckled softly at the memory of how adept his mother had grown at whisking it away when Da had no choice but to take it off. He also remembered, with even more delight, Da trying to wear it into the shower once, just to avoid her treachery. The image of him standing in the bathroom door, his deep brown eyes sorrowful, his red curls wet and tousled, and the cardigan stretched nearly to his knees, had floored them all with laughter. He'd looked like a guilty little boy caught wearing his father's sweater out in the rain. Mathair had tried to keep her gaze stern, but even she could not help chuckling. After that day, by mutual agreement, the sweater stayed outside the bathroom door when Da took his showers.

With a faraway smile, Patrick shook out the sweater and buried his nose in the crisp cedar smell of its folds. Closing his eyes, he slipped his arms into the age-softened sleeves and settled the cardigan across his shoulders. A deep sigh escaped his lips as he sat down on the bed. He felt closer to his parents now than he had in the fifteen years since they'd placed Da beneath the sod—two years after Patrick's mother had passed away. This was the first time he'd been able to bring himself to actually put on the cardigan. It was strangely comforting, forced, as he was, to confront his own mortality.

Settling back against the smooth wooden headboard, the sweater wrapped around him and pillows propped behind his back, he pulled the battered box onto his lap. With all thoughts of breakfast wiped from his mind, he sat for a long time just staring at the lid, as if it would lift off on its own.

His motions hesitant—as if the box might contain more than he wanted to know—Patrick carefully lifted the lid and placed it on the bed. Inside the creased and dented box were the usual black-and-white photographs and random trinkets of aged memories. As he lifted the items out one at a time, he rediscovered his parents.

It was amazing how much could fit in a shoebox. By the time he finished walking through his parents' past, the pictures, keepsakes, and papers covered the bed in a single layer. Most of the photographs meant little to him—in fact, they would have meant nothing without the carefully penned names and dates on the backs—other than the tiny pile of those featuring Mathair and Da. The souvenirs meant even less, though he was sure that Kara would be happy to have something more to remind her of her grandparents. The papers were another matter; those he must sift through carefully in search of any options they hadn't known were there. Carefully placing the photographs and trinkets back in the box and closing the lid, he then reached for the documents. A noise from the door interrupted Patrick's perusal.

"If I'd know this was going to be breakfast in bed I would have brought it to you outside...and saved myself the effort of getting the crumbs out of my nice clean sheets!" Barbara stood there with a breakfast tray in her hands. "Come on...move it over. I'd like to eat, too. Besides, the tea is getting cold."

"Sorry, love," Patrick quickly moved the box to the bedside table and gave his wife a wry grin. "I guess I got lost in the past."

With a glance, she took in the sweater and the dusty box. Wisely, she kept silent, merely crossing the room to place the tray over his now-vacant lap. He appreciated her sensitivity. It had taken a long time for him to find the courage to open up to his past. He could see she was making every effort not to disturb his tentative peace by calling attention to it before he opened the discussion himself. Settling next to him on the bed, she slipped one arm around him and reached for her teacup with the other. Patrick sighed and leaned into her embrace.

The mingled scents of cedar, Earl Grey, honey and orange, and the faint lilac of his wife's perfume filled Patrick with warm contentment. There were no demands on him today; he could sit here cuddling with his Bobbi half the day, if that was how he chose to spend his time. Patrick reached for a golden honey cake with one hand and gave Bobbi a squeeze with the one that was free. For a moment, she nuzzled closer, rubbing her head against his shoulder, then, tension pulling her shoulders taut, she straightened up against the headboard and twisted to search his face. Her eyes were wary as she watched him, as if trying to gauge the wisdom of whatever she was contemplating.

"Come now, Bobbi," Patrick prodded her gently. "Is it all that? I promise not to bite ye, whatever ye say."

His wife scarcely looked reassured. She took a deep breath and began. "I think we need to talk about what Kara has done," she paused, waiting for the re-action that would tell her how to proceed.

Patrick sighed, expecting his fragile peace to desert him. The silence grew heavy as each second passed; he could feel the rising of his chest take that much more effort with each breath. With a *whoosh* he exhaled, letting the forceful release sweep away the built-up tension of that brief pause. He expected to be furious, or at least depressed. And, if this had happened before he'd looked through the box of memories, he probably would have been. But no, each item in that box reminded him of the many sacrifices his parents had made for him, because love would accept no less. *How could he fault his daughter for the sacrifice she was willing to make?*

"Aye, my love," he finally answered. "'Tis the last thin' I'd ever have asked o' her, but the very solution we needed."

Patrick was aware this conversation could have meant the quick death of his good mood, but it wasn't. Any anger he had felt the night before had drained away.

"I'm glad you agree," she briefly smiled in relief, before becoming solemn once again, "but do you realize what this means? She never expects to get it back, and even if she does, it will be too late. With nothing to play on, she'll have to resign from the center."

Pulling his wife back to rest against him, he held her tight, basking in her warmth. There was a tiny frown creasing his forehead, but he did not feel the same panic he could hear in Bobbi's voice; those thoughts had crowded his own mind ever since Kara had revealed what she'd done. He'd no idea how or when she'd reclaim Quicksilver, though he trusted her promise that she would. Patrick sipped his tea as he formed his thoughts carefully before banishing his wife's fears.

"Love, where did we put Kara's old fiddle?" he asked his wife, an ingenious gleam to his gaze.

CHAPTER 6

Despite the windows running the length of one wall, high up toward the ceiling, the room was thick with smoke and darker than twilight. Heavy incense, mingled with the nicotine fog, obscured the majority of the room, leaving only a glaring island of light in the very center. Tony DeLocosta crept in the door, trying to glance around cautiously without shifting his eyes from the desk just barely visible across the pool of light. Did he see a movement in the shadow to his right? There was a disturbing sound from above; did it come from the rafters of the unfinished ceiling, or the rooms beyond? He dared not look closer; he dared not remove his gaze from the hard, glittering eyes he knew were watching him from the far side of the room. Whatever lurked around him, it could not be more dangerous than the man sitting there in silence, waiting.

Stopping in the center of the room, unable to move away from the false comfort of the light, Tony watched as the tip of a cigarette flared an angry red when unseen lips inhaled. He stood there coughing nervously into the uncomfortable silence. A billow of newly released smoke swirled around him as he fought not to quiver. In the end, he lost the battle.

"And where is my prize?" demanded the man after a calculated pause. His voice had a curiously cold, flat quality. "Answer me."

The young hood couldn't respond. It would be deadly to admit that he hadn't even found out what the item was. Running trembling fingers across his slicked-back hair as if reassuring himself that at least one thing was still in place the way it should be, he reflected on how nightmarish his life had become. Never before had lifting an item been the difference between life and death. Never before had he been required to steal something without even knowing what it was. It used to be that when he stumbled on a guard animal...he could recognize it, at least. Now, in this brief moment of reflection, he realized the answer he made would decide if he would ever wake from this particular nightmare. The rest wouldn't matter, only his answer was important.

"Well?" The voice and the crimson embers shifted closer. "Are you indispensable...or ineffectual?"

Subconsciously responding to the direct challenge, Tony straightened from his defensive slouch. The look in his eyes bordered dangerously on a glare as he hooked his thumbs in his pockets and shrugged.

"There was something blocking me," he answered. "I couldn't get past the counter, and whatever I was supposed to bring back wasn't where I could see it, let alone get it. I could feel something odd though."

When there was no answer from the shadow-shrouded desk, he dropped his gaze and resisted shifting his feet only through a supreme effort. "The lady, she wasn't fooled by anything. I think she was ready to take me on," Tony paled and took a deep breath before continuing, "before whatever was in the back room came after me."

Tony went silent. A bit of hell played across the surface of his mind. The thing that came after him had been vicious. He could still feel it tearing at the surface of his shields. *What would have happened to him if it had gotten through? And would it really have been worse than what might still be brought against him?* The man he faced now did not seem the type to forgive a failure.

The smoke-filled silence, combined with the weight of his boss's stare, made breathing a chore. It was as if he was gripped in an immense fist and brought closer for examination. He could breathe, but it was far from comfortable. The thought of that imaginary hand even slightly tightening its grip sent Tony into a fit of uncontrollable trembling. Darkness closed around him, leaving him staring at a pinpoint of light. Just moments away from a labored sob, he shook his head sharply and the dark drew back, leaving his eyes dazzled by the hazy light. Tony found himself on his knees, quivering violently. From the shadows, he thought he heard the faint echoes of chanted words at whose meaning he couldn't even guess.

"Yes," the darkness replied, as the sullen red glare of the cigarette tip came to rest upon some unseen ashtray. "It seems that not all is as it appears." The man stood and came forward, nearly obscuring the light completely, before reaching down to grip Tony's chin. With a most uncharacteristic gentleness, he forced the boy to look up. "Is it?"

The ice-blue eyes Tony encountered held his attention tightly as his head was gripped by the long pale fingers only inches from his throat; Tony could not respond. Fortunate for him, he was not expected to.

With a piercing gaze, his boss examined his features, as if for the first time. Tony's hard black eyes met that gaze for only a second before dropping away from its intensity. Tony's tanned face would have gone pale, had it not already done so. He closed his eyes tight, bracing for a painful blow he didn't want to see approach. Instead, he could feel the man's other hand come up to trace the surface of his face. Outlining his lips, the sharply angled cheekbones, and the strong stubborn chin, the fingers lingered over the not unpleasantly prominent nose, all of it the legacy of his Gypsy blood. If he hadn't been so terrified, the situation would have reminded him of his blind cousin's efforts to "see" his face.

The blow he anticipated did not come. Tony's eyes flew open as the icy hands drew away.

Once more withdrawn into the shadows, the man who moments before had been in a position to crush him now backed off and watched the realization of his pardon flow across Tony's face. The man just stood there behind the desk, his pale face floating in the darkness, his black turtleneck barely distinguishable from the shadow itself.

"Come, I must prepare you for your next task." Tony couldn't refuse the command; instead, he left his circle of light and followed. Beyond the desk was a spiral staircase leading to the floor above, its black, wrought-iron steps invisible in the darkness. He found himself practically praying that the unsettling sound he'd heard when he'd entered the basement wasn't from up there.

As they reached the top step, Tony could see that true night had fallen. In fact, the moonlight pouring through the window provided more light than the periodic ceiling fixtures lining the hallway. How much time had he lost in the shadows? How long since he'd entered the basement? It had still been light then. He realized that the hour hardly mattered; he had nowhere he needed to be, and after leaving behind the television and the knife—something he had been afraid to mention downstairs—he would have to stay out of sight anyway. Bad enough the woman could describe him, but his prints must be all over those things; he'd been sloppy.

Pushing away those thoughts, Tony stepped quickly to reach the door where the man waited.

"You would do well to remember," the man paused significantly, "it is not wise to wander from my side within these walls."

Quietly following the man through the dark wooden door, Tony's thoughts were drawn back to the only other time he'd entered this disturbing room. One week ago—it was hard to believe that was all it had been. Only a week had gone by since his life had been ripped out from under him. In seven days, he had gone from a tough who sneered at anyone's attempt at authority over him, to cringing before this man like any dog he had ever kicked.

The man had been tailing Tony all day. In the morning, he'd brushed past *Tony's arm in the corner bodega, startling him into knocking over a shelf of cans...the man stopped to watch with a smirk on his face, then turned down an aisle and was gone before Tony could confront him. In the afternoon, he had swiped a cab Tony had hailed. He hadn't even known who it was until the man turned in the back seat as the car pulled away, making sure Tony saw it was him.*

Seething inside, Tony was on edge the rest of the day, catching glimpses of what may or may not have been the stranger every time he turned. A patch of silver-blond hair, a distinctive stance, the flicker of a profile...there was always something. Finally, as Tony's temper went beyond control, there he was, standing in the entrance of a blind alley. Without a clue that he knew he had been seen, the stranger walked out of sight between the buildings. Tony signaled to a few of his friends before moving after the man, confident that they would follow. It was time for the stranger to learn a lesson.

As his eyes grew accustomed to the gloom of shadow and indirect light, Tony heard an umph behind him. He whirled to look for his crew just in time to see the look of panic and confusion on their faces as their way was inexplicably blocked by nothing more than air.

"You were thinking perhaps, that I am foolhardy and unwise?" As Tony turned toward the speaker, the man appeared much more imposing than he had in the light of day. "I think it is time for discussion, my young friend.... What possible use can you be to me, that would persuade me to keep you alive?"

Tony could not answer, attempting instead to back away and regroup with his friends. No matter how tough he was he knew better than to face a guy like this without his gang there to bail him out if things got out of hand. No, he was too smart to be caught in less than favorable odds...yet here he was, as good as alone anyway. What was worse, he found he couldn't move.

"Fortunately for you, my friend," the man gave him a calculated look while reaching for the basement hatch in front before them, "I had plans for you before this began. Follow me, Anthony. We must discuss our new association; I am sure you will prove most useful to me."

That was the first time Tony had entered this place; he didn't recall walking, yet a door had been before him and the stranger ushered him through it. Tony couldn't remember anything beyond that point, and he knew that there were many things he couldn't explain. One of those things he was distinctly grateful for: the shields that had kept his skin in one piece last night. Shields placed on him here, by this man. Now he was entering this room a second time. *How would his reality twist around him with this visit?*

Standing just inside the door, Tony caught himself once again unbalanced by his expectations. He stopped abruptly, his eyes reflexively blinking in reaction to the well-lit room. Given the atmosphere of the basement they'd just left, and the very attitude of the man before him, Tony would have expected the room to be ominous and dark, full of odd smells and barely perceptible movement in the shadows. There would be dusty old books along the walls and arcane symbols on everything—so much for Hollywood's depiction of the mystic arts.

The walls—where they weren't covered by neatly ordered and dusted bookshelves—were the off-white color one got when subjecting white paint to a chronic smoker. Besides the bookshelves, the room contained an old wooden cabinet, a large battered desk, a scattering of chairs, and a table by the window that had obviously had a variety of tasks carried out upon its surface. Nothing hung on the walls, other than a few framed documents that were too far away for him to read. As for the smell, not much could compete with the nicotine stench that permeated every item in this room.

"You seem disappointed...again." The boss did not bother masking his contempt. "Has my den let down your trite imagination? As if I require the trappings of stereotypes."

Tony flinched as the door closed with a sharp click. He couldn't help his preconceived notion of what this room would look like. The guy was creepy, and hell, just the fact that Tony couldn't remember what it was like after being in here before.... Having a blank spot in a man's memory was often more than enough to start his imagination running.

"Wait, while I consult my library." The man caught his eye, as if to imprint the fact that it would *not* be a good idea to distract him.

Tony stood nervously in the center of the room. Once the door closed solidly behind him, there was nowhere to go. He wasn't asked to sit. The man moved past him with purpose, first to the bookcase, and then to the worktable. After a moment, an acrid waft of incense mingled with the permanent scent of tobacco that filled the den. A toneless chant grew from a muted whisper. Bit by bit, it reached for Tony. Like steel bands, it held him immobile. As each heartbeat slowed, time meant less and less for him; whatever gripped him held him away from such linear things. Finally, as if in response to the claustrophobic quivering Tony could no longer hold back, the force eased off enough for him to again feel the current of time.

With a shudder, Tony looked up into the appraising eyes of the man, finally recognizing him as a true worker of magic. His head swirled with vague memories of yesterday at the pawnshop. It was all there: the woman, whatever attacked him, his flight. Everything had been sifted through, including the fact that he had left things behind. The discomfort was reassuringly real.

"You are quite accommodating, young man," the man's eyes flickered with resignation and contempt. "But you have a lot to learn. I think it's time for you to go back to work."

He pushed a key on his desk closer to Tony.

Disoriented, Tony merely stared at it, the full weight of the man's quip closing in on him. *What had happened? And most of all, what work was he supposed to be doing?* His fleeting memories were gone; he no longer recalled anything since stepping into this room and being told to wait. He was left with the feeling that he had been evaluated and labeled "substandard, but necessary."

"Well, go ahead and take it. It is the key to this building. You are to finish your task and return here. Come in the front door and right up the stairs to this room." Here the man paused, as if to let everything sink in. "You will knock on this door and wait until you are given permission to enter. Do you understand me? You will *wait*...no matter how long it takes me to answer."

Tony found it hard to swallow, but he managed to answer. "Yes, sir."

"You are never to enter this room without my permission," a particularly nasty expression crossed the man's face, "of course, I probably didn't have to tell you that, did I? I rather doubt you particularly care to be here even *with* my invitation, let alone without it.

"Now leave!"

Tony did not wait to be asked a second time. Shoving the key into his pocket, he didn't bother to mention that he had no idea what his task was. He left the building by the front door and was halfway to Queens before he realized it. As the A-train stopped at Broadway–East New York, Tony began to swear nervously, trying not to tremble. He lived in Manhattan, down in Alphabet City. Why was he on his way to Queens? Reality had definitely left the building.

Confused, but driven, Tony moved quickly and with purpose when the train opened its doors at the Lefferts station. With fear and determination battling for expression on his face, it was no wonder the people on the platform stepped aside to clear his path. He moved with the surety of a bloodhound on a scent trail as he descended the stairs and made his way deeper into the quiet Queens neighborhood. He had only a vague idea of where he was, but something inside him had no doubt of where he should be. Almost painfully, he was led through the back streets, where tall, narrow houses stood close in each other's shadows and counted themselves lucky for their wealth of space. Tony moved quicker and quicker as his internal guide told him their objective was near.

He was so fixated that when the force that dragged him to his goal gave way with an almost audible snap, Tony crumbled to the sidewalk, as weak as wet paper. Huddled in the dark, he hung his head, hoping to bring himself around with a blood rush. Breathing deep, he leaned back against the gnarled remains of an old and dying oak. In his dizziness, he imagined he felt a faint tingle where he touched the tree stump, as if someone had run the barest tip of a fingernail across his skin. Tony leaned away to break contact with the bark and willed his equilibrium to return. He was uncomfortable with all these tingles and tugs and other "feelings" he'd been getting lately. He wanted to finish this business and free himself from the chaos that had taken over his life.

He recovered more quickly with each passing second until he was able to pull himself to his feet. He would have to backtrack his way to the train platform and hope his "radar" locked in on something soon. Somehow he had been blocked, but he couldn't give up, not when the boss was waiting. He had to hope the interference would fade.

Kara paced a tight, little path as she waited on the elevated platform of the A-train. Where was it? After looking at her watch for the fifth time, she began to wish she'd remembered to bring a book to read. There was no cause for the tension across her shoulders or the dull ache behind her eyes, other than the fading wisps of her dreams, but still the feelings persisted. Her hand found its way into her pocket, absently reassuring her that the brooch, in its tiny, crinkly bundle, was still there. It was her only distraction.

At last she felt the vibrating rumble of the incoming train and turned to watch the nose of it coming around the bend. It was early on Saturday and there were only a handful of people with her on the platform. As the doors opened, a warm waft of air carrying the stench of bleach and acid engulfed her. Kara quickly moved on to the next car. It was the conductor car, which was where she preferred to be in the train, anyway. Cool air greeted her and any odors were barely noticeable. Carefully avoiding the occasional sticky spills and garbage on the floor, Kara moved closer to the conductor's booth and sat down to wait. The train seemed to fill slowly, but by seven o'clock they were pulling away from the station.

Once again, with nothing to distract her, Kara's eye wandered back to her watch. She would be much more comfortable when this was all over. Not just the matter of the brooch, but her resignation, the worry over Papa, her responsibility for their finances....

Oh my god! Kara felt the blood drain from her face as she realized what she'd been thinking. *No*, she told herself, *I don't mean that, I would never mean that!*

She burned with the shame and struggled to put it all aside for now. It was the strain, her weariness, making her think such shockingly selfish things. What she needed was a break, to put it all from her mind, if even for just a little while. That was what her music had...no, definitely not what her thoughts should be dwelling on. She had to find something else. Perhaps after dealing with Maggie, Kara would catch a movie before going to talk to Mr. Cohen.

For lack of any better distraction at the moment, Kara thought again of Maggie's brooch and the letter. Nothing about what the woman had written was threatening or necessarily sinister, but, combined with the situation, it left her wary.

Taking the bundle from her pocket, she turned it over and over in her hands. It was such a small thing; and yet it, and the woman who had given it to her, had dominated her thoughts since she rescued it from Pixie's clutches. Against her better judgment, she unfolded the crisp parchment to reveal the glittering pin. The rising sun was at just the right angle to strike the crystal through the train window. Even with the dirt and scratches on the glass, the resulting sparkle was breathtaking. Several people in the car looked up at her unconscious gasp. Even the conductor glanced out of his booth at her.

Kara blushed furiously and she slipped the brooch into her pocket before it caught anyone's eye. Muttering an apology, she focused herself on the paper in her hands, fervently hoping everyone would look away. Not even focusing on the words, she ran her hands across the creamy, slightly rough texture of the page. It was very high quality, too fine to be used for just a casual letter. Apparently, Maggie felt differently. Reading it again, Kara still could find no fault with the words themselves. It was just, well, the whole thing gave her a feeling that something loomed in her future and that reparation would be expected of her at some point. It was an uncomfortable thought. She'd already had enough of responsibility in her short life.

Leaving the train at Canal Street, the girl was too caught up in her thoughts to notice the young man slyly watching her depart. He was watching everyone who got off the train with a bored, disinterested mask that didn't quite disguise his keen gaze. No one paid particular attention to his hesitant move toward the door until he cursed and slammed his fist against it when it closed in his face. The remaining occupants of the car jumped, shifting nervously in their formed plastic seats, sliding him furtive glances, as any cautious New Yorker would.

As the conductor bounced just that door open, the passengers settled back with relief, watching but a moment as the punk darted onto the platform. But he was already too late. While he stood there, glancing sharply down the length of the crowded station, he missed Kara exiting the subway. His quarry disappeared into the bustling chaos of downtown.

An hour later, with a dry muffin and weak tea heavy in her gut, Kara once again stood nervously in front of Yesterday's Dreams. When she had gotten here earlier she found the place closed. Breakfast had filled the time between, but she questioned the wisdom of that now.

She tried to ignore her upset stomach as she peered through the glass door, to little effect on both accounts. The room beyond was dark and shadowy, barely touched by the morning light. There was no movement, though the posted hours of business were from 8:30 a.m. to 5:30 p.m.—seven days a week. She glanced around for some sign informing the public that the shop would be closed today. There was nothing.

Kara's unease threatened to flare into full-blown alarm. Perhaps it was her dreams, or Maggie's odd letter, but deep inside she was sure something was wrong. Backing away from the building, she looked for signs of life in the rooms above the store. The upper windows were as lifeless as those directly in front of her. *What if the thug from last night had come back? What if Maggie was hurt, lying there somewhere in the darkened building unable to help herself?* On the surface of Kara's mind flashed a persistent image from last night's dream—Maggie sprawled on the floor. Kara's hand subconsciously made its way into her pocket, clutching the comfort of the warm crystal brooch.

Clammy with the fall morning chill and her own dread, Kara rushed from window to window of the darkened storefront. Repeatedly, she knocked and pushed the doorbell, which was tucked unobtrusively in the side of the doorframe, which produced no other results than a tingling hand and finger. Then a screen door slammed somewhere to her left, bringing Kara's attention to a tiny side alley she had not noticed before. Approaching the squeeze way between the pawnshop and the pub next door, it was no surprise she had initially overlooked it; a slender tree in a massive cedar tub partially obscured the opening. She didn't recognize the tree, but it was full enough to overshadow the entrance. That, and the way the fronts of the stores protruded slightly beyond the actual building, hid the opening from anyone who didn't already know it was there.

Kara peered around the bole of the tree just in time to see an ancient, wrinkled woman glance nervously around before carefully placing a large, brimming bowl upon the ground. She straightened and, in a crackling whisper almost too low for Kara to hear, she called out, "Fair one, my lady...I've brought ye yer due. Do'na let it be said that Molly Kelley was forgettin' her place."

How odd...the woman must be a bit touched in the head to leave offerings to the faeries in a New York alley. If there were any place less magical than faerieland, Kara would have a hard time naming it. It seemed it wouldn't be a good idea to approach the neighbor, then, but Kara did see a private entrance to Yesterday's Dreams where she might get a better response than she had at the front. Keeping behind the tree, she waited but a moment for the woman to disappear behind her own door. Only then did Kara creep forward.

Once past the opening, she could see that the space was just wide enough for the side doors in each building, which faced each other, to open at the same time and not touch.

At her feet she looked down to see the old woman's bowl. It was filled to the rim with rich, creamy buttermilk, from the smell of it. It was a little weird to see something right out of Grandda's faerie tales. Carefully skirting the dish, Kara approached the door that was Maggie's. She looked with hope for some indication someone was there. There was nothing. She glanced down the length of the building, seeing no other windows lower than two stories up and that one was dark. There was an intercom, but no one answered when she pressed it. She couldn't even tell if it was working.

She felt strangely uneasy about knocking on the side door, but there was no other option. The feeling of intrusion she experienced the night before overwhelmed her once more. It was almost as if the sensation were outside of her, surrounding her in a disapproving cloud. *What right did she have to infringe on this woman's private space, after all? What if she'd had a long, tiring night, or a touch of a cold? There were many possibilities for why the store remained closed. Whoever said that the owner must leave a note to take a day off?* Everything seemed simple when she stopped to think on the situation logically. Yeah, real logical...then why did she grow more uneasy with each moment? It was no longer just about returning the brooch; Kara was anxious to make sure everything was okay within.

She put her doubts behind her, took a deep breath to try to slow her rapid pulse and settle the clenching in her stomach, and placed three sharp knocks on the aluminum door. The clatter should be enough to reach even to the third floor of the building.

"Sure and 'tis mischief yer up to!"

Kara spun around, startled by the sudden, unexpected reprimand. There behind her, livid with an Irish temper none diminished by the onset of age, was the old woman from across the way. Stooped and wrinkled Molly Kelley might be, but Kara could see that her eyes snapped like black fire beneath the silvered, white curls that framed her face in deceptive softness. The woman brandished her broom like a familiar weapon, obviously ready to drive all trespassers away.

"I'll na have it said I stood by while ye intruded on my lady's domain!" The lyrical brogue did nothing to soften the threat of the woman's warning. "Away with ye! An' mind the bowl at yer feet or sure an' ye'll visit her wrath on me as well!"

If the situation weren't so serious, Kara would have had a hard time not laughing at the feisty image before her. She respected the damage the woman could do with a good, stout broom handle, but the picture itself was quite comical, or would have been without the dead certainty in the woman's eyes. Slowly backing away, Kara tried to explain.

"I'm sorry I disturbed you, ma'am," she said softly, putting every bit of her good intentions behind the words, "I've come to see Maggie McCormick, the woman who runs the pawnshop."

The end of the broom rose ever so slightly and Kara bowed to the futility of convincing Maggie's neighbor of anything. She wasn't about to get into a fight with the woman, and standing here at an impasse was accomplishing nothing. "Well.... Thank you, I'll come back later, then."

Kara retreated, but only as far as the sidewalk in front of Yesterday's Dreams. She stood there frustrated and uncertain of what else she could do. She didn't like that the morning and her effort had been wasted. Her fists clenched as she tried to think of some alternative she may have overlooked, only a sharp pain in her palm disrupted her focus. Kara looked down to discover that the brooch, originally tucked in her pocket, was now clutched tightly in her hand. Without realizing it, she'd taken it out, holding it like some kind of talisman. When? She couldn't even remember doing it. Already unsettled by the encounter, Kara felt off-balance as she shoved the bundle back among the folds of her silk scarf, all efforts to return the brooch thoroughly thwarted, for now. She no longer had interest in a movie or any other distraction, and it was too early to head for the Music Center, even if she were dressed for work. Instead she headed home.

Tony was taking too long; it was morning already and still no word. Lucien seethed at having to wait for the prize he knew was out there; it was like a hunger constantly distracting him. Tony had amazing raw potential, but unless he brought something soon, even that wouldn't be enough to ensure Lucien's tolerance of him. If he could not be useful...then he would be used. There was enough latent power there to more than make up for the expenditure of harvesting it.

No longer able to take the waiting, and not wanting to destroy something important in his workroom out of sheer impatience, Lucien grabbed his trench coat and headed for the stairs.

"I'm going out," he called over his shoulder to what lurked in the darkness. "Tony may enter, but no other." As he passed through the front door, runes on its surface flared momentarily into existence and faded once again from view. Every window and door on the brownstone had similar protections. They lay dormant and waiting, poised for the moment a stranger tried to enter. It was always wise to be prepared for unexpected guests.

Skillfully blending into the sidewalk traffic, Lucien moved off toward a certain pawnshop in the Village. Perhaps the boy would prove superfluous after all. Besides, Lucien wanted a better look at this "lady" himself.

As he approached his goal, the tranquility of the street proved immensely irritating. Quiet little brownstones sitting side by side, shadowed by the stately oaks lining the street, seemingly untouched by the air of disregard that covered most of the city. Here and there, undisturbed plots of pansies dotted the curb where patches of sun pierced the boughs above, and stray cats, not looking in the least as if they were on the cusp of starvation, sauntered across the street. With the sidewalks clear of litter and the walls unadorned by graffiti, anyone—resident or tourist—would have questioned if they were still in Manhattan. In the middle of it all, like some nauseatingly serene focal point, sat the pawnshop. Its windows were dark and its blinds drawn, but it invoked a feeling of awareness...as if something benevolent kept watch.

Lucien wanted nothing more than to disrupt the peace that hovered over this neighborhood, anchored in that little shop. It was a challenge to his power; the tranquility that surrounded him was, in every way, a territory marker shouting louder than words: "Be gone. No harm will be permitted here." That alone did not sit well with him; it inspired in him an overwhelming need to wreak havoc on the place.

Like a spoiled child, drawn to certain acts precisely because they are forbidden, Lucien breathed deeply, preparing himself for an act of pettiness that would stir things up without draining him. Focusing his mind, settling on just the perfect affront, he pushed with his will to spread a little hate, a touch of fear, and the seed of suspicion. He wasn't able to continue. The only outward sign of his failure was the poisonous look of absolute fury that flashed across his face. So powerful was that glare that an older couple, out for their afternoon walk, immediately crossed to the other side of the street in attempted casualness.

Lucien's anger grew exponentially as he searched for more acts of defiance to throw in the face of this area's protector. Any action that he could put into motion without extensive preparation he tried, all to the same effect. The man's rage reached explosive proportions with each failed effort, though not again did it show on his now-cold face. Even worse, his unseen opponent apparently held him in utter distain. Not once did she come forth at his challenge of her boundaries. She had made a fatal mistake discounting him so easily. This little event served to focus his attention on her. He would give this shop and its owner his complete concentration until they relinquished the prize he knew was hidden inside and he had crushed them both. Spontaneous acts had no effect? Well, he would see how the place faired under his dedicated efforts, reinforced with the strength of precise ritual.

Lucien turned away, conceding this round. Let the witch think she'd won. He would see her brought low in their next bout. In the meantime, his lingering rage was a distraction. He gathered it into an icy ball and forcefully expelled it. As he turned and stalked away, purposely trampling the pansies, he once again composed himself so that his expression showed nothing. Behind him—the sole evidence of his visit—he left flattened flowers on the ground and pure fury hanging in the air like pollen on a humid spring day. Each person who breathed in the hateful miasma was filled instantly with animosity for all they encountered. Lucien smiled tightly at this small triumph. Finally, he had chanced upon the one thing that the protections could not thwart...pure and forceful rage.

CHAPTER 7

Lying in the cool darkness of her workroom, Maggie drifted in and out of consciousness. Vague memories danced around her awareness, pools of emotion strong enough to penetrate her lingering exhaustion. She figured she must be close to recovered, especially if she were coherent enough to puzzle at the imprints left on her defenses. She would have to check them to see what had taken place while she was...indisposed.

Without a glance, the woman reached out to the base of the pedestal beside her. She did not wonder that her hand encountered cool, moist fruit; she was well aware that Beag Scath was taking care of her. She settled back in her blankets, head resting on cushions she didn't even remotely remember climbing onto, then Maggie brought the rough, papery-skinned pear to her lips. Her only concern for this second were the demands of her parched throat and empty stomach. After only one bite, every one of her senses came into a sharp, clear, overpowering focus. This was what her body craved; the texture of the browned skin was delightfully at odds with the firm crispness of the ripened flesh. Each bite released a stream of juices and slightly tangy perfumes. Breathing deeply, Maggie closed her eyes and savored the sensual feast. Her tongue darted out to catch the drops of moisture poised on her lips, preparing to escape down her chin. Such pleasure from the fine, pebbly flesh, feeding her immediate need, even as it kindled her body's greater hunger. She barely noticed that she'd reduced the fruit to a close-cropped core in mere seconds. It was definitely time to reclaim her daily life.

Slowly stretching her length, muscle by muscle, stirring the rest of her consciousness, Maggie opened wide a set of eyes that seemed on the verge of subtly glowing. She stared at the tracework of veined rock above her head, focusing...reaching out for the barest trickles of energy. Hardly more substantial than the condensation dripping down a rock, the energy stream she grasped was almost more than she could handle in this state...almost. Drawing it in, it lent her the strength to rise and take herself to a more reliable energy source—the refrigerator.

Instantaneously, Beag Scath was at her side, his hair tousled even more than usual by sleep. The eager look on his face clearly expressed how tired he was of the spare rations she kept below. If she had not been so weary she would have felt more remorse at his being trapped down here while she recovered. Of course, she also knew that even had the way been open for him to leave, he probably would-n't have. Maggie leaned heavy against the pedestal as the sprite hugged her leg; she bent down, letting her hand rest briefly upon his head before gently re-leasing herself from his grasp.

"Hallo, my friend." She chuckled roughly as she took in the carpet of flowers that, with the exception of a Maggie-shaped hole, covered the floor. "No need to ask what ye did to keep yerself amused. My thanks, Scath, ye've cared for me well." There was no answer—the sprite rarely talked except to sing—but he hummed contentedly at her praise.

Making her way toward the stairs, Maggie carefully shuffled through the blos-soms. There was no telling what the sprite might have innocently buried beneath his amusements. As she moved, Beag Scath morphed to the needed height and slipped himself under her hand, understanding, in his simplistic way, that she needed support. Only once was it necessary for Maggie to stop and rest before they made it to the top of the stairs.

With barely a twitch of will Maggie brought down the barrier keeping them in and the world out. *How much easier it was to unravel the spell than it was to erect it.* Not for the first time, Maggie found herself regretting that the energy released was not hers to reclaim. Tormented by a deep hunger, she watched the energy of the locking spell drain back into the feral currents from which she'd diverted it.

The moment the way was clear, the sprite rushed off. Feeling sadly abandoned, Maggie slowly climbed the stairwell. The light pouring through the second-floor window nearly blinded her; she had been in the dark too long.

After checking the lock on the door to the shop, she turned to find the sprite, wearing the regal form of a cat, waiting impatiently at the door to the alleyway. Maggie slipped on a tired smile; old Molly must have left her daily offering. The woman had enough of the sight to catch the barest glimmer of their magical na-ture through the protections. Maggie did what she could to refute the claim, but still her neighbor left tribute each day.

As she leaned briefly against the side door, Maggie closed her eyes and extended her senses. Something nagged at her, but she couldn't place it. Her resources required replenishment before she had the strength to examine the residue clinging to her defenses. All was safe enough for now, so she reached forward and let her friend out to reap the benefits of Molly's superstition.

Thankfully she could allow the sprite to roam the alley. The defenses Maggie had erected made it an extension of the house, as far as the sprite was concerned. Beag Scath could prowl the alley as much as he liked, just short of approaching the way to the street or old Molly's door. Though she was careful not to let him out when the old woman was around, she would not take from him his small bit of freedom. Whenever Molly mentioned the vague glimpses she caught, those listening always discounted them as quaint ramblings, anyway.

Maggie sighed as she watched the sprite devour the twig-filled saucer of cream. Such simple pleasures seemed so great, the way he savored them. Well, it was time for her to think of her own needs. Scath could find his own way back into the building.

With a groan, she assaulted the next set of stairs—the final obstacle between her and food. Once again, the thought occurred to her that she should keep more substantial stores below, but she needed them so rarely that by the time she remembered, it no longer seemed important. Normally, Maggie didn't need to keep supplies at all; she just conjured what she wanted as the need arose. In fact, the only reason food was stored in the apartment was in case someone else might be around to notice, or for those times—like now—when she lacked the energy to even conjure a meal. By use of a minor amount of outside magic, she'd even managed to store her groceries in such a way that they never spoiled, so there was no need to replace them regularly, unless they were used.

Heading straight for the too-pristine kitchen, Maggie found herself craving honey-laden, orange and cinnamon tea, with its soothing sweetness and its sharp, lingering scent. She put on the kettle before absently reaching for a couple of bananas and sliding into a seat at the table. Her eyes focused just beyond the windowpane at the bright blue sky. Without the aid of a clock, she knew it to be about two in the afternoon, by mundane reckoning; her only concern was which day? How much time had she spent below? She didn't think it had been long. If she was lucky, she had only lost one day.

As the kettle reached a boil, Maggie finished the fruit and moved on to a muffin from a basket on the table. She fixed her cup and went to the sofa in the other room. If she were going to take inventory, so to speak, she would need to make herself comfortable.

She settled herself on the faded cushions of the overstuffed sofa and tucked her feet beneath her, resting her head against the high back. Her hand ran absently across the soft, floral print of the upholstery as she pulled her thoughts together. The fabric, with its dips and creases, served as a tactile focus. Relaxed but alert, she closed her eyes and pushed against her inner senses. With deliberate slowness, she allowed her consciousness to expand; first she was aware of only the texture, then the fabric, the couch, the room, the apartment, and the building itself in a series of ripples. At last, completely in tune with her surroundings, Maggie's mind encountered the layers of her shield.

There were drawbacks to working with outside magics, but only a few...if you had the power to control them. Maggie faced one of those drawbacks now—since this particular set of shields was woven from outside magics, Maggie wasn't instantly aware of anything that might have impinged upon them. Or, at least, not in the state she had been in for the last day or so. Of course, if she had used her own energy to create them, they would have failed all together with her complete exhaustion. She would have been forced to rebuild them now, if that were the case, but all she had to do was restore her connection.

Exerting a mental effort akin to walking a perimeter, she examined the entire shield. There were the usual traces of city wildlife, which she allowed to pass through the first layers of her defenses to give them a safe haven from the city. In the back, a vagrant had attempted to force the gate to the yard; he'd proved no match for the shield's outermost layer. Not much else of what she discovered concerned her...until she reached the section of shielding across the front of the building.

As Maggie's awareness glided across the storefront, only her extreme control of the trance state kept her from trying to send out a challenge flare. Just outside her defenses, the air vibrated with frustrated malevolence. Even more disturbing, some fading wisps of the anger were on the inside. Something more underpinned it, something vaguely familiar, but the anger nearly obliterated every other signature. Maggie was sure, if she stretched herself further, she would still find it pinging off the surface minds of the unsuspecting residents of the street. There must have been many senseless spats recently. Breathing deeply, she paused in her examination. The attempted invasion had triggered in her an aggression as forceful as a badger defending her hole. She must regain her focus or she could miss something important.

As she continued the perusal of her shields, Maggie extended a bit of her will, dissipating the anger in the air. She couldn't undo the damage, but she could prevent more. It was also clear that the front of her shields would require some repair; the surface was a bit rough in spots. Much more and the intruder might actually have made it through. Maggie was almost done, only the alleyway remained. She continued her circuit.

A second telltale hit her! Something *had* gotten through the shield, and at the spot most heavily defended! It was too much for her to take. Maggie trembled in reaction, her face alternately going cold and hot. She dropped into an instinctive rage. *Who could be powerful enough to pass her defenses?* Then an anger rose from her that was completely her own; who would dare?

In her current state, her fury was enough to unseat her focus. Her eyes opened, burning with a frosted glare, as her expanded awareness snapped back into the confines of her body. Someone had invaded her sanctuary with impudence; they would not do so again. Moving with a quick and frightening grace, she grabbed an intricately carved quarterstaff leaning in the corner. She was halfway down the stairs between one breath and the next.

As Maggie burst into the alley, adrenaline coursing through her veins in the place of blood, Beag Scath looked up from his lounging in the small patch of sun that had found its way between the tall buildings. Pleased, he sauntered to her, innocence and complete trust leaving him oblivious to her fury. Ignoring the raised quarterstaff, he wrapped his cat form around her ankles and purred. The peacefulness of the alley and the contentment of the sprite confused and disoriented her. She had stormed to the defense of her domain, only to find no threat. Lowering herself to the stoop, Maggie trembled violently as the force of her fury sought some outlet.

Like anyone recovering from exhaustion, she found her reactions amplified out of proportion. She also suspected that the anger she'd dissipated moments before was having its final effect on her. She closed her eyes and returned the sprite's hug tightly. Between her lack of focus and his excitement, there was no communicating with him in this form; she would have to content herself with the fact that he wasn't alarmed. Whatever the cause of his excitement, it meant there was no threat inside the shields. Any danger would have severely agitated the sprite. As drained as a convalescent, Maggie leaned back against the door with Scath in her lap. Both of them were content to soak up the warmth of the sun for the brief time it flooded the alley with its warmth.

The chill of the shade and the screech of a screen door slamming finally woke her. Opening her eyes and stretching to relieve the tightness of her back, Maggie looked up into the meek gaze of Molly Kelley. Maggie sighed; she much preferred old Molly with the Celtic fire that was in her eyes when she dealt with everyone else, but even Maggie couldn't defeat the might of superstition. No matter how often she tried to muddle her true nature to the old woman's sight, some glimmer still came through. Molly would always treat her like one of the Gentry, the fair ones. She would have much rather been treated as a friend.

"Good evenin', Molly," Maggie wielded smiles and pleasantries as deftly as she had wielded the staff earlier, trying to put the woman at ease. "Seems I've taken an unplanned nap."

Molly smiled tentatively in response, looking as nervous as a hare wanting desperately to act like it wasn't there. "I do'na know what happened, La...Maggie," the old woman muttered, just on the edge of a fear inspired by innumerable conflicting tales of the temperament of the fae, taken in over a considerable human lifetime. "'Twas a frightful racket I heard, an' her traipsin' around like she owned the place. I raised my broom an' she took off straight away."

There was a silence as Maggie tried to absorb the woman's rushed words. *What was she talking about?* Her neighbor's expression seesawed between anxious and eager, and she clutched the bit of crockery that was thankfully keeping her hands from fluttering. Maggie had never given the woman cause to fear, but her actions apparently could not stand against Molly's bred-in caution. It had taken the pawnbroker years just to convince the woman to call her Maggie, instead of Lady, and even now she slipped from time to time. Particularly when something had her as agitated as she was now.

"Calm, Molly, calm! What are ye talkin' about, love?" Maggie had the irritating feeling that something was just on the edge of coming clear, if only Molly could drag her eyes from the staff resting against the wall. Had she been watching when Maggie burst into the alley?

"Um...the lass...the one as snuck back here, rappin' on yer door an' eyein' the house," Molly answered, as she unconsciously gravitated closer to her own door, "but ye need'na worry now, I ran her off."

Maggie felt foolish as she saw now what had eluded her before; Beag Scath wasn't alarmed because the only people who'd been inside the shields were allowed to be! Their visitor had been Kara and she'd passed through the shields because she'd had the "key." Maggie was embarrassed to think she had missed the clues that would have told her who had entered her domain. A glance toward the entrance of the alley showed her the traces of the brooch's ancient signature.

The artifact was very old, so old that she didn't even know who had constructed it. That was why she had chosen it as the girl's protection; it was ancient enough that none could unravel its spells, and strong enough that very few could break them. The only drawback was that it would protect anyone holding it—but once it was keyed to Kara, she was the only one it would let through Maggie's shields. There were only a few of those that the girl could not cross, unless Maggie specifically keyed them to keep her out.

Between the magical signature and the calmness of the sprite, Maggie should have known not to worry. There were even traces of the girl's own power, raw and unshaped, which should have clued Maggie to the fact that all was well. The traces of anger, though, those weren't Kara's, or even Molly's; those concerned Maggie greatly.

Sighing softly at her own state, she looked back to her neighbor. "My thanks, Molly," she replied, "I believe I know who ye mean. If I'd known she'd be around so soon, I would have warned ye. 'Tis fine, she's a good lass," Maggie paused to choose her words carefully, "a friend...I'm helpin' her out a bit."

"Oh dear," Molly stammered, her fair skin going as white as her snowy hair. "Lady, I did'na know! Please forgive me! I'd never a done it if I'd known, truly I would'na! I was just so angered to see her there, disturbin' what she ought'na."

Letting the woman grovel, for the simple reason that nothing she said would stem it, Maggie hid her own burden of sorrow. She didn't like to see Molly act this way, but she seemed even more frightened whenever Maggie tried to reassure her.

Why couldn't the woman see her benevolence? Molly Kelley had no reason to cower from her. She wanted to pat the woman's shoulder to comfort her; instead, she refrained. Truth was, she couldn't bear that Molly would most likely flinch away in fear. It was a burden those like Maggie had born for untold centuries—those with the sight to see their power invariably feared them.

Rising slowly to her feet, Maggie focused once again on the bit of crockery in Molly's hands. The hearty smell wafting from beneath the foil caused her to breathe deeply in appreciation.

Noticing, Molly quickly held out the offering. "I did a bit o' cookin' this mornin'...I thought ye might take a mite for yer supper." Her eagerness to please was stamped unmistakably in her eyes, doubly so now that she knew the "trespasser" she'd run off was actually a friend with the right to be there.

"Why thank ye, dear, ye're too kind." Then, pleading a weariness that was unfeigned, Maggie moved to her own door, hands warmed by the cottage pie old Molly had brought to placate her. As she opened the screen, Beag Scath darted past her, anticipating his share of the feast in her hands. She barely noticed that she was halfway up the stairs before she heard Molly's door close.

Poor Molly. Ever the good peasant, she waited for "the Gentry" to take their leave before going to her own rest. Maggie sighed again. No effort of hers would change the old woman's opinion. *Who was she to refute centuries of folklore?* There was nothing more she could do.

Setting the dish on the table, Maggie scooped out a bit to cool for the sprite, then sat down to enjoy her own. It would have been nice to share this meal with Molly for a change, but that would never happen. She would reap what comfort she could from the present situation and hope that somewhere along the line Molly just might get over her unjustified fear. Either way, at least Scath and herself would remain well fed. Finished with her meal, Maggie put the crockery with the few others she'd yet to return. She would have to think of some way to repay the woman, without perpetuating her superstitions. The protections she had extended over Molly's tavern were a start, but not nearly enough.

As she relaxed, a corner of her mind couldn't help but replay the earlier scene with Molly. One phrase just kept repeating itself, 'I was just so angered,' she'd said. As fierce as the old Irishwoman could be defending her own ground, it didn't sound like her to be angry. Remembering the wisps of anger she'd diffused, Maggie was glad that more damage hadn't been done while she was recovering below.

With weary sigh, Maggie pushed her worries aside for the time being. Selfishly she decided tomorrow was soon enough to toil once more. It was too late to open the shop today and it was beyond time for her to catch up on some real rest.

Agitated, driven by ruthless compulsion, Tony found himself back at the pawnshop. It was so frustrating to pursue something and not know what it was. For a brief moment on the train he'd thought that whatever was guiding him had locked onto its prey. There hadn't been too many people in the car, a few kids, an old couple huddled on a two-seat bench, and a girl by the conductor's booth that would have been something to look at if she'd cut out the wholesome bit.

From the start, his attention kept going back to the girl. He'd watched her through the reflection in the window until she'd gasped. Panic momentarily filled him, though he'd calmed quickly enough, once he realized she was looking at something in her hand, not at him. Becoming aware that she'd gotten everyone's attention, she'd shoved the trinket into a pocket and hid her face behind a piece of paper she held. That was when his reflexes told him he could relax again. When he turned away he noticed his "guide" was no longer tugging at him. Once again, the trail had been lost.

Only an act of extreme will kept Tony from cursing loudly, even now. It was bad enough being controlled, but what was worse was knowing his "boss" wouldn't wait long before demanding to know why Tony had not returned with the information he wanted. On instinct, Tony had decided to follow the girl. Too bad he hadn't made up his mind quick enough. Nearly trapped by the closing car doors, he'd lost her at Canal Street. Then he decided to come to the shop.

Now, lounging on the corner of the block opposite the pawnshop, his instincts proved true. He'd been there half-an-hour and was about to give up when the girl from the subway came up the street heading toward the store. Tony watched her determined efforts to get the attention of someone inside. He'd already scoped out the place when he got here and it seemed vacant to him. With a practiced eye, the young man categorized the tell-tale signs that separated opportunity from risk: no lights were on, there was no movement from any of the windows, the recessed door was partially blocked from all but those directly across from it, and, with the exception of himself and the girl, there was no one around.

Noticing a phone kiosk a few steps away, Tony looked at his watch for the benefit of anyone looking out onto the street from the nearby windows. He carefully arranged his face with an annoyed expression, and walked over to pick up the receiver. If anyone was watching, he hoped they would think he was waiting for someone that was late.

A simple call to 4-1-1 gave him the number for the pawnshop, and the quick-dial had the phone ringing in a matter of moments. After a few minutes without an answer, Tony was assured that no one was there. Too bad he was here for other business; this place definitely had the marks of opportunity.

Even as he had that idea, memories of the other night arose to taunt him, making his thoughts a lie. Whatever outward signs pegged this as a reasonable hit, he knew inside there lurked a guardian who would tear him, body and mind, to shreds. Tony resisted the onset of tremors he knew he could not control by reminding himself he was here for other reasons today...reasons that did not require him to walk through the door of that shop.

As he focused once again on the girl, Tony cursed. *Where the hell was she? How could she have managed to disappear so quickly?* He forced himself to lean casually against the phone kiosk. Taking out a cigarette, he considered the situation.

If she hadn't gone into the shop, how could she have gotten away in the short time he wasn't watching? Glancing quickly around, Tony was about to cross the street and look closer when he heard the sound of a screen door slamming. An angry voice rising from the vicinity of the shop convinced Tony it would be better to stay where he was. Getting caught nosing around would only hinder his efforts further.

His decision paid off. After backing out of a hidden alleyway next to the pawnshop, the girl from the train moved purposefully in his direction on her own side of the street. Wrapped up in whatever had taken place, she never noticed when she acquired a second shadow.

This was too much of a coincidence. Some intuition told Tony this girl knew about whatever the boss wanted from the pawnshop. All he needed to do was follow her and see what he could learn.

He took a bandanna out of his back pocket and wrapped it around his head, pulling it down over his forehead. Not wanting to risk the girl recognizing him from earlier, he also took out a pair of sunglasses and slipped them on. She probably wouldn't notice one person out of many, even if she had gotten a good look at him this morning, but it was better not to chance it. To complete the picture, Tony dropped into a slouching, relaxed stride. Not only did it give the illusion of casualness, it also made him seem shorter than his height of 5'9". Using this deceptively slow-looking pace, he could follow her all day and never lag further behind than he intended.

As he trailed his prey back down into the recesses of the subway, Tony found himself once again on the A-train headed toward Queens. Perhaps this wouldn't be a long day; it appeared the girl was returning home. With a growing feeling of triumph, Tony hoped that she was. Once he knew where she lived, it would be so much easier to find out about her, and her connections to the pawnshop and the treasure locked inside.

He settled back, leaning against the door of the train car to wait out the ride. Behind the dark lenses of his glasses, he sized up the unsuspecting girl. Wholesome was the first word that came to his mind, followed by sheltered and obedient and uptight. She was pretty, in a boring sort of way. Everything about her was commonplace except for her eyes; they were gorgeous and different. A wild, orange-gold color he didn't have a name for, her eyes were the most exotic and expressive part about her. Even from here, Tony could see the worry and determination in them, and below that, something more: a flicker that surfaced sporadically, like a banked fire, as if most of her was hidden deep.

A twinge of guilt nipped at him, only to be immediately repressed. Okay. That was enough. Self-preservation was his philosophy. It was the only thing he held sacred. He hadn't picked her and he wasn't here by choice; Tony wasn't about to go soft on this girl when he was the one who would answer to the boss for it. He tucked away the meager information and refused to consider it again before the time came to pass it all on. It wasn't much, but the boss would want every possible detail when Tony finally returned.

I can only hope that I come up with more before then, he thought as he followed his mark through the quiet back streets of Queens. He was careful to stay a good bit behind her, on the opposite sidewalk. He didn't want her or anyone else getting suspicious. Nothing could point to him, if he were required to take decidedly more aggressive steps. As it was, Tony seethed inside at the familiar twists and turns the girl was taking. He out and out cursed when she turned into the front yard of a narrow two-story house he recognized all too well. There was no doubt now that the girl he followed must have been his objective last night. They were just half a block away from the tree stump that marked the point where he'd lost the trail when his guide failed him. So close! He'd spent the night on a train platform when he'd been this close to his goal. His temper didn't improve with the knowledge.

Down the street he could see a corner store that afforded a clear view of the girl's front door; he headed for it. Quickly, he went inside for a soda and something to eat, then set himself up out front. He would be glad when this was over.

Half an hour later she came rushing out the door, her face glowing and her hair swept back in an elegant twist, which was set off by the classy outfit that replaced the jeans and sweatshirt she'd been wearing earlier. The radiant smile as she looked back toward someone inside the house completed the transformation. Over her shoulder was a messenger bag and in her hands she cradled a worn instrument case as if it were something fragile and precious. As she moved off down the street, an old-looking man moved into the doorway to watch her depart.

Something about the guy stopped Tony from following her. As he turned his head to scan the street, Tony slumped back against the storefront, doing his best to look disinterested. Those piercing eyes swept across him and left him feeling completely exposed. He waited several minutes after the door closed before moving to leave.

The girl was still visible several blocks away but Tony didn't follow her; he had enough information for now. He strolled past the house, taking a quick, sideways glance to note the house number. At the end of the block, he checked the street number. He moved on with the girl's address firmly set in his memory. He would take what he'd learned to the boss and let him decide what to do with it all.

Agitated after her futile excursion to Yesterday's Dreams, Kara went home. She had been worried about Maggie at first, but now Kara wasn't sure. The brooch weighed down her pocket and dominated her thoughts. It was a symbol of futility; the focus in a dance of dark and roiling emotions. She could handle the doubt and uncertainty, they were fleeting; the despair was harder, but she refused to give in to it. What tormented her most was the growing tang of bitterness she could not evade, coupled with suspicion. Maggie McCormick wanted something, but how much did Kara have left to give? She was so tired.

All my efforts, all the sacrifices, and they never seem to be enough, she thought bitterly. *And now I have to give up my music altogether.* There is nothing left. Kara settled into the hard, unyielding train seat in a funk. She had nearly an hour ride ahead of her to sort herself out before she had to face Mr. Cohen with her resignation. Letting the dark curtain of her hair fall across her face, she tucked her hand into the pocket containing the brooch and settled back to let her mind try and unknot itself.

Why did life have to twist her about so? What had happened to her dreams? She had given up Juilliard and settled in at the Music Center with no more than a wistful look back, all to help her family in the time they most needed her. Now she'd given up Quicksilver and the Music Center to save their home. At that thought, she let her shadowed eyes close, rested her head against the cool window, and fought the despondency once more. *What had happened to the hope that sustained her in those beginning days?* If she were to find it again, she could not allow herself to get wrapped up in her own disappointment; the weight of melancholy would crush her if she'd let it.

Where once she had dreamed of the symphony, first chair status, and even soloist, now all she wanted was a quiet, peaceful existence, with health and family to comfort her. Instead, her life was a spinning coin, with the heads and tails blurring together to the point where she couldn't tell which one was being offered up to her at any given time. Whenever she felt the tight, merciless grip of despair, life casually laid before her a solution that appeared bearable, if not ideal. She wrestled with herself to choose right, and within a breath of doing what was needed, she discovered the new problems brought about by the very solution that was going to "solve" everything.

Just look at the state she'd walked herself into now—it had seemed so simple a choice, though she'd agonized over it for two weeks before taking action. By sel...pawning Quicksilver (she must never even think in final terms, or she would truly lose herself) she had solved some of their worst problems. With just that one simple act, Papa would have his medication, Mathair would be relieved of her financial worries, and they would not lose their home. Everyone could relax and be at ease again.

At least, that was how it was supposed to work.

Reaching her free hand up to her head, Kara rubbed across her temple and back along her neck, all of it tight with the strain of the past few days. Now she could admit that her actions had pushed back her worries for a while, but not solved them. The other day, even as she felt the pressure lift from her heart when she accepted the check, new worries lurked in waiting for her. Now she fretted about how to reclaim her violin and what she would do for a job. She was torn between trying to second-guess Maggie McCormick and her intentions, and hoping desperately that the woman was okay. On top of that—and here her heart clenched—the loss of Quicksilver had been more of a blow to her father's morale than she had thought it would be. Kara had to keep telling herself that he would eventually forgive her; for the rest of her journey home that was her only thought. It didn't help.

Wrapped up in her worries, Kara barely noticed as she reached her stop. Lucky for her it was the last one. Walking through the quiet streets of her neighborhood, she fervently wished she were on her way home to stay, and not just to change before she headed for the Music Center to quit. There was no avoiding it, though. She needed her own instrument to demonstrate and to lead her students through difficult pieces, to teach them the dynamics of harmonizing and playing in a group. Without Quicksilver, she could not teach, or at least, not for long. Kara wasn't even aware of it when her mournful sigh startled a passing couple.

Kara turned onto her own front walk and stopped at the door to compose herself. Things were bad enough without encountering her parents while her face looked like the embodiment of doom. After several slow, deep breaths, she moved through the door and into the dim foyer, where she hung her coat on a peg on the wall. She turned to go upstairs.

She didn't even manage one step before she swayed, put off balance by a rush of love for her father. There he sat in the kitchen, just visible through the archway. The sleeves of Grandda's cardigan were pushed up to his elbows and the belly of a familiar violin was cradled carefully in his lap. Beside him on the table there was a pile of old, brittle strings and a fresh tin of fragrant oil. Feeling as if her legs would not support her, Kara leaned against the wall, barely daring to breathe. She watched as he carefully drew an old, soft cotton cloth across the wood of the instrument, making it glow a warm mahogany. His eyes closed in a moment of priceless peace as he drew a relaxed breath and paused in his task.

"I-I thought we gave it away." Kara could hear the awe in her own voice and felt a rush of shame at the selfish, uncharitable thoughts she'd entertained all the way home. Fast on its heels was a flood of joy; She wouldn't have to quit the Music Center!

"Give it away, yer own first fiddle? The very one as learned ye to play?" Papa chuckled dismissively at the thought as he glanced up from his task. The look in his eye was one Kara long remembered; it made her feel like the center of the world and more precious than diamonds. *Of course her parents would not have given away such an important part of her childhood. Why had she ever thought they would?*

Her heart pounded eagerly in her chest and her eyes ached with tears, but the grin on her face, joyous and massive, said it all, which was just as well because Kara did not trust herself to speak. *What if this was a dream, one that would disappear the moment she spoke?* Not able to bear the thought, Kara simply beamed at her father, too happy for words.

"The poor fiddle needed a bit o' work, but shall we see how she faired in exile?" Papa didn't wait for Kara to answer. He set down his rag and took up a bow from somewhere at his feet. Carefully, he tuned the violin, adjusting the pegs as needed. Her father seamlessly slipped from tuning the instrument to playing it and the restored violin's voice rose like the irresistible song of Greece's mythical siren.

As a muffled sob escaped Kara's lips, Papa stopped mid-note and stood with an almost forgotten ease. Grinning, his self-pleased Celtic charm for once completely intact, he held out the violin without saying a word. She simply stared at the instrument as if it were an illusion that would disappear the moment she touched it.

"Papa...." There was so much she wanted to say, but joy robbed her of the words. Kara could think of nothing else but this reprieve from the dreary life she had imagined without Quicksilver. It wouldn't quite be the same without her friend, but at least she would be able to play, and able to teach!

"There's my lass, we've been here before, I think." Eyes dancing with amusement, Papa stepped forward and once again placed a violin in her arms. As his arms came around her in a hug, Kara realized the irony of the situation. Through streaming tears, her own eyes danced back at her father's. Setting her down at the table with her arms wrapped protectively around his peace offering, Papa reached down for the leather case he'd propped against the back of his chair. After giving it a quick wipe with his discarded rag, he presented her with the well-worn case.

Her tears fell a little faster, but her smile grew as she gazed fondly upon a pair of brass nameplates that sparkled in the sun pouring through the kitchen window. Once again, the engraving on the first plate was her name. On the second plate was the newly bestowed name of the violin: Papa had named it Hope.

Watching his daughter make her way down the street, Patrick sighed in contentment. By his simple act of restoring the violin, the balance of their household had been set aright. Now that Kara was off to work he could hear his wife coming up from the basement with the laundry. Wise, sweet Bobbi, she had understood better than he had that this act needed to come from him; anything else would have left the rift between father and daughter unmended. Before turning back to enter the house, Patrick took one last look around the neighborhood. Though things had always been quiet on their street, one must always watch for possible problems. Nothing really triggered Patrick's wariness, though he did notice there was a young man loitering in front of the store across the way. He wasn't one of the normal crowd that hung out there, but that was not too unusual, and he was only standing there. Content that all was well—at this second at least—Patrick went back inside.

"Well, with that smug look on your face," his wife greeted him cheerfully, "I don't really have to ask how things went."

"No," Patrick grinned mischievously. "I do'na guess that ye do."

Throwing a damp sock at him in retaliation, she expectantly held out the laundry basket. "Well, if you aren't going to entertain me with your tale, you can at least hang these on the line so I can get started on lunch."

Deftly relieving her of the basket, he pecked her on the cheek and headed out the back door. Only a small part of him was being contrary in not telling her what had taken place between Kara and himself. Mostly, he waited because the experience was still too fresh for him to discuss it casually, and his wife had had enough of tears for now...even happy ones. Without a doubt, he would tell her, but it would be later when they were under their down comforter, in the dark where silent tears would go unnoticed. Patrick broke into happy whistling as he strung the clothes up on the line. For now, all was well.

For a brief, perfect instant Kara's was a world at peace, as if the moment the mass of bills disappeared from her desk, it had taken with it the poverty in South America, the terrorist plots in Afghanistan, and the entire problem of global warming, not to mention all the other problems with the world, both near and far. And, in a rare twist of fate, she had some time to herself and a violin in her hand that begged to be played.

Kara stopped abruptly, her hand on the door of the Music Center. Why not? She was early...way early. There was nothing stopping her from taking some time for herself. The emotional whirlwind her life had become lately left so little time for relaxing; there was always something else that needed her attention, some obligation that must be dealt with. But not right now! A little quiet time alone would be wonderful. Assuming there was a practice room available, she fully intended to spend that time indulging herself in music for music's sake...for her own sake.

Besides, she and Hope needed to reacquaint themselves.

Her breath came out in a quaver. She couldn't even remember the last time she had played just for herself. Consciously taking a deep, steadying breath, Kara decided the moment was long overdue.

"Hey, Bert," she called out cheerfully to the custodian moping up a spill in the front hall. "How are you doing today?"

Bert looked up, his bushy thatch of salt-and-pepper brows drawing together in a scowl over his eyes. He looked as if he had a particularly sour lemon drop tucked beneath his tongue today, but Bert always looked like that. One had to look for the twinkle in his eye to know when he was in a good mood, which was nearly always, though he preferred to keep that to himself most of the time.

His eyebrows shot up as the thought caused Kara to chuckle and give him a brilliant smile. It hurt a little that her good mood drew such a startled reaction from this man who saw her nearly every day. While she hadn't particularly shared his regular sunny disposition over the past months, she made every effort to be pleasant even on the worst days. Of course, Bert was nothing if not observant. She was pretty sure he caught most of what she diligently tried to hide.

He looked almost wary as he peered closely at her eyes. "G'mornin', girly. You're not due in for another two hours."

Good ole Bert, she thought. *He still knows every little thing going on within the center's walls.* She treated him to a conspiring wink reminiscent of her days as a student, something she hadn't done since the concerns connected to her father's illness had begun to weigh her down. Bert opened his eyes wide with surprise before giving a pleased chuckle. She had always been one of his favorites and she knew that he worried at how somber she had been lately...but not today!

"And as far as anyone else is concerned, I won't be here for a couple of hours, either." Kara's voice was warm and happy, buoyed by her father's love. "In the meantime, I'll be lurking around the practice rooms."

"Just so, then." Bert went back to his mop as if Kara no longer stood there.

She giggled again and slipped away, taking the first available stairwell down to the basement to avoid as many people as possible. There were practice rooms on every floor, including those for the express use of the teachers, but all of them were too public. It suited her better to disappear into the less popular nether-regions of the school, where teachers never went and students only went if they were unfortunate enough not to find a practice space on the upper floors.

Just the same, Kara did not duck into the first room she came across; no, she took herself to the farthest one, tucked in next to the near-forgotten storage room and Bert's spare broom closet. Closing the door on the world, she turned and sighed, content with the solitude.

The room contained a music stand, a couple of chairs, and a single table off to the side, where personal items could be left out of the way. Laying down her bag and instrument case, she ran her hands across the newly oiled leather, noting the care Papa had taken to restore her old violin. She felt the smallest twinge of guilt, but quickly doused it. She was claiming this time for herself. She needed it, both to reacquaint herself with the newly christened Hope and to become comfortable in her own skin, something she hadn't been for quite some time. Fingering the clasps, she palmed the edges of the lid, and finally pushed it open. The violin inside was no Quicksilver. It was unfair to expect it to be. But that did not mean that Hope did not have a sweet tone.

With gentle, loving hands and the image of her father in the kitchen still blazoned on her thoughts, Kara lifted out the fiddle and carefully tuned it. She cradled it beneath her chin and ran through a few of the warm-up exercises she taught her own students. The room filled with sweet sound and Kara felt her heart respond. It was just her and the music: no demands, no expectations, and no obligations.

That last realization stripped away any inhibitions Kara might have had. She turned her back on the music stand and ignored the sheet music peaking out of her workbag. Now was the time for the music to move her, for her soul to pour itself out, as it had not been free to over the past two years. At first, she merely let the music flow from the strings with no guidance. Her eyes drifted closed and she swayed and dipped on the current that swirled around her. It was not enough, though.

Next she drifted into Bach, and Mozart, and then Handel, and all the pieces she taught her students, remembering the long-ago time when Hope had not had a name. When Hope had been the only instrument she had ever played. This violin might not possess the magical spirit Kara had always sensed in her Grandda's violin, but it had something more to recommend it: history. She had learned her skill in this very building, from some of the very teachers she taught beside now, on this very instrument. It was beyond time they got to know one another again.

But it was still not enough. Something in Kara ached with a longing that the classics and the popular music did nothing to ease. These were not things that she played for herself; they were merely the pieces she had grown accustomed to, compositions she equated with her time at the Music Center as both student and teacher. She thought again of Grandda and knew what she must play...what she had been afraid to play, fearing that something would be missing with a violin other than Quicksilver cradled beneath her chin.

So far she had not dared to play her cherished Celtic music, the music that meant the most to her, if for nothing else than her love of the man who'd taught it to her. Her bow hand fell to her side and her memories drifted to Grandda and one of the last times they had played together just for themselves.

The fancy stuff never interested her. Sure, it was neat to learn and oh so beautiful, but the works of the men her teachers called the masters only touched her briefly. What the sonatas and concertos inspired in her while she dutifully played was an aching appreciation of their beauty. They taught her form and style and intricacy, and she even lost herself among the climbing notes as her awareness danced with the melody until the world surrounding her faded away. All undeniable marks of a master work...but they couldn't compare with the wild, throbbing magic of the Celtic tunes Grandda taught her as a reward for the effort she put into her other lessons. The jigs and reels and haunting airs lingered once they'd been learnt, filling her with constant wonder and making her tremble at the bond she seemed to share with a land clear across the ocean, a bond that grew stronger every time she played the music. Her Celtic melodies didn't just lend passion; they woke what was already inside her.

"An' what are ye thinkin' o' so fiercely, my wee faerie?" Grandda's burr was like the warm buttered rum he'd let Kara taste last Christmas—when Mathair wasn't looking, of course.

"How Miss Frieda's music starts fading away with the last note, but yours stays inside me long after I'm done." Kara answered as she looked up from the patch of clover she hunted through. She smiled at him, her tongue peeking through the gap left by her most recent lost tooth. "Actually, the Celtic stuff never goes away."

He stared at her intently a moment before laughing richly. "Ye precocious little imp, 'tis started already, has it? An' yerself only all o' seven years old?"

Kara could see wonder in his warm brown eyes as well as sorrow. Not that she understood the cause of either one any more than she understood his comment. Both were gone quickly, though, as Grandda smiled back at her. "What do ye say we give the wee folk in that clover patch a break from tryin' to hide from yer keen eyes, an' go indulge in a bit o' buskin'?"

"Ooh! Yeah! Yeah!" Kara loved to play in the subway and in the parks with her Grandda. It was a real treat and she could barely contain her excitement. They didn't do it very often, though, because he said they didn't need the money people dropped on their case even when it was closed and it wasn't fair to draw attention away from those that did. As she waited for him to climb to his feet, Kara could not help but bounce up and down with glee.

"My! Get a look at ye, now!" Grandda exclaimed. "Ye certainly are excited. I best get ye away before ye squash all those Little People beneath yer feet."

Kara laughed merrily but immediately stopped her bouncing. She'd never seen one of the Little People Grandda described so clearly in his stories, though they both often pretended to. Grandda would point them out and Kara would greet them every time. While she was sure it was just make-believe, all the same, she found even the slightest possibility of doing harm to one of the magical beings very upsetting. After all, what did she know? Perhaps they were there and it was just that she couldn't see them. Kara would be careful where she jumped and played and go on looking for faeries in the clover patches. Maybe one day she would see one.

Grandda picked up his violin, Quicksilver, and handed Kara's own violin over to her. Standing on the sidewalk, she watched as he made a show of bowing to her clover patch, and then turned to look in both directions down the path. "Well, an' where shall we set up today?"

"Columbus Circle!"

Kara felt a thrill of utter joy as she slid her tiny hand into the work-roughened warmth of Grandda's. She smiled up into his solemn, dignified face and giggled as his merry brown eyes betrayed his true feelings. Grandda gave up his pretense of a gentleman escorting a lady and together they hurried toward their favorite spot, below ground by the southwest staircase that climbed out of the 59th Street subway.

"An' what shall we start off with, m'dear?" he asked as they set themselves up. Kara stood in her customary place at Grandda's shoulder as he sat cross-legged upon the ground.

One of the violin cases was open at their feet this time, the other tucked at her grandfather's back. "Well then, what is it to be?"

Kara pretended to consider the matter quite seriously though they both knew the answer. "First My Love from Tír Tairngiri and then Finnigan's Wake! An' ye must sing."

Her imitation of his brogue made Grandda laugh, his snowy white curls bobbing as his shoulders shook, which in turn caught the attention of many passersby. The two of them took up their fiddles and did their darnedest to hold that attention, if only for a few moments more. Soon they'd garnered quite an audience.

"How's about Scarborough Faire?" someone called out, as the last notes faded on Finnigan, and another suggested the ever-popular—and much overdone—Greensleeves. By unspoken agreement they went with the former. The crowd came and went, but their audience stayed consistent.

Kara watched the crowd as she played and her searching gaze was not disappointed. Hovering around the fringes was a man with a wild, matted mane and a thoroughly soiled leg brace. Despite the hindrance, he was bobbing anxiously from side to side. "Morning, Gerry." Kara called out to him, a sweet smile on her lips. "Do you feel like singing today?"

Before she even finished asking, he opened up and revealed himself a glorious baritone. Those around him shifted uncomfortably and a murmur traveled among them. It happened every time; even Kara could recognize that they found their awe of this person— whom many of them were conditioned to either pity or condemn—a source of uneasy embarrassment. What a shame they assumed the unfortunate had no kind of skill.

As the song ended and Gerry came back to himself, she could see him shift nervously beneath the stares of those around him. Not liking the way they looked at her friend, Kara gave a rousing cry particular to the Celts and launched into a lively jig. Grandda companionably followed her lead.

As they drew the piece to a close, Kara caught a barely perceptible nod from Grandda indicating an hour of performance was enough for one day. She obediently ended with a flourish and a bow and tried not to look too pleased as a shower of coins and even a few bills joined those already in the violin case. As Grandda emptied their take into his hat Kara occupied herself with putting their violins away. Finally, she could contain herself no longer.

"How did we do?"

"Quite respectably," he answered with a smile. Reaching out, he tucked one of the bills in her pocket. Kara's eyes burned bright and she wrapped her arm around his neck. Leaning into his shoulder she planted a kiss on his smooth cheek. She didn't know what figure "respectable" translated into but they must have done quite well for her to get part of the take as her own reward. They usually spent it all on Gerry when they were done.

"Well, shall we round up Gerry? I expect he could use some groceries about now." As Grandda spoke Kara thrilled in the love and pride wreathed around his words.

Kara came back to the here-and-now with the sound of *Finnegan's Wake* fading into silence and her cheeks wet with tears. Even after fifteen years she missed Grandda terribly. He hadn't been an old man—though after Mamó died, behind every laugh and every smile his eyes were ancient and weary—but suddenly one night he had been singing Kara to sleep, and the next morning Uncle Arn was there and they would not let Kara into Grandda's room.

She had not played this particular song since that day, and never had she gone back to Columbus Circle or her friend Gerry. Now she could see how foolish that had been. Sorrow was one thing, but she had allowed her grief to deprive her of the things that made Grandda seem so close to her, even now. Kara felt such love and pride in this instant that it was like he was there in the room and cradling her. She allowed herself to savor it a moment, but a glance at her watch revealed that it was also nearly time for her first lesson of the day. Quickly Kara gathered her things and hurried to her office.

CHAPTER 8

Lit by the warm, rich light of the autumn sunset, Maggie walked out onto the roof, leaving the door propped open behind her. After Molly's wonderful meal and a yet another nap, Maggie felt much restored. She couldn't fully enjoy the view though; she was here for a purpose. Maggie had many ways of finding out what went on beyond her quiet shop. She had her own little network of informants, one could say. In the hope that one in particular would arrive this night, she'd climbed these steps.

Settling against the still sun-warmed concrete wall, Maggie closed her eyes and breathed in deeply. She spread her awareness slowly, letting it move out like a ripple on a pond while she gathered in the counter-ripples set off by each object her senses brushed against. Things were quiet this night.

Ah! The one she'd hoped for was coming near. Drawing her senses back, Maggie opened her eyes just as she heard a soft thud on the roof in front of her. There, sitting calmly, almost as if she hadn't traveled across two boroughs and into a third, was a little marmalade cat. As their eyes met, a deep purr rumbled from the cat's tiny chest and Pixie sauntered forward to drape herself across Maggie's lap, butting her head against the woman's chin.

"Well, hello to ye too, puss." Maggie chuckled at the little hellion's sweetness. It had been some time since they had seen one another. Apparently, Pixie missed her. "An' what have ye to tell me today?"

Here was one benefit of Maggie's home being a haven for the animals of the city, they were a wonderful source of information. In this particular case, she couldn't have hoped for a better way to watch over Kara; Pixie was a special cat given to the girl by Maggie herself, though Kara had no idea, since the kitten had merely shown up on the O'Keefe's doorstep one day. Thanks to Maggie, the little puss traveled quite a bit faster than a normal cat, making conferences like this possible, despite the distance from the pawnshop in the city to Kara's home in Queens. If Pixie hadn't shown up tonight, Maggie would have made it known that she needed to see her.

Holding the tiny head between her hands, Maggie looked deep into her visitor's eyes. She chanted quietly to align her awareness with Pixie's. She could almost feel the little one trying to help her, twining around her thoughts exactly in the way she would have twined herself around Maggie's legs if she'd been trying to guide her physically, rather than mentally. Within moments they achieved rapport.

Slowly opening herself to the cat's awareness, Maggie waited for the creature to come forward and share what she would. Always, especially with felines, communion must begin on their terms; anything else conveyed aggression and a betrayal of trust. Maggie did not have to wait long. A feather-light touch brushed across her surface thoughts and in an instant her mind rumbled with a complex symphony of acceptance/comfort/pleasure, undercut by a dissonance of concern.

Maggie arranged herself for a prolonged sit and cleared her mind as much as possible of other matters, so as not to distract Pixie from her own stream of thoughts. She left only her own image of Kara, hoping to draw the cat's thoughts to the girl. Gradually, the images flowed, following no particular relevance or order. Some of the thoughts had the indistinct edge of second-hand information Pixie must have picked up from other cats on her way to Maggie's; these were full of vague scents, muted sounds, and flat images. Others were crisp and almost painfully clear, visions of the cat's personal experiences. Maggie could see into Pixie's mind almost as if it were her own. What she saw made her tremble. Danger had come closer to Kara than Maggie wanted to think.

Here was a sharp image of Kara sleeping, twisted in sheets that reeked of sorrow, small moans escaping her lips; there was a second-hand image of the would-be thief who'd come to the shop, slumped on the ground near Kara's house. Next was an older man's face—pleasantly familiar, though it was harsh and ugly with petulance and anger—surrounded by a blanket scent-marked as Pixie's chosen nest. Many images followed, including Pixie's courtship, paid by a black tomcat in some Brooklyn alley as she made her way to Maggie's roof.

Only two more memories caught Maggie's attention: The first was a complex memory of Pixie experiencing joy/surprise/confusion at sensing a certain "Maggie-ness" in Kara's jacket pocket, and the cat's excited discovery of the bundle with its crackly feel/sound and its familiar scent, the joy of the hunt and pounce, and the displeasure when it was taken away.

The second memory almost startled Maggie out of the rapport, something that could have bruised her mind and would have totally shattered Pixie's. With the sharpness of a memory newly imprinted, Maggie saw through Pixie's eyes an unfamiliar man who would have been called beautiful, if it weren't for the cruelty in his eyes and the hunger for power that dominated his face. This man bore the stench of evil. Ill intent filled him to the edges of his shadow. What was more, at this moment he waited just outside the sidhe's shields, anger slowly building in his heart because his very nature stopped him where he stood. Maggie recognized the feel of that anger; she had felt its remnants on waking from her earlier exhaustion. She must diffuse the power she felt him gathering before it contaminated her neighbors once again.

"Inside with ye, love. Run!" Already sensing her adversary, Maggie released her hold on the cat and was across the roof in one quick motion. As Pixie, with the excellent instincts of her kind, rushed out of the way and through the open door to the building, Maggie gathered the loose threads of magic that she'd carefully prepared long ago. There was no use trying to hide her nature; this man was likely gifted enough to sense some of what she could do, if not precisely what she was. Maggie would use this to her advantage. On these grounds, the stranger was no match for her. She knew the feel of her home and neighborhood, and, in its abstract way, it knew her. Anything she attempted would have the strength of her domain behind it. If he tried to use the local magics, he'd have to fight to bend them to his will...if he even could.

Unsure what training he had, Maggie was cautious as she peered over the edge of the roof's parapet wall. After strengthening her defenses, she reached out a tendril of her will to tug at the growing cloud of anger. Her purpose—to get her opponent's attention.

She succeeded. With a violent jerk he brought his head up to find the source of distraction. The man's angry face flushed as he snarled in response to her probe.

Woman, he thrust his thoughts toward her. *You have something I want, and I will have it!*

His actions gave much away. Maggie relaxed slightly behind her shields; this man had power but, compared to her, he wielded it clumsily and without finesse. By that alone, she would classify him as self-taught and not much in control of his potential power. Leaning forward on the wall, she continued to look down at him calmly.

I do? Maggie whispered into his mind. *An' what is it that I have? Anythin' in my shop is yers...an ye can best me.* Her mental tone made it quite clear that was unlikely. His lack of any reaction at all told her that this man could not even hear her thoughts.

Using a soft hum to direct the image in her mind, Maggie nudged the man's shields with the slightest pulse of power. Though it was just a small show of force, it curiously had the effect of physically bumping him. Apparently, he sustained his shields with personal power—any impact against them moved on to him. Maggie smiled, as this discovery strengthened her suspicions. He may have power, but had little idea of how to use it, let alone maximize it. He most likely only assumed she could read his thoughts because of something he read somewhere.

Come on, laddie buck, show me what ye can do....

"Are you too arrogant to even answer my challenge, witch?" The would-be invader growled up at her aloud. His eyes had gone dark and hard, lethal. Maggie still was not impressed.

Heaving a burst of sheer, manhandled power against Maggie's shields, the man snapped in impotent fury. Dazzled by the violent ripples of his magic breaking against her defenses, Maggie simply smiled. She didn't want her assailant to know his blow had struck in any way.

The man glared and thrust one more thought at her: *Know that your enemy is called Lucien Blank, and every time you turn I will be there, waiting for your misstep.*

As he whirled dramatically and stalked away, Maggie laughed out loud at both his pretension and his retreating back. With a thought, she turned the melodic laughter into enough force to dissipate the anger that still hung heavy in the air.

Maggie reflected, as her adversary stormed away, that no matter how crude his command of his talent, she would have to take care around him. She could remember times when brute force had been enough to overcome masters of the art. If she had been any less restored from her recent trials, he might have been able to force his attack past the shields that held against his evil intent. Tomorrow she would take steps to strengthen her defenses; she had a feeling that, with his reckless use of power at the end there, he would be of no threat to her tonight.

Carefully focusing herself, Maggie gradually released the strands of power she had taken up, allowing them to flow back to their paths. After the events of the past few days, she felt wrung out by the efforts of this confrontation. Maggie returned to the roof door to find Beag Scath just inside, in his tomcat seeming, curled around the anxious Pixie. Both of them rushed to twine around her ankles as she closed the door. Rather than attempt the stairs with them dancing about her feet, Maggie stooped to pick them up. Scath scampered to his perch on her shoulder, and Pixie curled against her ribs in the hollow of her crooked arm.

"Well, my children," Maggie sighed, "there's always somethin' to make life interestin', is'na there?" They merely purred in response, and huddled closer. "Shall we see if Molly has left her normal offerin'?"

Climbing down three flights of stairs encumbered with twenty pounds of cat and sprite was enough to make Maggie long for her bed. She hadn't realized exactly how drained she was, and the episode on the roof had sapped the bit of strength she had succeeded in restoring. On the ground floor, she carefully set her friends down and opened the door to the alley. There on the step was a healthy bowl of buttermilk, which cat and sprite immediately set to emptying. Beside it sat a second, towel-wrapped bundle, its steam rising in the chilly October night.

Bending down to retrieve the meal, Maggie caught the barest flutter of a curtain out of the corner of her eye. Straightening up with the care of a convalescent, Maggie turned toward her neighbor's house.

"My thanks, friend," Maggie raised her voice enough to carry across the narrow alley, and no more. "Ye canna know how much I needed this sustenance tonight." With a gentle smile on her lips, she gave a half bow, and turned to go inside. She knew that old Molly's awe would keep her behind her curtains. In this weary moment, Maggie wished she'd lose her fear enough to come and talk on her stoop, or even through the screen. It had been too long since Maggie had a friend that she could talk to.

Hovering behind her faded kitchen curtains, Molly watched Maggie accept her offerings, and heard her hail of thanks. If her neighbor were mortal, Molly would have thought there was weariness and sorrow beneath that voice. But no, this was one of the fair ones, a child of Danu, wasn't she? Molly had her doubts, but doubts were dangerous, even fatal, if she were wrong.

No. Any mortal feelings she thought she heard must be the folly of her aging mind, the exhaustion a ruse. Molly would not be deceived. She had seen what she knew to be the sidhe before, beautiful and cruel. They never wearied and their hearts were too cold for any mortal emotion to take root, save for vengeance. She'd learned that on a long-ago night back in Eire.

Anxiously making her way home through the darkening twilight, Molly swore at the ewe that she attempted to herd before her. She had turned thirteen today and she'd been allowed to claim one of the herd for her own, with any profits she could glean from it hers to do with as she pleased. It had not been as easy a choice as she had thought it would be. She had left the pasture much later than she should have, not realizing how long it would take to herd her prize home. Da had to be worried by now. He'd wanted to come with her, but she didn't want him to influence her choice so she'd gone alone. She was surprised that she hadn't encountered him yet, coming to see what kept her.

As the black-faced ewe began to stray once more, Molly rushed to turn her back. Sighing deeply, she noticed that they were just passing the place where Seamus McGilacuddy lived with his Da. She liked Seamus something fierce, but he was eighteen and not much interested in her.

Almost home, she thought as she looked longingly at the smoke wafting from the McGilacuddy's chimney. That was when she noticed something odd. Just beyond the cottage itself she could see their smokehouse with its door hanging wide open. With no further thought for her sheep or for getting home, Molly found herself walking toward the outbuilding, unconsciously compelled to look closer. Her gaze was transfixed by an eldritch glow that reminded her of the foxfire growing in the forest.

Moving forward to the doorway in a dazed, trance-like shuffle, Molly peered inside. Hanging from the rafters was a doe carcass waiting to be dressed and cured, its golden brown hide smooth and perfect, save for the hole an arrow had left in its throat. Deep inside herself Molly quaked with fear. Not knowing what possessed her, she moved forward to run her hand down the side of the carcass.

With a strangled scream, Molly stumbled backwards and fell across the threshold. Now on the ground, lit by the pool of greenish-white light pouring through the door, she tried ineffectually to scramble away from the sight before her. That one touch had newly awakened in her a frightening gift—the second sight.

On the hook in front of her hung not the carcass of a doe, but the remains of what could only be one of the Gentry. She was dressed in the finest doeskin leathers, leathers stained by the crimson flow from her pierced throat. Shaking with the knowledge from this new gift, Molly somehow managed to gain her footing. Longing to be far from such an ill omen, she turned to shoo the ewe home.

As she started toward them, her sight revealed, in the shadows by the house, a beautiful, inhuman glare. It resided on the face of another sidhe, this one tall and pale, his chestnut hair curling about his shoulders behind one ear.

"Be gone, child," the sidhe ordered in a deadly but musical whisper, "my wrath is'na for thee."

His hands flared in an instant with a frightening light. Though he held nothing, it was as if he wielded a fiery brand. He looked once more at Molly, expectantly, his eyes burning with both grief and fury. She knew she must flee now; he would not stay his hand a moment longer.

Her courage fled. Though she tried to stumble away, the world spun crazily as darkness rose up to overtake her. Falling to the ground, faint with fear, she thought she heard a brutal chanting before she knew no more.

When she came to, it was to the sight of angry orange flames edged in blue light devouring both cottage and smokehouse, punishing all within because one unknowingly took the life of a sidhe. Her father appeared seemingly from nowhere to grab her up from the ground across the lane, well away from where she had fallen. She hardly noticed as he clutched her to his chest.

"My darlin', my wee precious darlin'!" Her Da's voice broke upon the words.

Had she been able to look at him, she would have seen fear and relief battling in his eyes, but she couldn't look away from the unnatural flames; no matter how the wind whipped them, nothing burned but the home of the McGilacuddys.

In the warm safety of her Manhattan kitchen, old Molly shook with the memory from her childhood. That was not the last time Molly's sight showed her the children of Danu, though it was the worst. Before she came to this new land she'd seen immortal acts of both kindness and cruelty. Only one thing had remained true throughout those visions: never could she recognize the difference between a sidhe that did good and one that did evil. Maybe those wiser than herself could tell between a light and dark sidhe, but with all that she had seen, and remembering that dark sidhe were known to do good acts on a whim, Molly would remain cautious in dealing with her neighbor.

Maggie finished her meal diligently, though with little interest. On occasions such as this, it occurred to her that a life measured in centuries merely meant one had longer to grow weary of living it. Staring at the empty dish before her, Maggie sighed. She climbed to her feet with tired slowness and put the crock with the others, vowing that tomorrow they would go back to their owner. *If na,* Maggie thought caustically, *old Molly might go buy more dishes, rather than ask for them back.*

Not bothering with a light, Maggie made her way toward the bedroom she rarely used. Generally, she slept below, in the rath she'd created, but she was too tired to go much further than the mundane bed. Climbing between good Irish linens, her body cradled by a true feather mattress and covered by a comforter of thick eiderdown, she gladly let her consciousness slip away. As faerie lights began to dance behind her closed lids, she felt two warm and comforting weights join her on the bed. Good, Scath and Pixie had come in. The sprite purred as he kneaded a nest for himself in the blankets. Apparently, he was enjoying the cat form enough to keep it for a while; or perhaps he was merely being polite to their company. Her last thought was a hope that Beag Scath had remembered to close the door.

CHAPTER 9

The jarring ring of the telephone called Patrick out of the depths of his nap. Groaning with annoyance, he reached for the phone, not even bothering to open his eyes. As he groped for the receiver he could hear his Bobbi puttering around downstairs in the kitchen.

"Hallo?" he muttered into the phone, his voice still husky with sleep.

"Hello, Mr. O'Keefe?" the woman's voice on the other end was pleasant and vaguely familiar, but he couldn't quite place it.

"Yes," he answered, "can I help ye?"

"Mr. O'Keefe, Dr. Barnert is on the line. Please hold while I put him through." Patrick was suddenly wide awake. The woman was Linda, one of Arn's receptionists. His stomach soured as he listened to the tinkly hold music. He wondered if it was his imagination, or if he really heard a sigh as the music cut off.

"Hello, Pat," the voice of his doctor and best friend came over the line, "you busy?"

"Just nappin', Arn," he answered cautiously, "what's on ye're mind?"

There was just a moment of silence on the other end of the line. "Are you and Barbara busy tonight? Carol and I were wondering if you'd like to come over for dinner."

Whatever vestiges of Patrick's sleep remained disappeared in the silence that followed that question. It wasn't that getting together for dinner was that unusual, but Carol was always the one to call, and never at the last minute. That, and Kara had not been included in the invitation. Unconsciously he gripped the blanket tight in a white-knuckled fist. His only thought in that second was to remember to breathe.

"How about it, Pat? Say, about seven o'clock?" Arnold asked again, his voice seemed strained beneath the surface cheer.

"So, Arn," Patrick finally responded, dread heavy in his voice, "what's the bad news ye wanted to tell me? Is it about those tests ye had to do over? Or are ye just raisin' yer rates again?"

"Pat," Arnold's voice caught slightly as he answered, "Patrick, I didn't want to do it this way."

"I know ye did'na, but if ye wanted this to work ye should have had Carol call Barbara like she always does, or just waited 'til I came to the office." He wished he could make this easier on Arnold, but he couldn't wait. If there was something to know, it was better to know it now. "Out with it, Arnold, I do'na have the patience for waitin' anymore."

"I'm sorry, Pat," his friend finally answered, "you've metastasized. The cancer has spread."

My God! Patrick nearly dropped the phone. There were so many questions fighting to be asked: How could this happen? What could be done? How I...."How long?" His voice cracked as the only important question moved to the forefront of all the others.

"Please, Pat," Arnold begged, "come over and let's talk about this, don't make me do it over the phone."

He thought about it for a moment, the last thing he wanted to do was be sociable.... No, that wasn't true, the *very* last thing he wanted to do was have to tell Barbara and Kara; to face them and tell them that all the past and present sacrifices had been for nothing. Climbing forcefully away from his self-pity, he made himself answer. "All right, Arn, tell Carol to set the table for four, but go light on the food. I'm afraid I'll na have much o' an appetite."

"Thank you, Pat," Arnold answered him, sounding slightly relieved. "Um, are you going to tell Barbara before you come?"

"No, Arn, I will'na do it," he answered firmly. "Ye have some questions to answer before I burden her any further. Besides, one o' us has to be in a shape to drive."

Tap-tap-tap. Kara pulled her attention away from the theory tests she was grading and looked up at the door to her office. Mr. Cohen, the director of the Music Center, was standing there looking grim. Motioning him to enter, Kara carefully pushed aside her papers.

"Good afternoon, Kara," he started as he closed the door behind him, "I need to speak to you.... How much time do you have before your next student arrives?" Kara could feel herself go pale. He was using the neutral, this-is-business tone that was completely different from the cheery way he usual greeted her.

"Please, sit down, sir," Kara rose to clear off the chair by her desk, her hands trembling. "This is my break period, Mr. Cohen. My next student won't be arriving for half an hour."

"This won't take that long," he settled into the chair and took a deep breath. "Kara, I'm here because some of the parents have expressed a concern." Mr. Cohen paused before going on, as if trying to decide how to proceed.

"Apparently, some of the children are being affected by your mood and recent distraction." Looking as if he was torn between reassuring her and doing his job as administrator, Mr. Cohen shifted in his seat. "They've become discouraged because they think they are the problem; they no longer want to practice or attend their lessons. The parents are upset because their children were showing both progress and enjoyment, up until now. They feel that you aren't giving your students the encouragement and quality of instruction that they are paying for."

Kara bit the inside of her lip to keep from crying. She couldn't even speak. Until today she hadn't realized exactly how much strain she was under, or how it had affected her unfortunate students. *But why did it have to come to a head now?* Everything was getting better, she had a grip on things and for the first time in months she had a new sense of hope. Was what was happening now going to take that away from her?

"Now, Kara," he continued, his eyes softening with compassion, "I understand what you have been dealing with in the past months. I know how hard it is to keep showing a good face with all the worry you have had," Kara trembled ever so slightly as she watched his expression return to sternly official, "however, we cannot have our students dropping out because our teachers are having personal problems." It was obvious by his attitude that she had his support, but nonetheless she saw the warning there.

When she didn't respond, he went on. "My dear, you are one of the best instructors we have and it is amazing luck for us that you have even come to work here with the talent that you possess, but you must pull yourself together if you are to remain with us." As if to soften his words and offer some comfort, Mr. Cohen took her clenched hands in his own. "If you need time off to compose yourself, or if you need us to lighten your load for a while, well then let us know and we will do our best to accommodate you." To further reassure her, he continued. "This is *not* an official visit, and nothing will go on your record. Up until recently we have been more than pleased with your performance."

"I understand, sir. I am so sorry that I let my problems affect my work," Kara responded as she found her voice. Even to her the response sounded numb and stilted. Her earlier peace had been cracked, if not shattered. "I can assure you my personal problems will never again affect my performance."

As the director left, Kara squared her shoulders and stiffened her resolve. She had let despair and worry bring her that low, but no more; from this day forward she would foster the hope she had been given and put the rest behind her.

Her long day ended, Kara cradled Hope and thought how nice it would be to play for Papa tonight, sharing some of her new-found peace. Her old violin's tone was nowhere near as mellow as that of Quicksilver, but that didn't mean it wasn't capable of soothing away woes. Already Kara's mood had improved since

Mr. Cohen's visit. Each time she picked up the instrument to demonstrate for a student, she had regained some measure of peace. She hurried home with that thought held firmly in her mind.

As she approached her block, Kara slowed. She couldn't be sure, but from the corner the house seemed awfully dark with only the porch light flickering on and off over the door as the motion sensor was triggered by incidental passings. She picked up her pace. If she remembered correctly, her parents had no appointments for today, and everything had been fine when she left for work. She glanced at her watch. It was eight-thirty; maybe they had gone for one of their nighttime walks. Entering the house concerned, Kara went straight for the message board in the kitchen. Wherever her parents had gone they would have left her a note...and there it was, propped against a covered dish on the table—*gone to dinner at the Barnerts', we won't be late. Left you some supper. Have a nice night. Love, Mathair.*

Her mind at ease on that matter, Kara laid the violin case on the table and hung the message board back on the wall. She was a bit disappointed she wouldn't get to play for Papa as she'd planned, but she couldn't help but be glad her father was up to going visiting; her parents were such homebodies lately that it would do them good to get out.

Kara flicked on the light and turned to see what her mother had left for her. The cover was still warm and steam billowed out as she lifted it up to peek. Her stomach grumbled as the scent of roasted chicken and baked apples tickled her nose. Mmm.... Not leftovers, then...curious. When she'd left for work there had been no mention of her parents going to the Barnerts'. It must have been a last-minute thing, especially if Mathair had already made dinner. Pouring herself a glass of milk, she took her meal to her room, her mind already wandering off to other matters.

When she entered the bedroom, she saw a small, orange-furred mound among the papers on her desk. Setting her meal on the table next to her bed she reached over to rescue whatever Pixie had decided to use as her bed this time. The cat muttered in protest and stretched full length in a display of passive resistance. Worming her hands beneath the cat in a way perfected only through much practice, Kara won the round by lifting the cat gently to the ground. Or so she thought.

"Ewww! Pixie!" Kara looked in annoyance at the smudges of unknown origin that now graced her hands. "What have you been getting into?!"

With a glare at the dirty wet streaks across the papers on her desk, she wadded up the unimportant bits and couldn't resist using them to pelt the cat. Pixie's only response was to drop her disinterested pose and pounce on the crumpled paper. Growling in frustration, Kara kicked the makeshift ball into the hallway and closed the door firmly when the cat went after it.

"One of these days...." Kara muttered out loud to herself as she turned to review the damage; there were little smudges on the monthly bills, but most of the stuff on top had been junk mail. As she was cleaning up the mess—dumping the majority of the dirtied mail in the wastepaper basket and trying to clean off the rest the as best she could—she could hear a faint clawing at the door.

"No way, Pixie! You are so lucky you didn't ruin anything." The cat's only response was a pitiful yowling and another attempt at getting in the room. Kara could see a tiny paw reaching under the door in a futile effort to pull it open. She had to laugh. So many times before the cat had succeeded in this, but from inside the room trying to get out. The poor thing had no hope of success this time, since the door opened in.

Taking a few more moments to repair the damage to her paperwork, Kara scooped up a towel from the floor to wrap the cat in when she opened the door. She stopped abruptly as a familiar ivory bundle tumbled from its folds. Kara dropped the towel again and forgot about the cat as she picked up the brooch she had yet to return. Perhaps she should try to call the shop. If Maggie were there, she could even return the brooch tonight. There was nothing else she needed to do, so it was worth the try. She rummaged through the papers, located the pawn ticket, and went into her parents' room to call.

As she settled herself on the edge of her parent's bed, something caught her eye that stopped her cold: there next to the phone was a battered shoebox, the outside familiar to her though she had never seen the contents. Now the lid was off, like some Pandora's box letting loose her fear and doubts, and yes, also some small grain of hope. It was now so clear why she felt she ought to have known the face in the photograph, the one she'd been drawn to behind the counter at the pawnshop. The same handsome, cheerful face looked up at her now from a different setting, slightly older and this time with Kara's grandmother encircled in his arms as they both stared into the camera. Kara couldn't think why she had not recognized him, except maybe that the brain occasionally chooses not to believe what the eyes tell it. The last place Kara would have expected to see her grandfather's face was in a picture in a Soho pawnshop.

Why did her world insist on changing its orientation every time she thought she had her feet beneath her? She reached out for the box and drew it into her lap.

Kara sifted through the photographs. There was no doubt that her grand -father's face had been the one staring at her from the wall behind Maggie's counter. But what connection did he have with the woman—and what did that mean to Kara? Remembering the look of adoration on his face, she went cold at the implications.

Staring intently at the paper-wrapped brooch in her hand, she turned it this way and that. Her course of action was no longer clear. Should she keep it, supposing that it came from one related to someone her grandfather had obviously trusted? Or should she return it anyway because it was still too valuable to accept? For that matter, had he remained on good terms with the woman from the photograph? Kara had never heard mention of any McCormicks in connection with anyone in her family, let alone with Grandda. Or was there more to it? Could the brooch be a gift from a relative, a sister Papa never knew he had? There wasn't any resemblance between him and Maggie, but that didn't really mean anything. After all, Maggie clearly took after her mother. Kara's stomach went sour as the thoughts surfaced unbidden. She didn't even know how much of this she should mention to her parents—if she mentioned it at all. Whatever she decided, she had quite a few questions to ask Maggie McCormick first.

Kara glanced at the bedside clock. It was nearly ten. Tomorrow would have to be soon enough. By the time she made it into the city it would be much too late to bother the woman. Cleaning up the photographs and placing the box back on the table, Kara returned to her own room.

Standing dangerously still in her doorway, she wondered if her parents would notice the permanent absence of the cat. There was Pixie, balanced between the edge of her bed and the table beside it, blithely tearing away at Kara's forgotten dinner. Deciding the trouble wasn't worth it, Kara settled for scooping up the protesting animal and depositing her in the hallway, once more closing the door forcefully behind her.

No longer interested in dinner anyway, she sat on her bed and let her mind wander through her memories of her grandparents. Kara had been young when they had died. She had been six when Mamó had been hit by a car and killed; and Grandda had passed away when she was eight. She hadn't known what he died of, though she could remember overhearing her parents say it had been heartache that killed him, having lost the last of his two great loves. Kara had been too young to understand what they meant; all she had known was that her beloved Grandda had gone away.

Her vague memories were mostly of the man himself: the sharp, crisp fragrance of his aftershave mingled with a clean, soapy scent; the springy white curls of his hair that had amused her younger self no end as she tugged them straight and let them go; and the maddening grin that rarely left his face, but often and easily slipped into hearty laughter. Kara could remember more clearly the extra bit of sparkle in his deep brown eyes as he got into some mischief, or the way they flashed when he was taken by some strong emotion.

There was always something wild about her father's father; you could never expect conventional behavior from him. He had been different, his view on the world slightly askew from everyone else's. It had seemed more as if his allegiance was first with nature, and then with mankind. The things he used to bring her weren't bits of candy or toys, but natural things that he would sit and tell her about for hours, gladly answering all the questions her young mind could find to throw at him. It was from him that she learned to respect nature.

She had warm memories of visits with her grandparents. Mostly she remembered walking in the woods for hours with Grandda and sharing his fascination for each different flower, creature, and natural beauty they encountered. She remembered rushing home to share with Mamó the findings of the day. And she remembered cuddling with Grandda on a blanket, cushioned by the soft sands of some beach somewhere, staring at the stars until the combined sounds of the *shushing* surf and her parents and Mamó murmuring around the bonfire lulled her to sleep. Even when the memories were not as clear, they left her with a feeling of love and warmth that didn't diminish with the passing of time or people.

There was no need to ask where Kara had gotten her love of music and her gift of fiddling: music, particularly Celtic music, had filled their time even more than storytelling did. Whether they were walking, working, or just sitting together, song generally filled any silences that weren't wanted. Even now Kara still hummed the tunes of the Celtic airs Mamó would sing, accompanied by Grandda and Quicksilver.

Most poignant of all were Kara's memories of when Grandda told her of Ireland—or Eire as he called it. Other children were put to sleep with tales of Cinderella and Snow White: Kara had heard Celtic tales, like the stories of Tír na nÓg—the Land of Youth—or of Oisín, the son of Fionn Mac Cumhail, raised by the deer that was his enchanted mother. When Grandda talked of his homeland a different light came to his eyes, one that otherwise was never seen—unless it had to do with Mamó. Those were his two great loves, and he'd never explained why they'd left the former.

Every memory Kara dredged up was pleasant and content. There were no clues there of why Grandda would have been dancing with another woman. It definitely didn't explain how he had been looking at her. It just didn't make sense. No mention had ever been made of any family friends named McCormick and her grandparents had never seemed anything but blissful. Could some infidelity have occurred and not marked one or the other of them in some way? It seemed unlikely, yet her father had never alluded to any problems, even old ones. Could whatever had gone on have remained a secret that Grandda took to his grave? Kara was uneasy with the idea. Her suspicions were adding a distinct chill to the warm, loving memories she had come to depend on. She was very uncomfortable with this shadow descending across her heart, though tomorrow would have to be soon enough to deal with these demons, to confront Maggie McCormick. Right now Kara would attempt to sleep.

Lying completely alert in the darkness, she knew she would mention none of this to her father. There was no need to add more weight to the troubles piled on his heart. Unaware that she still clutched Maggie's brooch, Kara was asleep in moments.

CHAPTER 10

Standing at the sink, the sharp, tantalizing scent of lemon wafting around her head, Maggie made a concerted effort to work her way through cleaning the crockery that had somehow piled up so quickly. She had procrastinated all day, but it was time to return Molly's dishes. The sight of her "Lady" at so mundane a task would have horrified old Molly. The truth was, Maggie found pleasure in the simple task, and cleaning them any other way would have been extravagant and wasteful. Besides, it was pure joy to watch Beag Scath dive at the soap bubbles. She laughed each time he darted away with the iridescent froth streaming from some part of him. With the last of the bowls scrubbed and rinsed, and the sprite chased off to the other room, Maggie headed over to Molly's to return them.

As she stepped out into the cool night and carefully closed the door, her heart clenched painfully. Upon the crisp autumn air rode the sweet sound of Celtic singing. Wistful thinking told her it might even be sidhe music, some of which had, over the millennia, found its way into the Celtic repertoire. Scarcely giving it a conscious thought, Maggie altered her path, choosing to enter the tavern by the front, rather than knocking on the kitchen door. She was so sick for her home and people that she could not resist the siren song that drew her along. Before going in, she closed her eyes a moment and fancied she was back in Eire; the scents were right, the sounds were right, and the hearty laughter and clamor was more than right. Patrons standing by the entrance for a bit of air turned to watch her with compassion as they heard her sigh. Her eyes flew open as they reached to steady her and draw her in, utterly moved by the soul-sick look on her face as she swayed outside the door. Even those who had never set foot on the homeland knew how she felt--Molly Kelley's tavern tended to draw those Irish folk who had the soul of Eire in their hearts no matter where they'd been born. Whether she willed it or not, Maggie found herself handed in until she stood, bag clutched convulsively in her arms, right up against the tiny wooden stage. Looking up, she was startled as her dazed, ancient eyes closed with a set equally as ancient, if not more so. She looked up into the face of another sidhe.

Worn down by the week's events and heartsick with loneliness, one sob escaped her lips and was mistaken by the audience surrounding her as appreciation of the music. They howled and clapped and patted her back in agreement, totally misinterpreting her true reaction. The musician on the stage did not miss the depth of her feelings; his eyes glowing warmly, he inclined his head a trifle, respectfully acknowledging her pain and her longing. As the song drew to an end, the immortal minstrel turned to the rest of the band—they were all human, sharing no more than a faint shadow of the gift between the four of them—and signaled for a break. As he jumped from the stage to land gracefully beside her, the musician's lips quirked in amusement at the bundle she clutched in her arms like an anchor to reality. He was about to take it from her and lead her to a quiet table in the corner when Molly, darting from the kitchen with a mixed look of horror and anger burning in her eyes, came rushing toward them.

"An' what do ye think yer about, young pup?" she started in on the strange sidhe before she'd even reached their side. "Maggie, are ye all right?"

Molly turned her attention back to the musician and continued her tirade, without giving Maggie a chance to reassure her everything was fine. "Ye just leave her be; yer here to play music, not force yer attention on the Lady."

Maggie was at a loss to respond, even if Molly *had* paused long enough to allow her to; something wasn't right here, but there was so much to deal with at once that she just couldn't figure it out. As she shifted her bemused look from Molly to the musician beside her, she realized what it was: The old woman was treating him as she would any young human she thought needed reprimanding. Molly spared the strange sidhe none of her anger or venom. In fact, if he had truly been human he probably would have slipped away long ago, his figurative tail between his legs. Turning to see his reaction, Maggie was startled to see a look of extreme patience and amusement on his face. She stared at him anew with awed comprehension; Molly couldn't see him for what he was or she would never have dared speak to him that way (as Maggie knew well from her own experience). This realization told her one thing, she was in the presence of one who was ancient even for a sidhe. Only the oldest could completely hide their nature from one with the sight as strong as Molly's.

In that one moment of understanding, Maggie could no longer fault Molly for the way she acted toward her. How could she when Maggie herself felt that same combination of reverence, uncertainty, and even fear in the presence of this ancient one? Wishing to diffuse the situation before the look on the musician's face changed from amusement to annoyance, Maggie turned to Molly with the bag of kitchenware.

"Oh, Molly," Maggie said with a ease that she did not feel, "there ye are! This gentleman was just offerin' to help me find ye. I was comin' to return yer dishes, when I heard the wonderful music."

As she diverted Molly toward the kitchen, Maggie felt a tension lift from the barroom that she hadn't even been aware was growing. Apparently, the regular patrons were prepared to come to Molly's aid at any moment. Even now, with Maggie "setting things straight," a few of them were giving the musician black looks as he returned to the stage. Following Molly through the door, Maggie was relieved to feel strands of power stir as the band struck the first chords for "Irish Eyes Are Smiling." Soon the patrons would forget there was ever a problem after the sidhe on the stage soothed away the anger brought on by alcohol and misunderstanding.

In the kitchen, Maggie smothered a sigh while Molly fairly groveled for forgiveness for what she imagined was the insulting "advances" of the band member. Maggie let her go on a bit before assuring the woman that everything was fine. Finally, unable to stand the cowering she couldn't end, she thanked Molly for the kindness of her meals and prepared to leave. Something tugged hard at her will, however, as she started for the side door. She did not *want* to leave this lively tavern for the loneliness of her own rath. Her heart ached to be surrounded by the pulsing beat of the music and the liveliness of the audience. And deep inside, deep down in a place she shared with no one, she admitted that she hungered ferociously for the company of the sidhe. Shrouding her eyes to hide the depth of their pleas, Maggie turned back to her neighbor.

"Please," she forced herself to calmness, "do ye mind if I set a bit in yer pub? 'Tis so like a bit o' our faraway home. I'd very much love to stay awhile."

She had no doubt the answer would be yes, but when she saw Molly's nervous smile and heard her stilted invitation, Maggie's joy was shadowed. She couldn't resist staying, but recognizing how strained her neighbor would be while she remained, she would stay just long enough to take the edge off her solitude.

Maggie stopped abruptly as she reentered the tavern through the kitchen door. Standing there, caressed by warm, intimate light and boisterous singing, she breathed deeply of the very atmosphere and couldn't help wondering why she had held herself in isolation for so long. Few were as gifted as Molly, and this wasn't the only Irish pub in the city. Maggie could have gone safely to any of them and felt the pleasure of a little bit of home. True, they wouldn't all have the spirit that this place seemed to hold, but it would have been something.

Maggie took another deep breath and opened her eyes. Relaxing into the unconscious welcome the place seemed to hold for all of Ireland's displaced souls, she moved to a barely empty space beside the stage. Tension she had not been able to shake for days faded. She ordered a Guinness and settled in to lose herself in the music. She even joined in when the audience sang their favorites with the band.

After an hour of absolute enjoyment, Maggie reluctantly turned to leave. She'd avoided looking toward the kitchen while she stood there, but she hadn't needed to; she was quite aware that Molly kept peering through the porthole-shaped window. Whether it was to see if Maggie had left, or to make sure that she was content and well served, it was unimportant why. Now that Maggie was strengthened by even an hour of relaxing companionship, it was time to leave so that Old Molly could also find some peace.

Only one thing bothered Maggie as she gracefully wove her way to the front door; she had hoped that before she left she would have another chance to speak with the musician. But they played nonstop and she wouldn't presume to soul-speak an ancient. Pausing at the door, she briefly looked back with an all-consuming longing. Perhaps she would have her chance another time.

Do'na be so much the martyr, young one.

Maggie stopped short in the cool darkness outside. She was glad that all the patrons had moved back into the pub. There was no one to speculate at the startled look on her face. She had gone so long without soul-speaking with any-one other than Beag Scath or a fellow guardian that she hadn't even considered that the ancient one might seek her out.

Did ye really think I'd ignore one so starved for companionship? Maggie could feel his gentle rebuke twined with amusement at catching her off guard. She flinched at his assessment, but it wasn't as if she could deny it.

I did'na wish to disturb ye, she answered respectfully. *I hoped for words between us, but did'na think to see it so soon.*

There was a silence, though she felt that he had not yet left her. She waited patiently for his next words.

I've but a moment, Cliodna, he told her with laughter in his thoughts, *Jimmy's almost through his solo.* An image of an over-enthusiastic drummer was placed in Maggie's mind, distracting her from the fact that he knew her true name. She couldn't help chuckling out loud.

'Tis yerself I'm here to see, he continued. *I'll come to ye in the place ye've made yer own...tonight, an hour after the pub has closed. Wait for me.*

Maggie didn't bother with an answer. There was no time; his thoughts had withdrawn. Apparently, Jimmy was indeed finished with his solo. How discourteous of her; she forgot to ask the ancient's name, and he had not offered. It could not be helped now. She used the feel of his essence to key the shields warding Yesterday's Dreams and the alleyway, fixing in her mind his physical image as she did so. It would be enough to allow him to enter.

She should go in now, if nothing else but to see what mischief Beag Scath was up to, but she was reluctant. The night was crisp and cool, the breeze for the moment smelt of autumn, more than it smelt of city, and Maggie was tired of feeling tied down, penned, even. Besides, she was still drawn by the rousing beat that beckoned from Molly's pub. It wasn't just the music, or even the people, though; something deep inside her was fixated upon the sidhe singer and she could not wait to speak with him further, to discover what linked them so thor-oughly that she felt a sharp tugging as she drew away.

Maggie experienced a burst of eager anticipation. Companionship!

Someone to speak with! No holding back...no hiding behind polite trivialities....
She was not the only guardian on this side of the ocean, but the others all had
their own duties to see to, and they did not get together as often as they might.
But here was one not bound to any one spot in the city. This one knew her for
what she was, and might even know why she was here. His visit would be like
sweet nectar to her parched spirit. She was not solitary creature. Her essence
wilted in prolonged solitude.

Maggie could not resist returning to the pub entrance for a last glance as the
music pulsed and trilled. Stopping just outside the front door, she peeked around
the frame, her gaze riveted on the stage. A warm smile lit her face as the vitality
of the music gripped the lead singer and he seemed to pulse with its rhythm,
head lowered over the mic, heel flawlessly keeping the beat. She could feel the
music reach out to take her again, as well, causing her to sway in the doorway.
Her light grip on the frame was all that anchored her to keep her from making
her way back toward the small stage, the way her heart screamed at her to do. But
no, she must think of Molly's peace of mind; it would not be fair to the woman
to disturb it further. Maggie kept herself to the shadow of the entryway and the
cool caress of the autumn air, her eyes locked on the lead singer.

For a moment her heart tripped delightedly as he tossed his long hair back
away from his sweat-sheened face; a moment later it clenched beneath her breast,
shattering completely. Slowly, she backed away from the tavern, her eyes never
leaving the tattoo on the stretch of neck behind the ancient one's right ear. There
were subtle differences, a not-quite-rightness about the intricate design, but she
recognized the spiky, interlocking spirals standing out in dusky black against his
pale skin, and not only did it steal from her all hope, it flooded her with dread.

It could not be...she would have sensed something. Her heart wanted to deny
what she saw, but her mind refused to let her. Quickly suppressing her outraged
betrayal—as if that were a strong enough word!—Maggie obliterated the safe
passage she had arranged for the deceiver. Not satisfied with that, she drew up
layer upon layer of additional shields before she was satisfied.

He could not be allowed to enter. Maggie's oath had not been the sole
reason she had exiled herself so far from her homeland. In the very depths
beneath Yesterday's Dreams, wreathed with countless safeguards, was the great
and deadly treasure of the Tuatha de Danaan: the invincible sword of Lugh.
Mortal and immortal alike had cause to fear its edge, the merest touch of which
slew instantly. It was a god-killer. The deceiver and his ilk would not claim it.

She was torn between the need to defend her sacred charge and an equal
desire to seek the council of her fellow guardians. The need for guidance won in
the end; after all, she had two hours before he would even seek her out. Because
it would not be possible to soul-speak the others without the foe potentially
sensing it, she would have to go to them, and quickly. She would be back well
before that time was spent. And should he penetrate her defenses, no matter his

strength, there were certain protections she'd placed on the sword none could breach, short of killing Maggie herself.

Anger still boiled in Lucien's blood. It would not be mitigated by anything less that death and destruction.

"Come, minions, feast upon this sacrifice, draw strength from her suffering, whet your urges and I will provide the means to satisfy them." Darkness surged around him in the greenhouse. Crimson light danced over the glass panes, deepening the shadows, rather than banishing them. They jerked and lunged, battling each other for access to the bloodied slave girl spread-eagle upon the altar stone. Lucien almost regretted that his anger had ruined her. He had intended to keep her around a while longer, but when he returned from his encounter with the witch, rage coursed through him unchecked. It had been unwise to retreat to his chamber where the girl waited obediently. He abhorred mess in his personal haven, and blood spatters, while holding a charm all their own, constituted a considerable mess. Though satisfying, the experience did nothing but cost him a well-trained slave and the effort it would take to clean up.

Well, it could not be helped. She would serve him one last time, though. Once the newly summoned demons feasted upon her, he intended to take his leashed hellhounds for a walk. He was overwhelmed by the desire to see the magical sites of the city. And to start planning how to claim their power.

His gaze flicked back to the scene unfolding around the altar. It was almost time; even now the life drained from the girl's eyes and her complexion took on the pallor that could only be claimed by the bloodless.

"Goodbye, my dear, it's been fun."

"Did he think I would'na see it?" Maggie was more than furious by the time she reached the Broad Street Free Clinic; so furious, she somehow managed to stalk the confines of the converted broom closet that served as office for the clinic's administrator. "That I would'na recognize it for what it was? The arrogance!"

"Few would, even among the sidhe," The voice of reason chaffed her. Miach's nature was ever objective. "'Tis'na seen much anymore, especially outside o' Scotland."

"An' what, will ye be tellin' me, has that to do with the matter?" Maggie kicked at a chair, more ready for battle than a debate. When soothing lavender eyes merely stared at her from behind the desk, Maggie groaned. "'Tis sorry I am, my friend. I should'na be takin' this out on ye.

"I just canna help but feel set upon. First this Alistair Crowley-wannabe, an' now a member of the Unseelie Court. Why now? An' what am I to do? One or the other an' I would'na be concerned, but both, an' I fear dealin' with one will give the other the advantage o' my divided attention."

"Ye are'na alone, Cliodna."

It was jarring to have her true name thrust at her from every turn lately. Decades she'd gone without using it even in her thoughts; now, three times in as many days it was resurrected. Perhaps she needed reminding, for she certainly wasn't acting with the confidence and clarity her birthright demanded. For too long she had been merely Maggie. It was making her weak.

"Forgive me, ye're right. An' even if I were,'tis no cause for such alarm. I would'na have been granted the honor o' this duty if I were'na fit to carry it out."

Miach smiled at her.

Maggie basked in the warmth of his benediction for a moment. Of all the sidhe, this one was graced with an ineffable aura of divinity and grace. Some of the superstitious claimed the Tuatha de Danaan were fallen angels; if they had beheld Miach, they would have been certain of all but the fallen part.

"'Tis'na to say we've no cause for concern, though." Miach fingered the long, thick tail of braided hair draped over his shoulder. Normally, she loved his hair; to Maggie's sight it was no single color, but simmered with iridescence, and was the most glorious she had ever seen, even among the sidhe. Of course, to those of the everyday world it appeared more "normal," considerably shorter, and pure white, thanks to Miach's skillful glamory. Such observations aside, Maggie felt a tingle down her spine. Miach seldom paid any attention to his braid...unless he was troubled. He fell silent, his focus drifting inward, and she wondered if he intended to finish.

"What?"

"Ye are'na the only one beset." His look caught her eye and Maggie felt her breath quicken. His eyes had deepened to violet, his gaze turbulent, without its usual air of serenity. "Mostly it's ineffectual plaguing, mischief an' malice easily deflected."

"Why have ye na told me before now?"

"At first, none o' it seemed to be related. 'Twas all spread out for years; odd encounters, the occasional breach o' boundaries, vandalism o' the sort no human gang would consider, let alone have the ability to carry out...ye had no complaints yerself, an' the incidents seemed petty an' no cause for alarm." Maggie watched him flick his braid back over his shoulder and lean forward as he spoke. "Four days ago Cian was challenged by a demonic. Since then, the attacks have been more frequent, an' more brutal. We've held them off so far, but now 'tis more like a siege.

"I sought to tell ye, but ye were deep within yer wards an' I did'na wish to disturb what was clearly serious work. All seemed well enough at yer little shop." As he finished Maggie steeled herself. Now was not time for doubt.

"So, what do we do now? The unseelie are no small concern. They might'na bother overmuch with the sidhe, but they certainly have it in for mortals." Righteous anger still thrummed through Maggie's veins. She knew all too well of the Unseelie Court and their animosity for humans, having lost kin to their hatred. So long ago it was, and yet the pain did not diminish. The memories must be put behind her for now, but she would not forget their lesson. Unseelie was synonymous with treachery.

"Meet with him, Cliodna..."

"Ye canna mean it!" Her resolve could not withstand the distaste of what he advised. "Do ye have any idea what they're about? Have ye na seen their black deeds? 'Tis myself that has cradled the evidence of their...." She choked on the words, unable to continue as the memories flooded back full force. Every muscle twitched as battle rage threatened her tenuous composure. The room dissolved around her until ancient memory took over and she stared once more at the base of the Cliffs of Moher.

Sheridan played along the edge of the cliffs, as she did each full moon, her *blonde tresses dancing in the wind, glinting like white gold in the moonlight.*

"Come away, my little pixie, ye have'na wings to save ye an ye find yerself over-steppin' the cliff." Cliodna softly called out her familiar warning. Sheridan merely laughed her bell-like laugh and continued to skip in dizzying circles, confident no harm could come to her this night. True enough, with as many sidhe around as there were, but Cliodna was uneasy nonetheless.

The child was moon-mad. She always was when the Clan O'Keefe came to visit their fae kin. Usually there was no harm in that. All took care to watch over the precocious girl and her exuberance spent itself by the time the clan returned home. But still, it was rash to let her lose her wariness of danger; the sidhe would not always be around to safeguard her from her folly.

"She calls to me, Clio, she begs me to dance for her!" The child smiled with the brilliance of the sun, putting the night's stars to shame. "Listen! 'Tis so lovely to hear her, like an angel singin' just for me."

Cliodna shook her head in amazement. The child was more an imp than the kin-cousins, and Cliodna would not have her any other way. She brought them all joy with her antics. But this was different; Sheridan always acted wild at these visits, yet never had she claimed to converse with the moon.

Perhaps it was the magic that charged the air, or maybe Sheridan had a touch of the gift seeking its way to the surface. Pure mortal magery was rare, but potent. If the girl had it, she could well end up more powerful than her cousins, who were at least waterkin—the product of coupling between sidhe and mortal—and nearly guaranteed to have some magic skill. It would explain why she was so affected by the full moon and the presence of the sidhe.

Watching the girl closely, Cliodna wondered. She wanted to believe this was merely burgeoning magery settling into its natural outlet; it would ease the doubts, the anxiety. But no, Cliodna's own gift whispered warning. The night took on a chill that had nothing to do with the breeze coming off the sea. Cliodna hurried forward to pull the child back, but she was too late.

Youthful laughter continued to ring across the cliffside and the dancing became an uncontrolled whirling. Sheridan's voice rose in abject wonder and dread blossomed in Cliodna's heart. "She comes to me! Look at my lovely lady comin' to me! She's come to dance."

So joyous a proclamation, that unwitting death knell.

A dozen O'Keefes and their sidhe kin surged forward. Cliodna could see her own fear written in the others' eyes. None of them were in time. Down from the clouds danced an ethereal beauty, all moonbeams and pearly mist, her eyes dark pools in an ivory face, her lips pale pink and shimmery. She drifted close to Sheridan and wrapped the child with graceful limbs, cloaking her with the silvery curtain of her hair.

Cries leapt from the lips of those watching, powerless to rescue their loved one from this cold moon maiden. Dark eyes flared triumphantly as the woman heard them. Her head flew back on that long, graceful neck. All Cliodna could see in that moment was the intricate tattoo behind the woman's left ear; spiky, interlocking spirals stood out in dusky black against her pale skin. She laughed at them, all sultry and spiteful.

The pale lips parted in a razor-toothed smile as woman and child danced on the cliff edge. Slowly, they rose in the air as if they would dance all the way to the moon, swiftly leaving the cliffs behind. Just as they hovered high above the rocky shore, the moon-maiden pierced those watching with a glare of exultant warning before twirling in a moon-mad dance, her tresses a cloud around her shoulders. The child's kin watched in horror as grace-ful, sinuous arms—first one alone, then the other joining—wove the air in a deadly dance, releasing their hold on Sheridan.

A collective gasp reached the child's ears, cutting through the magical fog that mesmerized her. Dazed, she twirled an instant by herself, supported by the powerful updraft the cliffs were known for. Her dress billowed and she swayed back toward solid ground. Those at the edge of the cliff drew a sharp, hope-filled breath. A laugh from the moon-maiden shattered it. She gestured with one hand and the updraft died away unnaturally. In that moment, Sheridan came back to her senses; her feet faltered and her eyes grew wide. Tears glistened uncertain in her gaze as she sought the face of the moon maiden, her personal goddess, her death. Then Sheridan was gone, plummeting to the rocks far below.

Cliodna looked in utter anguish at the base of the cliff, her eyes, with utmost clarity, locking on the broken body of her little pixie. When she glared up at the foe there was murder in her eyes.

"There are but three kinds," the woman taunted as she drifted away on the wind, quite out of reach, "Seelie, unseelie, and mortal prey."

Maggie came back to herself with a gasp. She was on her knees, clutching the edge of the desk. Memories could be brutal. Her breath came fast and her pulse faster as she relived the horror. Miach crouched before her, one arm cradling her and the other running light caresses over her brow and down her cheeks, wiping away the tears as he calmed her.

"Shhh...shhh, my friend, shhh...." His voice was like the sound of gentle waves on a soft, sandy beach. "'Tis two centuries past...ye bear no blame for unseelie treachery. They are twisted an' hateful an' way too clever, but that is why ye must consider meetin' this one, if we are to figure out what they're up to now, ye ken? Ye're sidhe, he will'na harm ye, but the choice 'tis yers."

She could not help but glare at him before turning silently away. She did not like this, but, as guardian, she would do what she must.

Darkness spread across the city in a wave having nothing at all to do with the setting of the sun. Malice walked the streets and a single man trailed twelve shadows, where there was light to see them.

"Can you taste it?" Lucien hissed. He didn't care that those around him gave him a wide berth, or that even in as jaded a society as this he garnered more than a few stares, as if his talking to his shadows were no different than the bag woman across the street yelling at her shoe. He was too focused for any of that to matter. "We are so close. Soon my creatures, we strike at the impudent, flaunting their power in my city. I am ready for a bit of mischief to relieve this hellish boredom.

"There...you feel it, don't you? I'm right. That is where we strike this night." Stopping a block away, Lucien ducked beneath the shelter of a faded awning, the letters peeling back upon themselves as if even they wanted to escape from the depressed environment. He scanned his surroundings, his eyes coming to rest upon the long line of vagrants and indigent waiting outside of the only building in the neighborhood that did not bear signs of vandalism or neglect.

The shadows expanded, detached. Lucien's hard eyes glittered and the barest corner of his lips twitched upward. He had no doubts there were protections surrounding the Broad Street Free Clinic, but there were ways around them. "Go along and play, children."

"Yer kin send ye greetin's, Cliodna," the sidhe started, as he ventured into the alley between the pub and the pawnshop, "an' I add mine—Demne o' Temuir asks leave to enter yer domain."

"Enter freely, Demne, an' count yerself both kith an' kin." Maggie answered, fighting to hide her animosity and slight unease as she ended the formalities. "I've gotten used to all callin' me Maggie, so ye might use that name, as well. No use confusin' myself." She forced a grin and motioned him to step through the door before her. "Up the stairs until ye canna go any further, then open the door before ye. 'Tis such a lovely night, I thought we'd enjoy it on the roof."

If Demne found this odd, he made no comment. In silence, they made their way to the rooftop, Maggie trailing tendrils of power, almost eager for the man to give her a reason to defend herself. Miach may be confident the unseelie would not strike another sidhe, but Maggie herself trusted nothing about them. Besides, Sheridan had never been avenged.

The night truly was glorious. Wisps of cloud drifted past a near full moon and a light breeze blew just enough to ruffle their hair. Few stars could be seen from the midst of the city, but the sidhe could hear their astral song just the same. Repressing her black thoughts, Maggie led the way to the small rooftop garden she nurtured in pots and raised beds of soil. She would learn nothing by antagonizing Demne; he'd already proven his power and skill by successfully cloaking his nature around Molly, so it was unlikely she could force his hand. This one would betray nothing he did not intend to. But still, the right atmosphere could help, or so she hoped. And thus their meeting in her little aerial garden. It wasn't much, for she didn't have the time to tend the type of spread she'd care to have, but at least it alleviated the sense of a concrete and mortar world that sometimes overwhelmed her. Now all it needed to do was put Demne at his own ease.

"Can I get ye somethin' to drink? Or maybe ye're hungry?"

"No. Molly's a good one for hospitality." Demne smiled wryly as he ignored the lounge and bench and lowered himself to the roof itself, close to where she sat.

At the mention of her neighbor, Maggie was dying to ask how Demne had cloaked his nature. But it would be foolish to do so. One did not trade secrets with the Unseelie Court. They chatted a while on inconsequential matters, such as the pawnshop and living in America, the changes in Eire over the past two hundred years, and the quality of the produce this year up at the Union Square Farmer's Market. Maggie thought she would go mad with the senseless chatter, until it ended abruptly.

So, what was she to do now? He had diverted all her pleasantries and exhausted the small talk, yet she was no closer to figuring out what he was doing there. To probe his thoughts would be folly; he was much too powerful. Nothing he had said betrayed him. Maggie could make no sense of it. Well, perhaps she would actually get somewhere by asking.

"The clouds have carried ye far from the land we call our own. Is anythin' wrong?"

"Do ye mean beyond the anguish o' Celt harmin' Celt an' the sidhe caught between? 'Tis enough. An' thin's are gettin' worse. They do'na understand, they're tearin' Eire apart." Demne sighed and laid his head back against the cool brick of the parapet wall. "It does'na help that some o' our own goad them into more violence."

His answer took her by surprise and set her even more on guard. One would think he actually cared about the mortal inhabitants of Ireland. *But the tattoo...it made no sense. Was he attempting to mask from her his intentions? And yet he did not bother to hide the mark of the unseelie...Surely that would have been the first thing he would have done if he intended to deceive her.*

Nothing was adding up.

"But why does that brin' ye to this shore? To what purpose are...." Maggie did not get to finish. As she doggedly sought to draw out his secrets, a shaft of pain seared her from heel to head. It was brief, but stunning. She braced herself and her eyes snapped shut. If she had been standing, she would have swayed.

"Are ye alright?"

As through a haze, she could hear the concern in his voice, but she could not answer. Not right away, at any rate. Sucking in a quick, ragged breath, she resettled her focus and sought the source of the sudden agony.

If she hadn't been so distracted by the enigma beside her she would have realized right away that what she'd experienced was a breach in the defenses she'd helped erect around Miach's clinic. She could kick herself! It was so obvious.

With extreme effort, she buried her intense anger at herself and the man beside her. *She was such a fool!* Demne was a distraction. For some reason the unseelie must have decided to claim for their cause the ancient treasures of the Tuatha de Danaan, for surely they weren't here to interfere with the guardians' efforts to aid the needy mortals of this city. It seemed clear to her that Demne's only purpose had been to keep her occupied so that she could not come to the others' aid.

"Maggie! Will ye na tell me what troubles ye?"

She shrugged off his hand and cast her thoughts toward Miach's clinic. She must know what was happening. She had to know if he needed her. If her visit were even remotely the cause of her fellow guardian's troubles, Maggie would never forgive herself.

As she pondered her dilemma—to go and help or stay and fortify her own position—she began to notice the renewed silence surrounding her. Demne had given up on his questions. He sat beside her, an intent look upon his face. That was when she felt his thoughts reach out and brush against her own. Maggie recoiled with a hiss, glaring at him, and all her suspicions flared with full force. This was not soul-speech, but clearly a probing, a violation of her thoughts... her trust...well, in theory anyway, as she had not trusted him even before this violation of etiquette.

"Here, an' what do ye think yer about, then?" Her eyes flashed as she drew her defenses more securely about her. "Have ye mistaken givin' ye leave to enter my home for givin' ye leave to intrude on my thoughts? I think ye best go."

When he merely stared at her, his features artfully distressed, Maggie ground her teeth. Did he think her a fool? Let him; her inner alarms screamed "Unseelie treachery!" and she was not about to ignore the warning. She betrayed none of this in her expression.

"Good night."

He looked about to argue with her, clearly taken back by the simmering fury in her voice. Perhaps her expression warned him how inadvisable that would be, for he said not a word as he turned and descended from the rooftop and out the alleyway, Maggie on his heels. She brought her shields to full force behind them and with a thought wiped away the allowances that granted Demne entrance. As she watched him leave from the shelter of her precious rowan tree, Maggie was torn. *What should she do?* Her place was here, guarding her charge, but Miach was clearly beset and part of Maggie's duties on this side of the ocean was to aid her fellow guardians.

Miach? Despite her turmoil, Maggie's thoughts had never been more focused as she tried to soul-speak her friend. *Come on, Miach...give me somethin' to know yer there, at least.* Utter silence was the only response; she could not even catch a glimmer of his awareness. "Dread" far too weakly described what she felt in that instance.

She really had no other choice then.

Triggering her most rigid defenses, Maggie transformed Yesterday's Dreams into an impenetrable box. Even she could not enter at this point, not until she brought the shields down, which would not happen until she knew the danger was past. She then slipped into the alleyway. With a flicker of thought, a mere nothing, she threw up a glamory even Molly would not see beyond and moved briskly to the far corner, where her neighbor would be less likely to see her should the illusion fail. Maggie did not have the time to traverse even the short distance between here and the clinic in a conventional manner, not when she did not know what means of attack her kin faced. Besides, approaching from the street would be foolhardy. She needed an instantaneous doorway into the heart of Miach's domain. *Her own participation in erecting his defenses gave her the key, but what would she encounter on the other end?*

Maggie's ears were assaulted as screams and roars and moaning cries broke through the lingering silence of the void she just left. Next was her nose, which could already distinguish the pong of terror and the sickly sweet stench of spilt blood. But none of it set her raging more than the wispy tendrils of smoke that seeped from the reception area, or the bewildered homeless lain out in the back hallway. None of them seemed to be fatalities, but she didn't exactly have the time or skill to confirm her initial impression.

The sounds, the smells, the sights, while appropriate to the field of battle, were distinctly out of character for a place of healing. Something had obviously gone wrong, but what? Something distinctly magical had tripped her alarms, yet the sight before her was more reminiscent of a gang war. Whatever had happened, she couldn't take the chance of causing it to spread. Maggie dove through her temporary portal and utterly shredded its weave behind her. She couldn't allow anything through to her own quiet, sheltered domain. Better to find another way home, than to shatter her neighbors' peace.

"'Tis about time ye joined the fun."

Maggie spun about, a whip of energy at the ready. She did not stand it down upon identifying her fellow guardian, Cian. With a quick glance she took in his seared cheek and singed hair. His silk shirt was torn and bloody from his collarbone up over his shoulder and his hand bore signs of having been gnawed on.

"Looks like ye've had enough fun for the lot o' us." She followed his bantering cue, but her voice was taut. "Did ye na get enough at yer own place, but ye had to pop in here as well?" Cian merely grimaced at the reminder of his recent troubles, so Maggie continued. "Would ye care to be tellin' me what happened?"

A dark glimmer of grimness deepened the green of Cian's eyes as he answered. "Why, I figured on comin' in the front door when I answered the summons, is all, an' started helpin' a few wounded inside. As for the attack, you know as much as I—that there was one."

"Where is Miach?"

"I expect out front, seein' his uninvited guests receive a proper greetin' an' showin' them the door besides. He sent me back here to protect his pets."

There was no malice Maggie could detect in Cian's comment, but there was frustration that he was not on the forefront of the defenses. And there was guilt.

She nodded her thanks and sympathy and made her way carefully past the wounded. As she entered the public area of the clinic, she could see that the smoke came from smoldering sections of the wall that glittered even as she watched. Someone was putting out the flames with a bit of magery.

Making sure her personal shields were at full force, Maggie scanned the room, trying to make sense of the chaos. Inside she got the impression that four homeless persons of indistinguishable gender were on a rampage, only something wasn't quite right. She could see terror in their eyes, but malevolence in their smiles. Each of them was wreathed in shadow. She didn't recognize the aura, but it appeared they struggled as much with an internal battle as they did with the physical fighting. Miach and a number of the other guardians had things well in hand here. She would not distract them.

Next her gaze traveled past the plate-glass of the front façade; what she saw lashed her emotions into a whirlwind. Fear, guilt, rage, wrath...all pounded against her skin from the inside. There were more berserk homeless out front—about six of them faced off against the rest of the New York sidhe, drawing a crowd besides—but this was not what had her teeth clenched or her blood burning. Standing across the street, with mage energy balled around his fists and his expression flat and focused, was Demne.

NO! She had led him right here! Whether he had followed her trail or tailed her earlier, she had led him to one of the very places she least wanted him to discover. The unseelie tattoo glowed darkly in her sight and Maggie could feel the local magics flood her awareness as she continued to draw them to her without conscious thought. In her mind she hummed a battle tune and readied herself to stand against the intruder and his minions.

Moving with calm purpose to the door of the clinic, all else faded from her focus; there were no hag-ridden homeless, there were no wounded huddling upon the ground or gasps from the growing crowd, no patrol cars blocked the road and no policemen calling out for the violence to stop. None of it existed for her. For Maggie, there was only Demne and her own guilt in leading him here, by whatever means he managed it. She marched past the skirmishes taking place on the sidewalk and she evaded the restraining hands of the authorities. Maggie stopped in the middle of the street and continued to call the magics to her.

"Ye do'na belong here spreadin' yer wickedness! Nothin' within these walls is for the likes o' yer kind." Maggie heard her own voice rumble in her head and out like a wave. It echoed in her thoughts and off the surrounding buildings. It was a voice that could, in that moment, change reality with the weight of her will behind it. All she had to do was unleash the power. The unseelie would do no more harm. "Away with ye, before I help ye along!"

She watched Demne closely as her words slammed into him, saw the confusion in the dip of his brow and the hesitation as the energy he'd been about to release was stayed for a fraction of a moment, but only for a moment. The intensity of his eyes nearly caused her to sway; his fury matched her own, as did his determination. Damn if he wasn't going to attack her now! So much for Miach's insistence that the unseelie would do no harm to those of sidhe blood! Shoring up her shields with just a touch of the power she had gathered, she readied the rest for her own attack.

"Maggie! Stay yer hand!"

The cry came from behind her, the familiar voice barely piercing the intense focus that gripped her. Her instinct to obey clashed mightily with her instinct to defend. Her body trembled and her head pounded. She had gathered so much power that it must find release and there was only one target upon which she wanted to loose it. Why?! Why should she stay her hand? This man was obviously a threat; just look at the horror the clinic had become, look at the wounded and the damage. Only one thing inside would draw such an attack, and none of them could allow it to fall into such evil hands.

Maggie felt the barely harnessed power surge against her grip. She'd already given it focus with her thoughts; it only sought to obey. More voices cried out, but there was no sense in what they said. It was all just noise, inside and out. She must release the power.

Suddenly calm tranquility settled like a blanket around her. She could feel strong but gentle arms wrapping her from behind and only Miach's mental reassurance saved him from loosing them.

Drain it away, Cliodna, do'na strike down one innocent o' the crimes ye place at his feet. Miach's thoughts were a soothing balm and though she did not know what he meant, she could not fight him.

It was a good thing he held her with his arms as much as he held her with his power. The moment she obediently released the energy she had gathered, her legs folded beneath her and her vision dimmed. The power had been so much more than her own that she felt diminished, if only for a moment. But she had no time to recover; even as she found her balance, once more a cry of rage rang out and behind it rose a wave of anger that felt all too familiar.

Things happened so quickly. All around her, the homeless and the gawkers collapsed or threw themselves to the ground, and from different directions two vast flows of mage energy converged upon the clinic; one burned with red-black flames and stung like acid in its wake, the other was a blinding white balm. Of the two, the dark wave stood not a chance. As Maggie lay stunned upon the ground, borne down by Miach's weight, she blinked in confusion. Demne rushed to her side, his eyes wide with horror and his hands still shimmering in an ivory glow. With each step he took closer, the darkness fled further away.

Maggie glared at both Miach and Demne from across the crowded examination room. With twelve of them squeezed in the tiny space, they were all close enough that she could do so without even turning her head or shifting her gaze. They were here to discuss what had happened and this was the only place large enough to hold them all. At least it offered some privacy from the poor, confused souls recovering all over the clinic.

The wounded had been seen to and the memory of the afternoon's events "blurred" in the minds of all mortals who happened to watch—a thing the sidhe found distasteful, but necessary to all concerned—and now the sidhe had to sort things out to safeguard against any future incidents. Only no one seemed inclined to speak. Maggie could contain herself no longer.

"Would one o' ye care to explain what the hell happened here?" Her outbreak was met for a moment by more silence, as if none of them wanted to consider the matter. On every face except Miach's and Demne's there was a hint of chagrin. On Cian's the guilt was more evident than ever. Slowly all eyes turned to Miach.

"Ye ken we open the clinic to those homeless without shelter for the night, after we close. Tonight we had quite number o' them waitin' to see if there was room." His voice was calm and matter-of-fact and Maggie marveled that he could talk about the evening's occurrence with such serenity. "At first there was nothin' amiss, but soon a squabble broke out.

"We thought it was a simple matter requirin' naught but an intervention; instead it became brutal." His tone may have been even, but as he spoke, Miach's expression grew grim. "One o' those fightin' tried to flee inside the clinic, only to be thrown back by the magical wards. The rest went wild until many lay wounded upon the ground."

"An' how did they make it past the defenses, then?" Maggie asked. She did not miss it when Cian's jaw tensed at her question. It was he who answered her.

"We all o' us felt the call to come once the shields repelled the intruders, triggered by the magic binding them, but only too late did we understand. We assumed the homeless were innocent victims o' a mage assault aimed at us, only it turns out they *were* the assault."

"I do'na understand...."

"Some o' the homeless were possessed of demonics...only na realizin' this, I pulled them to safety along with those untouched.... By drawin' them in myself I gave them a way through the defenses." Cian's eyes were haunted by the truth of his words.

"Could ye na tell when ye touched them?" There was something of exasperation in Maggie's tone that she could not suppress, "We're none o' us half-trained youths!"

"That'll be enough o' that, Maggie." Demne's rebuke was swift and startling, "The possessed were shielded. None knew the truth until they were already inside."

His intervention made Maggie seethe. What right had he to reprimand her? What was he even doing here? Had he followed her? She couldn't help wondering again. Or had he plucked the information out of her mind back at Yesterday's Dreams when he took the liberty of brushing his thoughts with hers? Either way, she bore the guilt of drawing him here and regardless of whatever had caused Miach to stay her hand she did not trust this man.

"An' who in the name o' the Mother Goddess are ye that ye bear such a black mark on yer skin an' yer soul, yet Miach would have me spare ye? How is it that ye pass the shields yerself?"

"A black mark upon my soul? Does this look black?" Demne answered her in deceptively soft tones, his eyes glittering as he crossed the short distance to her. She could not look away and as he drew closer, his intent gaze pulled her in until it seemed to her that she shared his skin. It was as if her very spirit was drawn into the heart of a fire, but one pure and golden-white, like the mage energy that had just an hour ago saved them all.

Though the sound was far distant from her awareness, she was sure she groaned...feared that she whimpered, but only for a moment. Why should she cower? Whether dark or light, this man was but another sidhe: older, certainly...more skilled, perhaps, yet still just a sidhe. What had she to fear from kin?

She was lost in the mingling of souls for but an instant before Demne drew back enough that the world once again surrounded them both. Maggie noted he did not relinquish the link that joined them.

"Does it?" he whispered.

"No..." her answer came out breathy but certain. There was no way she could honestly claim there was any darkness in his being. And still, she could not help but reach up and touch the mark behind his ear. "But what o' this? I know what it stands for.... I have seen this before on one with a soul black as pitch. What makes ye different when ye both hold to this?"

"Ah!" Demne murmured and Maggie saw the understanding in his eyes. "'Twas this that has set ye against me? What ken ye o' this symbol?"

"'Tis the mark o' the Unseelie Court."

"After a fashion, but what else?"

Maggie drew a sharp breath and felt her temper rise. Did he toy with her? "I know nothin' more than that."

"This was'na always a mark o' pure blood an' a black heart." Demne raised his voice, speaking to all in the room. Maggie could see that her words had brought doubt to all their eyes. "I have been upon this earth for millennia, well before the Unseelie Court was ever conceived. What ye see beneath my right ear is the ancient mark o' a warrior sworn to the Mother Goddess, a mark given by Danu's very hand as she charged us to rescue the fallen from the ancient lands our kind once called home. I am a Soul Savior, one o' the last."

"But that is the mark I saw!"

"Is it? Are ye sure?" Demne returned his unwavering gaze to her and Maggie felt her own conviction sway. "Shall I show ye what ye saw?"

He, this insufferable, arrogant, cocky ancient, would not daunt her! Maggie met his gaze and lifted her chin in challenge. As he prodded her thoughts with his own mind across the link he'd held open, Maggie felt her breath quicken. It felt so right, no matter that all he sought to do was put down her claim; his soul was like silk against her awareness, the subtle friction setting off tiny sparks along every nerve. His mental search was pure distraction in itself.

And then it was before her, in her mind's eye, the proof he sought. The memory surrounded her like a fun-house mirror, only without distortion. She could see once more the tattoo of the moon-maiden as if the woman hovered right before her. Likewise, as her true eyes focused, she could see Demne angle his neck to give her an unobstructed view of his own symbol. They were close; there was no denying that. None could blame Maggie for believing them one and the same. Yet where Demne's was all rounded edges and graceful arcs, and located beneath the right ear, the moon-maiden's was all sharp points and lines, and beneath the left. There was one other difference; of its own volition, Maggie's hand reached up to trace the outline of a heart at the center of Demne's spirals. It was open and perfect and pure. In her memory, she could see that the heart at the center of the woman's tattoo was red-black in color and pierced by spikes.

As Demne gently withdrew from her mind, openly relinquishing his mental grip upon her, Maggie felt a keen loss and could not help but look at him in bewilderment. She blinked it away and met his gaze. "Forgive me, I allowed my own prejudice to cloud my judgment. I have never sensed the darkness in ye that I found in her. I would have seen that if I was'na blinded by intolerance."

His smile was like sunshine. She found herself turning toward it like a flower.

CHAPTER II

"Does she toy with me!?" Lucien screamed his rage, the words filling the small space. "Does she dare toy with me? Bad enough to treat me with such irreverence at her precious little store, but apparently she must interfere in all of my endeavors."

He could still see her, the witch from the pawnshop, striding out of the pathetic little clinic. Very likely, she was the reason he had detected power in that place to begin with, but she had to thwart him yet again, without even the sense to show some fear of him. She would learn her mistake. Yes...very soon she would learn. From now on she had his full attention to the exclusion of all else.

Lucien, his face scarlet with fury and his cold eyes sparking with an insane glint, stood in the midst of a scene of mass destruction. All around him, the contents of the storeroom showed the force of his ire. Splinters of wood that had once been chairs and tables, shards of glass from shattered bottles, and the twisted wreck of former metal shelving made the place seem like the aftermath of a tornado. And yet this violent indulgence only added to his rage; he could not stomach that any woman had enough power over him to drive him to this thorough loss of control.

"I will utterly destroy that place!" he roared to the shattered room, "I will leave Yesterday's Dreams a pile of rubble! And I will make that woman watch!" His hands flexed unconsciously as he looked around him for something else to destroy. As his gaze settled on an empty bookcase with subtle cracks already running down its warped oaken sides, faint red strands of light trailed from his clutching fingers, variegated from an angry black-red where his hands clutched them to an unhealthy pink at the loose, somewhat ragged ends. With a great deal of force, the man gathered the sullen energy as quickly as a politician acquired sycophants, crushing it together until it fused into one large mass. The entire time he pictured the woman's face.

Not content with the throb of power in his hands, he tore more from the streams of energy around him. Each strip that he ripped away from its source took on the same ugly red pulse as those Lucien already held. No longer able to keep his rage in check, he lashed out at the bookcase with the full force of the perverted energy.

While the dust settled, Lucien slumped against the nearest wall, completely drained from the manipulating of all that raw power. "I will have my prize," he muttered, now to himself. "And my revenge. She will be less than nothing once in my hands. Perhaps she will take the place of my slave...or as a plaything for my little pets." Opening eyes that had drooped closed on their own he looked around him. It was a good thing he'd had enough restraint to head to this room of unused junk. Had he gone to the rooftop, or to his library, in his fury he might have done serious damage to things more costly to replace. Taking several deep, slow breaths, Lucien pushed those thoughts away. It was time he returned to the workroom to see if the boy had shown up, but that was something he couldn't risk if he were still gripped by wrath. There was too much of value in that room to take the chance.

Composing himself, he closed the door on the evidence of his rampage and headed down the hall. There, by the workroom door, was the boy, waiting in nervous patience. With the mood that Lucien was in, he hoped—for his own sake more than for Tony's—that the boy had something of value to tell him. After all, he had invested so much energy finding and preparing the boy as a tool that it would be a shame to waste it all by killing him now.

"You certainly took your time," Lucien said in icy greeting, "I hope it has been worth it." Tony paled as he followed Lucien into the room and wisely said nothing in response. Following the familiar pattern they had established, Tony stood waiting in the center of the room as Lucien moved toward the scarred table. Once there, the resemblance to his previous visits ended. Rather than losing a measure of time and coming to his senses in a chair he never remembered sitting in, Tony watched as Lucien Blank prepared an innocuous cup of tea and sat down with it at the desk. Somehow this event was all the more unsettling for its lack of threat.

"So, Tony," Lucien began, his cold, hard voice betraying none of the weariness visible in his eyes, "have your efforts today justified my sparing you?" His scowl deepened as Tony remained silent.

Unsure of where to begin or the exact importance of what he'd discovered, Tony hesitated. Finally deciding that the girl had to be in the center of it all, he told his master everything that he had discovered about her: where she lived; how his "guide" led him to follow her to the pawnshop (he faltered as that comment brought a faint flush of anger to Lucien's face); he even mentioned his thought that the girl might have been the one behind the curtain that night at Yesterday's Dreams. He didn't mention how he'd lost the scent that first night, or how he lost it again the next day on the train. It was enough that he had something to tell the man. Much better to see the eager glint now in his master's eyes, than the smoldering anger that had been there moments before.

"It will do," Lucien responded. Tony did not miss the hungry look in the master's eyes as he sat forward. "The girl, what is her name?"

"The name on the box was O'Keefe," Tony shifted in discomfort, "I don't know her first name. Her old man came out the door when she left and might've seen me. I didn't wanna make him suspicious." When the master didn't explode in irritation he continued carefully. "I figure I can ask around in a bit. I have some buddies from that neighborhood, maybe they know something about her."

Tony couldn't identify the look that flashed across Lucien's face when he mentioned the girl and her connection to the pawnshop, but for some reason it left him wanting to tremble. He wasn't given a chance to dwell on it, though. For the next hour-and-a-half Lucien put him through a round of intense interrogation, extracting from him details Tony hadn't even known he'd noticed: What did the girl look like? How tall was she? Where was she going when she left the house again? What was the design of the house? He kept at it until Tony's screamed from the tension of constant standing and his head pounded with the effort to provide answers for every question. He almost longed for Lucien to pluck the memories from his mind as he usually did...almost. Each time he could not respond, he braced himself for a blow as Lucien's gaze hardened. But the blows never came, just more questions, and something told Tony that it was just possible that the master was as tired as he was.

Eventually, his questions ran out and the man turned away with a thoughtful look on his face. Tony swayed in the silence, glad only that Lucien hadn't been looking. The young man braced his legs and waited for some direction. Just as he was beginning to consider that he might have been forgotten, the master turned toward him once again.

"Forget about the pawnshop, for now," he ordered, the barest undercurrent of strain in his voice. Tony wondered what could have worked him up so much. "Follow the girl. Find out what you can. In fact, you would do well to find a way to bring her to me. Do you understand?" Tony nodded, feeling uneasy about the orders he'd just been given.

"You will bring her to me at this address tomorrow night," Lucien pushed a slip of paper toward Tony, and with that final order, turned his back on him—an obvious dismissal.

Tony had no desire to argue and removed himself from both the room and the building with all haste, shoving the paper into his pocket. Once outside, he staggered against the handrail, clutching it convulsively. As much as he wanted to be away from the cursed place, he was forced to rest a moment in the shadow of the doorway. He desperately willed strength into his weary legs. He hadn't slept or eaten much since beginning this odd pursuit. He figured he could get away with making a few phone calls to his friends in Queens on his way home for some much-needed rest. With that decided, he dredged up some extra energy to get himself home.

As dawn painted the sky in brilliant colors, Maggie found herself once again on her rooftop with Demne seated across from her. She wasn't quite sure how she felt about that. Her heart still churned over the conflict between what her eyes and memories told her, and what she now knew in her very soul. Demne was not evil; though others had perverted his symbol of honor very much in the way the humans' *swastika* went from being a symbol of life, to being a banner of hatred.

"Tell me again, will ye, what has brought ye clear across the ocean?"

"Unrest...in the mortal realm an' our own," he answered, his words so soft Maggie wondered they had been uttered out loud. "It canna all be explained. Sacrifices on sacred lands, defacing o' monuments, scrawled threats. No sign if 'tis the work o' man or sidhe. An' now I come here an' find more o' the same. We'd feared as much...an' the seers warn o' far worse to come."

"I figured 'twas too much to hope that good news brought ye here, or even no news an' merely some harmless errand." She tried hard not to think of what her first impressions had been. "An' what would ye have o' us?"

"Soon Danu must call her Children home," Demne sat up and watched her face with care, his eyes blazing as he continued, "before all is lost an' Eire falls at the hands o' her own...mortal or sidhe. All must be ready to return. The first oath comes before all others." In his passion he gripped her hand, only to recoil at the unexpected turmoil he encountered. "There are rumors that *Gearoidh Iarla* has been seen ridin' like the devil 'round the Curagh o' Kildare. His horse's shoes were worn fair thin, it canna be long before the Miller's son blows the trumpet to herald his final return. *All* the people will be called to join the battle." He subsided, his face a beautifully composed mask while he waited for her to speak.

Maggie sat silently a moment, her mind roiling with many concerns, not the least of which was that he would now judge her by her response, just as she'd judged him by his markings. What could she say to him? Could he understand how torn she was? Far away, her people and the land they'd made their home were in jeopardy; right here, there was a threat to both her new home and those mortals who she sought to protect. There was no question of her taking her place in Eire, but how much time would she have to settle matters here?

Drawing all of her dignity around her, Maggie likewise gathered her thoughts. "I have held my oath in this place for two centuries past," she paused, selecting most carefully her next words, "what was placed in my care has been guarded without fail, waitin' to be called upon.

"In that time I've taken to protectin' other items that crossed my path," Maggie allowed the shifting thoughts in her mind to focus into an image of the shop and the significance of some of what it held. She left her mind accessible to her judge. "Mostly none o' it matters to any but they who pawned it, but some rare bits...they need guardin' near as much as that already in my care." Here she allowed Quicksilver and Kara to fill her mind along with a select number of her other treasures.

"I'll answer the call, an' gladly, when it comes, but I worry at the time I have left an' if 'tis enough for all I must do to safeguard what must'na fall into sinister hands," she finished with a burst of her encounter with Lucien. "Can ye see my dilemma?"

Demne's gaze clouded as he digested all she had thrown at him. She feared that he had indeed begun to question her status of guardian. Dared she hope those doubts had been satisfied?

Chapter 12

The silence hung thick and alien in the warm comfort of their bedroom. It was maddening how sleep danced out of reach. The softly illuminated dial of their old-fashioned alarm clock glared brightly in the darkness, taunting Patrick as he lay stiffly beneath his covers, afraid any movement might rob his wife of her chance at sleep. At least, that's what he told himself as he tried not to acknowledge her equally false repose.

"Turn on the light, Patrick," Barbara's words cut through the dark with a weariness no amount of sleep would cure.

"Watch yer eyes." Patrick squinted against the violent radiance of the sudden light and sat back against his pillows. He waited for his wife to voice the thoughts that plagued them both. Rolling over carefully, she curled up with her head resting gently on his chest. Patrick closed his eyes and forced the tightness in his throat to ease. Things weren't quite as bad as he'd feared if she was willing to be held in his arms. He held her close and allowed himself a fleeting moment of peace. Very fleeting.

"Before today, did you know?" Barbara asked in a voice barely above a whisper.

Patrick shook his head, forgetting she couldn't see it, trying to be hurt by the question but knowing he had no right. It would not have been the first time he'd kept things from his wife, all with the good intention of protecting her from something that couldn't be changed. God, how he wished that was the case now; it would have been so much easier to deal with if he hadn't gotten his own hopes up. He had felt so much better recently. And, thanks to Kara, money was not a concern. Of course all would be well; after all, they had what they needed, and hadn't he already beaten cancer once? This morning, the biggest worry he had had was how to help Kara get back Quicksilver; he couldn't say the same tonight. Too bad he'd let down his guard.

"Did you know?!" The hurt and impatience that were now clear in his Bobbi's voice tore at his heart. At his silence she made to pull away, turning angry eyes up at him.

"No! No, love, I did'na hold out on ye!" Patrick clutched her as tightly as the pain in his chest would allow. "I did'na know 'til Arn called today.

"I did'na know, I did'na know...." The soft-spoken words hung in the air like a mantra until Barbara finally clung to him with more care than he took himself, gripping her tightly in return. She murmured to him gently, soothing away the tight sobs that caught in his throat. Patrick buried his face in her shoulder and tried to swallow his grief. Muffling the sounds he couldn't hold back, he rocked back and forth as he hadn't done since childhood...as he hadn't done since they'd taken him from his home in Ireland and put an ocean between him and the land he loved. For the first time since learning of his illness, Patrick O'Keefe let the barriers crumble, letting out more than half a lifetime of grief that he'd never released.

As his broken gasps became once again smooth, Patrick lay back, clammy and exhausted, with his wife in his arms. She pulled away a moment, reaching out her hand to smooth back his sweat-tangled curls. Leaning forward, she kissed the signs of his tears away, showing him in the simplest way that she held him in her heart...that she was there for him. He brought his hand up to cradle the back of her neck as his forehead came to rest against hers.

"A ghrá mo chroí, love o' my heart!" he whispered. Weariness faded away as his love looked up at him with an answering heat in her eyes. With the threat of death once more at the forefront of both their thoughts, Patrick drew his wife to him, driven to reaffirm life.

Drained, but with renewed hope, he lay in the comfort of their room, which once again held the solace of sanctuary. Faint snores beside him finished the job his emotional purge and physical exertion had begun. Within moments he too was asleep, with his wife's head pillowed upon his chest and the lamp keeping away the shadows.

If it weren't for the draft that found its way through the cracks around the smoke-clouded windows of the basement, the shadowy chamber would have remained absolutely still; a stagnant and lifeless collection of musty boxes and unidentifiable clutter. The only motion in the room was the reluctant waft of stale smoke that hung permanently in the air. In the darkest corner of the basement, the flare of a match cast demonic shadows across the face of Lucien Blank. The stale smoke thickened with a fresh infusion and the burning tip of Lucien's cigarette seemed to glow brighter as the night sky darkened, depriving the room of even indirect light. He had been sitting there for hours now, lost in his thoughts ever since the boy had left.

It all came back to the girl; he had to see her, he had to know if she was worth claiming. Lucien's mind repeatedly cycled through the information he'd gleaned from his interrogation of Tony. His descriptions matched enough of what Lucien had seen the other day at the pawnshop for him to believe that she had something to do with the power he craved. Of course, he had only seen the girl from behind, and his attention had been more on the awesome trail of power that had actually drawn him to the pawnshop door. In the darkness, the red glow of the cigarette trembled at the memory of that power. His hand unconsciously clenched the edge of the desk as he thought of what he could do with such energy at his disposal. The possibilities sent such a wave of obsessive longing through him that his body quivered. In this thirst the master was the slave; whenever he encountered such strong magical potential, he needed it with the strength of an addiction.

Yes, there was no doubt; this girl was the key. But the question remained: did she possess what he must have, or was she herself the prize? Lucien could think of some delightful opportunities should she prove to be the source of the coveted power. The texts in his private collection spoke of many...interesting ways to stimulate magical potential. Sex and pain generated quite satisfying results, and combining the methods led to even more possibilities. Should those efforts prove insufficient, there was always death. A frightening, torturous death with the proper rituals could release an amazing amount of energy for one who knew how to harvest it.

Lucien's pulse quickened dangerously and his loins tightened in response to the mental image of the ravaged and hoarse young woman bound to a table, surrounded by the trappings of ritual magic. It would be quite interesting to see how far he could go before the pain sent her into unconsciousness. None of it would be quite as satisfying without her emotional feedback to motivate him to greater efforts. Vividly, he pictured himself, almost lovingly separating her skin from her living flesh in a moment of agonizing ecstasy, his own body vibrating as it absorbed the overflow of energy that his power objects could not store. He could visualize the look of utter, hopeless terror in the girl's eyes when his final stroke plunged in her heart and she saw the orgasmic pleasure on his face as her last pulse of blood flooded him in a wash of death energy.... Of course, death was so final, and not nearly as satisfying as the other options. Besides, it was wasteful; the first two methods had a nearly infinite potential for repeat performances, as long as he was careful not to do too much damage; with death magic there was but one opportunity.

An extremely nasty chuckle broke the silence in the basement as Lucien leaned forward to switch on a light on the scarred desktop. Tony would soon bring him this girl—or die explaining his failure. In either case, Lucien couldn't risk any questionable events taking place in this building. Nothing must happen to cast a shadow over the respectable reputation he had built up over the past ten years. That reputation was his security, his protection against those elements of society he couldn't possibly control the way he had the people in the auction room earlier that week. Lucien Blank was above reproach as far as the world was concerned, and it must remain that way until he'd gathered enough power that all of humanity would be helpless in his grip. That was why he'd acquired a number of properties with no paper trail leading to him, such as the one Tony was to take the girl to. Now to make sure the place would be ready. Lucien reached for the phone beside him.

The soft light of dawn nearly overwhelmed Tony as he made his way back to the girl's house. Rested and fed though he was, it was never his habit to be up and about before the sun. He couldn't remember the last time he'd been awake this early, especially on a Sunday. It was just the beginning of his irritations that day.

Pulling a faded ball cap further down to shade his eyes, he took up his position at the bodega across from the house. An idea had come to him last night when he was calling around to his friends. None of them had known or heard of her, no one could tell him her name; but there was someone he could call guaranteed to have that information. It just might work, but only if the girl was not home.

At about eight o'clock, Tony decided it was a good thing he'd dragged himself out of bed so early. Across the street, the girl left the house and headed purposefully down the block. Grabbing the phone book chained to the wall beneath the pay phone, Tony flipped quickly to the listings for O'Keefe. He picked up the receiver and wedged it under his ear, his finger on the entry for P. O'Keefe at the address across the street. Dialing quickly, Tony held his breath as the phone rang. He didn't have much time if he was to meet Lucien tonight...with the girl. Tony spared an anxious look for the retreating figure as he listened to the phone ring. At this rate she'd disappear before he hung up.

"Hello?" The woman's voice on the other end sounded fuzzed by sleep.

"Good morning, Mrs. O'Keefe," Tony answered in his best effort at politeness. "May I please speak with your daughter?"

"I'm sorry," the woman answered. "Kara's already gone out for the day. Can I take a message?"

"That's okay," he answered, keeping his voice carefully pleasant, "I'll call back." Not even waiting for a response he hung up the phone and ran after the girl...Kara. He could just see her turning the corner at the end of the block; if he could only keep sight of her he might come out of this with his skin, and everything beneath it, intact. Tony tried not to think what that would mean for her; he was too terrified of what would happen to him if he did not meet Lucien's demand. But as he sprinted down the street, he couldn't suppress the memories of Lucien Blank standing over him as some force held him in suffocating immobility. He could still feel the chill of that finger tracing the features of his face. Tony nearly faltered at the thought of what might happen to Kara.

Shaking off those feelings, Tony focused only on the rise and fall of his legs.

Sheesh! He didn't even know the girl, why should he care? Right now he would tail her; later he would decide what else to do. After all, the right situation might not even present itself. Catching up with Kara...with *the girl*—better for him not even to think her name...it made everything too personal—Tony slowed to a comfortable walk about a half a block behind her. This neighborhood was too quiet and open. If he tried for her now, someone would notice. He would watch for his moment and see what he could learn in the meantime.

CHAPTER 13

Until she stood before Yesterday's Dreams, Kara hadn't considered that the shop might again be closed. Fortunately, the knob turned easily beneath her hand and the anachronous bell tinkled merrily. It was an instant replay of her first visit here; there was singing in the back room and Kara had an overwhelming desire to be elsewhere.

What was she going to say to this woman? Would she find the answers she had so determinedly come here to get, or more evasion? As she waited, her eyes fixed on the photograph. Kara stepped behind the counter and lifted the picture down from the wall. She was there, transfixed, when Maggie walked through the curtain.

"Hallo, can I h...." The woman stopped abruptly as the scene before her registered. In an instant the carefree gaze and easy smile were gone, replaced by a dignified and respectful look from eyes that seemed suddenly ancient. Maggie's lips set in a sad little smile, barely lifting at the corners, as if pride and resignation fought each other for expression. Moving with a grace only hinted at before, she walked to the door, leaving Kara with the feeling that royalty had swept by. "If ye wait a moment, child, I'll just lock up so we can talk in peace."

Clutching the photograph, Kara felt as if her balance were completely swept away. She didn't know whether to be anxious or angry. Who was this woman and what part had she played in her Grandda's life...all their lives? Whatever answers she expected to find, something told her the reality would be something else altogether. Waiting in a heavy silence where breathing was no longer an autonomous function, Kara looked down at her grandfather's face, feeling oddly reassured by the joy there. He looked so happy...so carefree...so innocent. Kara rather liked the picture. Some detached and perverse segment of her brain plagued her, wondering who the photographer had been—as if that mattered.

As Maggie turned and came back toward Kara, there was a distant look in her eyes and her face glowed. "'Twas yer Mamó took the picture."

Mamó? Kara jerked back as her very thoughts were answered without her voicing them, but either Maggie didn't notice her reaction or she chose to ignore it. The pawnbroker acted as if her own thoughts were far away and long ago. Her gaze traveled across the photographic timeline on the wall behind the counter before coming to rest on Kara. With a contented little sigh, Maggie returned to the here-and-now.

"Turn an' look at them, Kara: they are the ones who reclaimed their dreams. Do yerself a favor...never forget the look on their faces. Some day I hope to see on yers the very one."

Not waiting to see if Kara did as she said, Maggie slipped past her and pulled aside the velvet curtain. "Well," she said, just barely turning her head, "come along an' ask the questions that are floodin' yer eyes, then."

Did she really want to know the answers? Could any good come of knowing, or would she just add to her own heartache? It scarcely mattered; Kara had a feeling there would be no halting the confrontation she herself had put into motion. She squared her shoulders and followed the woman, giving only one quick glance at the locked door behind her.

Rather than lead her into the office as Kara had expected, Maggie moved beyond it without even a glance and made her way to a security door in the far corner of the back room. The pawnbroker took out a cluster of keys and opened the door, motioning for Kara to precede her. They entered a small space, a landing between two other doors at the bottom of a narrow stairway. Maggie locked the door to the shop behind them and Kara wondered why she wasn't more nervous. She should be, going deeper into this woman's domain, with locked doors between her and the outside. But she wasn't. Whatever else Maggie was, she was not a threat; of that, Kara was certain, though she would be hard pressed to explain why.

"Go on up, dear," Maggie said as she turned around. "I'll brew some tea an' we can talk." Silently, still cradling the photograph she had appropriated from behind the counter, Kara made her way carefully up the stairs. At the first landing she turned to Maggie with questioning eyes. Did she continue up the stairs, or was this floor their goal?

"Right here, love; that way leads to the roof." At the woman's response, Kara stepped to the side, allowing Maggie to precede her through the door.

Anxious as she was, Kara couldn't help but admire Maggie's apartment. Everywhere she looked something fascinating waited to catch her eye. As if she were again reading Kara's mind, Maggie chuckled. "Ye tend to collect an unusual array of items when ye're a pawnbroker—even in yer home."

The moment she began to speak, a blur of motion streaked from the other room, aimed right at Maggie's legs. The woman laughed and bent to scoop up the largest cat Kara had ever seen. It arched its neck and fairly rumbled with purring as it watched Kara out of bright, burnt orange-colored eyes. When Kara did not immediately move to pet it, the feline meowed demandingly and jumped to the table beside her.

Maggie laughed, "I do believe, Kara, that Beag Scath has decided to like ye."

Kara forgot to be anxious as she set the photograph on the table and obligingly pet the cat's soft, silky hair. She had never seen such unusual markings before and she stared in fascination at patterns that shifted prismatically as she ran her hand across the cat's thick coat. In that single instant, the tension that had dominated the room faded to almost nothing. Kara sat in the chair conveniently positioned in front of her new friend as Maggie busied herself with refreshments.

"So, would ye care for some tea? Or would ye rather have somethin' else?"

"Tea would be fine," Kara answered distractedly; she didn't shift her eyes from the cat's acrobatic expression of its pleasure at finding someone who knew where to scratch. "What's its name again?"

"*His* name's Beag Scath," Maggie responded. "It means Little Shadow." There was mischief in the woman's eyes as she brought the tea to the table and set it down next to Kara. "Shall I tell ye the tale o' how he came by his name while we drink our tea?"

As much as she would have loved to hear the tale, Kara did not care to put off this reckoning. "Perhaps later, Maggie, after we've talked about what I'm here for."

"Fair enough." Lowering herself into the chair facing Kara, Maggie drew the now-forgotten picture toward her. Silence settled about them as she looked thoughtfully back and forth from it to Kara, as if deciding how much to say.

"He was'na much older than yerself, ye know," the woman began after a moment, "the first time he came to my shop.

"The burden on his heart so heavy an' his eyes so bleak." A sad shadow of a smile slipped by on Maggie's lips, "I'd have helped him even if I had'na already given my bond to."

Reality seemed to fade as Maggie's implication penetrated Kara's efforts to focus on the cat. Some part of her hadn't wanted to know what Maggie would say; now there was no question of her complete attention. All was quiet, as if Maggie knew a moment was needed for Kara to grasp the significance of her words.

Kara's stomach fluttered violently as she got the feeling that the world as she knew it was about to be stripped away. What startled her most was her own lack of shock. She couldn't say why she knew that Maggie would recall that long-ago day firsthand. The realization came to mind that she would have been more startled if the pawnbroker hadn't started off the way she did.

Feeling the need for something to hold on to, Kara pulled Beag Scath toward her and held him tight. Within seconds, reality shifted. Preceded by a squeal that seemed like nothing that had ever come from a cat, there was an odd ripple of fur across Kara's arm and her stomach lurched. Looking down, startled, Kara swayed unsteadily on the straight-backed chair. Indignant burnt orange eyes stared back at her as a miniature hand pushed firmly against her chest. As the foundation of her understanding shattered into blackness, Kara slid quietly toward the floor.

Maggie cursed vehemently to herself. The moment she saw Kara reach for Beag Scath she knew what would happen. For the sprite, contact was on his terms or not at all, even if he liked you. When Kara threatened to tumble to the floor, Maggie was already at her side. Glaring at the now-freed sprite, the sidhe caught the girl as she fell and lifted her effortlessly.

"Now what shall I do?" Maggie said out loud as she adjusted Kara in her arms. "Thank ye very much, little pest! Now ye can go open the door to the rath for me."

Looking totally unrepentant, Beag Scath scampered down the stairs in front of the burdened Maggie. Not knowing how Kara would react when she came to, it was safer to take her below where, if the girl woke up hysterical, the neighbors would not hear and get the wrong idea. As she maneuvered the steps, Maggie lightly hummed Kara into deeper unconsciousness using the tune she had used days before to put the sprite to sleep. It was best if the girl stayed out until they were situated in one of the rooms below.

It was taking considerable effort to put the sleep on Kara. In fact, Maggie had the suspicion that it wouldn't have worked at all if the girl weren't already passed out and in physical contact with her. Maggie shivered at the implications.

"Well, it looks as if I'm to tell ye more than I'd planned to from the start," Maggie spoke casually as Kara opened her eyes. She gave her visitor a moment to adjust and take in her surroundings before going any further. The girl didn't scream, as Maggie had feared she might, but her eyes were still dazed.

The sidhe did not drop her human seeming; it was too clear that Kara's reserve balanced precariously. Instead, she waited patiently as the girl grappled with this sudden overturning of the world as she knew it.

"Do ye need some water before I explain, or perhaps a fresh cup o' tea?" Maggie put every shred of reassurance she could into her voice.

"Kara?" The girl had gone very still on her pile of cushions, her eyes focused just beyond Maggie's shoulder. The sidhe had expected nothing less, but as the girl spoke she was totally taken by surprise.

"Silly me.... I always searched the clover patches."

What in Danu's name...clover patches? Maggie prayed to the goddess that Kara hadn't gone mad, though she suspected what had inspired the odd comment. Maggie turned to look behind her and sure enough, Beag Scath was leaning on the doorframe.

"He's real enough, Kara," she said soothingly, keeping her voice low and relaxed, "Beag Scath is my friend an' ye need na fear him...or me. If ye let me, I'll explain; if ye'd rather leave, that's okay as well." Maggie was taking quite a chance here, but something told her that Kara's need to know would win out over any fears the girl had. Kara blinked and gave a brusque little shake of her head. All Maggie could read was a sense of wonder as the girl met her gaze. Perhaps all would work out well.

Moving leisurely, Maggie turned and motioned for the sprite to come to her. With all the overwhelming curiosity of a wild creature, he eagerly left his perch in the doorway and came to stand at Maggie's side, half-hiding behind her arm. He lowered his eyes in a look that might have been contrition, but which Maggie recognized as intense concentration. After a moment, he held out his hand to Kara. There, resting lightly on his tiny palm, was a perfect, blinding-white rose with just the faintest hint of violet edging its velvety petals. The tableau held for several minutes before Kara, with an astounded look in her eyes, gave a joyous laugh and edged hesitantly forward. Her hand seemed to rise on its own, as if it would have the flower whether Kara willed it or not, or perhaps, in the fear that the flower were an illusion, she did not want it to shatter. Maggie held her breath as Beag Scath approached the girl as solemnly as a knight on quest, holding the rose before him as his standard. Only after Kara, with equal reverence, accepted the blossom did the sprite's usual impish smile resurface. Kara smiled widely in return.

Maggie exhaled gently, not wanting to disturb the tentative peace. She had taken a calculated risk by keeping Beag Scath with her while she waited for Kara to come back to her senses. She had finally decided that the girl would need something to prove that what had happened upstairs was real, and not just the current strain of life overcoming her. Maggie looked on joyfully as Kara watched the sprite in astonishment. Impatient with the slowness of it all, Beag Scath climbed into Kara's lap and settled down to play with her dangling curls.

After giving Kara a moment or two to absorb the new reality of things, Maggie made a small noise to bring back the girl's attention to the situation before them. Kara's eyes came away from the disarming presence of Beag Scath to focus on Maggie. She did not, the sidhe noticed, make her earlier mistake of gripping the sprite tightly.

"We must talk, my dear," she began gently, keeping her voice soothing and low. "There is much I find I must tell ye, without the luxury o' goin' slow."

At Kara's cautious nod, Maggie breathed deeply and tried to gather her thoughts. She had not been prepared to tell so much, though now she must. "I am o' the people called the *Áes Sidhe* or the *Tuatha de Danaan*—elves, I believe they're calling us now. Beag Scath is kin, though not kind; he is what ye'd call a sprite or a faerie.

"We share this world with yer kind in many different guises, mostly across the ocean. I myself hail from Eire, Ireland, but my kin are found in every country. Those who still believe often count us as dark—for they think anythin' they do'na understand must be evil. They tremble if they think we are near, though they've only cause to fear a few o' our number," Maggie paused to smile sadly, remembering too well the treatment that had forced her kind beneath their hills. "The legends that have grown 'round our name are numerous, an' some even bear a shadow o' truth. We are creatures o' magic an' death does'na take us, except by accident or violence. We are few an', as with yerselves, there are those among us who are either kind or cruel, an' most often both."

Maggie's heart ached at the emotion battling in Kara's eyes. The girl drew in on herself as doubt and belief both sought supremacy within her. Beag Scath had abandoned Kara's lap moments before, as things got too close. Maggie knew how unsettling all this must be, but with what Kara had seen it would be more harmful not to explain.

"The name given me by my clan is Cliodna. It is a name shared only with kin." Maggie held her breath, waiting to see if her unsettled visitor would grasp the true importance of that statement. Maggie thought she saw a flicker of understanding in the wary eyes that wouldn't quite meet her own; it was a subconscious recognition, as if Kara was not yet ready to acknowledge what had just been said.

"The Tuatha de Danaan have always given aid to their human neighbors; those who were worthy. Those o' my line have sworn to aid an' protect yer kin, who have ever seen the goodness o' our kind. I am the bean sidhe o' Clan O'Keefe." With those words, Maggie fell silent. From this point on it was up to Kara to give the cues, to ask her questions. As the silence grew, the sidhe wondered what damage her revealed secrets would do in the end.

Kara stared appraisingly at the woman before her, the one claiming to be an elf. Every logical neuron in her brain wanted to denounce that claim as an unstable person's fantasy. There was one problem: with all she had seen—was seeing—it was impossible to deny that there was something extraordinary about Maggie McCormick and her "pet."

Reared on Celtic mythology and tales of the sidhe, Kara had heard the good and bad of what mankind claimed of the fae. From literally the day she'd been born, Grandda had filled her mind with the wonder, magic, and respect commanded by the Gentry. Those memories now surfaced, bright and fresh as the day they'd been made. No matter how she tried to convince herself this was all madness, she couldn't help remembering that each time he'd told her another tale his voice had brimmed with feeling. Now, thinking back, it had always seemed more that he was speaking of a rich and treasured history, not distant folk tales. Only now did she realize how much of that proud belief he'd managed to instill in her.

"Cliodna...I know that name." Kara's voice was strong despite the shock she had experienced. Her brow drew down as she concentrated fiercely and she sang under her breath.

> Beneath the waves a faerie land
> Filled with magic and great beauty
> lo, deep in the heart of the deep
> Lovely Cliodna saved my life
> there in fae Tír Tairnigiri
> Beneath the waves I met the sidhe
> And looked I there on a goddess...

"My Great Grandda wrote that song...about you?" Kara waited for an answer.

"Aye, long ago...longer than ye would imagine possible, I saved the life o' Ryan O'Keefe. He was fishin' an' a storm blew up. The boat was lost an' nearly himself with it, but I drew him into my home in Tír Tairnigiri...the Land o' Promise."

"I always wondered at the words, they didn't seem right. Grandda said it was a poor translation...."

Maggie smiled at that and Kara marveled that she had not seen before now the otherworldly qualities in that face. The woman engendered something more than any human could ever aspire to. "A poor translation, indeed; no mortal words can compare with the Old Tongue, but 'tis a fair enough attempt."

Again, Kara wondered if this were insanity. And if so, whose? Was she the crazy one, or was Maggie? Realistically, sprites and magic did not exist. In actuality, Kara had seen—or thought she'd seen—both today. As for Maggie, other than her now regal demeanor, she'd yet to offer any proof of her professed heritage. Where were the pointed ears and cat eyes of popular fiction? Where were the fantastic underground chambers that looked like a transplanted summer meadow or the court of a king? It was insane. Breathing deeply, searching for some internal center to strengthen her failing balance, Kara finally met Maggie's eyes.

"So, how much of your blood runs through my veins?" As the words left her mouth, Kara jerked back as if hit. That was not what she'd intended to ask! The dumbfounded look on her face must have shown quite well her own confusion. Even more so when the instant Kara spoke, Maggie's dignity fell away. She tossed her head back and somehow made a roar of laughter sound musical.

"Oh my! Love, 'tis amazin' how our minds an' mouths conspire to show us what we refuse to see." Taking obvious care, Maggie composed herself. Kara shifted uncomfortably on her cushions as she waited. She could see the woman watching her, seeming ready to speak several times over, though she remained silent. Finally, as the silence was about to shatter on its own, Maggie sat forward and began.

"Your grandfather's grandfather was my kin," Maggie paused, as if searching for the next path for her words. "Sometimes our oath to the clans awakens more in the heart than fidelity."

"What does that make us?" Kara asked, feeling safer in mundane topics, regardless of how fantastic the answer had to be.

"Who would think such a simple question would be so difficult to answer?" There was an undercurrent of laughter beneath Maggie's voice, though she allowed herself only to smile. "We do'na call our kin as yer kind do, thin's are different with us in a way I do'na know that ye would understand without more time for me to explain than we have. By yer terms, I would most likely be yer several times great-aunt."

"Does my family know?" Kara asked, finding it hard to imagine her down-to-earth father believing in anything so fanciful. The only magic he believed in was the magic of music.

"Yer grandfather did." There was the warmth of memory radiating behind the slight widening of Maggie's smile. It made Kara think of the photograph of this woman and Grandda. Seeing Maggie's look of fondness, and nothing more, Kara blushed now to think that she'd suspected Maggie was Grandda's child from an illicit affair. Kara brought her attention back to the conversation as Maggie continued. "Without revealin' what I was, his father told him to look for me, should he need help. Yer Grandfather saw my nature through my seemin' in this very shop, the first time Quicksilver came to me." Kara's pulse skipped as those words sank in, startled that her actions had unknowingly mirrored those of her grandfather.

Maggie's head tilted thoughtfully, "I doubt he ever told yer father, or Paddy would have come to me for help himself."

Not sure how much of her grandfather's tales were fable or fact, Kara thought on what Maggie said before forming her next question.

"Does that mean we can't die?" Kara's thoughts were on her father. Even as the question left her lips she sighed, knowing what the response would be. After all, she had been at Grandda's funeral. The look of compassion in Maggie's eyes was almost too much.

"It sorrows me that ye were parted from yer grandfather so soon," Maggie finally answered. "Those with the blood o' the sidhe in their veins, the years o' their life can still be counted—particularly when that blood has thinned—but the span is generally longer than that o' one who is merely mortal."

Maybe it was just her imagination, but Kara wondered at the pause before Maggie responded. Was it just a fraction too long? Was there something this odd woman wasn't telling her?

Then what she said registered and Kara bristled at the term "merely mortal." Up until moments ago, she believed herself "merely mortal." Perhaps she still was, depending on how much she chose to believe after a night's sleep. She didn't care for this woman's attitude, at times, as she unconsciously belittled the human race. Having grown up with the knowledge of the power and capacity for vengeance the Tuatha de Danaan were capable of, but not knowing how this sidhe would react, Kara withheld her objection.

"What does it mean to be a sidhe?" Kara continued, carefully pronouncing the word correctly—*shee*.

"Well," Maggie answered. "That depends on who ye ask." An impish glint kindled in her eyes as she continued. Kara already knew that others didn't always speak favorably of the race. "As 'tis me ye asked: we are magic-touched; beautiful an' eternal an' capable o' great emotion, despite what many o' the legends say. Both good an' evil are found in us an' we each have our virtues an' our failings." Kara watched Maggie as she spoke, fascinated by the passion that propelled each word. "Music is important to us; 'tis how we record our past, teach our young, an' fill our unwanted silences—'tis counted as one o' our greatest gifts."

Here Maggie grew silent. Kara sighed. Something inside of her longed for what had eluded explanation. She knew that the essence of what the sidhe were could not be captured by words. Listening to Grandda had told her that, though then she'd had no idea that the stories he'd told her were true. And yet there had always been some rueful quality to his voice—a quality mirrored now in Maggie's—that spoke to Kara's heart, telling her how insufficient words were compared to the reality.

"Ah, lass," Maggie said as if she understood the sigh, "do ye know the legacy yer grandfather left ye? 'Tis'na just the music or the tales; there's a world out there waitin' for ye, an' 'tis so much more than ye expected."

Kara relaxed on the cushions, resting her head against the smooth rock wall as she listened to Maggie's soothing voice. She could find nothing to fear in this woman and what she was learning did much to dispel the misgivings she'd had earlier. In a way it was ironic; all those years Grandda had told her tales of the sidhe, and now a sidhe was telling her tales of her Grandda.

Maggie told her how he had come alone to America to find a new life for the family he had started, how he despaired of making enough to bring over his wife and young son to the security of this new land, away from poverty and persecution. He had worked hard enough to make himself ill and still had not earned the money even for a steerage crossing. Ready to give up hope, he remembered the words of his father; if he found himself in trouble he should seek out Maggie McCormick at a pawnshop called Yesterday's Dreams. Taking the only thing he had of any value—the violin his father gave him as he left Ireland—he searched for the pawnshop, desperate and heart-sore. That had been the first time Maggie had exchanged a ticket for Quicksilver.

Remembering many nights of sitting at Grandda's feet as he made Quick-silver sing, Kara would have understood how hard it was for him to give up the violin, even if she hadn't done the same herself just days ago. She could still see the joy light up his face, sparkling through the beads of sweat that dotted his brow; and she could remember the way his eyes glistened, his ruddy cheeks glowed, and the music pulsed through every inch of him. With such an example to learn from, it was no wonder Kara shared his passion for music.

In her mind, she could see the photograph that had been left upstairs and she understood much better how her grandfather had come to look at Maggie as he did; she was the one who'd given him back his family. Kara also remembered what Maggie had said about the pictures on the wall behind the counter...those were the people who had reclaimed their dreams. Even had she not already prom-ised her father, Kara was determined that her own face would join that gallery.

Maggie's voice drew Kara from her thoughts. Though her first words were missed, the grave tone behind them commanded Kara's attention. "...so much more complicated in this time. There are laws an' taxes an' paperwork, all drawin' unwanted attention if each detail is'na satisfied." Maggie shook her head impatiently at these human conventions. "'Tis why I could'na simply help ye outright, but must go through this charade."

"What do you mean?" Kara asked bemused.

"I mean," Maggie looked kindly at Kara as she answered, "ye need'na pay me to get back yer Quicksilver; what I gave ye was yer grandfather's, though that's a story for another time." Here Maggie paused, a concerned and thoughtful look creeping into her eyes. "But first, there are thin's ye must know about yer grandfather's legacy...an' yer violin. Most important o' all is that I canna return Quicksilver for now."

Kara grew anxious as Maggie spoke. There was much that did not seem right about what she just said. Could such mundane things as government and laws have any bearing on a creature out of myth? If they did, then how could they avoid the formality of payment? Maggie couldn't just record phantom payments, because there would be no corresponding record of Kara earning enough to make those payments. And the sidhe couldn't just make it appear the transaction had-n't taken place because then there would be no explanation for the large sum of money Kara had deposited in her bank account. Kara's stomach clenched as she thought of all the possible complications.

"Kara, I have been doin' this for far more years than can be accounted for in the photographs behind my counter. Do'na fear that I would cause ye trouble with the law."

Kara blushed furiously as anger and embarrassment warred across her face. She had surprisingly little trouble accepting that the woman across from her wasn't young or human and that somehow magic was involved, but what did that mean to her? Fine, she had been raised on Celtic fairy tales. Yes, she had seen things that couldn't be explained in the narrow confines of her reality. Despite all of that, Kara felt adrift here, not knowing what to expect or what was possible. Some part of her couldn't help but bristle at Maggie's attitude, even knowing that no offense was meant.

"Oh, dear!" Maggie looked chagrined at Kara's expression. "It appears my people skills need more than a touch o' work.

"Let me explain." Kara couldn't deny the entreating look in Maggie's eyes. "When ye reach home, take a look at yer pawn ticket an' ye'll see 'tis no such thin'. What ye have is a rental agreement—with myself doin' the rentin'...if ye'd read it days ago 'twould have appeared as proper a pawn ticket as ye could hope for, but now that ye know it for what it is, yer eye'll see it true."

Before she could say anything more, Kara thought she noticed a flash of alarm travel across the pawnbroker's face. The woman's eyes seemed to flare bright green and her mouth grew tight at the corners, as if she restrained herself with great effort. From what, Kara could not say, for she heard nothing and the moment passed in seconds. Almost like a backdrop being lowered on a stage, Maggie's expression relaxed and the fire in her eyes faded. With all that had happened, Kara came close to wondering if the transformation had truly taken place at all. Only the slightest tension as Maggie adjusted her position on her own cushions betrayed her readiness to move at a moment's need. Something had just happened and, seeing how quickly Maggie poised herself to strike, Kara dearly hoped she hadn't been the cause.

"Please, Kara," Maggie leaned forward in earnest, continuing in a more considerate tone, "there is much I must tell ye an' not enough time to do it now; can ye come back tonight, after four?"

Not quite understanding why she did, Kara agreed. Immediately, Maggie led her up a carved rock staircase she didn't remember descending. At the top, by the side door Kara had banged on days before, Maggie all of a sudden stopped and stared at her intently.

"Quick, the brooch I gave ye the day ye left Quicksilver in my care, what have ye done with it?"

On its own, Kara's hand slipped into her coat pocket where the brooch lay in its paper wrapping. She had forgotten it. It had been the reason for her return and she had forgotten it. Nodding, she emptied her pocket, pulling out her scarf along with the bundle.

"I was coming to return this," despite her intentions, Kara's voice sounded uncertain to her own ears. "It's much too valuable...."

Kara's voice trailed off as Maggie's hand darted forward to grab the scarf. A musical string of syllables filled the air surrounding them, making Kara's ears burn. She didn't need a translator to know the sidhe was cursing.

"By the silver hand o' Nuada! 'Tis a fool, I am." Maggie peered so intently at her that Kara began to tremble. "Lass, 'tis a silk scarf...ye could'na have known, but the pin, 'tis magic an' any good it would do ye is hindered by silk. Every time the brooch went into the pocket, the scarf insulated it so it could'na protect ye."

Kara just stood there staring back at her, trying to control her trembling. The situation kept getting more and more weird to her. How could a pin protect her?

"Listen to me." Maggie's intensity nearly overwhelmed Kara. Eyes wide and every muscle tense with the desire to flee, Kara had no choice but to give the sidhe her complete attention as Maggie held her gaze. "Whatever ye do, no matter how much ye may na believe me, ye must wear this brooch until I tell ye otherwise...an' keep it away from silk! 'Tis the most I can do to keep ye safe, short o' hidin' ye away below."

With no recollection of agreeing—other than finding the brooch pinned at her throat–Kara looked around the alley in a dazed sort of way. It hadn't changed much since the old woman chased her out of it with a broom. The only difference seemed to be the china pattern on the bowl of buttermilk. Carefully stepping over the offering, Kara left the alley feeling chilled to the core by all that had been thrown at her today.

Well, what was she supposed to do for the next six hours? She apparently hadn't thought of that when she agreed to return. Unsure of what to do next, Kara paused beneath the tree guarding the mouth of the alleyway. She rested her hand on its slivery bark and was startled at the gentle tingle that traveled up her arm. It was almost as if the tree acknowledged something about her, something of which it approved. Kara remembered the significance of certain trees in Celtic lore and shivered. Was this her imagination running wild? Or was it an unexpected affirmation of everything Maggie told her?

Dwelling on such things for the next six hours would only stress her out beyond belief. Kara pushed the thoughts away. Not wanting to travel back and forth to Queens all day, she began walking purposefully toward Soho to find something to occupy her time.

CHAPTER 14

Tony was really not surprised to find himself back in front of Yesterday's Dreams. The pawnshop was turning out to be a nexus for all that had happened in the past few days. He positioned himself a little ways down the street and prepared to wait. Once again hidden beneath the bill of his cap, he watched the storefront carefully while whatever internal sense had propelled him the other day hovered in an agitated hum at the corner of his awareness. More than a guide, it was a constant reminder that there was nothing in the world Tony wanted more than to be free of Lucien Blank. Three things appeared to be the key to that goal: Kara O'Keefe, the pawnshop, and some unknown object inside its walls. With that in mind, it was all he could do to stay where he was. Patience and caution were traits that Tony had learned well growing up on the streets of Alphabet City. As much as he wanted to rush across the street and claim the keys to his freedom, there was no chance that tactic would work. It would be foolish to walk into a place where he could easily be trapped without knowing if anyone else was inside. *Let's face it*, he thought. *I don't even know what to grab besides the girl.*

Movement across the street caught his eye. He watched closely as the pawnbroker turned the sign to "closed" and locked the door. Tony cursed beneath his breath and started walking casually across the street toward the storefront. He couldn't take the chance that Kara would leave by some other exit. Stopping in front of the window as if something caught his eye, he looked the place over. Inside there was no sign of anyone around. The lights had been left on, though he had seen her lock the door. Apparently this was a temporary closing. It bothered him that he could see no one. After a moment Tony continued on. He would walk around and see if this place had an entrance in the back. Maybe he could get in without being noticed.

Near the end of the block he found the entrance to a service alley wide enough to allow a garbage truck in with a little room on either side. The dark, cramped alley was empty when Tony made his way to where he figured the back of the pawnshop was. Passing door after nondescript door, he wondered if this was a good idea. *What if someone saw him? What if Kara left by the front while he was back here?* At that thought, Tony shook his head. Whatever guided him seemed to know that that wouldn't happen. He had a feeling it would let him know when he was about to screw up.

Looking warily around him to see if anyone was visible in the surrounding windows, Tony noticed the periodic sign wired to a grating or nailed to one of the back doors that opened onto the alley. Most of these were residential buildings, with only the occasional small shop on the street level—all he needed to do was look for some kind of sign. As he worked his way past tumbled garbage cans and other discarded debris, he started paying closer attention to the buildings to his left, the side where he would find the pawnshop. He'd kept count of the buildings on the front end, but it was harder to tell where one ended and the other began here in the back.

Tony was so focused on his search that he was startled by a gate latch being lifted behind him. Ducking into the shadow of a large battered trash bin, he swore at himself beneath his breath. He had been so concerned with who might be looking out a window that he forgot to watch for those coming out of doors. Tony peered through a gap between the lid and the bin, watching as an old woman tossed a couple of bags into her dumpster. He caught a glimpse of the faded sign on her gate when she disappeared back inside. This was the bar next to the pawnshop; he had overshot his goal. He caught a fading whiff of good cooking as he backtracked past the old woman's fence. Tony's stomach rumbled in protest, but he continued on and approached the tall fence blocking the way to the back door of Yesterday's Dreams. He didn't know why he hadn't noticed this place to begin with, the building did not extend all the way into the alley the way its neighbors did. It was the only one with any kind of a "yard," hidden behind a tall chain-linked fence with green plastic privacy strips woven through the links.

Glancing once more around him, Tony reached for the dangling lock, accessible on either side of the fence. Once more—as it had done so many times in the past week—Tony's life spun crazily around him: Before he even touched the cheap padlock, he found himself thrown across the alley, landing with a thunderous crash among the empty garbage cans that faced the gate. Every instinct told him to run, to get out of there before someone came to look. Whatever rode him was stronger than his gut feeling. Despite himself, Tony approached the gate again, whether to rip it open or climb over it he couldn't say—he was no longer in control. Intentions didn't matter, though; once again he was thrown back.

With his vision red-clouded and the aches of his body distanced by adrenaline, Tony felt himself rush the gate with a chilling single-mindedness that left him unaware of the faint humming from beyond the fence, the angry shouts from above him, or the sudden hush that cut across the alley.

"Ah, 'tis a mooncalf thinkin' himself a bull."

Whether it was the chill of the words that stopped him dead, or the invisible granite fist clutching both him and his "guide," Tony halted in the alley without even the ability to sway. All around him the world froze in tableau; no wind tugged at his clothes and no sounds waited on the threshold of his hearing to be filtered and identified. Even the sunlight seemed more solid, as if held in the same grip. His eyes locked forward, he could focus on nothing but the gate. And yet he couldn't say when it sprouted its new ornamentation. Impossibly balanced atop the high fence was a strange sight. A man perched with the ease of a cat. Whatever else he looked like, all that registered to Tony's dazed mind was a pair of cool green eyes, watching him from behind a fringe of hair that could not seem to decide what shade it would be—appearing at once sandy, and in the next breath silver blond. But those eyes, they skewered Tony until he could not look away.

"Ye'd do best to buck what rides ye, mooncalf, though I daresay ye've not a hope on yer own." The imposing figure before him leaped lightly from the fence, leaving some corner of Tony's mind to wonder if the stranger had really floated down, as Tony's eyes swore he did. "But I see ye have no ken o' what I'm talkin' about," the strange man continued, a mix of anger and pity dancing through his words though the eyes remained distant and frozen. "Away with ye, there's no place for ye here with yer black ways, an' tell Lucien Blank that we now have yer measure...an' his. What we have, 'tis'na for him."

Tony fumed in his immobile state. His pride wanted to pound in the face dominating his vision. *Why was it that everyone he encountered lately seemed to have the power to freeze him where he stood?* The arrogance on the stranger's face invoked an equal, rebellious response in Tony. If he could have moved, his chin would have jutted and his chest would have puffed itself into an aggressive pose. He thought he could feel the phantom of a sneer on his lips, though he couldn't say if his lips had actually cooperated enough to show it.

A look of scorn flowed across the guardian's ethereal face; apparently Tony's intent was clear to him. Dismissively flicking his fingers, the man was there and then not there. Tony's knees trembled at the sudden release of the force that had arrested him. Careful not to touch the fence, Tony looked over it to the other side. He could see no sign of the stranger. Huffing subconsciously in frustration, he hurried from the alley.

"So, Maggie, it appears yer rival is gatherin' forces," Demne greeted Maggie gravely as he returned to her modern rath. She had rekeyed the shields to allow him entrance and he had been coming and going all day. Right now she was doubly glad she had done so, having caught some of what had taken place upstairs. She had felt the conflict in the alley as she'd talked with Kara, and had shooed the girl away as quickly as possible. She did not want Kara anywhere nearby if there was a confrontation. Maggie stood in the doorway of her most secure work chamber, wondering what Fate had in store for them. She looked up to where Demne still stood in the stairwell leading to the surface. It was clear he shared her concern. "Will ye show me?"

Nodding solemnly, Demne projected the face of a young man across the surface of her mind. "There's power there, but little control. Whatever he has he is unaware o', or 'tis put upon him by his master." Once again Demne made a gesture of contempt with his free hand at the thought of the one he'd encountered in the alley. "He bears watchin'. 'Tis my guess his only chance to harm ye is if ye're not payin' attention, an' then only physically."

Now more than ever Maggie was relieved she'd convinced Kara to return later that evening. Of course, if she had known who'd assaulted her defenses, she most likely wouldn't have sent the girl away at all. The cruel face hovered in her thoughts without Demne needing to project it. What troubled her greatly was that she knew this face. This was the man from the other night, the one who had threatened her on her own ground, until Beag Scath chased him off.

Presented with his second assault on her domain, she wished she'd had the forethought to examine the knife he'd abandoned before turning it over to the police. Any personal trace would have helped her set up specific signals to alert her should he return. Without a doubt, any traces were gone now. In fact, if her rival had even a basic understanding of his craft, she doubted the fingerprints had been of any use to the police—just a bit of magic would have been enough to smudge them beyond recognition.

In view of these new developments, Maggie was actually glad Lucien had shown up to challenge her yesterday; that little bit of contact had given her what she needed to key Kara's brooch against him and any bearing his magical signature. She had taken care of that before sending the girl away.

Sighing deeply, she met Demne's eyes and forced herself to relax. "At least I'd a chance to add my own tags to the protection I gave Kara. If anythin' happens, I'll know."

"Ah, but have ye convinced her to wear the bauble?" he asked in return. Maggie knew he was thinking of the doubts that grew in human breasts and caused them to disregard sage advice merely because it came from a source they didn't understand. She did not respond right away, caught up in watching as Demne walked idly over to the marble pedestal. He ran his hand across the surface as if expecting to feel at least the remnants of the magic that held the violin hidden. She knew he was fascinated by her tale of Kara and the violin, and the lengths to which Maggie had gone to protect both. His face showed both respect and reassurance as he turned back to watch her expectantly, waiting for an answer.

"I can only hope," was Maggie's worried response. "I think she took my revelations well, an' the brooch itself has a certain power o' compulsion. I doubt it has left her possession since I gave it to her, even if she would'na wear it.

"My own energy feeds the line I attached today. Should anythin' go wrong, it will draw me there, should she need me. If na, I can at least keep track o' her."

Demne nodded grimly as she spoke. "Are ye sure that's wise? Can ye afford the draw on yer power an the demonics attack again?"

He was right; using personal energy could be quite a drain, but in this case Maggie had little choice. They could take no chances; this girl was important to them all, human and sidhe alike. With luck there would be no need for the world to know exactly how important. These early days would decide how much the impending conflict would impact on them all.

Maggie slumped a moment, her forehead resting against the cool, rough surface of the chamber wall. She should return to the store above—it was important to maintain appearances—but she was so weary with the weight that rested upon her. With a sideways glance she looked up the many stairs leading from the safety of her secret place. She felt something touch her and jerked upright, blushing at her own lack of grace; it told how weary she was to lose awareness enough to be startled. But Demne gave no sign of disapproval. He gently rested his hand on her slouched shoulder, drawing her back to the world of pawnshops and human cities—back to the world of her oath. With care he slowly turned her so that they faced. His hand brushed across her hair and down to cup her chin, ever so gently. It did not occur to her to resist.

Maggie's eyes widened and electric fire skipped across her skin where he touched her. The ghost of her earlier doubts surfaced fleetingly, only to be torn apart by the irrefutable feel of his untarnished soul dancing across the connection to mingle with her own. She could feel the beginning flow of power like sweet, warm honey. Whatever this bond was, there was nothing casual about it; there was too much intensity as Demne tangled himself deep within her heart. Maggie felt the thrill of union so deep it was rare even among her kind.

Demne continued to caress her hair as if wiping away the strain of solitude and concern. Before she even realized it, he'd drawn her back into the chamber and toward the newly placed cushions in the seating nook she'd carved from the living rock—perhaps it had been wasted energy at a time when she would need all she had, but she also had the feeling this magical workroom would see much more use in this troubled time. Better to be prepared, rather than suffer as she had just a few days ago.

"So much ye've shouldered." He sat down and gathered her in his arms, his hand guiding her head to his own shoulder as he smoothed back her wild curls. "Ye just rest yer head an' yer heart. The sleeping one still rests, an' the call has yet to go out. I'll help ye as I can, Maggie, until it does."

They sat in the silence of the rath, undisturbed by the mundane world. Maggie let herself go, basking in the joy of companionship as Demne sang softly of their homeland and beckoned her to walk through his fresh memories of green hills and wild flowers; of cool mists and shrouding fog; and of craggy cliffs coming right up to meet with the sea. The people of Eire marched past Maggie's closed eyes, going about their everyday lives. Each memory he shared was like a perfect jewel to her, priceless and breathtaking. Maggie breathed deep in contentment and adjusted herself for comfort, letting Demne's gift flow over her. Fresh memories made the pain of separation fade. Her guest had given back to Maggie her home, in every way possible to him, short of rescinding her oath. Resting in his arms, peace descended upon her, smoothing the lines of her face and relaxing her limbs to the point where she couldn't tell where Demne ended and she began.

At some unrealized point, as Demne's soul caressed her own, his thoughts shifted from those images of their people and life in the rath, which had so comforted her heart, back to the beauty of their homeland, which offered a different kind of comfort. The music of running water and courting birds filled Maggie's ears. Romantic landscapes of beautiful bowers hidden in the forest and majestic cliffs overlooking the silvery, moon-gilded waves of the ocean were painted across Maggie's mind.

She couldn't say when the caresses moved from the mental realm to the physical—or even which of them had initiated that move—but she thrilled to find an end to her isolation. Demne's fingers sent trails of tingling fire across her now-bare thigh and her own ran like smooth water across his sculpted chest. Their oaths prevented the joining from being anything more than brief—for now, at least—but she would lose herself in the offered paradise for as long as she was able. Comfortable in her decision, Maggie abandoned thought for the moment, allowing herself to drown in the sensations Demne introduced to her starved soul. Maggie wasn't alone...for now. She would rest easy in that fact, knowing how fleeting this time might be.

Later, as she and Demne lay wrapped in soft robes and complete harmony, sharing songs of their homeland, Maggie felt a twinge of guilt. She was unsure how long they had been below, but Beag Scath was alone all that time. There was no reason for his continued isolation, especially when he loved nothing more than listening to songs of Eire. She reached with a thought to open the way for the sprite to join them. He would enjoy the company and the song, and it was wrong to leave him out. That taken care of, she abandoned herself once more to Demne's rejuvenating companionship.

While they sat there, alternately singing together and talking, Beag Scath crept down the stairs timidly. It was most uncharacteristic of him. Pulling himself into her lap, he sat quietly, his wide-open eyes following every move of the strange sidhe. Experience had also taught the sprite caution around those he didn't know. It had been quite a while since he'd been in the company of others of her kind and not all of them had treated him kindly. Some few of the Áes Sidhe had too much pride to acknowledge the thread of kinship they all shared with the sprites and the other little folk; to them, the sprites were just a nuisance. Maggie found herself hoping fervently that such would not be the case with Demne. It was important to her that these two be companionable. Already she cared for Demne deeply, even beyond the closeness her kind had for each other. She was confident she had found the mate of her soul.

As if he sensed the little creature's uncertainty, Demne held out his hand palm up. Maggie sensed the calm assurance that he projected. She smiled contentedly and relaxed in his arms. From all she had felt in their sharing of memories and more, there was goodness in this one that was not shallow or feigned. No darkness hid behind his smiles. The sprite reached out his tiny hands and gripped the edges of the sidhe's much larger one, tilting it toward him and peering intently into it as if he would find something of interest there.

Maggie fought to hold back her laughter as Beag Scath lowered his head to sniff at some remnant of scent. The little mooch was looking for a snack! The sprite gave a trill of laughter himself and relaxed enough to settle in for a nap—without, however, relinquishing Demne's hand. Content to leave things as they were, the sidhe continued their conversation. Maggie went into more detail of her time on this side of the ocean, in particular the events of the past week. Perhaps a new outlook would help her to figure out what to do next. After all, her time was much more precious now than it had been an hour ago.

As pleasant as the unexpected interlude was, it was time to venture back above ground. Neither of them spoke a word as they dressed once more in the clothing of the mortal world and left the rath, returning to their duties above. At the head of the stairs they parted, she returning to her store and he going out the back of the alley to his interrupted business: to reinforce the original protections placed long ago on the dwellings of each guardian.

The moment Maggie unlocked the door, her thoughts drifted once again to Kara, wondering what the girl would do until the time of her promised return. In an instant, information swarmed across the link she had made with the brooch; confusing images of people hurrying by, the tumultuous sounds of city traffic, and a bouquet of smells that simultaneously clashed and meshed in a way that should have been impossible, but was a particular trait of any large city. In the center of it all was a certain "Kara-ness." Reassured by the lack of distress and the slightest hint of hunger conveyed by the link, Maggie reopened the shop and waited patiently for the time to pass.

CHAPTER 15

Burning with anger and frustration, Tony waited at his new vantage point with something less than patience. He resented every moment he spent watching for the girl his extra sense told him was still within. He didn't know how it could tell but, but since he had no better lead, he would stay where he was—for now—and see if he couldn't think of some way to untangle himself from the events that had taken over his life. Then, all of a sudden, Tony's link to his prey was again severed.

This was ridiculous! What good was a guide this undependable? Every time he turned around, it stopped working. Tony was about to stalk away and forget the whole thing—he would ask his grandmother to give him a protection so Lucien couldn't find him. As afraid as he was of Lucien, he trusted that Gypsy Rose was more than a match for him.

The pipedreams ended when he saw Kara; with the slow, relaxed quality of one recently asleep, she materialized beside the odd tree that hid the entrance to the space between bar and pawnshop. Watching from an apartment lobby down the street, Tony held himself back with effort. It wouldn't do to be noticed by someone inside the pawnshop, or anyone else on the street, for that matter. He allowed himself to exit the building only after she was halfway down the block. He would follow for now, watching for the moment where he could strike unnoticed. Meanwhile, he would learn all he could from her actions.

Patrick woke just as the soft golden glow of dawn began to tint the window shade. He was surprised to feel well rested. Last night's tearful release must have left him too drained to be plagued by the doubts and worries that had crowded his mind, so that for the first time in weeks he could rest as he slept. Lying there in near silence, the only sound the soft, rhythmic breathing of his still-sleeping wife, Patrick couldn't quite bring himself to rise and start his day.

As he glanced around the room, the battered box of his parents' memories caught his eye. *Was it really just yesterday that he had brought it out?* He had not gotten the chance to look through the papers, as he had meant to. Who knew what he might find? He had even entertained the hope of a forgotten will or rich relative—if he was going to daydream, he might as well do a good job of it! Patrick reached carefully for the old box. At least it was something to do that did not require leaving the comfort of his warm bed. He gently pulled himself up on his pillows with the box in his lap, removed the papers, and set the rest back on the nightstand.

There wasn't much in the jumble of clippings and notes. Only two things seemed of any interest to Patrick at all: a time-yellowed newspaper clipping from one of Kara's early recitals, and a rich, ivory-colored envelope with his name written neatly across the front. Gathering everything else and returning it to the box, Patrick settled back and laid his two treasures in his lap. He looked from one to the other for a moment before he reached for the newspaper clipping.

Patrick gazed fondly at a faded, newsprint photograph of his daughter's sweet little eight-year-old face. Kara's eyes were closed in peaceful concentration, her bow frozen in its graceful glide across the strings of her old violin—the one recently christened Hope. Patrick smiled at the intense concentration captured on a face still wrapped in the soft roundness of childhood. It had been her first student recital, the event that had led to her teachers raving about their new prodigy. It had also been her only public performance with her Grandda present. Kara had been so excited to show off for him. Her teachers had allowed her to choose his favorite song for her performance piece and she had thrown herself into perfecting it. A week after that performance, Conall O'Keefe—widower of Moira, father of Patrick, grandfather of Kara—faded peacefully away in his sleep. Patrick closed his eyes at the persistent, fifteen-year-old ache. He missed his father. Shrugging off the melancholy mood he couldn't afford to indulge, Patrick opened his eyes and once again examined the clipping. What had caught his eye to begin with was a bit of writing along the edge of the photograph; in his Da's own hand was a note in some Gaelic script that Patrick had long ago lost his skill to read accurately. The only words he recognized were the ones for fulfilled gift.

Patrick set aside the clipping and reached for the envelope with a hand that trembled. With the edge of his nail, he carefully lifted the old wax seal from the paper without damaging either it or the envelope. As he pulled out his Da's final message something small fluttered to the bed. The letter still in his hand, as if laying it down would allow it to disappear, Patrick reached for the bit of paper that had fallen from the folds. It was a pawn ticket: an old, faded pawn ticket. Across the top was the name of the shop—Yesterday's Dreams—and below it a number. On the back of the soft, creased paper Da had written an address, this time in English. Most likely it was the address of the pawnshop. Patrick couldn't think of anything his Da would have pawned—or even why—but perhaps it was important, if only in relation to family history. Perhaps the letter would explain.

Unfolding the stiff folds of the parchment paper, Patrick settled down to read his father's final words: a letter that had waited fifteen years to be opened.

With a coffee and a new book she'd been meaning to buy for months, Kara lounged on the grass in Washington Square Park, her back against a convenient tree. It was early in the day and not many people were around. A few runners went by—with or without various-sized dogs keeping up or being dragged behind; a performance artist or two staked out separate corners of the park to vie for the attention of the thinly-spread crowd; and a scattering of children and people like herself were enjoying this island of green in whatever way suited them.

Bracing her coffee against the knob of a root, Kara opened the still-stiff cover of her book and lost herself for a couple of hours. It was no use though; with all that was going on in her life, she found it impossible to stay focused on the fantasy plot without wondering how closely it mirrored reality. While the hero on the page roared around in a Ford Mustang with a ghost in the passenger seat, Kara's mind kept bringing up uncomfortable questions that had nothing to do with the author's story line: Were there such things as unicorns and chimeras? Did magic flutes open up doors to fairy realms? Would that little, white-furred dog full of matts sitting on the bench beside the old lady suddenly come over and declare in a human voice that it was an enchanted princess and the old woman a vile witch? Why not? She'd already seen a pixie pull flowers from the air and a perfectly ordinary woman of about thirty that claimed to be an elf hundreds of years old.

With a slight shiver, out of place in the still-warm autumn afternoon, Kara let her head fall back against the tree with a little more force than she intended. Wincing, she closed her eyes and sighed. She had not asked to have her definition of reality drastically altered. She had only wanted some way to help her parents. Giving up on reading for the moment, she sat there and tried to empty her mind of fantastic thoughts. The book lay forgotten in her lap and her hand had found its way to the brooch at her throat. The smooth, intricate detail of the enameled bronze was soothing. Her fingers almost tingled with the sensation. Uncontrollably, her thoughts went back to Maggie and Yesterday's Dreams. When she'd left the alley it had felt much like this, comforting...accepting. *What was the brooch? Why had Maggie given it to her?*

Suddenly, Kara's eyes snapped open and she looked around her. Her senses prickled even more, only darkly. She felt exposed, as if someone's eyes were on her. The air seemed still with waiting and the brooch beneath her hand burned the now-chilled skin of her palm. Kara blushed furiously as she settled back against the trunk. Nothing around her had changed, people lounged and ran and performed without a single thought for the girl sitting quietly under the trees. Glancing at her watch, she decided she'd sat and pondered long enough.

It was two-thirty; if she couldn't focus enough to read she'd walk off the nervous energy that had her very skin vibrating, though she wondered where she'd end up with an hour and a half to fill.

Tony's temper grew fouler with each hour that passed as he tailed Kara. Most of the day was gone, and after forcing him to sit in the park for hours she had then led him down more city streets than he ever cared to know...crowded streets, leaving him no opportunity to grab her. His feet were sore and he had to piss in the worse way. He didn't dare stop, though; he couldn't risk missing his chance. The boss wanted the girl and had "requested" Tony bring her tonight. A tingle worked its way across the back of Tony's neck as he thought of what would happen if he failed. Needless to say, he would no longer have to worry...about anything. He wasn't thrilled with the prospect of kidnapping, but Kara was nothing to him and his own skin meant a heck of a lot more. He would follow Lucien Blank's orders because he didn't stand a chance against the man otherwise.

Glancing at his watch, Tony cursed beneath his breath. He didn't have much time. Occasionally looking around him, Tony waited for a moment of isolation where no one would be around to notice if Kara struggled. His chance came along a stretch of Hudson Street, just below Houston. Stealing up behind her on the empty sidewalk, with a convenient alley to his left should he need it, he reached for Kara's shoulder as he palmed the knife from his pocket, shielding its open blade from view between the two of them.

Before Tony even touched her, the world erupted around them.

It was hard to tell exactly what happened; when he was a mere inch from grabbing her shoulder, Kara jerked around as if shocked. The moment his finger brushed her sleeve a blinding flash exploded before his eyes, followed by a shockwave that bashed Tony flat, sprawled across the sidewalk. With every inch of his body aching from the impact, Tony faded away into the whiteness that engulfed him.

Chilled to the bone and trembling in reaction, Tony shook his head to clear the daze. Sitting up with care, he looked around him, hoping not to have drawn anyone's attention. He expected to find himself alone. Instead, he saw Kara lying only inches from him. The sight of her curled on her side, her face sickly pale, made him feel anxious and ironically protective. Scanning the area to see if all was still quiet, Tony climbed quickly to his feet. He swayed slightly for a moment before locking his legs beneath him. In seconds, all sentimentality fled as he realized his good fortune. All he had to do was scoop up Kara and get her into a cab. They could be at the address the boss had given him in minutes; Chinatown wasn't that far away.

As he bent to pick her up, a stinging sensation in his fingers stopped Tony dead. He had no idea what had happened a moment ago. What if touching her triggered it again? That was one experience he wasn't anxious to relive. Grinding his teeth in frustration, he leaned over the girl just a moment too long. Even as he made up his mind to chance it, Kara's eyes fluttered open. She looked up at him, confused, with no recognition in her eyes. Feeling his chance slip away, Tony scrambled to reclaim it. Perhaps he could convince her to go with him.

"Ya okay, miss?" Tony asked, doing his best to fill his voice with concern. "That guy hit ya pretty hard."

"Y-yes, I think so," she sounded dazed as she answered. "What guy?"

"Some big guy came up behind ya," Tony improvised. "It looked like he was trying to grab your purse. He ran when I hollered.

"Ya know, ya shouldn't wander around down here, it ain't the best neighborhood."

Tony relaxed as the look on Kara's face went from bewildered to a blend of frightened and grateful. Now if only he could convince her to climb into a cab, maybe he could still pull this off. "Are ya sure you're okay?" Trying to look anxious and contrite, he automatically offered his arm. "I'm sorry I couldn't catch him...I didn't want to leave ya like this."

Still looking unsettled, the girl reached for his outstretched hand. Tony nearly jerked it away as her fingers settled on his wrist, but other than a weak shock, nothing happened. Whatever had knocked them on their asses apparently hadn't recovered as quickly as they had. Relieved, Tony made his next move.

"Please, I feel bad," Tony pushed on, fixing a sorrowful expression on his face. "Let me hail a cab and take ya home..."

Though she stood unsteadily on her feet, a look of wariness crept into Kara's eyes. He watched her as she hastily released his arm and dusted herself off. She stiffened as she ran a hand over her head. Tony held his breath and tried to project innocence and concern. He relaxed when she winced; apparently she'd banged her head when she fell.

"What's this?"

Kara's question as she stooped carefully to retrieve her bag made Tony tense up once more. He glanced where she pointed, already knowing what he would see. He scrambled for something to say. "It must be the guy's—he probably dropped it when I yelled." He moved forward as she picked it up. "Here, Kara, let me take care of that."

"No," she answered him with a look he couldn't quite figure out, kind of cold and intent, "I know someone who'll take care of it for me. Thank you for your help, I'm fine now."

She hailed a passing cab while Tony fumed. She closed the door before he could grab it, leaving him no chance to make an excuse to join her. As the cab pulled away, he saw her turn back to watch him furtively. She looked pale and tense. Tony cursed violently as once again she slipped away from him.

Kara trembled uncontrollably, collapsing in the back seat as the cab headed off in the direction of Canal Street. So much for taking self-defense classes, in this instance they'd been completely useless. She couldn't quite tell if it was fear or anger...no, that wasn't true, she knew it was both. Up until this moment she hadn't really taken Maggie's warning seriously. Why would someone be after her? What did she have to be afraid of? Well...now Kara knew better. That man had known her name. How? Her skin crawled and her stomach clenched at the close call. She didn't know who she was more furious at: herself, or the guy who had tried to grab her. If he hadn't slipped up there at the end, she would have believed his story about her mysterious attacker. She might have even gotten into a cab with him. Where would she have ended up then?

Trying to calm herself, Kara closed her eyes and focused on the mix of strident and melodious sounds of Indian music coming from the speaker by her head. Presently the cab slowed. She could feel it pull to the side, and tried to decipher the driver's heavy accent as he told her the fare. Opening her eyes, she recognized Maggie's quiet street. Handing the driver some cash, she pulled herself from the car and swayed on the sidewalk as the cab pulled away.

The world went grey for the third time that day. Kara wondered if she were seeing double when her muddled senses told her two Maggies were rushing to her side. One of them caught Kara and swept her up. Her last conscious thought was that soft arms were much nicer than rough concrete.

Maggie knew immediately when Kara was attacked. She herself had been stunned momentarily by the unexpected backlash from protection colliding with protection; only the fact that most of the shields were powered through the brooch had cushioned Maggie from a worse reaction. Maggie could also sense—through her own connection to Kara's brooch—that the girl had evaded whatever pursued her and seemed to be returning to the pawnshop. Relieved but fretfully impatient, she stayed behind her counter waiting for Kara to arrive. She hoped fervently that the brooch was still protecting Kara and that it hadn't been shorted out by the impact; that could happen if the impacting force was the stronger of the two. She focused every bit of her concentration on her connection to Kara, hoping to learn as much as possible about her condition. Just one thought did Maggie spare: she soul-spoke Demne, warning him of what had happened. She knew he would hear her, though he couldn't respond from far away. No matter, he would return if he could. If not, Maggie was used to dealing with matters alone. Cursing herself for not thinking to warn Kara of impact shock and how to prevent it, Maggie waited for the girl to arrive, hoping that all was well.

Finally, after an eternally long twenty minutes from the time of the attack, Maggie could feel Kara draw up in front of Yesterday's Dreams. Maggie was watching from the door as the cab stopped out front to let the girl out. Kara swayed on the curb and Maggie rushed to her. She was so focused on the girl that she barely noticed as Demne emerged from the alleyway just steps behind her. He drew level with her as she caught Kara up in her arms. The two of them exchanged looks of concern over the head of the trembling human; this reaction was much more intense than anything they'd encountered in one of their own kind. Was something else wrong? Was this normal? They couldn't say, or even guess; neither one knew of a hybrid or a human who had ever been caught by a spell backlash such as this. Maggie's eyes burned with guilt. She was so anxious to protect the girl that she hadn't anticipated the possible effects. A failed effort to skim the surface of Kara's mind for details of what happened concerned Maggie even more. Either this untrained mortal had strong natural shields capable of thwarting a skilled sidhe, or whatever trauma Kara experienced had been enough to totally disrupt the girl's thoughts. Either way, they had to get Kara down below where they could care for her.

Chapter 16

Sitting in the soothing, engineered peace of Dr. Barnert's waiting room, Patrick absently flipped through whatever magazine he'd picked up. As he mechanically turned the glossy, idealistic pages of advertisements and grooming tips, he struggled to keep his mind off the letter he'd discovered that morning. Vague memories battled with the carefully constructed reality Patrick had been so confident of for a major portion of his life. Each time he shifted in the squeaky vinyl of the chair, the faint sound of crinkling paper drew his thoughts once again. Compulsively, his hand slid into his pocket, slowly drawing forth a folded sheath of ivory-colored parchment. He abandoned his magazine and toyed with the thick, fibrous pages. Finally, with careful precision, he straightened the letter across his knee. Patrick looked at the words without focusing and let his eyes travel down the page, reacquainting himself with his father's flowing script. What did this letter mean? So many emotions battled within his heart. He kept coming back to the first paragraph:

> My Son,
>
> > Forgive me. Time suddenly rests its heavy weight upon my shoulders and I find that without my Moira beside me I lack the will to bear up both it and me. Duty has held me here two years. Two weeks ago it released me. I am weary. My heart longs for peace and my soul for those who have gone before. Save for one more duty I must discharge, I would join them. Here I pass to you my knowledge; accept it if you will and share it with Kara. If you decline then the legacy is Kara's alone and I charge you with its delivery.

Patrick didn't want to dwell on what he thought those lines were saying. It didn't make sense. He knew Da had taken Mathair's death hard, but he hadn't given up. It had been difficult in the beginning, but each day had been a triumph. Da struggled with the grief and put it behind him. He spent his days with his music and his granddaughter, showing no less exuberance for life than he had before the accident. Nothing at all in his behavior even hinted that he might take his own life. Now Patrick had to wonder and it made him furious. Da had always told him every life was precious; that he might have taken his own was the worst of all betrayals. And yet, what was the truth? Before this letter, no evidence even suggested Conall O'Keefe's death might have been a suicide.

Struggling to control his anger, Patrick let his eyes travel down the rest of the unbelievable letter:

> My words should wake in you old memories; after all, you were raised on the legends. Now I tell you of our part in those tales: blood more than human runs beneath our skin. We are sidhe–elves–at least in part. The rules as understood by humanity do not always apply to our nature. The years touch us less than they might were all of our blood mortal; our five senses are refined, and occasionally augmented by others not enjoyed by the common man. Also, there is often a magic about us that shows itself in too many possible ways to tell in this letter.
>
> You have never needed what I had to offer, Patrick. I have taught you what I could, and simply loved and cared for you after that. You and Barbara–the daughter of my heart, if not my blood–gave me my greatest joy in Kara, a joy intertwined with responsibility. What your heritage did not wake in you bloomed powerfully in my granddaughter, even more so than in me. I heard in her music the other night a power well beyond my skill to shape further. I have given her a history she will not know she can lay a claim to, I have taught her what it is to be as we are, and I have given her my love and knowledge of music. The rest of her training must fall with those more skilled than I.
>
> There is a woman you might remember by the name of Maggie McCormick. She is sidhe of undiluted blood and her knowledge and powers span centuries. You must go to her for Kara's sake, no matter what you choose to believe. The gift is a dangerous thing without a trained hand to guide it; it is both a power and a beacon. Find Maggie in Soho, at a pawnshop called Yesterday's Dreams. I have entrusted her with things you need to reclaim. Let her help you. She will know how to keep our Kara safe.
>
> Love Eternally,
> Da

Patrick was confused; he didn't know what to think of what he had read. He loved his Da and, up until this morning, he'd no reason to doubt the soundness of his father's mind. After reading this letter, Patrick was no longer so confident.

Wearily, he leaned his head against the wall behind him. The polemical letter fell from his limp hands to the floor. *Why, of all times, had he picked now to look back on his past?* Patrick fervently wished he'd left the dusty box in the back of the closet.

"Pat?" Arn Barnert's concerned voice broke through Patrick's introspection. "Pat, are you okay?

"Katie, help me get Mr. O'Keefe inside, please."

"Do'na be daft, Arn," Patrick opened his weary eyes and sighed, "I'm quite all right. Can I help that ye left me waitin' long enough for a bit o' a nap?" Firmly lifting the doctor's hand off his shoulder and bending to retrieve the letter, he continued. "Did ye finally decide to see me then?"

The doctor watched him with troubled, unconvinced eyes. Without another word he motioned Patrick to join him in his office.

An uncomfortable silence hovered in the wake of Patrick's quiet-spoken words. Arnold Barnert sat behind his desk, a perplexed look on his comfortably lined face. Trying to reconcile the sudden accusation with the treatment options they'd been going over, Arn couldn't help wondering if the stress of recent events hadn't been too much for his friend and patient. "What do you mean how did your father die?"

"I mean, did ye hold out on me," Patrick answered, his face a stony mask. "Did ye tell me false o' Da's passin'?"

"What in the world are you talking about?" Arn replied, shocked and startled by the accusation. If it weren't for Patrick's dead-flat tone and the look on his face, Arn would have thought this was some kind of a joke...true, a twisted one, but what other explanation could there be? Of course, looking at his best friend, there was no doubt Patrick was as serious as it got.

"Did ye lie to me, Arn?!" Patrick's eyed had grown so dark as to appear black. "Whatever yer intentions, did ye lie? Because this little letter right here seems to imply ye did!"

"Letter? What friggin' letter? What is your problem?" Maybe he should have answered differently, but he could feel the emotional maelstrom sweeping him up. Patrick and he had always been like that; for good or bad, their emotions set off an amplifying feedback in the other. It had always seemed cool...when they were boys and getting into high-spirited mischief. It most definitely was not now.

Patrick shoved a creamy sheet of paper beneath Arn's nose, but he was jerking it around so much there was no hope of reading what it said, of making sense of whatever had Pat so agitated, but one thing was clear: at the bottom of the page was a large, graceful 'Da'. Oh my...where had Patrick found that, and what the hell did it say that had him making such accusations? "Of course I didn't lie to you. What's going on here, Pat?"

His friend glared at him fiercely, his brow drawn down and his chin jutting. It did not seem he could speak, though. The letter landed on Arn's desk and he could not help but stare at it as he would a venomous creature within biting distance. He couldn't bring himself to touch it. The world narrowed down to him and that little bit of paper. *What did it say that had his friend so wild?*

Before he brought himself to reach out and pick it up, Patrick's massive hand snatched it away. Arn's head snapped up and what he saw frightened him more than the anger. Patrick had gone pale and a shudder went through him. Wheeling away, he slammed the door behind him without another word, taking his letter with him.

What the hell? Arn shot out of his chair and stared at the closed door in disbelief. What had just happened? "Patrick! Patrick, wait!" Beyond worried, he hit the intercom. "Katie?"

"Yes, Dr. Barnert?"

"Has Mr. O'Keefe left the office?" Arn caught himself holding his breath as he waited for the answer, even though there was no question of what it would be.

"Yes, sir," she answered, her calm voice drifting from the speaker. "Would you like me to see if I can catch him?" The intercom fell into the particular silence that told him she'd turned it off without waiting for a response. Arn nearly jumped with tension a moment later as the door to his office swung open.

"Sorry, sir," Katie's expression was neutral as she stood alone in the doorway, "he's already gone."

"Damn!" Arn slammed his hand down on the desk, forcing a startled expression from his receptionist. "Do I have any urgent appointments for today?"

Katie went to her desk without a word. Arn could hear the turning of crisp pages as she consulted the schedule. "Only a couple of check-ups," her voice drifted in from the other room, still composed in an attitude of neutral professionalism. "What would you like me to do?"

"Reschedule them...if possible, for some time this week—tell them an emergency came up," Arn paused, glancing at his watch before he finished working his way into his jacket. "It's three o'clock, I'll be out of the office for the rest of the afternoon, if anyone calls. If it's an emergency, page me."

Saying nothing more, Arn hurried out to his car. He would catch up with Patrick at his home. Things couldn't be left as they were; for some reason Patrick didn't believe him. No...because of the letter Patrick didn't believe him.

They had to sit down and work this out. Arn didn't even understand what had just gone on in his office, but he couldn't let it come between him and Patrick. Besides, the entire situation made him worry about his friend's state of mind. It could very well be that things had finally become too much for the proud Irishman. The very thought frightened Arn more than anything else as he sped toward Queens.

"I just don't understand what happened, Barbara," Arn confessed as he sat perched on the edge of the soft, faded couch. So he wouldn't have to look into Barbara's eyes, he watched the cat torment the dangling sash from his trench coat where it hung from a hook by the front door. "One minute we were going over his treatment options, and the next he was barreling out the door."

In the following silence, Arnold Barnert fidgeted. He didn't know what was going through Patrick's head, but Arn couldn't help but think that he could have handled the situation better himself. Reaching for the cup of tea Barbara offered him, he finally looked into her eyes. It deepened his guilt that all he saw there was compassion and understanding.

"Things have been a bit crazed here lately," Barbara began thoughtfully. "It's difficult to know how he's going to react to anything. I don't know about any letter, but I'm sure he will be fine by the time he gets home."

"I'm just worried that he isn't home yet," Arn admitted. "I left just after he did; we should have gotten here at the same time. Where else would he have gone?"

"I couldn't say. He's had something on his mind all day. I don't even ask when he's in one of his moods," Barbara shook her head and sat back in her own chair. The look on her face hinted that those moods had been more and more frequent. From the moment he'd arrived, Arn thought she looked tired and worn by the entire situation.

"Would Patrick go anywhere specific to cool down?" Arn did his best to keep his concerns out of his voice.

Barbara looked confused a moment before shaking her head. "No. He usually takes himself to another part of the house when he's feeling antisocial, but he's never gone off somewhere. I'm sure he'll be home soon, though."

Her smile was shaky. He knew that she was trying to hide her worry. That made him all the more glad he hadn't told her of Patrick's suspicions. She had loved her father-in-law deeply; it wouldn't do to open her to unfounded doubts as well. Arn had been the first person they had called when they'd found Conall O'Keefe passed away in his bed. There was no doubt in the doctor's mind that the man had died of natural causes. No matter what implications Patrick chose to read into the old letter—the contents of which Arn still wanted to know—there was absolutely nothing to substantiate the death as a suicide. Now how to convince Patrick of that? Bloody stubborn Irishman! Arn thought to himself as he wondered what the hell to do next.

CHAPTER 17

As she effortlessly carried Kara inside, Maggie visually traced the pattern that
ran unobtrusively around the ceiling of the shop. There in the intricately carved
molding of the woodwork, at a height where most people gave it little attention,
was Maggie's contingency plan for when things rapidly went to hell. The carving
was a trigger that instantly focused her thoughts no matter what her condition.
By tracing the woodwork in her mind, the sidhe released a spell that both cleared
the way before her and secured the shop behind her. She had never needed this
particular precaution. Today she thanked the sun and the wind that the spell
was in place, for Demne did not know Maggie's defenses and they would have
wasted precious time if she'd needed to see to each one herself.

They made their way quickly down into the rath. Demne rushed ahead with
Beag Scath, keeping the sprite out of Maggie's way.

The chamber on the left-hand side, the first one ye come to, Maggie guided him
through soul-speech, *ye'll find blankets an' such tucked in a nook in the far corner.*

She was about to tell him where to find her cache of supplies, but as she descended the stairs her nose caught a whiff of her special blend of reviving tea. If
they were fortunate it would help Kara snap out of her reaction shock...if they
could get it into her. Maggie hoped he'd thought to prepare two cups, at the very
least, for she could use a pick-up herself.

She turned off at a landing some flights above her workroom, carrying Kara
into a room nothing less than magical. It reminded her, as it was meant to, of Tir
na nÓg; a bit of home to ease her in the lonely times. The crystals imbedded in
the ceiling glowed warmly and the walls of the chamber were intricately carved
in Celtic knot work patterns reminiscent of those of Mor Halla, Goibhniu's great
hall. For comfort, the floor was carpeted by a vibrant green moss, thickly grown
and soft. She'd worked nooks in the stone for storage, but they did not disrupt
the smooth flow of the room. And best of all, a velvet curtain pulled aside on the
back wall revealed a second chamber where a miniature subterranean waterfall
drained into a pool large enough for two or three Maggies to comfortably
submerge. Along its edge, lush ferns allowed for some privacy—not that Maggie

had ever needed any—and other than a path of moss to the pool, all that could
be seen of the floor and the other three walls of the waterfall chamber was
covered with flowering vines. Other curtains led off of the main chamber, but all
of these were drawn closed.

It gratified her to find Demne standing in the middle of the first chamber,
a look of awe and respect, mingled with concern for Kara, in his eyes. He had
already prepared a resting-place beside the tiny fountain that bubbled from a
crack in the chamber wall. The folds of an immense comforter were laid across
the thick cushion of moss, ready to receive Kara.

"I heated the waters o' the pool," Demne greeted the two of them out loud.
"Perhaps 'twould draw her out o' her trauma."

Maggie thought hard on this before deciding the warm bed would have to be
enough. "'Tis just the thin' to help, but ye know how mortals are about flesh,"
Maggie looked regretfully through the curtain at the pool. "She would'na
understand when she came to, whether 'twas one o' us holdin' her above water
or a bit o' magic."

With extreme care, Maggie laid Kara on top of the blanket. Slipping off the
girl's jacket, belt, and shoes, Maggie had to be content with those small efforts
at making the girl comfortable. Anything else could be misconstrued. They had
a fine line to walk until they gained Kara's trust.

All they could do now was treat her for shock and wait for her to come back.
Kneeling gracefully beside the unconscious girl, Maggie accepted the damp rag
Demne held out to her. It was with a practiced hand that the sidhe drew the cool
and soothing cloth across every inch of Kara's exposed skin. Maggie had treated
this kind of reaction before, though never one this severe. When a person was
unprepared for a magical impact, the refracted energies could "short out" the
person's own system. The severity of the response was often proportional to
the degree of talent the person possessed. It was bad enough in an educated
individual, one who would knew the tricks for minimizing or avoiding the shock
altogether; but with a totally inexperienced person like Kara, the defensive
shutdown was nearly complete. Frankly, Maggie was surprised the girl hadn't
gone fetal. By the magnitude of ripples that radiated from Kara's own energy,
much had been disrupted by the magical collision. Handing back the rag, Maggie leaned forward and literally swaddled Kara in the blanket, tucking it firmly
around her until only her face was exposed. That done, she sat back and looked
thoughtfully up at Demne.

It occurred to Maggie that it was a good thing she didn't depend on the
pawnshop for her existence, considering how little time she'd spent running it
lately. Someone had to stay with Kara until she woke, and Maggie was afraid that
no one other than herself would do. Kara might be amused by the sprite, but not
comforted—and the girl had never even met Demne. Maggie would have to stay.
Something inside of her was uncomfortable about closing the shop though.

"Demne," Maggie ventured. "Is the business I called ye from pressin'?"

"I've a bit o' time. Already I've reinforced the shields on the major artifacts, includin' yer own. The rest will wait another day," Demne answered with solemn understanding. "Have ye a way to contact the lass's kin?"

"Aye, but I've a suspicion that will'na be needed. If ye'll tend the shop I'll shield the chamber an' care for her," she explained. "That should calm thin's enough for Kara to come to herself." Maggie wished she were as confident as she sounded. Demne nodded once and rose to comply.

"Are ye sure ye can handle the shop?" she half-teased, trying not to sound too concerned.

Giving her an overly patient glance and no answer, Demne turned and walked from the chamber. Concern for Kara and the events of the past few days had addled Maggie's thoughts that she would have asked such a question of a fellow sidhe. Or perhaps it was that she'd been "Maggie" for far too long, isolated across the ocean from her kin and her home. Sighing, she put the thought aside and wove a shield around the two of them. That taken care of, she dimmed the glow of the crystals and settled herself on the moss beside Kara to wait. Beag Scath curled contentedly in her lap.

Lying in a crumpled heap in the middle of his workroom, Lucien experienced ultimate terror as he gasped for breath; he clutched spasmodically at his motionless chest, as if he could force it to perform actions that should have been automatic. Just as his sight began to fog over and his world drifted toward blackness, every nerve ending crackled. Lucien's back arched painfully as he was hit with a massive seizure, like a circuit breaker had been thrown, resetting his system.

He breathed heavily and for once did not take the action for granted. It took a moment for him to realize he was now in a twisted heap on the floor. His head throbbed, but it ached less than his pride. He was ever conscious of his dignity. Right now it had suffered, no matter that he was alone.

As he climbed back into his chair every muscle trembled. Clenching his jaw, he forced his body to obedience. No more shakes. No more labored breathing. There was little he could do about the pounding in his head, though, other than to ignore it while he tried to make sense of what had just happened. Inhale and exhale became less ragged as he closed his eyes and dropped into a trance, an exercise mastered from one of his many books. Once more settled, Lucien extended his thoughts to trace the path of the episode.

"That fool!" Lucien snapped back to full awareness, his pulse throbbing in his temple. "All the power I exerted to equip him, and he ignores the warnings!"

Still clear in the man's mind was the image of Tony climbing to his feet, and Kara sprawled unconscious across a sidewalk. Lucien was pretty sure he could piece together what had happened; Tony had attempted to take the girl with a physical attack and had ignored the magical warnings of his protections. Apparently the girl carried shields, too. They collided, and the shock of their collapse had traveled down the line to Lucien, since he actually powered Tony's shields.

Rubbing at the back of his neck in an attempt to relieve some of the tingling caused by the backlash, Lucien smiled in a very nasty way.

"Well, Anthony," the man said with a sneer to the not quite empty air, "you may be inept, but today you have provided me with some very invaluable information."

Lucien restored himself to order, and settled back in his chair in to wait for Tony to arrive. Or that was his intent. But his energy was drained and his eyelids weighed down. He was loathed to show weakness of any kind, yet once again unconsciousness overcame him.

As Lucien fell into a backlash-induced doze, slowly slumping over the scarred surface of his desk, Olcas—the Power that dominated him—filled his head with violent, angry images. Flashes of lightning and apocalyptic thunder set off tremors through his tool's body. Throwing in images of the woman and the girl, using jolts of phantom pain to force the message home, Olcas expended more energy than he liked to ensure that Lucien realized the significance of the pair: one represented sweet revenge; the other, a strength and power that must be absorbed to make that revenge a reality.

Olcas hated the woman and all her kind, with very good reason. At one time Olcas had a form, a body of his own; he'd had a family and ambitions. Thanks to the Tuatha de Danaan, all he had left were the ambitions. Long ago across the ocean, Olcas and his family had been a mighty force dominating the land of Eire, crushing it beneath their mighty heel. No mortal could stand against the Athenian goddess, Carmán, and her sons, Calma—Valiant; Dubh—Black; and Olcas—Evil.

No mortal, Olcas thought ruefully. Ah, but that was the key—the Children of Danu were not mortal and their treachery had put an end to his family's rightful conquest.

The night sky was torn ragged by devouring flames, and the rousing battle cries of desperate Celts mingled with the piercing screams of wounded peasants. The resulting din rang across the hills of Eire until it must have echoed in the very halls of the sidhe themselves—and yet the fae ignored the challenge, for challenge it was.

Carmán and her children descended on village after village with the wrath of gods, only to be met by farmers with scythes and wood axes and children and women armed with cooking knives and whatever else came to hand. It was an uneven battle, without doubt; the green hills of Eire were bathed in the blood of her people.

As they strolled through the middle of their latest conquest, Carmán and her sons surveyed their work. Their eyes reflected the fires consuming the thatched roofs to either side of them, lending their faces even more of a demonic air. Calma, the oldest of the goddess's sons, ambled forth with all the confidence and swagger of any warrior, though his heart was blacker that the soot blown about by the evening air. The hint of cruelty about his hard mouth gave lie to any smile that did not reach his eyes...about like the one gracing his lips now.

"Are they cowards then," Calma sneered, "that they would hide from us? They must be wise cowards, to know they cannot stand before the might of gods."

Carmán came to stand beside him, her face expressionless but for her eyes. Her eyes reflected her boredom. "Wise and foolish both then, if they think hiding will do them any good. All they do is delay their destruction, forcing us to waste our time on these mere wisps of potential. I grow weary of this...we should kill them all."

Her words were Calma's actions. Ever the dutiful son, he immediately, almost casually, brought his sword about to thrust it in the pregnant belly of a peasant woman who cowered all but unseen in the shadow of a shattered doorway. Drawing her shuddering body toward him, he placed a gently deceptive kiss on her trembling lips, holding her terrified gaze until he had suckled the full measure of the meager magic that clung to her. As the spark dwindled from her eyes, he dropped her carelessly to the ground. Carmán laughed at the heartlessness of her son. The remaining villagers scattered before them, not even stopping to drag away their dead.

Following ever in their brother's wake, Dubh and Olcas walked side by side. In the shadow of Calma's greatness, Dubh was as black as pitch in every aspect. Frightening to behold, peasants quailed before him. Some—woman, child, and man alike—froze in place for the terror of him. When they stood transfixed by horror, Olcas, with the golden beauty of an angel to mask the darkness within—but for the betrayal of his cold, ruthless eyes—stepped forth, offering false hope. Even now, a child cringed before them.

"Come, little one," Olcas moved between Dubh and the boy and beckoned the lad into the visible protection of his open arms. "All will be well."

Only too late could the child see the hunger in the veiled eyes, too close to the deceptively divine face. From the cradle of Olcas's powerful arms, the victim let out a tortured keen as both brothers had their first savory taste of the ambrosia of sidhe power, for this boy was a halfling—the mingling of mortal and immortal blood.

Observing them with a look of mingled pride and unholy amusement in her eyes, Carmán laughed heartily at the clever cruelty of her sons, the way they drained Eire and its people of their power. Little did she know this cleverness was their downfall. In seeking to lure the Tuatha de Danaan from their protected lairs, they did the one thing that would incur their wrath—not only slaughtering children, but one of sidhe blood, however diluted.

And so Carmán and her sons began their fall as the very hills of Eire rose against them. The treacherous sidhe—an immortal race who fairly glowed with that power that the goddess and her sons craved above all else—descended upon the Athenian deities and extracted revenge for the halfblooded bastard and the devastated Celts.

The memory of that defeat was nothing compared to the details of Carmán's death—she'd died of a mother's agonized grief. Swathed in chains and tethered to the ground, she had been forced to watch in horror as her children were destroyed. He could still see her tormented eyes, even millennia later.

The bloody sidhe had supreme confidence in their triumph. Assured of their might, the bodies of Carmán and her sons were burned to cinders. Not that the measure had proven effective at all. Very soon the Tuatha de Danaan would learn the folly of their disdain—Carmán's death had preserved the souls of her sons, if not their bodies. The day would come when the Children of Carmán would rise up from where they waited and crush the Children of Danu beneath their heel. All the better would the satisfaction be if it were a sidhe that proved the key to their destruction!

All of this reminiscing made the botched efforts of Lucien and his selected tool all the more infuriating. It was bad enough to have to work his vengeance through others; even worse that they were incompetent. For good measure, Olcas sifted into Lucien's dreams an overwhelming sense of power-hunger in the hopes that the man would go for the woman and girl even without knowing what they were, just as he had gone after the other sidhe in the area.

That all-important task accomplished, Olcas extended his thoughts across the city. Out there, in the smothering greyness generated by the close proximity of millions of mundane, ungifted souls, a handful of brilliant points flared in a psychic parody of the faint, scattered stars of the city's night sky. These were not the only sparks in the metropolis, though they invariably were the brightest. Each point was the immortal flame of a member of the Tuatha de Danaan. Hatred ate its way through Olcas's thoughts like bitter acid that those fires still burned. He longed to see each of them prone before him, eyes drowning in despair as he drained away their vibrancy; what joy to savor the utter hopelessness on the faces of their fellow sidhe as he snuffed each soul like a guttering candle. Oh the joy, to see his ancient foes so fallen, knowing he himself had left them no more than empty husks.

But now was not the time to daydream. If he was to succeed, he could not allow himself to become distracted by a petty vengeance, not when he was so close to claiming a grand one. And yet, he must ensure they could not interfere with his plans for the sidhe witch from the pawnshop; he would have her, and through her the girl...the delightful, untrained, utterly powerful, and, above all, malleable girl.

The rest of the sidhe in the city must continue to be distracted. Ah, but perhaps in this Lucien would be useful, not by his own actions, but through the network of tools he had established in the past ten years, and the pathetic demons he insisted on summoning. Carefully constructing the images he desired, with more subtlety than he'd taken before so as not to dislodge the importance of the two women, Olcas laid a web of thoughts that would torment the man to no end: constant reminders that the sidhe in the city possessed items of power that Lucien craved. Careful to weave in the need to send henchmen—Lucien must be discouraged from wasting precious energy on such secondary pursuits...no more effort would be diverted from Olcas's goals—he planted the need to harass those individuals for the coveted items they hoarded.

With an economy of effort, Olcas sent the thoughts like a spear to painfully pierce Lucien's unconscious mind, laying further torment on his own disappointing tool. Olcas savored the bittersweet irony—the only dreams Lucien had were these nightmarish visions. True dreams required a soul; something Lucien hadn't possessed since the day he had been "born." Whatever soul had inhabited the form in the chair, it had fled before Olcas' possession, providing an unoccupied body for "Lucien." Seemingly, it was a perfect situation. The thought was a galling one. Here was Lucien with a perfectly good body but no soul, and Olcas was a soul without a body...and no way to mate the two.

What a miserable choice this one had been. Not for the first time, Olcas felt deeply frustrated with this creature's inability to communicate nonverbally. It was questionable that Lucien even realized how much of his power and personal achievement came from outside himself. Because he was blithely unaware of his benefactor, these dreams were the only way to convey important instructions. Perhaps Olcas could have found a more useful tool but, at the critical time, this man had been the only choice. With enough latent power to be tempting and such a weak grip on what mortals called reality, the target had suited the purpose. Or so it had appeared.

Clearly his less-than-suitable nature had not been evident. Telepathically mute and psychically blind, Lucien presented a constant draw on his master's energy reserves. His body, actions, even his thoughts could be guided in subtle ways, but more cerebral manipulation required draining efforts like tonight's. Their plans would have progressed much quicker if "speaking" to this one were easier and less vague. It was impossible to even "tell" Lucien that the woman he kept challenging wasn't even human. And the girl...she was the key to all their goals. Her massive potential was overwhelming, even if it was as yet unexplored. She would make the perfect vessel...but not for him. The girl was destined for another. Until then, what couldn't he do with those two in his control! What *wouldn't* he do to obtain them!

As an hour passed and nothing changed in the girl's condition, Maggie's concern grew. Despite the centuries she had behind her, there were still things she didn't know. Unfortunately, how to counteract mage-shock in a not-quite mortal girl was one of those things. Drawing on her vast knowledge of herbs, magic, and even music, Maggie sought to draw Kara from whatever inner place she cowered from everything that had assaulted her senses in the past few days. When all of her efforts produced no more than marginal improvement, Maggie felt an ache inside that was nothing less than maternal.

With a tenderness made all the more touching by her ethereal beauty, she gathered Kara into her arms in the hopes of waking in the girl a sense of safety and security that might draw her to surface from the depths where she was lost. Resting against the cool stone of the chamber Maggie sang to Kara haunting lullabies in the private language of her own kind. In half a millennium, human ears had heard neither that language nor the songs. The angelic sounds wreathed the two in a spell of peace ruffled only occasionally by their own thoughts.

Maggie had never had a child of her own—pregnancies were so rare for her kind—but all children were precious to a race that so seldom experienced the joy of parenthood firsthand. It was at once a blessing and a curse for the Áes Sidhe: their numbers neither shrank nor grew. Time did not ravage the Children of Danu, only accident or malice could sever their lines of life.

A blessing to be immortal? Yes, but at what cost? Sidhe souls were finite in number; no sidhe child was born without the death of another in that line. Maggie sighed and faltered in her song. There hadn't been a sidhe death in at least a century. There had also, perforce, not been a sidhe birth in that time. It was a hard thing to long for a child of one's own blood yet know that to realize that dream meant the loss of another kinsman.

The only solace for such longing was mortals: the prolific race of humans. Matings between sidhe men and human women were more fruitful than among human couples, with conception occurring even in women whose wombs were thought to be barren. When the pairing was a love-bond, mother and child would move to the father's rath, blessing all there with the joy and laughter of childhood. That was one way the sidhe satisfied their longing for children of their own.

Maggie clutched Kara closer as cruel memories rose to remind her of her own heartbreak when she learned that the opposite pairing did not have the same effect. In her youth, she hadn't realized a child gained its soul through its mother. A sidhe woman could never bear a human soul; one of many lessons young Cliodna had foolishly insisted on learning on her own.

There was another way that the sidhe gathered children to brighten their halls with laughter, a way shadowed with immortal anger. The Áes Sidhe considered the bonds of parenthood shattered once mother or father chronically raised an abusive hand to their child. Such a child could be secreted away, a dead or dying seeming left in its place. Maggie herself had rescued a child or two from unworthy parents, leaving a changeling as a fitting punishment for the crimes visited against one to whom love and care had been due. Some few of the Tuatha de Danaan were bitter to the point of hatred at the often-unappreciated wealth of children born to humans.

Caught up in the ancient and righteous anger of her race, Maggie didn't notice immediately when Kara transitioned from the shallow, labored breath of shock into the guarded stillness of the newly awakened. As Kara became more alert, she stiffened in Maggie's arms. Only then did Maggie realize the danger was past and that they had entered another phase of conflict.

"'Tis good to see ye awake, dear," Maggie spoke with careful casualness. "We had a concern for ye. Can ye be tellin' me what happened, then?" While she waited for some comment from Kara, Maggie kept completely still, but the girl fought to release herself both from the folds of the blanket and from the sidhe's arms. "Carefully, love, ye've had a rough time o' it."

Kara scrambled to her feet, then swayed with the sudden change in elevation. Immediately Maggie stood next to her, offering her arm for the girl to lean on. Kara stared at it with a panicked look in her eyes, backing into the center of the chamber to avoid it. Maggie's heart ached to see Kara's fear. The sidhe knew the emotion was only reflexive, and not personal. It had not occurred to Kara that she was now safe.

"Please, can ye tell me what happened?" Maggie did her best to project calm and concern. As she waited in stillness for Kara to answer, she noticed the girl's hand move unconsciously to rub the back of her head. Almost like the action had triggered it, Kara's face flooded with relief, mirroring Maggie's own. She was confident that the trust she'd built up with Kara had survived whatever ordeal the girl had gone through. Still moving cautiously, as if with a nervous animal, she motioned for Kara to sit down and turned to retrieve another cup of the tea that Demne had left steeping. A small burst of power reheated it before she handed the mug to Kara. Maggie waited patiently.

Curling herself once again in the warm blanket, Kara clutched the mug of aromatic tea in her hands. Without its comforting weight, she had no doubt they would have trembled uncontrollably. She gathered her thoughts in silence; Maggie sat just beyond reach. It was almost as if she knew Kara needed space after the fright she'd had. Kara looked around the fantastic chamber for something to help her make sense of the jumbled flashes of memory that were all she had left of the afternoon.

Locking her wild eyes on a bit of shimmering crystal embedded in the far wall, Kara began, "Someone tried to grab me. A man hit me on the head and then tried to convince me he'd rescued me." Her voice was steady enough to be disturbing even to her as she told Maggie what she could remember. There was no emotion behind her words, almost as if they described something that had happened to someone else. Kara wondered at how distant everything felt.

"I never would have known until he'd gotten me into a cab, if he hadn't slipped." Here her eyes held a terrified glint and a tremor ran through her voice.

"He knew my name, Maggie. He knew my name!" Kara felt her composure fail the moment she slid her fear-maddened eyes away from the crystal. Tears slid down her face as she absorbed the frightening reality of her close call. She was safe now...it was okay to let go of the terror, to purge it from her.

With the tears drying on Kara's face and the chamber silent save for the sound of tinkling water, it was difficult to know what to do next. Maggie had never been a mother, or any other figure so commonplace in human experience. It seemed the spooked look was fading from the girl's eyes, but some remnant still lurked. A diversion...that was it! Sending out a tendril of thought, Maggie summoned Beag Scath to her side. She could tell he wasn't far away. His presence had flitted on the edge of her awareness the whole time they'd been below ground. Wisely, he had kept his distance. But that did not suit Maggie's purpose now.

Come along, Little Shadow, Maggie enticed him. *Now 'tis the time to earn yer saucers o' milk.*

From around the corner of the doorway, the sprite came scampering in...looking like a perfect, dainty unicorn, with a hide that was all browns and reds and a delicate golden horn! He bleated most musically and gamboled about the room, clearly showing off for Kara, and just as clearly taking a purposeful tumble to land before her in an endearing heap, his tufted little lion's tail tickling her bare feet.

The girl's startled laughter at the sight was worth any amount of impish shenanigans. Summoning the puckish creature was just the right move to make. For a short time they sat and chuckled together as Beag Scath transformed from one magical beast to another, in all of them playing the clumsy fool. Clearly the sprite cared less for his own dignity than he did for this new friend; Maggie could read that quite clearly in her little companion's mercurial thoughts. Finally, Kara expended her nervous energy and no longer seemed even the slightest bit brittle, as she had such a short time ago. Sensing that the need for extreme measures had passed, Beag Scath crept into Kara's lap and burrowed under the comforter. Kara clutched the cover around her shoulders, but could not hide the occasional tremor that still ran through her. As Beag Scath made himself comfortable, the girl sat very still, wonder and delight filling her eyes. At last, the sprite snuggled in against her chest and drew her arms tight around him, settling in for a nap.

"Would ye care to hear the tale o' how I came by that little scamp?" Maggie surprised herself by asking Kara that question a second time. Generally, Maggie didn't talk about her time in Eire; generally, she avoided all mention of it, considering how much the longing to return ached in her breast. But this was different. Kara was kin, and she was hurting.

"Yes, please." Kara didn't sound shocked anymore, or fearful. No, she just sounded really tired.

"He found me in County Cork," Maggie began, her voice drifting into the soothing rhythm of storytelling, "well before my time of oaths...in the youth of my magic. It was in a time even before I'd acquired the name Maggie. I have both fond an' frightful memories o' that time."

She watched without watching as Kara settled in for the tale, clearly mesmerized by the proposition of a story. The melancholy shadow in the girl's gaze was quite clear, though perhaps few others would have caught it. Maggie could empathize...she missed Conall O'Keefe, as well. In his memory, she continued her story, bending to it with all the skill of a master bard.

As she made her way down the back tunnels of the rath, young Cliodna's heart raced. The surface was nothing new to her, but the forbidden was always a savory spice. Wandering the moonlit nights, she thrilled at her single rebellion. Creeping from the mound in a shift and leggings of mottled greens and browns, she didn't heed her elders' warnings. Their talk of magic's pulse that, unshielded, rippled the flow with its very existence made no sense to her; she didn't believe such a thing.

That night it was Abarta who approached her. Always before it had been one of the more compassionate or persuasive elders. She would listen to their words and their wisdom, not understanding but diverted from her path, nonetheless. Most of the elders had a way of capturing one's attention and gently clasping it in an iron grip. When they spoke, if it was their wish, hours flew by like minutes. Dawn always broke before they were done, chasing away another of her chances at dancing across the moors in the moonlight. If Abarta possessed this skill, he chose not to exercise it.

"Come join us in the singin', Cliodna," Abarta had called to her as she tried to slip unnoticed from the hall, his hand patting the satin cushion in front of him. "The night is no place for half-trained sidhe who leave more ripples than a leapin' trout."

Cliodna's face went cold and pale with fury. "That would be why ye are singin' then, Abarta?"

Some of the younger sidhe had chortled at the sting of her retort. However, the looks of disappointment from everyone else dampened Cliodna's joy in the evening.

"Excuse me, all," she addressed the room, "an' ye, good Abarta. Perhaps I am in need o' some solitude. I will find myself a quiet place to meditate on my behavior."

As she'd walked slowly from the room, it was all she could do to keep herself from crowing. Yes, she would meditate, but it would be with a clear sky above her head, not emtombing rock, and none would know the difference.

If she hadn't run off so quickly to savor her triumph, she might have wondered at the mischief glittering in Abarta's eye.

As she loped through the tall grasses that carpeted the land some distance from the rath, Cliodna allowed her hands to trail at her side. The young sidhe thrilled in the chilling impact as the dew-bejeweled stems slapped against her open palms. She threw herself down amidst the grasses, causing the surrounding blades to shower all of her in dew. Lying dazzled on the hillside, hidden from the sight of all but the owls and bats, she closed her eyes and let her senses wander through the land around her; she caressed the minds of sleeping rabbits, and listened to the murmuring of the trees. Everything around her seemed so still, so quiet. She marveled at the hush of the evening landscape.

Allowing her attention to spread across the meadow, Cliodna learned the folly of her rebellion. Though she did not move, the utter stillness that surrounded her made it seem as if she were aquiver. A tinge of anxiety took root in her subconscious. As she arose from the crushed grass, pulling her mind back to itself, she encountered a presence that chilled her heart; something out there was marking her, something with an intense hunger.

Torn between facing the anger of the elders, and her terror at what she sensed, Cliodna held back her call for help. Perhaps it was pride, or even a fear of punishment, but she couldn't bring herself to reveal her disobedience. Focusing her thoughts on getting back to the rath, Cliodna tried to think of her best path of escape. Whatever tracked her drew closer, unfortunately, and its path placed it directly between her and the rath. She tried to picture the tunnels beneath the mound, wracking her brain for an alternative route. She did not think they extended this far, or, if so, they were long disused. Cliodna only knew of one tunnel that might take her safely home, if she could reach it.

As she prepared herself for a dash to safety, she also readied every bit of defensive magic she had been taught so far. Her heart sank at how little there actually was–she was fairly young for her race and had just begun her serious training. Cliodna crouched in the tall grasses trying to glimpse her hunter. When she cautiously extended just a bit of herself, she recoiled at the voracious hunger she encountered. It was so overpowering that she could get no sense of what lay beyond it. If she were to escape, it would have to be now, before that force drew any nearer.

She darted away, using every one of the tricks she knew to avoid capture, leading her follower on a frantic chase across the moonlit moors. She dodged through the trees and hid in the cover of the shadows, but Cliodna felt dread claim her. With each step that brought her to the tunnel, she could sense her pursuer draw near. Almost, she thought she could feel the heat of breath on her neck. The idea was enough to inspire her to a burst of terror-fed speed.

All around her the landscape blurred; so focused was she on her mental image of the half-remembered tunnel that she nearly ran past the vine-draped reality. With a tortured sob, she fell through the vines and lay panting against the cool cavern wall knowing she was safe–even unused, this domain of the Tuatha de Danaan still bore the protections that all their mounds were laced with; time itself could not enter unbidden. Willing her heart to calm, she extended a thread of her awareness to explore the way she had come. It seemed as if her pursuer had gone away.

"Aauugghh!" a scream ripped itself from Cliodna's tortured throat, raspy from her flight. As if her tendril of thought had been a beacon, the voracious hunger returned and gave her no time for more reaction than the one startled from her. The moment she probed outside the tunnel mouth whatever had followed her threw itself through the opening. She was so frightened that she couldn't even gather herself to call for help. Sobbing with fear and vowing by every god she could imagine that she would never disobey again if only this would turn out to be a dream, Cliodna closed her eyes and waited to be devoured.

The shock was almost too much for her when, instead of experiencing intense pain, something small and warm climbed into her lap and began projecting immense contentment as it ran miniature hands along the tear trails coursing down her cheek. The creature fairly purred as it ran those same salt-dampened hands across her forehead and through her tangled locks, instinctively trying to calm her.

Cliodna's clenched eyes flew open and she stared in confusion at the creature before her. A sprite! She had known such things existed, though she had never seen one near the rath. The creature was kin-cousin to her kind, but that was all she knew of it. Reaching out to touch it, she once again sensed its almost painfully crisp emotions. First and foremost was a sense of devotion that made Cliodna wonder exactly how she would explain her new companion to the others. Already she could see the look on Abarta's face. No...now was not the time for that.

Experimentally she lifted the sprite off her lap and rose. The moment she moved away, it followed right on her heels like a second shadow. Whether she liked it or not, for now she had a new friend.

Behind the devotion, she could once more sense the hunger that had pursued her; an appetite that seemed linked to her ability for magic. This more than anything forced home the lesson the elders had been trying to get into her head. Surrounded by magic, as she'd always been, how could she know the way of things above? How could she know how thinly the surface magics trickled? How could she know her own aura would be an ever-present hum, like a small sound echoing in an empty cave? Simple: they told her. It had been easy to laugh away their warnings; there was no hum amidst the deep and ever-present magic of the Áes Sidhe and their world.

Possessing a new sense of respect for the elders and of affection for the sprite, Cliodna picked up her little shadow and began to make her way home down the long tunnel.

"The irony," Maggie went on, "was that the next day my teachers taught the shieldin' I needed to journey safely above, never sayin' a word about the 'shadow' I'd acquired."

Kara laughed. It was a weary laugh, but reassuring, which was why Maggie had brushed the dust off the tale. More importantly, though, it was time to make several things very clear for Kara, starting now.

Maggie dropped her vital bombshell, "Which is why I'll be teachin' ye that shieldin' spell as soon as ye can stand without swayin'."

"What?" There was no doubt she had startled Kara, though confusion and doubt were not the only emotions surprisingly conveyed by the girl's single word. Maggie could sense Kara's guilty excitement as well.

"Ye heard me...I was lucky that night; only Beag Scath was drawn by the rhythm o' the magic in my blood." Maggie captured Kara's gaze and would not let it go. "Ye might'na be so lucky yerself. There are many a creature—some mortal, though most na—who feel the irresistible pull o' mage energy. Most are merely a nuisance, fawningly in the way until they catch the waftin' o' stronger magics; others stop at nothin' to claim whatever energy attracts them.

"Most noted for this in all o' the history o' the Tuatha de Danaan is the Athenian goddess, Carmán, an' her bloodthirsty sons, Calma, Dubh, an' Olcas. They were na contented with the magics o' their own land; their cruel heels crossed oceans to descend on Eire with no mercy. Lone sidhe an' mortals in any number were na safe from that unholy family. 'Twas said they caught the very scent o' magic on the air, trackin' anyone bearin' even the faintest whiff o' power. All o' enchanted Eire—whose very soil, stones, an' streams were steeped in magic until even the ungifted mortals were faintly tinged with it—was laid waste by Carmán an' her children...until the sidhe stepped in.

"But that's past," Maggie forced a cheerful note. "No Tuatha de Carmán tracked me that night, or anythin' more harmful than Beag Scath, a lovely, if mischievous sprite who buries me in flowers, not salt-sown soil."

Once Beag Scath's antics and Maggie's subsequent tale banished the final remnant of the terror, Maggie was able to settle Kara down to rest, making appropriately soothing sounds and maintaining a steady stream of the soporific tea. Finally she left the girl to soak in the subterranean pool and to rest however she liked.

Maggie went upstairs to the shop to touch base with Demne. She was disturbed by what she had learned. The entire time Kara told of her encounter, Maggie opened herself to the mental images the girl had unconsciously projected at her; the clearest image was the face of her would-be abductor, who also happened to be both the thief from the other night and the would-be intruder from earlier today. Unfortunately, she couldn't say she was completely surprised by what had taken place or who was involved. The moment Kara had entered the store for the first time, Maggie had known what a tempting target the girl would make to the wrong person. She could kick herself for not making the correlation earlier, though; she'd had no idea her challenger had already associated Kara with the pawnshop. Maggie had thought she was being overcautious when she'd keyed the protections against Lucien, but from what Kara told her now, those protections had been all that had saved the girl. Maggie had been so sure that she herself would be the target that she hadn't protected Kara nearly well enough. By the time the girl went home tonight, that would be rectified.

She extended a trail of thought to Demne, just enough to give him a bit of warning of what had taken place. She could feel him recoil, startled and enraged all at once. There was something more though, some other distraction. Maggie hurried to see what demanded her attention now.

CHAPTER 18

Eager for this opportunity to glimpse Maggie's day-to-day life, Demne wandered the shop with a dust cloth in his hand, his gift extended to its fullest as he explored the pawnshop and its contents.

He wished to become familiar with the world that occupied so much of his Maggie's life. First he explored the pictures on the wall, experiencing a twinge of jealousy toward strangers who were nonetheless close enough to Maggie that she kept their images as a constant reminder. Pushing the irrational feeling aside, he drifted through the shop, exploring with fascination all that it held.

His main talent lay elsewhere than Maggie's did; if he wished it, his touch could provide him with instant flashes of an item's past. For objects he knew well, he could focus on specific points in time; otherwise, he saw whatever fate revealed. On very rare occasions, his gift could even tell him something about a person he happened to touch.

This skill had proven quite useful. Demne had often been called to bear witness to events that none had seen. With his gift and a link to another sidhe, proof could be gathered and presented indisputably, for one could not lie successfully when soul-speaking; the other would always know a falsehood from a truth by the liar's own emotions. In this way, those accountable for a deed done in secret were faced with their responsibility, and the truth of unwitnessed tragedies was revealed.

In fascination he worked his way through the main room. As the hours passed, he glimpsed fragments of many centuries of personal history: An antique fountain pen revealed to him the treachery of a long-dead noble; a mahogany armoire shared with him its ancient secret—a fortune in confederate dollars hidden in its false sides and back by a frightened southern belle and her maid just before Yankee soldiers carried them away; and an exquisite, time-worn quilt spoke of the throes of both labor and death for generations of a single family. There were many untold stories here, known now only to Demne and those long-dead humans who had lived them. He found it tragic that no one would ever know the wealth of history contained just in this one room.

Slowly, once he'd fully delved into the wondrous physical items the shop contained, he tightened the focus of his viewing to summon Maggie's yesterdays. As he moved about, everything around him became as a ghostly image, overpowered by the visions of his other sight. He saw her wearing many of the clothes that now hung on cedar hangers in the corner of the room, always with compassion on her face, as she greeted two centuries of people for whom hope had fled and only desperation remained. Demne watched as she restored their faith in the future and gave them the means to carry on just a little longer...long enough for their personal shadows of ill fate to pass. He watched her smile and cry and fly into rages, but never for herself; all the energy she expended was for those fleeting mortals...what was there in this life for Maggie? For Cliodna...he loved this woman already and feared that in taking up her duty, she had set aside her life. The only vision that showed a true spark of his lover's soul was some thirty years past. Demne returned to the photograph of that moment to call forth the memory again.

Before he could summon it, Demne heard the tinkling of the bell on the front door. He quickly turned to greet the person who had joined him in the shop. Just as quickly he drew back, wondering if he was still engaged in visions.

"Can I help ye?" Demne managed to smile at the gentleman, who stood uncertainly in the center of the room. While the man shifted uncomfortably, Demne saw his mistake. This was not the man from the photograph, but the similarity was such that he could only be a relative. A son, perhaps? No matter, Demne told himself, he must act as if he knew none of this.

"I'm here to see Maggie McCormick," the man answered stiffly. "I'll be appreciatin' it if ye'll fetch her."

"I'd like to oblige ye, sir," Demne answered politely, though the man's abrupt attitude made it difficult, "but I'm afraid she's busy an' canna be disturbed."

The set of the man's jaw warned of his building belligerence. Only the hint of desperation in the stranger's eyes stopped Demne from exercising his own arrogance in response. Throughout the centuries, the sidhe had encountered many humans who blustered their way through resistance by the sheer volume of their objections. Demne had no patience with such tactics, which were generally fueled by manipulative and bullying personalities; this didn't seem to be such a case, though the man's bleak gaze was the only proof.

"Please, sir," Demne pushed on before the man could gather breath enough to start bellowing, "I really canna interrupt her now. Maybe I can help ye?"

Just as it seemed that polite firmness wouldn't work, the man's face paled and he swayed slightly where he stood. His eyes grew wide and slightly crazed as if they had seen much more than his mortal mind was willing to comprehend. Reaching out a hand to steady the man, Demne experienced a startling flood of images...images he would have to examine more thoroughly later. He turned to follow the stranger's fixed stare just in time to see Beag Scath poking his nose thorough the velvet curtain. Though the sprite was cloaked in his cat seeming, Demne had the sinking feeling that their visitor saw something more than he was meant to. Demne was about to soul-speak a warning to Maggie when he sensed her approach. Discreetly he stepped to the side, allowing her room to pass into the shop. The first visible sign of her came when the "cat" was scooped into the air by unseen arms. With the effortless grace expected of an angel or a queen, Maggie glided through the curtain with the "cat" climbing to her shoulder.

"An' why did it take ye so long to return, Pádraig O'Keefe?" Maggie's words floated in the silence of her entrance. The man flinched at her use of the Irish variant of his name, a purposeful reminder of where he came from. "Welcome are ye on this side o' the threshold."

Maggie could have wished for a better opportunity to reveal her nature to Kara's father, but leave it to Beag Scath to force her hand. Gently prodding the sprite with a thought, she encouraged him to drop his seeming. Then she let her own regal nature show through. Demne followed her lead seconds later.

Without the veils of their seemings, any mortal could see them for what they were. Whether or not they would believe their senses, or even recognize what they were looking at, was another matter. The difference wasn't so much physical, as it was manner. They were not seven feet tall with pointed ears (embellishments of hundreds of years of human imagination and expanding myths), but there was a clear alteration between their human seemings and their true appearance as sidhe. The only physical distinction was a fair, translucent glow to the sidhe's skin, a lean, deceptively delicate frame, and a brightening of the color of their eyes to shades of blue and green and orange never imagined by mankind. The rest of the transformation could only be called a difference in attitude—though that was an inadequate term, no other came closer, unless it was perhaps intensity. They were so filled with life and connected to the world that they gave the impression of not quite fitting in their skin. When a sidhe looked into a mortal's eyes, the human was left with feelings of awe and wonder. They also felt guilt to varying degrees, depending upon the humans in question and their attitudes regarding the world and all it contained. The ancient wisdom of the Tuatha de Danaan went beyond experience or simple knowledge; it was as if they were born knowing the answers to every question in the universe. A false impression, but one that struck ages of mortals dumb regardless. With a lifetime of dedicated meditation and study, a man might gain for himself the merest glimmer of the serenity that characterized the sidhe, but if ever faced with one, that man would only understand how he paled in comparison.

Anyway, there could be no doubt that the pair was not human.

The look on Patrick O'Keefe's face before they'd revealed themselves told Maggie that he'd suspected, though he'd probably been ready to label it a case of illness-induced insanity. The pallor he wore afterward assured her that all doubts were gone. Putting down the sprite and shooing him into the back room, she reached for a nearby chair and pulled it toward the shaken man.

"Patrick, I think ye need to be sittin' down," Maggie suggested, this time using the Anglo version of his true name, as she gently pushed him into the chair. She then turned to Demne. "Please fetch some water from the back while I lock up."

At her last words, Kara's father rose in protest, his eyes nearly rolling like those of a panicked colt. "What do ye mean, lock up?"

"Do'na argue. Ye might'na remember much o' me after thirty years, but we've thin's we must discuss an' we canna do that here." When his face showed no sign of losing its stubborn set, Maggie took a calculated risk. "Besides, I think Kara could stand to see her father after all that's happened to her today."

In mere seconds, a flood of emotions rippled across Patrick's face almost too quickly for Maggie to note them all. Watching him go from confusion to fear to anger, all leavened with a steady stream of concern, Maggie reached for nearby tendrils of magic to defend herself. Some small part of her mind noticed Demne was poised to physically restrain their visitor, if necessary. The room vibrated with tension for several minutes before the remnants of color drained from the man's face and he slumped to the chair. With a thought, Maggie assured Demne he could now go for the water. She knelt beside Patrick and searched his face, trying to find reassurance that her gamble hadn't proven too much for the man.

"What do ye ken about Kara?" The anxiety on Patrick's face was plain to Maggie. "What have ye to do with my daughter?"

"There's a lot to explain, Patrick," Maggie answered him reassuringly, "Kara is fine, just a bit shaken. Do ye feel up to goin' to her? We can talk downstairs." When he hesitated, she continued. "My word o' honor ye'll both o' ye be safe."

Patrick rose from the chair before Maggie could say more. She had to smile at his resilience. Leaving Demne to close up the shop behind them, Maggie led Patrick to her subterranean chambers, followed by a small shadow.

In the gloom of the smoky basement, Lucien furiously pawed through half-buried boxes containing what he had considered the obsolete volumes of his mystical library. Already the cellar floor was littered with journals and grimoires recorded on a fantastic array of materials and in an equally bizarre variety of "inks." He had spent the past ten years gathering and painstakingly deciphering any ancient text he could find. Those that he'd found valuable crowded the shelves of his workroom. A few—more precious still—were hidden away in his secret sanctum. These were treasures that woke in Lucien an unfocused, yet murderous, jealousy, which alone told him they were worth any number of lives (other than his own) to protect. Everything else—those read no more than once before being set aside—found its way to the basement. Somewhere in these discards there was an obscure reference, a description that now nagged at him, something about a race of magical beings. His vague memory of that passage meant nothing to him at that time, but now it spoke to his craving for power. If he could only find it, he might gain the key that could turn the woman from the pawnshop to his purposes. He had a feeling she and the girl would be most valuable to him.

Growling viciously, Lucien extracted himself from the jumble of boxes and glanced at his watch. Where was that pitiful young man? If this incompetence went on much longer, he might have to consider discarding that particular tool and find someone else to handle the more questionable details of the plan. It was bad enough that Tony had failed so miserably today in trying to take the girl; it was even worse that his blunder had affected Lucien personally. With extreme effort, he restrained himself from taking out his anger at that thought on the scrolls and books at his feet. If there was one thing he had learned, it was to discard no tool until it ceased to be useful in any way. That went for books as well as people. Tony was just lucky that his failure had at least given Lucien some very valuable information.

Impatient with his search, not to mention recent events in general, Lucien peered into the shadows pooled around the edges of the room. Tracing an intricate pattern in the air, the man watched with satisfaction as part of the darkness shifted and moved slowly toward him. Here was one benefit of his study of ancient texts, this...familiar, one would have to call it, was quite adept, among other things, at prolonged, detailed searches and similarly tedious tasks. One had simply to implant an image as clear as possible in its mind of what was wanted, including any exact details that were known, and show it where to look. It wouldn't stop looking until the item was found, the search area was exhausted, or someone called it away from its task. Lucien wasn't sure what the creature was—some lesser demon or elemental, he supposed—but it was quite a useful tool.

"I need something found," Lucien told it tersely. "I am looking for a particular text. It is very important." The man called to mind every detail he could remember of the passage and thought very hard at the shadowling.

"I will be in the workroom if you should find it." Lucien paused, trying to decide the impact this specter might have on Tony...if he ever arrived. He wasn't sure how much of his own power he wanted to reveal; after all, Tony had abilities of his own. It wouldn't do to open his eyes to that fact when Lucien wasn't sure of the extent of that power. "I will be with the young man; I do not wish him to know of you."

Not waiting for an acknowledgment, the sorcerer mounted the spiral staircase. His head had begun to throb once again, and he decided it would be better to wait for Tony upstairs. Once Lucien had all the details of today's events right from the tool's inept little head—not to mention the text his minion sought even now—he might have enough information to firm up the vague plan that had been taking shape since the magical impact.

Working through a shell was so frustrating, particularly when that shell was too dense to even realize it was being used. Not for the first time, Olcas regretted the circumstances that had made it necessary to choose this current vessel. It had worked through many people over the centuries, but none as psychically blind as this one. Not only was the situation maddening, it was almost painfully limiting. While the creature now called Lucien Blank had plenty of latent potential, it was very difficult to access. It was possible, but it cost Olcas much power. It meant that Lucien didn't have the finesse and control that came with trained ability or even the instinct that came with raw talent. He reached blindly for power because the books he had hunted told him it was there and what signs to look for, not because he could sense it himself. At times, working through Lucien was so tortuous that Olcas longed to shatter his creation and seek another. Perhaps the creature Tony; he would be a very useful tool. His banked potential made Lucien's ability look like a dying ember by comparison.

But no, things had come too far. Such a change would cost Olcas greatly both in time and mage energy. Tony was strong with natural protections that would make a takeover such as had created Lucien impossible. Besides, too much had been invested in this tool and the connections he had forged as Lucien Blank. No, things would have to remain as they were for now. Fuming at the necessity, Olcas was tempted to vaporize a scroll Lucien had discarded as worthless. In actuality it was more powerful than anything in the coveted collection hidden upstairs. He held off. While that particular scroll was of no use to Olcas, destroying it would waste energy and accomplish nothing to forward his goals. Best to find the reference Lucien sought to further guide the incompetent in the right direction. The fact that Olcas's surest way of guiding Lucien was to pose as a harmless familiar galled Olcas more than the need to work through the man at all. The indignity infuriated Olcas even further as it searched for the elusive tome. A brief puff of black, acrid smoke in the corner of the basement was the only sign that Olcas had indulged in petty revenge.

Patrick watched his daughter with concern. Her face seemed twice as haggard set off as it was by the fantastic backdrop of this faerie haven. She seemed fragile—emotionally and physically—as she huddled in the folds of a soft blanket, though the chamber was quite comfortable. Each time he looked at her in this unbelievable setting, hysteria and fear battled in his heart. Thirty-three years ago he had left the world of magic and the sidhe behind him in Ireland; thirty-three years ago he had distanced himself from all that reminded him of his home. All that he had fled, both good and bad, came flooding back now with a vengeance as he saw in his daughter's pensive face a pale reflection of the ethereal beauty that blazed in the two sidhe sitting beside her.

In this cold, modern world of America, where the word "dreams" was synonymous with "ambition," magic was something found in Hollywood, and fantasies were *not* discussed, it was difficult to keep faith in the legends that had been such an integral part of life in Ireland. The stories Patrick had grown up with, and believed just as vigorously as his father, became nothing more than the silly stories Da whispered to Kara at twilight.

Patrick had become quite comfortable in his new life. He'd purposely forgotten the speculating whispers that, culminating in a brutal attack, had driven his family across the ocean. Along with that purging, he'd banished his childhood beliefs to the realm of myth. Only now could he see how much he had diminished himself by pushing his heritage away. Even his name had changed from the Gaelic Pádraig to the more recognizable Patrick, a necessity even his parents had seen the wisdom of. With that change he had immersed himself in being American. The only thing he hadn't obliterated upon coming to this new country was his brogue.

Now, over the course of just a few hours, Ireland had reclaimed her own. His life had turned into one of those fantastic stories from his childhood and he hadn't the faintest idea of how to deal with it. It brought back dark memories of the persecution he'd endured as a boy. Unconsciously, Patrick rubbed at one of the whisker-thin scars running down the blade of each hand. What would become of Kara now that magic—wielded by those both "evil" and "good"—had entered her life?

Reaching out to take Kara's hand, Patrick did his best to cover his own anxiety with reassurance. "How are ye holdin' up, lass?"

Kara lifted her eyes to focus on him with just a little effort; giving his hand a gentle squeeze, her only answer was a wan smile. She looked so tired it made his heart ache. At least he reassured himself that she did not look frightened or confused, just a little dazed, as one would expect when hit with so much at once. And all he could do was hold her hand as she turned her attention back to what the sid...Maggie was saying.

"I wish that one o' ye had come to me sooner." The look of concern on Maggie's face took Patrick by surprise. He wouldn't have expected such emotions from one of the Gentry. As if she knew his thoughts, Maggie favored him with a wry smile and continued. "Paddy, I could have helped ye long before ye got yerself into such trouble. I do'na know what good my help can be now; perhaps 'tis'na too late to do somethin' for ye."

Patrick reached over to pat Kara's hand lightly as she unconsciously gripped his more tightly. He hoped she wasn't getting grand ideas of him being magically cured—for that matter, it was all he could do to keep himself from that unbound hope—nothing of what he could remember of Celtic lore spoke of such powerful healing, short of the intervention of a god.

"An' as for Kara," Maggie continued, "there's no doubt I need to be teachin' ye; but it would have been a mite easier if ye had'na first drawn the eye o' the dark mage that seems to have his sights on ye.

"The very first thin' we need to do is protect ye better than I already have." The sidhe continued looking at Kara thoughtfully, "an' second, I think, is to teach ye the trick o' avoidin' the overload that floored ye today."

She held her hand out to Kara. "I know ye're weary, love, but it must be done. If ye come with me I'll show ye what I can for now an' we'll all rest a bit easier."

Kara released his hand and rose smoothly and gracefully to follow. Wanting to go with her, but knowing that he would be in the way, Patrick reached up and grabbed her hand back for a moment. "I'll be right here waitin' for ye."

It was the hardest thing he had ever done, just sitting there as she followed Maggie out of the chamber. But the longer he sat, the more memories surfaced to reinforce his feeling that he could trust this woman. As he turned, preparing to thoroughly interrogate the sidhe who stayed behind, he hoped he was right and that this wasn't just a sample of the charismatic power of these living legends.

Drained by the turmoil of the day and the bizarre twists her life had taken, Kara allowed her father to guide her up the stairs after her lesson with Maggie. Some oddly detached portion of her brain wondered how Papa could be so unfazed by everything. She barely remembered leaving the chambers below, yet he was chatting pleasantly with Maggie's friend, who preceded them.

A headache throbbed at the base of Kara's neck and all she wanted to do was get home to Mathair and the nice, normal world she'd thought they lived in. With one hand on the smooth rock wall and the other lightly gripping her father's arm, Kara tried not to wonder about the warm glow that lit the stairwell, though there was no visible sign of a light or torch. Keeping her eyes focused on the rise and fall of the man's legs in front of her, Kara settled into the rhythm of the climb.

"Careful, lass." Papa caught her before she stumbled into Demne. She was so numb she hadn't realized they'd reached the landing. "Welcome back from where ye were off to."

Kara blushed as Demne turned to see if they needed his help. Mumbling an apology, she found it difficult to meet the gaze of the otherworldly man. Uncomfortable, she slipped her hands into the pockets of her jacket because she had nothing else to do with them. She encountered the chill of metal.

"What's this?" Kara knew the answer before she'd even finished the question. Immediately, the memories that she had been trying to bury from this afternoon came into painfully crisp focus. Not wanting to explain, she merely pulled the knife from her pocket with two fingers. She didn't even want to touch it.   It hadn't been easy to calm herself down from the anger and fear she'd felt earlier; the knife only kindled her emotions once more.

Slowly, as if he were afraid of startling her into panic, Demne reached for the switchblade. For a long moment, none of them said a word. Then Demne spoke gently.

"Can the two o' ye manage goin' back down to Maggie? I imagine she'll need to adjust yer shields usin' this little bit o' nasty business to key them against our friend."

Kara looked at her father as he slipped his arm protectively around her. He looked like he was about to object, but that wouldn't be wise. Her luck was a blessing from the very beginning: finding the knife led to her escape from abduction, and now it would ensure that an evil man could not come after her again. Squaring her shoulders, Kara turned and started down the stairs once more, before Papa could say a word against it.

Even as her father began to protest, Kara found herself reaching back for his arm and tugging him after her. If there were anything more Maggie could do to protect them, then Kara was willing to walk down these stairs a hundred times over for the much added peace of mind.

When Tony let himself into the apartment he shared with Gypsy Rose and dropped into the faded, over-stuffed chair in the living room, the soft singing in the kitchen abruptly halted, followed by a clattering noise as some utensil fell to the floor. For the first time in weeks, both he and his grandmother were home and awake at the same time. Sitting there, without even the energy to lift his hand—let alone his entire body—Tony had an overwhelming feeling that he should have gone right to his room to avoid his more-than-slightly eccentric grandmother. Or better yet, not have come home at all. Maybe he should go out again. No. He was too exhausted. After his encounter with Kara, he already felt like he'd slam-danced with a wrecking ball. Of course, he didn't feel like dealing with Gypsy Rose either, not when he could quite clearly hear a rapid stream of burning, liquid syllables pouring out behind the kitchen door, among them at least one declaration of "stupid, foolish boy!"

He could clearly picture in his mind's eye the bent and ancient woman peeling the paint off the walls with her language. She was really his great-grandmother and her name wasn't Rose, though that was the name on the storefront below where she liberated vast amounts of cash from bored housewives and love-anxious teenagers. But she was a Rom, a gypsy, and he respected her even when he was ready to tell the rest of the world to go to hell. Though he had to admit, some portion of that respect was healthy fear. What she did in the store below may or may not be chicanery, but he knew the power that lay beneath her deceptive appearance. With that in mind, it was time to drag himself off to his room. It was the best way to stay out of Gypsy Rose's way. In fact, as he sat upright, Tony realized that the only person he feared more than his gypsy grandmother was Lucien. Both of them were frightening in the grips of anger, but Lucien....

Lucien! Tony jerked to his feet and stumbled back out the front door in an exhausted run, letting it slam behind him. He had been so fried by what had happened earlier that he'd automatically gone home. Here he had been sitting, idly thinking of his grandmother and whether it was worth the effort of walking across the apartment to avoid her, while down in Chinatown Lucien waited for him to show up with the girl. He had to get there fast. It was bad enough that he was showing up alone, without adding to the situation by being late.

Tony was so caught up in his panicked flight once he reached the sidewalk that he collided hard with a steel-framed door that appeared out of nowhere. A battered cab idled on the curb beside him. Its back door had opened in his path.

Enraged, he turned on the passenger. "Hey! What the hell's your problem, ya jack..." He stopped dead in the middle of his tirade as his battered senses absorbed the face of the man leaning out of the open door. Unnoticed tremors, an equal mixture of adrenaline and fear, ran through Tony's body as he met Lucien's icy gaze.

"Get in...*now*."

Chapter 19

Bone weary and with the depths of her gut roiling with turmoil, Maggie slumped against the spell-wreathed pedestal in her workshop. She could vaguely sense the pulse of Quicksilver beneath the surface, but only because her own magic was so tightly woven around it. Its energy practically mocked her exhaustion. After dealing with Kara and her father, she couldn't have felt more tired than if she'd sparred with the great hero Cuchulainn himself, and yet, she still didn't know what to do about the situation she faced. On every level, she felt drained: emotionally, physically, mentally, and magically. Some selfish part of her ached to lay her burden down, but long ago her kin had sworn an oath to watch over the Clan O'Keefe; she herself was one of those sworn to the duty of Bean Sidhe. That very oath had brought her across an ocean. Now it called on every resource she had to protect Kara and her family. Besides, some part of Maggie was deeply afraid that whatever conflict was growing would impact even on the sidhe themselves, if left unhindered.

She was alone now, except for Beag Scath. Demne had left with Kara and Patrick, vowing to see them both home in safety. Maggie was grateful he was gone for now. She needed the solitude to recover. It bothered her that she was so drained. Every time she gained back some of the energy she'd lost confronting the entity residing in Quicksilver, something happened that caused her to spend it again.

There was no denying it, though; after this afternoon, it was absolutely necessary to reinforce Kara's protections. At least this time Maggie had been able to work directly with the girl to pull the raw mage-energy from Kara herself, which ensured that she was still protected if something happened to Maggie. She also placed protections on Patrick and provided him with a second protective bobble for Barbara. Finally, once Demne got them home, he promised to add his own shields to those Maggie already had on the house itself, reinforcing them as he was those on the sidhe strongholds throughout the city. It wouldn't do to safeguard Kara, only to have her coerced by threats on her home and family.

Yes, Maggie was weary, and rightly so. But she had some time to rest and she most definitely was going to take advantage of it. Something told her she was soon going to need all the energy she could gather. The waterfall chamber beckoned her and she was more than willing to answer its call.

As she turned to leave the workroom, she nearly groaned aloud. There, just reaching the bottom of the stairs, was Kara. Patrick and Demne were right behind her. Looking from one to the other, Maggie noticed a wicked little knife in Demne's hand.

"'Tis our friend's," Demne said, without need of further explanation.

Taking a deep breath and shaking loose the tight muscles in her shoulders, Maggie held out her hand for the knife. All she wanted to do was go back to her chamber and soak in the pool until she was so relaxed every muscle was limp. Instead, she had more work to do.

No rest for the weary, eh? Maggie soul-spoke her mate so the mortals would not hear.

Aye, and weary ye must be an ye're resortin' to cliché, he answered her. *The lass chose to come back down. I think it'll ease her heart, knowin' he canna harm them once yer done.*

Demne handed Maggie the blade. Too tired for words, she motioned Kara and her father forward as she mentally prepared to adjust the shields. How fortunate that Kara realized she had the knife, Maggie thought as she keyed the protections against the young man; he would be unable to even touch her now, magically or physically.

"Do'na worry, Kara," Maggie finally spoke as she finished her adjustments, "yer safe from any direct attempt that young man can make." She gave Kara and her father a considering look. This lesson was one they both needed to learn; best teach it now, while the situation was fresh in their minds and the consequences vividly clear to them. "Ye need to know, if ye had kept this in yer pocket, it would have provided the enemy a way past yer defenses. The shields would have proven useless...this knife servin' as a foot in the door."

She let her warning sink in, noting Patrick's tight-lipped anger reflected in Kara's expression. They were so new to this, for all the influence Conall O'Keefe had on their education. It was one thing to be raised on tales of faerie and magic, quite another to realize the relevance they had in one's life. Maggie prayed to the Mother Goddess that she would have the chance quite soon to set their minds at ease and educate them in their newfound magical heritage.

"Does that mean the shields are useless?" Kara asked, her tone grim and her eyes betraying a bare glimmer of fear. Maggie could see the girl once again battled uncertainty.

"Na if ye watch me closely." Maggie answered. She then turned to Demne. "Hand me the knife once more."

Kara watched curiously while without a word Demne did as Maggie bid him. Tension shivered beneath her skin at the sight of the wicked thing. It was not a pleasant blade, and, if she looked at it just right, it seemed as if shadows clung to it, dulling the shine of the metal.

A glowing ball quickly formed before Maggie, and as they stood there, the sidhe slowly drew the nasty blade through it. Kara was fascinated at the way the woman's mind molded the magic around it so that it clung to the steel. She could see the energy intensify and condense, thickest around the weapon's surface, and instinctively, Kara understood how Maggie did it. In fact, it was as if Maggie went in slow motion, no doubt ensuring Kara missed nothing.

Kara released a slow, steady breath as the blade emerged on the other side glittering with motes of magic still caught upon it, but with all trace of the thug's energy wiped away. There was no connection left by which the man could slip past the defenses against him.

"Paddy, hand Kara somethin' from yer pocket ye carry regular." Maggie ordered, her attention still focused on Kara. "Now, Kara, do as I did."

Kara accepted her father's wallet. Her senses were so in tune with what Maggie had done that automatically Kara looked for and felt his essence sunk well within the leather. Slowly, hesitantly, she mimicked Maggie's actions. Instead of a tight, condensed ball, hers resembled more of a wispy, cotton-candyish puff, but as she drew the wallet through and focused her mind on molding the magic around it, she was relieved to see her clumsy efforts were at least successful.

"Very good...now if ye sense their touch upon anythin', walk away from it. If 'tis something ye canna leave behind, cleanse it like ye just have that wallet."

That was it? That was supposed to reassure her? She was supposed to either walk away, or hope a spell—sheesh! A spell...real magic—she had just learned would keep her safe? No...no pressure here! Maggie was right...her people skills needed some work.

For a moment there was a pronounced silence as Demne and the mortals stood beside the parked car. The O'Keefes still looked stunned by the massive overload of all that had taken place that day. Demne was merely concerned. Frankly, he wouldn't trust either of them behind the wheel in city traffic at the moment. Gently clearing his throat, the sidhe offered an alternative.

"Why do'na ye leave the drivin' to me?" he exerted a bit of his ethereal charm to soften the suggestion. "That way ye have some time to relax before ye reach home."

Even as he made the offer, Demne knew what must be going through their thoughts. It was almost priceless to watch the perplexed look spread across their faces as they struggled with the concept. It was an old car, still made out of steel and iron, instead of composites and fiberglass. Clearly, Kara and her father wondered how one of the sidhe would not only enter a vehicle of cold iron, but also propose to drive it. Kara was the braver of the two, or simply the more curious.

"How can you even ride in a car?" Kara's forehead was creased ever so slightly. "Doesn't the iron and steel hurt you?"

"When ye're a creature o' myth, child, not all that's said o' ye is true," Demne reached for the keys in Patrick's hand, reinforcing his words. "We do'na fear iron, an' it does'na harm us; we merely respect it."

The humans watched him expectantly, obviously wanting further explanation of his cryptic remark. Demne simply stood there, waiting for them to respond to his offer. Maybe someday he would tell them of Goibhniu the Smith and the gift of immortality he'd given the Tuatha de Danaan, but not tonight. Their minds were too full with all that had taken place. They did not need to know that sidhe, dark or light, out of reverence for the Celtic god, would not harm anyone "protected" by a token of iron. Fortunately, for the safety of the sidhe themselves, not much was made of iron these days.

The look on Patrick's face was something between relief and rebellion. He glanced at his daughter before stepping aside from the front door of the car. Demne offered the man what he hoped was a reassuring smile and slipped into the driver's seat. With mild interest he watched the humans through the side mirror as Patrick opened the door for his daughter and climbed in beside her.

Demne experienced a twinge of envy as Kara settled in beneath her father's arm and noticeably relaxed in the comfort there. He had had children—both sidhe and mortal—in his time, but the last had been born centuries ago. Sidhe children were never so dependent; his own young hadn't needed anything so basic from him as comfort. As for human children, his only one had been very like this Kara, loving and sweet, full of energy and charm. But his daughter was not gifted and had not thrived among the Children of Danu; the mortal world had always called her soul. Her life had been rich and full and she had welcomed him as a part of it, but in the end his little Kelly faded away, like all mortal flowers. Most sidhe could accept the brevity of mortal offspring, but for Demne losing Kelly had been too much.

No matter how he longed to be a father again, he couldn't bear the pain that would come with another mortal child, and wishing for a sidhe child would be like wishing death on one of his kin. For one brief moment his heart betrayed him: he could not suppress a flood of joy at the dream of Maggie heavy with his child. Then, full of guilt, he forced the thought away. His only course lay in cherishing his memories. Demne aimed the car toward the Manhattan Bridge and firmly focused on his driving.

The already tangible silence solidified even further as the O'Keefes' car pulled to a stop before the driveway. Once Kara got out to open the gate, Demne turned slightly in the front seat to look into Patrick's shadow-shrouded face. The sidhe was the first to speak.

"I'm afraid I must enter yer home," he said, "to set the final protections." Patrick felt a chill. Somehow it didn't seem right, letting the Gentry into your home. It was an irrational response—especially after having spent the last three hours rather pleasantly in this...man's company—but that made it no easier to overcome. "An it'll make ye feel better, Patrick, yer missus'll have no idea that anythin' is happenin', but either way, I must come in."

"W..." Patrick's voice stuck as he tried to speak, his throat dry with the exhausting strain of the day. He tried again. "Why? Canna ye do yer business from the outside?"

"Were I to set the shields from outside I'd also be outside their protection, leavin' me vulnerable to any with the power to sense what's goin' on," Demne answered, a neutral look settled across his eyes. "If ye do'na mind, I'd rather na call down an' attack upon myself makin' sure yer safe inside."

There was a strained moment while Patrick felt himself flush. He thought he saw a glimmer of pity in that inhuman face. He could only imagine what the sidhe saw in his own. *Could he trust the safety of his family to a creature whose expressions he could barely read? Was the man really dedicated to the safety of Patrick's family?* It took the opening of the front door to break the stalemate. Kara, still standing beside the gate, jumped, and the two in the car unlocked their gaze.

"Patrick? Kara?" Barbara called from the open screen door. "What in the world is going on?" She fell silent in confusion when she noticed her husband wasn't the one behind the wheel. The porch light revealed her expression—and the color of her face—going through a rapid series of changes, none of them boding well for Patrick. That helped him make up his mind.

"Fine then, I'll trust ye," he answered the waiting man, pushing away the moment's doubt and fixing a grateful look in its place. "Yer welcome in my home." As Patrick climbed quickly from the car he was startled to realize he actually meant it.

Moving aside so the sidhe could pull the rest of the way into the driveway, Patrick turned toward the house and his wife waiting by the door. He sighed as he realized that he was more afraid of being alone in the house with Barbara, at that moment, than with any number of the Gentry. At least the presence of company would keep his skin intact for a little while, but from the look on Barbara's face he was in for it once Demne left.

"Patrick Kyle O'Keefe!" As he came close enough to hear his wife's ominously low voice, Patrick didn't need magic to confirm he was in bad graces with Barbara. "You have exactly the time it takes that man to get within hearing distance to explain what possessed you to pick a fight with Arn—who's not just your doctor, but your friend—*and* then disappear to goodness knows where for the entire day without even a phone call—and finally show up at home with a stranger driving the car!"

Thinking back on the events of that day, Patrick shook his head ruefully. "'Tis sorry I am, love, but that's in no way enough time." His wife must have seen in his face some fraction of the tale he would tell—as well as his fortunate willingness to tell it—for as they waited for Kara and the sidhe to join them on the steps Patrick could see her composing her expression into something suitable for greeting a guest.

"Barbara, this is Demne, one whose recent an' future efforts toward us place us in his debt." Demne solemnly bowed his head, shaking hands not being a custom of his kind. Then Patrick turned to the sidhe, who stepped forward with the dignity of ceremony.

"A blessin' upon yer hearth," Demne intoned.

Something about the sidhe's delivery gave the greeting a distinctly formal feel. Not exactly sure how to continue, but guided by some fragment of memory no doubt gleaned from the tales Da used to tell, Patrick responded, "Ye're welcome on this side o' the threshold. Enter freely, an' count yerself both kith an' kin."

As the words left his mouth he could feel they were the right ones. He felt almost as if he had passed a test. A quick glance at Demne's eyes betrayed a glint of mirth and mischief that had for a moment triumphed over the seriousness of their purpose. Patrick was almost annoyed that the Fair One had felt the need to remind him of the tradition he had forsaken when he'd taken up his new life this side of the ocean. Laying his arm across his wife's shoulder, he motioned for Kara to lead the way into the house and let Demne follow her before he allowed himself to ever so slightly rest his weight on Barbara. He was so tired, and the evening wasn't yet over.

The moment Kara entered the house a blur of motion hurled toward her. She cringed back against Demne, who spoke to her in a low voice that only she was near enough to hear. "Calm yerself, love," he said softly, his words already settling her, "'Tis only yer wee friend, an' a lovely, irrepressible catling she is." Kara's body trembled in reaction and her face grew hot with embarrassment. She exerted extreme will to calm herself as he laid a soothing hand on her shoulder, steadying her against the tremors. "There's a lass, ye must be strong just a while yet. For yer parents' sake, if nothin' more."

Her legs now under control, Kara bent down to scoop Pixie into her arms. Without a word she nuzzled her face into the cat's thickening, pre-winter coat and moved on to the living room. More than anything, she'd rather be climbing the stairs to her room, the sanctuary she'd been craving lately. Instead, Kara curled herself in a corner of the couch and waited for the others to join her, her ears filled with the soft rumble of Pixie's purrs.

"You can sit if you like," Kara told the sidhe as her parents entered the room. She tried not to look at her mother, tried not to notice the worry, bewilderment, and annoyance that crowded her face. In fact, she couldn't even meet her father's gaze and the unsettled glint of his tired eyes at having his world turned askew once again. "I think Mathair would appreciate it if we all did some explaining."

Kara's words left a heavy silence in their wake. The mortals in the room were stilled by the uncomfortable prospect of where to begin and how much to tell. The sidhe merely waited, conscious that it wasn't his place to make either decision. The tension in the air grew more tangible as Kara and her father exchanged uncertain glances and Barbara O'Keefe's exasperation flooded her face. As Kara cleared her throat to speak, however, she was interrupted first by a sudden feline growl from Pixie and then by her own amazement as Demne flowed to his feet in one graceful, dangerous motion that was mirrored by the cat beside her. Two sets of green eyes stared intently toward the back of the house; two lithe forms—man shape and cat shape seemed to almost blur before her startled eyes—stood poised, defensively gauging their surroundings with every sense at their disposal. If Demne had been equipped with a tail, Kara was confident that it would have been thrashing as violently as Pixie's.

Letting loose a string of liquid syllables whose beauty was at odds with their obvious intent, Demne was instantly at Kara's side. So quickly it was hard for her to say when he began to move, the sidhe pulled her from the couch, barely allowing her to gain her balance before turning toward the front door with her arm still in his grasp.

With fear for her clear on each of their faces, her parents lunged into his path, mistaking Demne's actions for the threat itself, rather than a response to the danger they could not sense. Though everything was happening too quickly for her to explain to them, Kara knew that the danger was somewhere beyond the kitchen, not right beside her; she could feel the weight of it upon her back in the same way she would have known if someone stared at her on the train. A sudden flash in the air left her parents looking dazed until Demne noticed they blocked his way. Growling he swept them before him.

"Out! The protections will'na last as ill-set as that, just long enough for us to get away. Move! *Now!*"

With a forethought that Kara couldn't believe, her mother grabbed the keys to her own car, fortunately parked in front of the house, rather than behind the driveway gate. That was all that Kara had time to notice as the five of them—Pixie had been waiting for them at the car—piled in. Somehow Demne again ended up behind the wheel and they sped away from the house. At some point Kara was sure she would be grateful for that fact, but right now she was cowering beneath the shields Maggie had erected just that day. Beyond her shields something voracious attempted to bring them down, intent—and she was sure of this—on devouring *her*.

CHAPTER 20

Alone in her pawnshop, making sure everything was locked up for the night and that the side door was open for Demne when he returned, Maggie was unprepared for the flash of terror that drove her to her knees. She was so tired and unprepared that throat-ripping sobs shook her without resistance.

The sidhe were a strong race, but Maggie had been running her resources to the dregs over and over again for almost a week. She was used to pulling the energy she needed from her surroundings, for it was put to passive purposes that didn't need her constant attention. Since she'd encountered Kara, most of what she had been called upon to craft were active defenses; spells that required Maggie to remain aware of all that occurred to those she was guarding.

Stumbling toward the stairs to her underground haven, Maggie wept uncontrollably as she struggled to regain her mental balance. She needed to compose herself enough to learn what happened, and what action it required of her. Several deep breaths settled her sufficiently to change her course. What she needed now was clear sky above and enough focus to allow her to read the threads that connected her to Kara and her family.

Maggie wasn't surprised when Beag Scath materialized at the screen door as she made herself comfortable on the side steps. Shooing him away with a thought, she began a series of meditation exercises to bring her thoughts to clarity. In less than a minute she was ready to reach out with her mind. What she sensed startled her completely out of the calm she had obtained, though not before she had seen all she needed to know. The enemy had struck sooner than expected, and Demne had barely gotten Kara and her family away in time. They were on their way back to Yesterday's Dreams...with Lucien and his man close behind them.

Lulled by Lucien's lack of formal training in the use of his powers, Maggie had assumed that it would be days before he was organized enough for an attack. She had confidently sent Kara and her father off with Demne, knowing that her mate would anchor the protections they had both prepared. Never for a moment did it occur to her that anything might go wrong. She had figured that they would all have a day or two at least to regain their energy—and in the case of Kara, to examine her own capabilities. The few things Maggie had taught the girl today were a start, but though her powers appeared greater than Lucien's, her control and understanding were less, and her instinctive ability was unreliable. Besides, Maggie was beginning to suspect that Lucien was just as much a tool as his henchman. While she grew more confident his incompetence was real and not feigned, she worried about the unknown force: she had no idea how much control it might have over him.

"Ahhh!"

Opening her eyes even as she stood in one graceful movement, Maggie nearly struck out before she realized the anguished cry had heralded no threat. Maggie calmed herself with a few deep breaths and, thinking of her tear-streaked face and prone position, she could forgive Old Molly the startling cry. Right then, Maggie came to a decision she hadn't known she would have to make. Neither of their interests was served by her attempts to maintain a charade of normalcy. Hoping it wouldn't be too much for the woman—who had clearly suspected anyway—Maggie drew her inhuman majesty around herself and dispelled the glamory that made her appear human.

Standing before Molly as Cliodna of the Tuatha de Danaan, she was careful to remain still and unthreatening as she spoke her calm, but urgent words. "Molly, 'tis time all were clear between us." Maggie waited as the woman's eyes took in her true form, tear streaked face and all, careful to keep her hands by her side and her body relaxed. Her mind was ready though, should it be necessary to cloud the woman's thoughts to preserve her sanity.

Molly trembled violently, but stood her ground.

"As ye see me, Molly, I am," Maggie continued, when it was clear that the strength was not with the woman to speak, though she had found enough to stand her ground, "an' ye had no doubts, I'm sure, but I'm showin' ye just the same ye were right."

"Why?" Molly found her voice to ask. "Why now, then?"

"Do ye remember the lass ye ran off? She an' her family are in frightful danger. What's more, they're headin' here with that danger quick behind." Maggie paused to allow the implications to set in. "I fear for ye, Molly, an' any others around. I can protect yer place, ye can be sure, but I wish ye away from the danger."

With those words, Maggie noticed several changes take place in Molly's expression. Fear and doubt and sheer stubbornness fought for dominance. Maggie actually couldn't tell which one had triumphed, for Molly carefully shrouded her eyes with a calm look.

"Ye can protect my place, can ye?" Molly cocked her head thoughtfully and looked first at the pub and then back to Maggie. "Grateful I'd be for yer protection, an' perhaps I'll be closin' the pub today, no need to be puttin' the custom in danger." Maggie felt unrealized tension pour from her limbs. She knew Molly fairly well, and had been expecting something of a fight to get her to go somewhere safer. Knowing how much she had to do in the short time before trouble arrived, Maggie smiled gratefully to the woman.

"If ye focus on the pub with yer sight, ye'll see a bit o' protection already in place." Maggie could hear a gasp of astonishment come from Molly as the woman did as she suggested. "Now keep watchin' an' ye'll see them grow brighter. I'm keyin' them against those I know mean us ill." She described what she was doing more to reassure Molly than out of any expectation that the woman would be able to recognize her spell.

"What do these blackguards look like?" Molly asked, her voice hardened by the steel of an Irishwoman protecting her own. "Is there aught they can do against what ye've worked here?"

Maggie described both Lucien and the boy, explaining that they were the only ones any of them had seen. "There's another who guides them all, but he has'na shown his face where we could see it." A thought occurred to Maggie; Molly had one of the gifts known to crop up in the Celts from time to time. Perhaps she had a bit of another.

"Molly, have ye've aught of the mind sight as well?"

The woman looked thoughtful a moment. "That I could'na say, though there was talk of a long-dead aunt who claimed it, may the good Lord rest her soul."

"Can we have such luck?" Maggie looked thoughtfully at Molly. "'Tis oft that one gift is'na found alone. I've somethin' I want to try, Molly, if yer willin'."

As Molly nodded her assent, Maggie focused her thoughts, calling to mind everything she knew of Lucien Blank and his tool: their faces, their voices, the feel of their "signature" to Maggie's own sight, what they'd done so far, and what Maggie feared their intent might be. Bringing all of that to the forefront, she projected it at Molly and watched her face for a reaction. The one she received was a disappointment.

"Well, then...will ye be doin' whatever ye planned?"

Maggie shook her head ruefully. "I already have, Molly. Looks like ye're blessed with but one o' the gifts...unless...yes! 'Tis worth a try." Maggie focused her thoughts again. This time she held them clear in her own mind and kept them there.

"Okay, Molly," the sidhe said in a vague voice, "try to look at my mind. Focus on the spot between my eyes an' then imagine lookin' beyond it."

For a long moment both women stood rigid, lost in their own concentration. Finally, Maggie let go of the images. Either Molly had read them or not. There was no more time to waste on trying. As her eyes focused once more, she nearly laughed at the look of complete astonishment on Molly's face.

"It worked! It truly worked!" Molly whispered. Her face was bright with the wonder of it all, though fear and anger still lurked beneath her eyes.

Already Maggie's mind had leapt to what needed doing next. She had warned Molly and armed her the best she could; now she must do the same for herself and those who rushed here with the thought of safety on their minds.

Leaving Molly to her arrangements, Maggie hurried to take care of her own. It was time to summon her fellow sidhe. Sadly, there were few on this side of the ocean close enough to come to their aid. Still, any help was better than standing against Lucien's forces with just two sidhe and whatever aid the mortals could lend. Knowing she would need all of her energy for the battle, Maggie hurried to the phone in her office to call the others.

They sped toward Manhattan. Behind them, the normal sounds of traffic were frequently punctuated by the screech of brakes, angry car horns, and occasionally by the torturous sound of collision. Amazingly, Demne's evasive driving wasn't responsible for any of the accidents. No, it was those hunting them who seemed to relish the mayhem their pursuit caused. Without a doubt they knew how it amplified the anguish of their prey.

Huddled in the back seat, Kara clutched Pixie in her arms, not quite sure exactly which of them she was trying to comfort. Though the cat's tail twitched violently, she didn't object to being held so tightly. Kara was relieved. In the midst of this insanity, it helped to have something to hold.

Other than the occasional, sub-vocal growl from Pixie, everyone in the car was silent. Looking at the others, Kara could feel her own fury grow toward the monsters in the car behind them.

Kara's parents were caught in the whirl of confusion caused by those chasing them. Mathair, seated beside her in the back seat, kept looking at the back of Papa's head as if she wanted to believe that all would be well as long as she could see him. Kara could barely see the outline of his face, but she could imagine from his clenched jaw that it was a fierce sight. It was probably a good thing her mother couldn't see his expression from where she sat or she might lose all hope, along with her illusion.

When she wasn't looking behind them, Kara glanced at the rearview mirror, trying to catch Demne's eye. Unfortunately, he was too preoccupied to reassure anyone. By the set of his shoulders, his nearly tangible concentration, and the shimmer of magic that danced around Mathair's car, Kara was pretty sure he was the reason for the miraculous way they avoided causing accidents themselves. It would be best not to distract him. She looked away, not wanting to dwell on his face when it was such a vague, disturbing mask.

Once again Kara glanced out the rear window and this time her heart lurched. Behind them, not more than two cars away, she could see a taxicab. From this distance, she could just make out the guy who'd tried to grab her this afternoon sitting in the passenger seat. As the cab swerved dangerously to pass the intervening cars, Kara could see the look on the cabby's face. That look of insane, helpless terror unnerved her more than anything else. Seeing her future in that face, should their pursuers take them, Kara shrugged off the paralyzing fear trying to root in her heart. She refused to have anything to do with that possible future.

A quick glance in the rearview mirror told her that Demne was well aware the hounds were closing. As their eyes met, an understanding passed between them; at all costs, they could not be taken. A burst of desperate speed and a moment's reckless driving helped them pull away.

When next she looked around, Kara could see no sign of the cab that had been following them. She then noticed that the sound of the traffic had settled down into its normal, disgruntled roar. Where had they gone? Somehow Kara found no comfort in their apparent escape; some part of her was sure it heard the snap of a trap in the sudden return to normalcy.

Even from three cars away, Lucien could clearly see the face of the girl named Kara, one half of the trophy in this race. Gripped by a desire that could have been called lust, had it been physical, the man tightened his control on the cabbie. They must not get away. He wished he had time to summon some of his fiendish pets, but he did not wish to lose their prey, and it took all his concentration to maintain his hold over the driver.

They wove even more recklessly between the intervening traffic. Some small, unoccupied segment of Lucien's brain noticed Tony's discomfort as the car they were chasing took desperate risks to pull away. Lucien was too contemptuous of the boy's flawed response to wonder at what motivated his feelings. Perhaps it was time to discard this tool. It was too weak for the plight of others. Almost as if he were reading Lucien's thoughts, Tony turned in the front seat to look back.

"Um, don't ya think...." Tony paused, his face taut with the knowledge that he was about to make an unpopular comment. "Don't ya maybe think if we chase 'em too hard they might have an accident? The girl could get killed or something. We don't wanna like permanently lose her."

Annoyed at the accuracy of Tony's statement, Lucien gave him a withering glance. Such logic disrupted his enjoyment of the chase. The only problem was, Tony was right; Kara was no use to him dead. "Slow down." Lucien growled and loosened his grip on the cab driver.

He cast ahead with a tendril of now-freed power and anchored it to the car in front of them. They would not escape him now. No matter where they went in the city, he would track them. Let the frightened rabbits think they'd gotten away safely; let them lower their guard even just a bit. When they did, Lucien would snap closed his jaws and claim Kara as his own. Once he had the girl, it was only a matter of time before he breached the stronghold of Yesterday's

Dreams and laid claim to its treasures. On that day, he would have the bitch who ran the place at his mercy; what a pity for her there wasn't even one hint of mercy in him. Laughing nastily, Lucien sat back and let his thoughts fill with images of his eventual triumph.

CHAPTER 21

"Greetin's, Cousin," Maggie's voice reflected her strain as she called her final number. So far, only four of those she had talked to could come to their aid; the others were faced with problems of their own that could not be ignored and could only promise to come once those troubles were resolved. "Are ye free? I have a bit o' a problem I could use yer help with." Maggie was relieved when the voice on the other end of the phone gave its assent, promising to be there upon the quickest wind.

Feeling slightly better about the situation, Maggie hung up the phone. Thanks to the marvel of speed-dial—and her short, grim list—she finished with her phone calls before the gel ink dried on the paper. Seven sidhe—counting herself and Demne—should be more than a match for anything Lucien could call to bear against them. She couldn't allow herself to think any differently, not if she was to keep her own spirits ready for battle.

Maggie made the rounds of the rath and the upstairs apartment, gathering every item in which she had ever invested personal energy. She needed every advantage for the upcoming battle. Then, settled on the couch in the apartment with all of the items around her, Maggie withdrew her power from them, replenishing her body's own depleted reservoirs. For the first time all week, she felt invigorated.

Just as she completed her own preparations, the sound of the doorbell summoned her to the intercom.

"Hallo?" As she answered it, she noticed the absence of Beag Scath. She wasn't surprised; the sprite generally became subdued when tension was strong in the air. He was probably holed away somewhere trying to avoid the confusion.

"Did ye order a couple o' barely controllable an' ever-hungry guard dogs?" An undercurrent of laughter could be heard behind the male voice on the speaker.

"Ye're both welcome on this side o' the threshold, Cian, as long as yer housebroken," Maggie answered them warmly. "Come along up, the door is open to ye."

Moving on to the kitchen, Maggie searched for something to offer the new arrivals and those that would follow. They would all need their energy for this confrontation. She took a moment to set out soft cider and muffins next to the bowl of fruit that was always present on the kitchen table. Then Maggie went to greet the two guests coming up the stairs.

"Ye're the first to arrive," Maggie said as they entered the apartment. Considering the situation ahead of them, she figured this was not the time for formalities. While she led them to the living room, she told them what had occurred in the past week, opening her mind to them so they could see whom they would face. In return, each of them shared with her further evidence of growing trouble.

"I canna say for sure if this Lucien has had a hand in our misfortunes," Cian added, when the two were done cataloging their own problems, "but ye'll forgive me if I hope he is; I'd hate to think there are two adversaries out there dividin' our attention." Eri, a quiet woman of the sidhe whom Maggie knew only in passing, nodded in agreement.

The ring of the doorbell interrupted any further discussion they might have had. Maggie didn't regret the diversion; she had enough to worry about with the threat of battle before them. It did her heart no good to think that this might not be the end of their troubles. Leaving the two to occupy themselves, Maggie went to let in the new arrival.

Demne's driving didn't slow with the disappearance of their pursuers. Even if the feeling of being hunted didn't still oppress him, he was getting disturbing feelings from Maggie. Not for the first time he cursed the limited nature of his soul-speaking ability. It was useless to him over a distance. He was hoping to find safety at Yesterday's Dreams. He wasn't completely sure his hopes would be realized.

"We'll be there soon." Everyone in the car jumped as Demne broke the taut silence. "Ready yerselves to move quickly, I do'na ken what will be waitin' for us."

Kara was the first to find her voice. "What about Maggie? She's had no warning."

"Ye're wrong there, love," Demne was proud of the girl's concern for Maggie. It heartened him that she was prompt to speak out for another. Not once had she complained or worried out loud about herself, though he was certain the thoughts were crowding her mind. "Maggie's had fair warnin' enough to ready a force o' our own, to be sure. She'll keep the way open for us, but we must be fast." The humans accepted his words without comment. They were very close now. He slowed the car a fraction to turn the last corner. After a moment, he continued, "We must ready ourselves as we can, for sure there's no doubt Lucien's readied his own atta...."

Demne's voice trailed off as he took in the sight before him. There, in front of Yesterday's Dreams were six very agitated sidhe, poised to strike. There was no threat in evidence, but there was some sign they'd already done battle.

What is it? he soul-spoke Maggie, his thoughts sharp and searching. *What has all o' ye bristlin'?* There was no response. Maggie was not an alarmist; something must have happened for the guardians to be at the ready like this. Demne sensed his love's turbulent emotions and grew puzzled. His agitation increased with each passing second. What were they waiting for?

As if in answer the air crackled and the automobile shook with the force of a collision, though there was not another moving car in sight, and they had not veered toward any of those parked along the street. Demne hit the brakes and looked around with sharp eyes.

Maggie, will ye be explainin' or na? What are we facin' here? He could see her gaze snap in his direction when his mental queries finally penetrated her focus.

Apparently more o' the same from the other day at the Clinic, only they are'na botherin' to hide themselves in the bodies o' innocents. A steady stream of images followed her thoughts: the sidhe arriving to lend their aid, only to be beset on the threshold by ethereal demonics. *Watch yerself!*

Demne cursed as dark and unnatural shapes converged upon their vehicle. It was as if the clouds moved to encase them. Again the car shook and Barbara O'Keefe moaned in terror. Another tremor racked them, as if boulders were tossed against the car's frame or wild bulls charged them. He watched as Kara released the little catling and wrapped her arms around her mother. Kara...this was no coincidence.

No wonder Lucien had not bothered to pursue them, he thought, *when he obviously had known where they would flee.*

Eyes glowing poisonous green and teeth that dripped noxious venom flashed across the amorphous forms that surrounded them; the demons tested their bounds. Before they could venture an attempt to breach the interior Demne drew power to himself with the speed of a cat materializing at mealtime. He caressed it, charged it, encouraged its glow until the car seemed filled with fire, to those with the right sight. While that blatant display distracted their attackers, he subtly drew more power beyond the immediate surface of the car, well behind the circling demons. He waited until their greedy eyes glittered and they began to lash out at their own numbers as each creature coveted the wealth of mage energy for themselves.

"When I tell ye to run, ye bloody well do it, ye hear?" Without looking to see if the humans acknowledged his order, Demne snapped in the outer ring of power until it crushed the evil ones against the all-steel body. For a moment they were held immobile and he seized upon that, using the opportunity to release his hold upon the awesome force he'd contained within the car. Like suddenly released insulation foam, the mage energy immediately expanded out, flooding over the trapped demonics, frying them in a brutal overload and scattering their misty forms like chaff on the wind. He did not delude himself that they were destroyed—it was deuced hard to destroy any creature of the sinister plane once it entered the mortal world. Instead, he took advantage of their disruption to get his charges to safety.

"Now!" he barked, and threw open all the car's doors with a thought, as he pulled into an empty space before old Molly's pub. They all moved in stunned silence as they leapt from the car and dashed toward the pawnshop, Kara carrying the cat in her arms. A second thought on Demne's part slammed the doors behind them and threw the locks. A silly measure, perhaps, but there was no need to call attention to themselves by leaving a literally open invitation for any local car thieves.

The once-calm street crackled with tension as they ran for the alleyway. Stopping beside the hawthorn tree, Demne scanned the street for any other signs of Lucien's forces, magical or otherwise. There was no one in mortal sight, and Demne could not sense anything gathering beyond the range of his eyes. He had no doubt, though, that Lucien was not far behind his demonic pets.

Turning to enter the alley, he found Maggie standing beside him.

"The others have taken Kara an' her family inside," Maggie's voice was calm, but her flashing eyes betrayed her temper at this further invasion attempt by Lucien and his ilk. Hah! He couldn't resist a moment of exaltation. Another failed invasion attempt. Perhaps the vile man would learn from this humiliation and give up his pursuit. Hah again! Demne thought, this time derisively. That most certainly was not very likely.

"I trust ye do'na mean for them to stay? We'll away with them, aye?" Demne allowed his eyes to trail once more over his beloved as he waited for her to answer. He found it was not difficult to smile, despite what had just happened and the implications behind it, not when he had been worried that Maggie would enter this fight already depleted. But no.... There was now a subtle glow about her, revealing that she had managed to restore herself. That eased his mind regarding their ability to stand against Lucien and his forces. Demne said nothing more in return; this mate of his soul could readily read his feelings for her from his very heart.

"An' where would ye have me take them?" Maggie's words were grim and her eyes like pale jade, hard and cold. His heart told him her harsh feelings were not for him. "We are none o' us in any state to be to be tryin' to defend those mortals here in the open, or anywhere else nearby, at that. An' we canna very well lift our roots an' flee back to Ireland over this, even if the O'Keefes would agree to come with us."

"Can ye na talk any sense into them? It need na be for long..."

"No." The single word was laced with steel, final and immutable. Maggie would argue with him no further.

"Wait, Maggie," Demne laid his hand gently but firmly on her arm, "there's somethin' I must be tellin' ye about yon Patrick."

Maggie turned on him almost impatiently; he could imagine how her nerves must be twanging with the effort to be aware of every minute particle of her shields, just waiting for the next attack to come. If his news had been anything less important he would have waited, but very likely this would be the last time before battle they could talk without being overheard—by their own kin or by the humans. It had to be now. Besides, perhaps the knowledge would help convince her that they should be fleeing to Ireland, rather than digging in at Yesterday's Dreams.

"Love, I've told ye o' my gift," he started, carefully choosing his words, "I know somethin' about whatever I touch—times are when I even see somethin' o' the people I touch. 'Tis rare indeed that'll happen, but it did tonight. Earlier in the shop when ye came through the curtain an' Patrick went unsteady, I reached out to him. I saw him as a lad in Eire playin' on the Rath o' Mullaghmast; Maggie, he was tootin' a toy horn—an' beneath the hill, the earl o' legend stirred as if to rise—but 'twas'na yet time an' he settled back to rest." Demne searched Maggie's face for some sign of surprise; he was disappointed.

Maggie finally spoke. "I'm aware o' what he may be; his Da worked the mill 'til he came across the water. An' have ye na noticed the scarrin' on his hands? It very well might be that our Patrick's the miller's son, then, with the fate o' Eire restin' on his shoulders. Whether 'tis so or na, we still will'na be hoppin' a cloud to Eire. 'Twould only lure that man after."

Demne grimaced but bowed to wisdom. Going or staying, in either case things were going to be tricky. Better to accept it now and ready themselves as best as possible for the impending conflict.

Lucien would be coming. The familiar weight of destiny pressed heavily on their hearts as Maggie and Demne turned to join their companions. It was time to prepare for battle.

CHAPTER 22

In the protected sanctum of Maggie's rath, mortal and immortal watched each other in wary and speculative silence. Scattered around the room where Kara had recovered only hours ago, unfamiliar sidhe sifted through a pile of hastily gathered weaponry in the corner, while others lounged gracefully on the moss-covered seats. The humans stood in a stunned cluster by the door, Kara and her parents watching the strangers anxiously, particularly those arming themselves.

Untouched by the tangible strain of the bipeds present, Pixie promptly extracted herself from Kara's grip and made a thorough investigation of the chamber and its inhabitants. Unable to resist the cat's regal charm, a sidhe woman sitting on the moss bed Kara had earlier occupied reached out to ruffle Pixie's fur. The feline leaned briefly against her knee before moving on to explore the rest of the chamber. As if that liberty had put her at ease, the sidhe's eyes lost their veil of wariness as she looked toward the humans.

"My name's Eri. Would ye be wantin' somethin' to drink, then?" The soft, lilting words filled the silence. With one careful wave of her hand she gestured to the rather ordinary cups stored in a cubbyhole beside the fountain that bubbled from a crack in the wall behind her. That simple kindness dissolved the tension gripping those present.

As the other sidhe relaxed they began to talk among themselves, politely directing their attention away from the nervous mortals. Kara slipped her arm through her mother's and guided her toward the fountain and the sidhe woman waiting patiently to see if they would accept her kindness. Her heart lurched to feel the tremors that shook her mother. Life had become surreal for the O'Keefes, and it wasn't fair that Mathair was more in the dark than any of them. She knew nothing of what had taken place recently and hardly more than that about the legend of the sidhe, let alone the reality. In the few seconds it took to cross the room Kara sent off a fervent prayer for both her mother's safety and her sanity.

"Thank you." She was careful to meet the immortal's eyes, wanting her to see the genuine gratitude there. "I'm Kara, and these are my parents, Patrick and Barbara O'Keefe."

Maggie and Demne appeared in the doorway in time to witness the sidhe forces cautiously introducing themselves to the humans. Their gazes met and they saw the reflection of their own relief in the other's eyes. The history of sidhe-human interaction wasn't an easy one, for all that the species had been known to find love in one another's arms and hearts. There was more of anger, fear, and hatred in their joint past than there was of harmony—on both sides.

Such was not the case tonight. It was clear that though the atmosphere in the chamber was uneasy, those gathered in it were there to fight side-by-side. As Maggie looked into their faces she could see the fierce determination there and it warmed her. Lucien Blank would have a rude surprise this night.

It was only as her eyes came to rest on Kara and her family that Maggie grew worried. These humans weren't equipped to deal with battle of any kind, let alone one involving magic, and yet there weren't enough sidhe to fight and protect them. Patrick could probably hold his own in a physical fight, but barely trained as she was, Kara was magically too vulnerable to outside influences, and her mother could be nothing more than a hindrance in the battle to come. Maggie came to the quick realization that the two women would have to be hidden below. A pressure on her leg caused Maggie to amend her plan; the women, the cat, and the sprite would have to be hidden in the rath.

"We do'na have much time, people," Maggie addressed the room, "there is no doubt Lucien's on his way, an' he will'na be alone. Once ye're all ready, gather yer weapon o' choice an' follow Demne here upstairs." Here she grimaced, "I do'na particularly care for Lucien to know o' my little haven below."

As the sidhe silently armed themselves with assorted blades and staffs and followed Demne out of the chamber, Maggie turned to the O'Keefes. With a wry amusement that could not be quelled by the seriousness of the situation, Maggie noticed that Kara had claimed a sword and Patrick had already helped himself to a cudgel from among the weapons assembled in the corner of the room. Watching him, she struggled with a tough decision; she knew Patrick must be protected, but she also knew their force was much too small not to take advantage of every able-bodied fighter. If they did not survive, there was little chance of him fulfilling his destiny, whatever it may be. How difficult it was to choose, when either option had possibly undesirable outcomes.

"Do'na be gettin' too comfortable with that in yer hands, Paddy," Maggie gave the man an appraising look, "I have'na decided if yer in any shape to be fightin'."

As she stepped forward with one hand reaching out to grasp his shoulder she noticed how he nearly vibrated with nervous tension. "Ye'll na find stoppin' me an easy thin' to do."

"'Tis'na a brawl we go to, Patrick, men will die tonight an' Goibhniu help ye if ye're na prepared to brin' them to such a state, for I have no doubt they will'na have a qualm to serve ye so."

"They come for my daughter, Maggie," Patrick ground out through clenched teeth. "For that I'll dance on their bones 'til there's naught but dust left."

"Aye then, let me get a look at ye."

Maggie was careful to catch his eye as he unconsciously began to raise the cudgel in a defensive move. She kept her gaze steady until his expression went from determined to contrite as he realized what he'd done. Gently pushing aside the weapon, Maggie laid her hand on the man's shoulder and opened her awareness, willing it to flow across the contact and explore the true condition of Patrick O'Keefe. Satisfied, she allowed her hand to fall away, though her heart moaned and keened silently at the hidden devastation the cancer had wrought in him. He was sturdy and steady now, but not for much longer. The warrior in her felt it only fitting that she grant him this chance to die in battle—though realistically it must never come to that—instead of dying so ignominiously, not to mention painfully, of his devouring illness. Aye, for him this wasn't about being needed, it was about a man doing something to protect his daughter. Silently, Maggie soul-spoke the rest of the fighters, warning them he was to come to no harm. If she hadn't understood the intense compulsion he felt, Maggie would have kept him below as well, but he was hale enough to fight and she knew the sidhe would stand by him should he falter. May she not live to regret this choice....

"Take yerself upstairs an' tell the rest I'll follow in but a moment," she murmured to him, "after I've safeguarded yer family below."

She watched him take the stairs two at a time with an energy lent to him by the intense dose of adrenaline coursing through his system. When Kara moved to follow, Maggie blocked her path. She could make a concession for Patrick, but there was no way she was letting Kara up those stairs, no matter how comfortable that sword was in the girl's hand. Maggie had watched over the O'Keefes for years and knew Kara had more than a little proficiency with a blade. That made no difference in her decision.

Turning back to the women, she could see Kara's objections clearly on her face even before she'd regained her composure enough to talk. Maggie didn't allow her to begin; there was no time to argue. Too quick for the girl to stop her, Maggie took the sword away. Stepping back from the doorway, she grasped the strands of magic that flowed around her and, mingling them with a thread of her own, she drew a hasty shield across the entryway, making sure to key it to let Beag Scath through when he finally surfaced. Perhaps he would entertain them enough that Kara's rage would fade before Maggie had to let her out again.

"I hope ye'll be forgivin' me, Kara, but even were ye na the very thin' we're fightin' to protect, ye're scarcely trained up for this type of battle." Maggie turned to the girl's mother and met her eyes with a knowing gaze. "Do'na fear, Barbara, ye'll both o' ye be safe down here until we come for ye." The sidhe didn't mention that should the defenders fall, the barrier would collapse on its own without her magic holding it in place, thus ensuring they would not be trapped in this room forever if Maggie fell.

Without another word, Maggie headed up the stairs, her every step punctuated by Kara's desperate, angry yells. Sparing one more thought—and as little mage energy as possible—the sidhe cancelled the spell lighting the stairs and erected a more substantial barrier across the upper entrance to the subterranean stairwell. Once Maggie gained the landing outside the basement door, she reached out with a thought and triggered the latent protections she had woven long ago, shields that hid the very presence of the opening she'd just come through. As she made her way up to the apartment, Maggie was confident that the O'Keefe women were as safe as she could make them.

At the sound of hurried footsteps on the stairs, those gathered in the small kitchen tensed, hands unconsciously gripping weapons and feet carefully shifting balance. Those in the living room flowed quickly through the doorway, battle-ready. The strain of not knowing from which direction the impending attack would approach had left all of them agitated. No one relaxed when Maggie walked through the apartment door, though all the weapons were lowered. As she came in, she laid the sword Kara had been holding on the table. Each of the sidhe settled back in their waiting places; only Patrick drew close to the new arrival.

"Will they be safe, Maggie?" The anxiety he felt was broadcasting from every inch of his body. "I could'na bear it if they came to harm."

"We'll all o' us see to their safety, Paddy." Patrick found himself reassured by Maggie's words and comforted by her grip on his arm. "Ye have my word on it."

Relief and determination flooded his veins as Maggie raised her voice to be heard by all those gathered. "Ye've all o' ye pledged to stand beside me to keep Kara from the hands o' Lucien Blank an' whatever force he brings against us." Patrick couldn't help feeling a little awe as Maggie paused to meet the gaze of each of those present; these sidhe, these lords and ladies of the Shining Court were here to protect his daughter. Patrick's confidence grew as Maggie continued. "My thanks to each o' ye."

"An' mine as well." All of the sidhe looked startled as Patrick spoke. "I know yer here because this Lucien's a danger to ye if he gets a hold o' my Kara, but the truth is, I do'na care why; ye're here to protect my little lass, an' I thank ye for it."

The dignity of Patrick's little speech dissolved in moments as something brushed against his leg. Startled, he yelled and jumped away, nearly trampling Pixie, who had resurfaced from wherever she'd been hiding and decided to twine herself between his legs. Between one second and the next, Patrick was faced with a room full of elven warriors with all their weapons trained in his direction.

He didn't know what was more unsettling: that sight, or the next moment, when they all dissolved into laughter bordering on hysterical.

Ting...ting...ting.... **With a ghostly flare of greenish light, the rhythmic sound** of pennies skipping out of sight down the stairs taunted Kara as she leaned against the cavern wall, contemplating her prison. She had already wandered the chamber looking for some way to get free. Nothing presented itself as a possible key, and the stairway landing was already littered with the few objects she'd tried to use to disrupt what blocked their way. She was only tossing pennies because the flash it produced gave her something to look at other than the lost, terrified look on her mother's face. Kara had already tried to comfort her, but drew away at the panicked shudder Mathair had been unable to control. Between the attack on the house and then the car, too much had happened that her mother couldn't grasp, but Kara's own efforts to escape using the little magic she'd learned agitated Mathair even more than being unable to walk through an open doorway. So, here they were trapped in a room by thin air, with Kara trying to pretend that she did not frighten her mother senseless.

Somewhere above her people were fighting to keep them safe. She had no idea how they faired and couldn't stand that she was not among them. That fact added to Kara's frustration. It didn't matter to her that she had never fought outside of practice bouts or competition—by magical or mundane means—there were people somewhere outside this room fighting, and maybe dying, for her, and Papa was one of them. As she fumed in her forced hiding, Kara continued to pelt the barrier with change. At least it gave her something to do...until the coins ran out.

Her actions became so automatic that she almost didn't notice when several pennies came shooting back through the doorway at her; only Mathair's startled gasp called Kara's attention away from wherever it had wandered. Curious, she tossed another coin, only to have two come sailing back. Their tinkling *ping* against the cavern wall was joined by little musical laughs from the shadow of the stairwell. As Kara peered intently at the doorway, Beag Scath crept forward, his bright eyes scanning the floor for more pennies. When he found none, he reached for a plastic mug she had tossed through earlier and threw it back into the chamber. The flash it produced was even brighter and the sprite filled the air with merry giggles. Apparently he liked this game.

Desperate for any means to get out Kara moved toward the door; if she could coax the magical Beag Scath closer, he could be the key she was looking for.

"Hello, my friend," Kara greeted the sprite from her new seat next to the doorway. She held up her hand to the invisible barrier and watched with glee as he mirrored her actions, his tiny hand disappearing from sight behind her own larger one. "What are you up to?"

Kara didn't expect a verbal answer, but the look of mischief in the sprite's eyes was answer enough; whatever he'd been doing, it wasn't what he was supposed to be. Suddenly, she could actually feel Beag Scath's hand connect with her own. As the barrier sparkled in a way that was different from the way it reacted to the objects she'd thrown through it, Kara felt a glimmer of hope, and something else. *Did she imagine it, or was the resistance weaker?* She started to step forward, hoping this was her chance to move through the barrier. Her need to get free caused Kara to move with less caution and her haste startled the sprite into stepping backwards, breaking his contact with her hand. With jarring abruptness and a dazzling light show, Kara found herself falling back on her ass with ghostly lights still dancing before her eyes. Shaking her head to clear the afterimage of the flash, Kara found her mother by her side ready to help her up, though she still had the look of a skittish animal. Once Kara was standing, Mathair backed away, love and doubt dancing around each other in her eyes.

Kara felt a surge of anger pulse through her body, throbbing even in her clenched teeth. It was the anger she felt for everyone who had played merry havoc with her life recently, methodically eating away at her support structure: at her father for being sick, at her mother for being weak, at herself for being helpless, and at the rest of the world for thinking it could do whatever it wanted, no matter how it affected her and her family. But at the moment it was mostly directed at Beag Scath, who happily dancing back and forth in the doorway, convinced that this new game was even lovelier than tossing pennies.

Surprisingly, her anger gave her the focus, the determination she needed. They would get out of here; in fact, Kara was getting out now. Keeping her movements extremely calm and slow, she stepped to her mother's side and gently reached for her hand. There was a slight tremor to the ice-cold fingers as Kara determinedly caught Mathair's eye, letting her own fill with all the love in her heart. She was her mother's daughter, no matter what a Grimm-variety fairy tale her life had become.

"I love you, Mathair, and we'll be okay," Kara did her best to project reassurance. She couldn't leave her here alone, but they would get nowhere if her mother didn't trust her. "Will you come with me?" She felt a surge of pride as she could see Mathair forcefully gather her courage, the pale blue eyes grew clearer, and her hand gripped back with comforting firmness. Now all they had to do was pray that Kara's instincts were accurate.

Moving once again toward the doorway, Kara took care not to startle the sprite. If she was right, he was the key to their escape; she couldn't explain how but something inside her, some instinct she hadn't needed before now, had shaken loose when their hands touched through the barrier. Besides, if it didn't work, she'd just have a bigger bruise on her tush.

Still gripping Mathair's hand, Kara stopped just short of the barrier and knelt down in front of the sprite. Holding out her other hand to him, she prayed fervently that he would not decide to be playfully coy at this moment. As she waited, her hope growing fainter and fainter with each passing second, she tried not to think how the hard stone beneath her made her knee ache or how keeping hold of Mathair's hand was wrenching her shoulder. It was so difficult to remain still when her body wanted to tremble with the tension.

"Won't you come to me, Scath?" Kara was ready to squeal with frustration; the sprite seemed to taunt her, coming near, and then backing away. "Come along, my friend, Mathair's waiting to meet you."

That was where it all threatened to fall apart. Before Kara even finished the sentence she could feel her mother try to pull away in panic. If it hadn't been for the intense flare of interest she saw kindled in Beag Scath's eyes the moment she used the Gaelic word for "mother," Kara probably would have let her go. As it was, she didn't need to. Stepping through the barrier with all the ease and dignity of an English gentleman, Beag Scath put an end to Mathair's fear by simply offering her his hand, or rather what formed upon it.

Familiar with the process, Kara held her breath and watched the mingled look of joy and concentration on the sprite's face as the air above his open hand began to sparkle and the sparkles grew denser. By the time the iridescent, orchid-like flower sat finished in his palm, Mathair had crouched closer, watching in fascination even before she realized his intentions.

Kara had never seen her mother more stunned than when the sprite turned his gentle umber eyes upon her and held out the flower for her to take. More than willing to benefit from the convenient distraction, Kara waited only until the flower was in Mathair's hand before scooping up the willing sprite and bracing herself for what she hoped was her final attempt to free them.

On the second floor of the building that housed Yesterday's Dreams, eight warriors waited, taut and battle-ready. Seven of the warriors were staggered as the building shook. Maggie had just enough of a warning to brace herself. She had been expecting it, though not from the direction from which it came.

As they all looked around, eyes narrowed and intent, the phone rang, and Molly's incensed voice could be heard over the answering machine speaker. "Maggie! Maggie, ye must pick up! Blast! Where are ye, woman? Those nasty blighters ye warned me o' just traipsed across my rooftop. They were'na alone an' they're headed yer way."

So...their enemy had come across the rooftops, where her shields were the weakest. Lucien was not as inept as she had first suspected. Maggie watched as those with the mage-sight blinked against the sudden flash that accompanied a second tremor. Maggie grimaced at the arrogance of such a wasteful use of energy; either their foe had such contempt for them that he felt no need to conserve his resources, or he'd had rather sloppy training. It was better to unravel defenses, not blast through them. Such a waste of mage energy!

"Well, my friends, shall we join our...guests?" The look on Maggie's face was wry as she turned to her mate. "It seems they could'na find the door an' came across the roof instead. Shall we make an impressive entrance? Demne, grab ahold o' Patrick an' brin' him along with ye."

There was no confusion or complaint as the fighters moved out with the speed and grace of great hunting cats, all except Patrick, who moved like an elephant in comparison. Of course, a charging elephant was a formidable creature, so Maggie didn't dwell on Patrick's chances in the coming battle. In seconds, the kitchen and other rooms of the apartment were empty of all but the O'Keefes' cat.

Maggie made her own way to the path she had chosen for herself. As she climbed to the field of battle, she pushed against the shields surrounding her building, repairing the rent, pushing the boundaries past the attackers, and strengthening them to the point where Maggie herself would have to be dead before they would give. With the barest of thoughts she shattered the plank of wood Lucien's forces had used to breach the eight-foot gap between Yesterday's Dreams and the building that housed Molly's pub next door. Combined, her efforts would ensure that no more of the enemy would come across, and any fireworks that occurred would not draw unwanted attention. With a mere thought Maggie made sure any onlookers would see nothing more than an empty roof, no matter what took place. Now was the time for battle and Maggie was determined that whatever her fate, this would be one fight Lucien did not walk away from; she couldn't allow anything to distract her from that goal.

In the dim, battered hallway the only sound was the steady jingle of coins in someone's pocket and the muffled, timid noises that occasionally betrayed those watching from behind the peepholes in each apartment door. Faded, yellowing paint chips littered the windowsill that had moments before been forced open from the fire escape.

As the silent, brooding men made their way toward the stairwell of the tenement building, they occasionally raised their makeshift weapons threateningly at a door; a silent message to the occupants that the men were "never there."

Making their way to the roof unnoticed by any but the cowed tenants, Lucien and his gang followed a street child showing them his particular aerial route through this part of the Village—for a price. Climbing from the stairwell into the open air as silently as they'd made the rest of their journey, the men waited expectantly for the boy to lead the way. With a shrewd look in his eyes, the child held out his hand for payment, evidently having no plans to move further without that assurance. Eying the deserted rooftop, Lucien, in no mood for such maneuvering, grabbed the boy by his collar and casually dangled him ten stories above the cracked pavement below until complete cooperation was restored. It didn't take long.

Somehow, from that point on, thirty-three men and their child-guide traveled unnoticed from rooftop to fire escape, down into derelict buildings, and across assorted caches of boards to other vacant, glassless windows, steadily making their way closer to Yesterday's Dreams.

With their goal in sight, the men carefully took no notice when the street child stiffened on the rim of their current rooftop, eyes wide with terror and every visible inch of his flesh quivering. Lucien himself watched with a kind of hunger, nearly shivering with delight as the fresh, youthful energy flowed into his own—it would come in handy when he breached the sidhe's defenses. Finally, the feverish light faded from the boy's eyes, leaving his face utterly blank. His body, well-fleshed just moments before, was starved and brittle. Those with the sight to see would have noticed as Lucien reached up and snapped the ethereal link he'd established when the boy defied him earlier. Without that link to sustain him, the child toppled from the rooftop, looking like nothing more than one of Dicken's damned souls.

For the first time in their journey, Lucien broke the silence, "Your payment." His tone was cold and disdainful as he contemplated the crimson splatter on the sidewalk below. "Coming, gentlemen?" None of the men mistook the suggestion for an invitation; they all followed him, still silent.

It was no use. Kara felt the same change in the barrier's resistance that she'd felt earlier, but it didn't seem to be enough. Instead of passing through the doorway—or at least being blocked by the barrier all together—they now seemed to be trapped within it; something like wading in the sea, the incoming waves keeping them from reaching deeper, calmer waters, yet the outgoing waves making it nearly impossible to make it safely back to shore. Ready to cry with despair, Kara felt as if she were smothering in the dazzling curtain that kept them from being in one place or the other. Even worse, the energy surrounding her seemed to be tripping every nerve ending in her body; she couldn't even tell if she still held her mother's hand, or if Beag Scath still rested on her arm. Slipping into sheer panic, she thought she was hallucinating when a gentle cooing reached her ears. By now she was sure it was just one more effect of the sensory overload that had her in its grip. If she could have moved, she would have jumped back a moment later when two tiny hands gripped her hair lightly on either side of her face, pulling it forward like two halves of a curtain to shade her eyes. In that soft shelter, all she could see was the brightness of Beag Scath's gaze. The expression it held was an odd mixture of ancient wisdom and simple innocence. He called her back from the precipice she had been about to lose herself over. Somehow that look was enough, in some unexplainable way Kara knew to stop fighting...so the sprite could lead the way safely through.

After the passing of several ages, Kara once again felt hard rock beneath her feet and her hand tingled from being held in her mother's viselike grip. Turning to look as Mathair took the last step through the barrier, Kara was nearly brought to her knees by a roar like a wall of shattered glass coming down, her eyes blinded by the accompanying supernova. Dazed she looked up a moment later into the confusion on her mother's face.

"Kara?" Kara could see that the fear was gone from Mathair's eyes, replaced with concern. "Kara, what's wrong?"

"I'll be fine, Mathair, the noise...the flash...it was just a little too much for me."

"Noise? Flash? What are you talking about?" Kara's heart sank as a bit of the fear crept back into her mother's gaze. Clearly, Mathair hadn't heard a thing.

That was went Kara noticed where her mother was standing: right in the middle of the doorway. It seemed that however they had gotten past the barrier it had come down in their wake.

CHAPTER 23

In the late-night darkness, what appeared to be seven moonbeams shimmered on the roof, sinking down and growing brighter. "*Pharo! Pharo!*" The ancient Celtic battle cry rang out fiercely into the night. The shockwave slammed into the humans trespassing on Maggie's domain. Several stumbled back and one fell over the parapet wall, plummeting to the ground below. All of them were startled for a long moment at the sudden appearance of seven sidhe and one human standing ready for battle in their own private pools of light. Taking advantage of that surprise, the sidhe converged en masse, lashing out so quickly that three of Lucien's men were crumbled in motionless heaps, blood pooling around them, and five others already bore the marks of battle.

Not for the first time in his long existence, Demne couldn't help but thrill at the fact that few aggressors could stand before the roaring, passionate fury of advancing Celts without even a ghost of a flinch among their forces. Alas, the initial response was short-lived; Lucien's forces laughed maliciously to see just the eight of them. The odds seemed too uneven to be taken seriously, as far as the humans were concerned. Regardless of the success of their initial strike, it appeared the defenders didn't stand a chance.

Of course, Demne thought with burning conviction, *the invaders would learn the folly of their contempt.*

By unspoken agreement, the sidhe and Patrick drew back into a loose circular cluster, spread out enough to not interfere with the next person, but close enough that their backs were guarded. As the sidhe silently dared the mortals to charge, the molten flame of anger that burned in their eyes gave them the look of avenging angels. Most of the intruders may have gained the rooftop, but they would not breach the building itself. Demne quickly wove a tight-meshed seal of magic across the access hatch. None would pass through, either in or out.

"Gentlemen, I'm afraid yer names are'na on the guest list," he taunted those left standing, then there was no time for further words.

Abruptly the tableau broke as one of Lucien's men roared like an enraged bull and came at them swinging what looked to be a massive, cast-iron pipe thicker in diameter than Demne's own thigh, its dull matte finish absorbing the moonlight. Also wielding weapons as eclectic as those of the defenders, the rest of the humans leapt into the battle with a brutish glee. It was difficult to count heads in the snarling mess of battle, but Demne figured they faced more than twenty men—and Lucien, of course.

And then there was no time for thought. His attacker reminded him of a bull mastiff...one with the temperament of a pit bull. He was huge, a veritable giant with a bald head that rested almost directly upon his muscled shoulders, and massive fists that created the illusion that the pipe was dainty in comparison. Demne ducked as the three-foot length came whizzing at his head. It was like a dance...or more honestly like a piñata party, with Demne as the papier-mâché target. He continued to dodge and weave as he calculated his next move, trying to maintain the loose circle while still avoiding a bludgeoning.

Immortal or not, if his attacker connected, it was going to hurt. So, how to deal with Bluto, here? The battle would be long and Demne did not want to squander his mage energy when cunning would serve just as well. His elven sword—hundreds of times stronger than Toledo steel—was more than a match for the pipe, but if they were to connect the metal would shatter beneath his blade, the flying pieces potentially wreaking more damage to those on Demne's side. Ah, but with just a trickle of power to immobilize the pipe...the concentration was fierce, then as the pipe froze in midair Demne thrust his sword up through the man's abdomen and into his heart, withdrawing it quickly as he pushed back on the mountainous corpse. It would be an embarrassment, after all, to have to be rescued from beneath the dead behemoth.

He gave the man not another thought, as two more men surged forward to engage him, only to be dispatched with disheartening ease. These were the foot soldiers, never expected to survive, but tossed in waves at the sidhe to wear them down. Lucien was a despicable leader.

Demne's eyes narrowed with distaste as they tracked the battlefield for that black-hearted creature; he spotted Lucien on the next roof over, his face a shiny mask of concentration, his hands weaving evil, sullen patterns in the air, patterns that were briefly visible to one with the sight. Surrounding him were ten to fifteen more men, all struggling to lever another plank across the alleyway to come join the fun. From what he could see from the enemy casualties on this side, the defenders would be facing about thirty attackers if they all managed to make it across. *What was Lucien thinking?* Even if he didn't know what the sidhe were, he still knew their side had some knowledge of magic. The humans didn't stand a chance.

He was mad! From the brief moment of attention Demne spared to watch, he could clearly see that this sorcerer was working from rote; he had little or no understanding of what he truly did. And thanks to Maggie's efforts to shield the conflict from mortal eyes, Lucien was within their defenses.

"Maggie! Look to Molly's rooftop!"

As Demne watched, Lucien completed his crudely constructed spell and unleashed it on the battlefield. On the other side of the rooftop there were horrifying screams as black, billowing smoke engulfed a handful of fighters—from both sides. Demne could see brief, bright flashes light up the black mass, but nothing else was visible. Looking away to defend himself as two more opponents presented themselves for the slaughter, he couldn't tell which of the sidhe dispersed the deadly cloud, but by the time he stole a glance in that direction it was gone, leaving behind several shaken sidhe and one dead attacker.

What kind of leader used such an indiscriminate weapon in a situation where it could harm his people right along with the other side? This man wasn't just heartless but also foolhardy; Lucien may have a larger force, but it made no sense to eat away at your own number. His loathing for the man as a person, a leader, and a mage translated itself into a vigorous attack, and the humans Demne faced were driven back. That was when he realized Lucien's ruthless cunning...the mortals were not meant to survive, they were merely the distraction that allowed Lucien the leisure to ready his magical attacks!

Even as he reacted, Demne recalled the foolishness of letting anger influence a fight. He may have forced his opponents to back away, but as the battle raged the sidhe circle had disintegrated and Demne's back was now unguarded; one of them was cagey enough to take advantage of the situation to slip around behind him. The surrounding battle faded away from his awareness as he focused on his own fight, hardly noticing when a foe had been dispatched, so quickly did another replace them. Only the occasional scream penetrated the density of his concentration; each time he heard one he couldn't help trying to see if it was a sidhe. Sparing a roguish smile for Cian, who came to stand back to back with him, Demne could not help but find some thrill in the confrontation. A good fight quickened the blood, the trick was for it to do so while keeping that blood well within the veins.

Minutes passed by in what seemed like hours as both sides grew weary. Without pause Demne's sword darted and slashed and thrust against humans armed with pipes, knives, and two-by-fours. For a brief moment, he couldn't help wondering why he heard no guns; after all, the humans seemed so fond of the cowardly weapons. Well, even small favors should be appreciated. Dragging his thoughts back to the fight at hand, Demne became aware of several things: there was blood on his sword; some of his own trickled from a cut on his forehead; and for the first time since they'd ascended to the rooftop, no one stood before him or looked ready to attack him in any way.

Using the respite well, the elven warrior wiped the blood from his face with a sleeve and caught his breath. His eyes wandered the horrible scene before him. With the exception of Lucien, no one on either rooftop was unscathed, and no few had fallen; dead—all fortunately from the side of the attackers, since their own forces had none to spare—or injured. Demne decided it was time to find Maggie, before someone else engaged him in combat.

He spotted his beloved making her way across the battlefield with her face set with purpose. While his heart told him she bore no injuries that were not minor, her expression told him she was determined to commit some rash action. Like personally confront Lucien and end all of this. Demne couldn't let her face him alone. He wove his way past those few still fighting, defending himself swiftly so that his progress not be hindered.

He could not watch her fall; should the brute force of Lucien's way of magic slip past her defenses, Demne would be there to fend the sorcerer off, or he would fall beside her trying.

Do'na go to him, Lhiannon, Demne soul-spoke Maggie so as not to startle her. She smiled as he called her 'sweetheart' in the language of the Celts.

"I mean it, Maggie. Find your high ground an' challenge him from there," he finished out loud, his battle-roughened voice coming out hoarse.

Clear our folk away an' I'll make my stand here, 'tis as good a spot as any. Her smile faded when he remained by her side.

Though it wasn't what she intended, he used soul-speech to warn the others away, trusting one of them to see that Patrick was safely clear as well.

With Maggie's fiery eyes locked with his, Demne could sense her efforts to not only prepare herself for mage-battle, but to do it in such a way as to force him back as she'd intended. It could not work, though; even if he weren't centuries older and more experienced in the technique, he was too much a part of her now. Their souls were so intertwined that any barrier she erected would work no better than a beaded curtain at keeping him away. Slipping past her efforts, Demne defiantly linked his arm through hers, replacing the energy she wasted trying to force him back with his own potential; he would face her wrath later.

"Look to yer defenses, love, an' stop wastin' yer time on me," he tightened his grip on her arm to gently remind her he was there to stay. "Ye'll be havin' more company soon, I believe."

Maggie's temper flared, along with her energies. A clear, if premature beacon to Lucien.

Demne was relieved to see Maggie turn her attention back to the dark mage, who still stood on Molly's rooftop. The look on the man's face was a mixture of hatred, contempt, and barely controlled rage as he stared at her, with something not quite like lust flickering around the edges.

Only the hold Demne had given Maggie by locking arms with her kept him from lunging across the chasm to go for the sorcerer's throat. Knowing the folly of such an attack, but finding the urge difficult to fight, the sidhe closed his eyes and relied on his mage sight to watch as the magical battle ensued.

It was quickly apparent that the two were at the moment equally matched; Maggie's adept grasp on the ways of magic was quickly being countered by the sheer volume and energy of Lucien's crude attacks. He would burn out quicker than Maggie, but that scarcely mattered if he overwhelmed her defenses first.

Most of those still fighting were unaware of the glorious display taking place around them, but any of them not in the midst of an attack couldn't help but notice the charge in the air as every hair on their body attempted to stand on end. Demne did not envy them the uncomfortable sensation as he stood protected within Maggie's shields, but then he had quite a lot more to worry about should any of that energy get through.

A mere moment later, Demne decided he'd need to have a serious talk with a chap named Murphy as the shields around him wavered and came down. Only his grip on Maggie's arms stopped her from falling as well and she staggered as if hit. One look at her dazed eyes told him he was on his own. Something had happened to one of her shields and this was the backlash of that energy snapping back to her.

Well, it was up to him then, was it? Instinctively reacting to the immminent danger about to descend on them, Demne did something he didn't even know was possible; he flooded Maggie's shields with his own energy, forcing them back up just in time for a massive mage bolt to blossom upon them with the intensity of a nuclear flash. The bolt was so powerful, everyone on the rooftop—with the exception of Maggie (who was having problems of her own), Lucien, and himself—was disoriented by the blast; some were hit even harder. Just beyond the shield, Demne couldn't help noticing the punk he had encountered earlier today in the alley behind the pawnshop; he couldn't help noticing him because the blast had left the boy in a crumbled heap, most likely comatose. Remembering the amount of mage potential the punk had, Demne had no illusions of what his own fate would be if the shields came down before the next blast.

Maggie! Come now, Maggie me love! If ye do'na come to yer senses 'tis the end o' us all. Demne's thoughts were tinged with desperation. He could feel her shaking off the shock of the broken shield, but it was taking too long.

He didn't know what warned him, it could have been the crunch of gravel or the man's excited breathing, but whatever it was Demne quickly released his grip on Maggie's arm, knowing she was still too stunned to stand on her own. Something told him she'd be safer on the ground. Taking his guard with practice easy, he spared one thought and one breath only.

"Pharo! Pharo!" he shouted with both voice and soul, desperate for someone to come to their aid, though he knew it would come too late for him. With the speed and precision only a sidhe was capable of, Demne used the sweep of the blade made in Goibhniu's own forge to deflect four bullets. Startled by a yell of pure, deadly rage, the beautiful sidhe missed the fifth.

As he fell to the ground, his body shaking with the pulse of blood rushing from his chest, the world around him erupted with sound. His failing heart ached as if it knew the hair-raising keen near at hand to be for himself, and that it was torn from the tortured throat of Maggie. While his lover clutched him to her breast he could hear Lucien's enraged voice yelling across the battlefield. Demne couldn't help thinking it was a good thing Lucien was a rooftop away.

"I said no guns!" There was the promise of painful death beneath the surface of their enemy's voice, and it was not directed at them. "The woman is no good to me dead!"

Demne was fading, but still he could feel the thud as nearby a body hit the ground. The clatter echoed in his skull as the gun followed. He watched with failing interest as Lucien yanked the thug from one rooftop to the other with nothing more than a lash of energy and a hell of a lot of will. Closing dimming eyes that no longer wanted to focus on such things, the sidhe would never know how long it took his slayer to die.

Climbing carefully down the dark stairway, Kara's need to get free increased with each passing moment. Escaping the chamber had been so deceptive. They had gone up the stairs only to find the shields there were so strong that not even the sprite could pass them. Instinctively, Kara wouldn't give up. Stories kept bubbling up from her memory, tales told to her by Grandda of the faerie mounds and the multitude of ways both in and out of them. Well, this was a faerie mound of sorts...and Kara *would* find the way out.

Behind her Mathair gripped her shoulder tighter and tighter until Kara reached up to pat her hand, trying to get her to relax her grip without speaking, for surely if she did it would come out shrewish. Kara's patience was fading quicker than a loose woman's blush. But suddenly an idea formed out of her thoughts of just a moment ago...stories...perhaps she could distract her mother's fear with a story.

"Mathair, would ye care to hear one o' Grandda's tales?"

Her mother didn't answer, but Kara figured anything would be better than letting her trudge through the unknown in frightened silence, with her thoughts free to fear the worst.

"Long ago Ireland was a land of warriors and kings. The country was ancient and wild and magical, and the only limit to a man's power was his ability to claim it." Kara let her voice fall into the cadence of the storyteller, learned long ago at her Grandda's knee. He would have been proud of her. "All were united beneath the might of the Ard Rí, the High King, and his bodyguards, the fierce Fianna."

A tug on Kara's other hand alerted her that she'd slowed down. This subterranean maze was so dark she was relying on Beag Scath to lead the way. Either the sprite had no trouble seeing, or he knew the way by heart, for his step never faltered. Kara just hoped that he'd understood when she tried to explain that they needed a way out. For now, she must continue her story. Already Mathair's death grip had loosened.

"Greatest of these fighters was Fionn Mac Cumhail, made wise by a taste of the salmon of wisdom and possessing the might and skill to lay claim to the title of leader of the Fianna.

"One day Fionn and his men spied a lovely fawn in the forest on their way back to his home, the Dun of Allen. He and his dogs gave chase but the fawn lay down and the hounds began to play and frolic with her. Fionn was astounded and vowed that there after none should harm the creature.

"As he and his men continued on to home, the fawn followed." Kara was relieved the story was having the desired effect and their progress seemed to pick up, though she did not know where they were going yet. *Now if only my breath holds out,* she hoped as she continued.

"That night Fionn woke to find the most beautiful woman in all of Eire beside his bed. 'I am Sadb, cursed by the druid o' the faerie folk—the one they call Dark. Until this night, when I drew nigh to the Dun of Allen, I was the fawn ye chased today.'

"That is the tale of how Fionn Mac Cumhail took Sadb to be his wife."

Kara dare go no further in the tale, as this was where things turned dark, with the druid spying Sadb and whisking her away, once more a fawn. The two lovers were never reunited, though eventually Fionn found a boy raised in the wild by a fawn and knew him for his son by Sadb. He took the boy home and named him Oisin—Little Fawn.

She would have begun another tale, only singing no less sweet than an angel's drifted to their ears from the darkness in front of them. Kara smiled as Mathair's grip grew gentler still and her step surer. It took less than a moment for the girl to realize it was Beag Scath singing, and something told her it was meant to reassure both of the women.

Just as it seemed the stairs would never end, the blackness gave way to shades of grey. It was so subtle at first that Kara thought it was her eyes playing tricks...that they were so desperate for something to see that they were creating it themselves. But no, as the rough stone walls came into focus Kara's confidence grew.

"See, Mathair," she said in an effort to draw her mother out of the numbness that seemed to engulf her, "already we see light. I'm sure we'll find a way out, too."

Kara knew something was wrong when her mother stopped abruptly and her grip once again grew crushing. She was not prepared for the crazed whimper that escaped from her mother's throat.

"What's wrong?" Kara tried to turn to look at her mother and couldn't move for the hand on her shoulder. She tried turning just her head and found that once again all was blackness. "Mathair?!!"

"There is no light! There is no light! No light! No light!" Kara went cold as the hoarse whisper reached her ears. They had to get out now...while Mathair still had her sanity. Letting go of Beag Scath, Kara used both hands to remove herself from her mother's grasp as gently as possible. It wasn't easy; she was startled at the strength in that small hand. As she struggled to sooth and guide her mother down the stairs, again the tiny hand reached up to tug at her. On an impulse she crouched down to try once again to speak to the sprite; as she did so, she couldn't help but notice that she again saw the light.

"My friend, what happens to the light?" Kara thought as hard as possible on what she meant, hoping either thought or words would get through to the little creature, and that for once he would answer. The singing told her he was at least capable of speech—he just didn't bother to use it.

She was afraid he still wouldn't. They stood there forever, but only silence greeted her. Breathing deeply, Kara tried to use one of the concentration techniques Maggie had taught her that day. She filled her mind with two images: the first, the vague greyish light in front of them; the second, the complete darkness she saw if she turned around. Kara concentrated so hard she nearly didn't hear the answer she was hoping for.

"No light...magic," Beag Scath said in his clear, liquid-crystal voice, "Soon." Suddenly, Kara's mind flooded with the simple, yet alien flow that was the way the sprite thought. She now could see that what she thought was light, wasn't...it was magical energy, and she wasn't even seeing it with her eyes. *No wonder Mathair sounded crazed; she's walking forever in darkness and I'm telling her there is light she can't see, she probably couldn't even see the flashes the barrier had made when we escaped the chamber.* Kara was so ashamed of the torment she was causing for her mother that she almost let the other message in Beag Scath's thoughts slip away unnoticed: somewhere close below, there was true light...and a way out. Kara barely noticed when the sprite left them behind; she only cared about relieving her mother's torment.

"Oh, my lovely Mathair," Kara tried to sooth her mother, "I am so sorry, I didn't realize you couldn't see what I could. Please, Mathair, please, just a little further and we can see again; a little bit more and we'll be out." Gently tugging on Mathair's arm, Kara managed to get her to continue walking downward.

With her own eyes dazzled by the mage energy growing brighter as they descended, it wasn't until Mathair gasped that Kara realized what was now before them was true light, and that the rough, sparkly surface of the rock walls was the most beautiful thing either of them had ever seen. Their flagged energies found a fresh burst from somewhere and they hurried down the stairs where Beag Scath danced merrily on the landing. Both women laughed at the little creature, and neither made any note that the laughter was slightly hysterical. They could see again, and if that was true then they had to believe there was also a way out nearby.

As they regained their composure and the mirth gradually faded, Kara couldn't help but look around at this part of Maggie's complex. She had already been down here once today—had it really just been today?—but only in the one room. There were several others on this level, and the farthest one drew Kara like a magnet. Glancing at her mother, Kara felt uncertain at leaving her here to rest.

"Mathair, I need to check out that room over there," she pointed it out to her mother. "Would you like to come with me?"

"But it's so dark...I don't think I could take the dark again so soon." At her mother's frantic words, Kara knew it was even more important to explore the room for that was what drew her. What's more, to her eyes the chamber seemed lit brighter than day.

"Okay...okay, Mathair. You wait here." Kara gave her mother's hand a light squeeze. "I promise, I'll be right back."

Moving toward the room was like being in a dream; Kara seemed to float across the distance to the bright chamber. By the time she stood in the doorway, she could barely see. The room might be as black as pitch to Mathair's eyes, but to Kara's sight it was like looking into the sun. The blazing light drew her. She went forward, confident that whatever drew her would not burn. She did need some way to filter it out or tone it down, though, so she could see what lay in the middle of that brilliance. Kara shielded her eyes with her hand and forced her way inside.

Once again Kara found herself caught in a sparkling curtain of energy, prevented from reaching her goal. But this was infinitely worse than escaping the upper chamber; this was like being slowly pulled apart, piece by piece, and examined. Everything Kara ever was—and, she suspected, everything she ever would be—was laid bare until she itched the way she imagined an animal in a cage must, with the whole world waiting to see what it will do. Afterwards, she couldn't say exactly what did the trick, but one moment she had been staring into a nova, trapped in space and time, and the next she was rushing toward a podium that seemed to almost cradle Quicksilver. Her precious Quicksilver. As she stumbled forward, she was left with a warm feeling of approval...surprised approval, at that. She reached out and took the cherished violin into her arms, lifting it reverently from the cold marble.

A gasp from the doorway brought Kara back to the here-and-now. There stood Mathair, white as a sheet, her eyes feverish. "I was worried about you here in the dark." She seemed almost ashamed that she had come to see that Kara was okay. "The light, the music...where did it all come from? It was so beautiful." Her eyes grew even brighter with understanding, "You are so beautiful."

Music? Kara hadn't heard any music. But she also had a feeling she hadn't been in the same place Maither was; Kara had been inside the experience, closed off from the physical world around her. She said nothing of what she had seen and heard because she knew the words would pale beside the reality of what had just happened. Something monumental had taken place here; some...power had judged her, and she had passed. There were no words for that, and somehow both of them knew it. Taking her mother's arm, they walked back to the main chamber, the room behind them growing once again dark. An ecstatic Beag Scath greeted them, looking with hungry eyes at the violin and prancing and scampering and dancing around them all the way to the dusty, forgotten stairway Kara now knew would lead them to the surface.

CHAPTER 24

A mournful keen rose to fill the air. Turning to find its source, Patrick was gripped by dread the moment his eyes locked on Maggie. His own Da had told him stories of the Bean Sidhe, the woman of the fairies, and her wail that warned of impending death. As his horrified eyes took in the scene before him, he recalled those stories in vivid detail; he had no trouble believing them now. Huddled in a corner of the roof, Maggie was the epitome of terrible grief. The intensity of what she was feeling warped her beauty, and her fingers were tangled in clumps of hair she had torn from her own head. Despite the lingering violence of the battle that surrounded her, she stayed crouched over something lying in the shadow of the wall, her wild eyes seeing nothing.

A quick look around proved that no one else was close enough to help her. Rushing to Maggie's side, he tried to catch her half-mad eyes and bring her attention back to the danger surrounding them. He was quite careful not to glance at the crumbled mass beneath her or else he'd lose himself in a similar hopelessness.

"Maggie," Patrick tried calling her back from her grief, "impossible as it seems, ye must set it aside for now. 'Tis'na safe to be standin' here." He put his hands on her shoulders and attempted to shake her out of it. Going so far as to forget his awe of the immortals, Patrick slapped her soundly, hoping the physical shock would free her from the emotional one.

"Och, Maggie, we need ye," he begged her desperately. As he tried to bring her back to herself he caught a movement out of the corner of his eye. One of Lucien's punks, with muscles that rivaled those Patrick had had before his illness, in his days on the docks, ambled toward them from the far side of the rooftop, a crowbar in his hands. He had the intense look of someone who wanted to smash something; what that something was didn't really seem to matter a whole lot. And it was clear he intended to put everything he had behind the effort.

Patrick positioned himself between Maggie and the new threat, and reached for the neglected quarterstaff beside her. Hastily Patrick scanned the roof for help to summon. Among the trampled remains of what must have been a rooftop garden, a sidhe of such ethereal beauty that it shone through his human seeming tended to the fighters that had been pulled to safety. If only he could get the man's attention. Patrick's attention darted back to the approaching attacker. The thug was nearly upon them. There was no time to summon the healer to come for Maggie and Demne.

Calling on years of experience in self-defense on the docks, Patrick set his stance, took a firm grip with both hands on the middle of the staff, and waited for the other man to swing, letting the punk commit himself to an action that prevented him from defending himself. As Patrick expected, his opponent charged forward blindly, flailing around with his length of solid iron. Carefully stepping into the man's swing, Patrick reached with his left to deflect the descending crowbar. At the same time he brought up the end of the staff into the man's groin. All too quickly, Patrick was reminded both of his age and his health. The second he connected with his attacker, he felt more than heard a sharp snap and his hand went numb with the impact. He watched as the punk crumbled to the rooftop, pulling the crowbar with him and momentarily trapping Patrick's staff beneath his weight. Now Patrick had control of neither weapon and his left hand was useless.

The punk recovered a bit more quickly than Patrick hoped, or else his blow hadn't been as hard as he thought. Looking up, Patrick searched the roof for his own salvation. Already a few of his fellow defenders were making their way toward him. Most of the attackers had fallen or fled, with only a handful left standing to engage the sidhe. Then, across the rooftop, a sudden flash of brilliant light caught his eye and a strain of furious fiddling slid past his ears. Patrick refocused and balked at what he saw: Kara stood by the stairwell door, shrouded in a glowing mist. He moaned and watched helplessly as she aimed a challenging flourish at Lucien, who at some point—how had he missed it?—had managed to cross to this rooftop. Right now, though, all Patrick cared about was his daughter. She wasn't supposed to be here! She was supposed to be safely locked away below with Barbara.

The brilliant, colorful glow that surrounded Kara dimmed and flared with the impact of unseen blows. Beyond the haze, Patrick saw a sight that made his heart clench with fear: two men crept up on either side of Kara, whose complete focus remain locked on Lucien.

"Kara!" The one cry was all Patrick managed to make. That brief outburst distracted his rescuers just long enough for them to hesitate a crucial moment. Patrick's only warning was a fatal sound of disturbed rubble before his side burst with agony.

Standing before the backdrop of a blood-red moon, Kara played Quicksilver with a ferocity she would have never imagined possible. Each flowing note stretched her skin taut across her body, growing tighter as the power continued to pour into her. As quickly as it came, she bent her will to it and instinctively lashed out at the malevolence pounding on her own defenses. Her unschooled efforts were keeping Lucien Blank at bay, but they weren't doing much to bring an end to his attacks.

Already it felt like she had been locked in the struggle for an eternity, but it could not have been more than five minutes since she had arrived. She had rushed up the stairs to the rooftop without a thought for the nightmare she would find.

Expecting nothing more than a rumble, she had instead stepped out into a war zone, complete with screaming wounded, motionless dead, and liberal amounts of blood everywhere. Oh yeah, and Lucien...Lucien had been right there waiting for her the moment she came hurdling through the door.

"Come now, my dear," Lucien's cold, contemptuous voice refocused Kara on the moment at hand, inspiring outrage and restoring her intense focus. "Think how you could benefit from my instruction. Why don't you stop wasting all of that glorious energy and join me, instead? Do you really want everyone to continue suffering when all I'm interested in is you?" She didn't care for the look that crossed his face during his little speech: it was a look that spoke of obsession and violence, of evil acts and ruthless misuse. Kara knew instinctively what sorts of lessons she would have at the hand of this man, even if her mind balked at providing the specifics. A fresh barrage of sickly red flashes impacted on Kara's shields, accompanying his words. As if to totally discount her abilities, Lucien kept his stance relaxed and his expression one of boredom.

Kara didn't bother with a direct answer. For the moment acutely aware of the mingled sounds of crashing blows and pained cries rising from the battle zone around her, Kara surged into pure rage. It was bad enough that her defenders bore the brunt of this fight while she stood protected beneath her glowing, technicolor dome. It was even worse that her attacks seemed to have little effect on an opponent who acted like he was humoring her before delivering a crushing blow. If only she knew what she was doing, but everything that had happened since she'd come through the door was instinct...and something else, almost as if a wealth of knowledge hovered over her head and each time she needed to counter something, what she needed dangled just where she could reach it. But it wasn't enough; none of it was enough. She understood nothing of what she was doing, and without understanding she could not act, only react. Eventually, her energy would drain away and he would have her. Meanwhile, she had to witness her defenders falling in her place.

Again, he mocked her with his laughter, and she wondered if it was her curse to never be of any use to those she cared about. Time and again, those she loved suffered while she stood by, unable to keep them safe, unable to help them. Kara was tired of feeling helpless. There was nothing more she could do about the events in her life that had entrapped her and her family, but she damn well could do something about the evilness before her. Lucien's would join the bodies scattered around her on the rooftop, even if she had to fall as well to make it happen.

❧

An anguished cry from somewhere beside her tore Maggie from her grieving. When one of pain followed, the sidhe automatically reacted, driven by a need to comfort that pain. *Demne! Demne is hurt!* Maggie's befuddled brain told her. Turning toward the source of raw agony, she was surprised by the sight of Patrick O'Keefe sprawled half-conscious beside her on the rooftop, the white of his face tinged green with pain-induced nausea and his forehead beaded with sweat. Some detached part of her brain noticed the odd contours of his chest. Crouched next to him was Eri, doing what she could to deaden the pain, while another sidhe stood guard over them all. *No, Patrick is hurt; Demne is dead. My love is....* She shoved the thought away and her eyes dropped to her clenched fists. She relaxed her grip and the torn locks fell away. She smothered a second keen.

When she could comprehend the effects of her own grief, she realized she could not afford to lose herself to it again. For now, at least, it must be put away so she could help those who needed her. First she dedicated herself to Patrick's aid, noting that Eri wasn't having much success alone. Closing her eyes to better view the energy flow surrounding Patrick, Maggie tried to evaluate the damage to her human kin. Her heart sank at the seriousness of the wound, but she was determined to begin her own healing by doing what she could for another.

"'Tis the lung pierced through by the broken ribs, Eri, an' the damage beyond yer skill," Maggie spoke softly so as not to startle her ally. "Aye, an' my own as well."

At the sound of her voice, Patrick's eyes flew open. His jaw clenched against the pain and he could not speak, but the pleading look he gave her was more than enough to tear at her heart.

"Sure an' that's clear to me, Cliodna, but there must be somethin' we can do." Eri's eyes were just as imploring as Patrick's when they met Maggie's.

After a moment of furious thought, Maggie grasped her fellow sidhe's hand. "Have ye anythin' left to spare?" The other sidhe nodded. "Draw it up an' we'll give him what we have to hold him 'til we grab one o' the kin with the gift o' healin'." They drew on their dwindling reserves, rested their free hands on Patrick's chest, and sent the burst of energy to the failing human to ease the pain. Patrick's eyes closed and a bit of the strain visibly slackened on his face.

Feeling mortally weary, Maggie leaned against the parapet wall, too tired to release Eri's hand. She allowed her eyes to survey the rooftop, praying all the while to Mother Danu that Miach and his gift of healing were nearby. As her gaze traveled across the nightmare before her, Maggie caught sight of the one she sought. Too exhausted to call out loud, she soul-spoke her plea and waited as Miach rushed to their side.

As the healer took up Patrick's hand and did what he could for the human, bright-colored flares from the other side of the roof finally caught Maggie's attention.

Kara?! The last crippling effects of Maggie's grief fell away, pushed aside by her fear for the girl. She had left Kara safely hidden below; how in the world had she gotten past both barriers? It was something of a struggle for Maggie to remember the moment in battle where the shockwave of one of her shields collapsing had laid her low. She forced the memory away. She had no difficulty remembering what that moment of weakness had caused; if she allowed herself to dwell on it now there would be more tragedy. More heartache. She couldn't bear more.

Maggie turned her thoughts back to the situation at hand. Even through the mental fog that hindered her ability to think Maggie had no trouble focusing on the uneven mage battle raging by the stairwell. Abrupt clarity returned to the sidhe's mind with one chilling thought: nothing but an amateur's shield stood between the nearly unschooled Kara and the evil man they were all fighting to keep from her.

Pulling energy from reservoirs she didn't know she had, Maggie grabbed her staff from beside the body of a slain attacker. As she climbed to her feet, leaning heavily on the staff, the sidhe tried to gather in the streams of feral magic that were stirred up by the fighting. Only her grip on the staff kept her from falling back to the ground when her effort failed. Fatigue dragged at her even harder. She did not have the energy to harness the power she'd summoned. It flared tauntingly in front of her eyes before drifting back off to its original lines. Burning tears streamed down Maggie's face as she realized exactly how spent she was. *How could she hope to save Kara from Lucien if she were as weak as an invalid?* She tried once more to bend the surrounding magics to her will, and this time Maggie was brought to her knees by the effort, again with no success. She felt so faded, as if one more attempt might make her disappear. The sidhe did not even have the energy to sob. *First Demne, then Patrick, now Kara...would she lose everyone she cared for?*

Lost in her despair, Maggie didn't notice the shadow that crept toward her, carefully avoiding those still engaged in combat. As she slid lower and lower down the length of her staff, the urge to keen once again rose from her aching breast. It took two hands gripping her face between them to snap her out of her daze. It took one of those hands waving an iridescent orchid before her eyes to prevent her from going into an uncontrollable battle rage and doing her best to slaughter whoever had gotten too close—friend or foe.

Rebounding into complete awareness, Maggie saw the answer to her dilemma. She pulled the sprite along behind her and crawled over to a sheltered corner of the roof where she had a clear view of the battle raging between Kara and Lucien. She settled the sprite in her arms, and dropped into trance as quickly as she could. Soul-speaking Beag Scath, she made it clear that she needed him to once again filter raw magical energy for her. While the sprite eagerly did what she asked, Maggie cast the growing thread of power to Kara like a lifeline, fervently hoping her own dwindling energy would sustain them both.

Reining in her fury, Kara ended her ineffectual attacks; instinct told her it was the right thing to do. Up until now she had thrown the power entering her body at Lucien as fast as it accumulated, trying to pound him down by the sheer barrage of her own attack. Obviously that wasn't working.

Somewhere in the background, the sound of shattering glass brought the ghost of a memory to the surface, a flash of inspiration that just might make up for her lack of practical knowledge. Here was something she understood, something she could use.

While the sorcerer lashed out at her with his own power, Kara tried to ignore the jolting impacts on her shields. She focused her entire mind on drawing in the flow of magic she sensed around her and this time holding it tight. It built up in every cell of her body, scintillating across her nerves. Once again she lost all notion of what took place around her as she willingly brought upon herself another sensory overload. And still she drew it in until it seemed she would burst with the effort to contain it all.

As she stood there serenely, feeling as if her very skin pulsed with the power she contained, some distant portion of her mind noticed the attack on her shields lessen, until finally it halted. When she opened her eyes, her veiled gaze met with Lucien's calculating stare. His eyes flickered to a point just behind her before he held out his hand, smugly overconfident.

It occurred to her that he'd interpreted her lack of action as willingness to join him. With a calm that did not betray her growing sense of hope, Kara simultaneously collapsed her shields and lowered Quicksilver toward the ground, but didn't release her grip on either. Eyes down in feigned modesty, she moved gracefully across the rooftop into Lucien's grasp. Not until she found herself within the compass of his shields did she look up into his cold blue eyes.

Her smile unfeigned, Kara held his gaze in an iron grip and watched with contentment as his confidence drained away to be replaced with horrified disbelief. If she could see her own face, she would have been surprised, and somewhat disturbed, by the fierce satisfaction reflected there. She could feel no regret when part of her own innocence died in the flood of raw power she let loose upon her foe. As the energy poured from her, leaving her like an empty husk, she took a single step back beyond Lucien's shields. Then she watched them shatter as completely as the barrier had below. One look at the madness in Lucien's eyes assured her he had fallen over the mental precipice from which she had been saved. As the last of the magical energy drained away, she crumbled to the rooftop, her gaze still locked with that of the gibbering shell that had for a brief time been Lucien Blank.

CHAPTER 25

Climbing from the blackness was the hardest thing Maggie had had to do in all of her centuries of living. She couldn't say what called her so strongly from the comfort of oblivion, back to the bitterness of a New York rooftop, where crumpled and bleeding bodies surrounded her—not all of them the enemy's. Haunting strands of melody seemed to wrap around her thoughts; soothing and persistent, they swathed her heart, cushioning it against the crippling grief she could feel creeping back alongside her awareness. Maggie could now feel gentle arms cradling her and hands smoothing her brow in the same way the music calmed her soul.

"Welcome back, *cara*," a warm voice greeted her in low, tranquil tones.

Friend...someone called her friend. The voice was familiar, though it wasn't the one Maggie longed to hear. Her entire body tensed, betraying her desire to resist their comfort, to return to the oblivion from whence she had been snatched. No, it was too late; she had nearly followed Demne from this world unwittingly, but to consciously do so now would be the true betrayal. Maggie was no oath-breaker. She had been robbed of her chance to follow her love, but she had not been free to seize it in the first place.

As she lay there, despondent and listless, the music grew more persistent and demanding. It chastised her for laying down her responsibilities and turning from those who needed and loved her. The melody forced her to honor the triumph of the day, no matter how tinged it was with bitter loss. Deep in her heart, she knew she dishonored those who had fallen this day with her grief and the extremes she had embraced to end her suffering. *Who was she to render their sacrifices meaningless, when they had fallen that she might stand?*

Maggie could feel the healing of her heart begin the moment she confronted her shame. The walls of will she'd withdrawn behind crumbled and her friends and kin reached out with hand and heart. Their comfort and strength, so freely shared, wrapped her in a warm glow of its own, different from, but as peaceful as the music she heard. She would still grieve, but it would be a healthy sorrow, and it would take its proper time.

"Where do we stand then?" Maggie whispered to the circle of Sidhe who greeted her as she opened her eyes. Apparently, at some point others had arrived to lend aid, for not all those around her had led tonight's charge. Beyond their shoulders, she could see even more new people cleaning up the evidence of battle. She was careful to avoid looking too closely at their expressions as she waited for someone to answer.

"We've won the day," Eri spoke up after the others remained silent for too long, "though three o' our number have fallen."

"Three? Which three?" Maggie became impatient as her kinswoman hesitated. She sat up from the cradle of Miach's protective arms and locked her gaze with Eri's. "Well, go on then, who do we mourn tomorrow?"

Eri looked wounded by Maggie's bluntness, but she continued. "Cian an' Demne have crossed over, an' Patrick will'na be long to follow."

The silence was long as Maggie fought once more against her grief. Now was not the time! Finally, as she won her inner battle, she noticed that the music continued. Maggie hadn't realized the song that called to her had been anything more than internal. Now that she knew otherwise, she had no doubt who the musician was, and for whom she now played.

Maggie's heart raced to think that even untrained Kara had been able to wield enough power to call a Child of Danu back from a death will. Maggie had no doubt whom the girl commanded with her music now. With the memory of Patrick's state coming abruptly to mind, Maggie couldn't tell how much good Kara's raw talent would do against such a mortal injury.

At that mingling of fear and impending loss, Maggie trembled with the whisper of recent memory.

Demne lay twisted on the ground beside her, the light in his eyes flaring bright as the last of his strength threatened to burn away. Maggie nearly flinched when his hand slid down her leg in an unwitting mockery of his past caresses.

"I'm afraid I must leave ye, my wild-eyed lass. 'Tis another dance I'm off to now." The lighthearted tone Demne tried to give his words was spoiled by his fading voice.

"No! No, do'na leave me behind, A chuisle mo chroí!" Words of entreaty and endearment poured from Maggie's mouth in a tortured stream, fighting their way past the lump in her throat. Her entire body shuddered with her sobbing. "Ye canna take my heart with ye an' expect me not to follow ye."

In violent fury, she kicked away the gun dropped by the human responsible for the pool of glittering blood in which Demne rested, a pool that grew larger with each second that passed. The creature had died much too quickly to suit Maggie, and not even by her hand. She sank to the ground next to her mate without a qualm about joining him in the gore. She was oblivious to everything: the crimson stain soaking into her clothing, the jarring sounds of the fight taking place around them, and the acrid odor of gunpowder still lingering in the air.

Pulling Demne half into her lap, she frantically attempted to close the wound in his chest both with her hands and the scraps of energy she ripped from the air around her. Her gift was not for healing, but, if that lacking could be overcome by sheer determination, she was certain she would do so. With extreme focus, she hunched over Demne, her hands beginning to glow with the raw power converged there. The growing light cast the coursing blood into ghastly, unnatural relief. Its continuing flow held her attention so raptly that Maggie didn't realize at first when her mate's limp hands sought to push her own away.

"Nay, love, 'tis too late for that." He pleaded with weary eyes when nothing else could get through. "My time is done, be turnin' yer will for those with still a chance for this world."

Maggie pulled her tortured gaze from the wound and sought her lover's face as she realized he resisted her with more than his hands; Demne was using the last of his energy to block her efforts. "Why?"

She searched Demne's face, watching in torment as the pain momentarily silenced him. "I know now what ye must do, my sweet Cliodna." Demne's use of her true name brought fresh tears to Maggie's aching eyes. "Ye need all yer energy to summon the clouds. Ye must take Patrick to Tir na nÓg, to the Fledh Ghoibhnenn."

Maggie went pale at what he asked of her. She couldn't remember the last time a mortal had been taken to the feast of Goibhniu, where the smallest sip of ale bestowed the gift of immortality. She went cold as it occurred to her that most gifts carry a price, for both the giver and receiver.

"Ye must, love, or the cancer will soon slay him." To Maggie's ears, Demne's voice surged with strength for an instant before growing even fainter. Her heart ached that he should feel such conviction that he squandered his strength to convince her as well. Reluctantly, she leaned closer as he continued, not really wanting to hear his words, let alone be swayed by them. "Patrick's part in this is'na over yet. He's as important to us as his daughter, in his own way. Swear to me you'll take him." Flashes of images in her mind told her all that Demne did not have the energy to put into words.

Swayed by the fervor of his voice and the intensity of his pain-fevered eyes, Maggie went bitter cold as she pulled Demne to her and whispered in his ears the words that to her heart were a betrayal, knowing the price she paid. "Aye, love, ye have my oath."

Battered by the memory, Maggie dug her nails into the palm of her hand to distract her from the ever-present anguish. *She knew what needed to be done, but did she have the strength?* The harm her own descent into grief had caused made it all the more imperative that she honor her final oath to Demne. Unless they journeyed to Tir na nÓg now, they wouldn't reach Goibhniu's table in time to save Patrick. She would have to find the energy because she was the only one left in the city who could call the clouds to carry so many. She climbed to her feet with the help of her quarterstaff, trying not to lean upon it too obviously.

"We canna allow death to claim more than the two that have fallen." Maggie looked carefully into each of their eyes so they could see her senses were sound and not warped with grief. "I've an oath upon me that I'll see yon Patrick to *Tir na nÓg*. 'Tis the feast of Goibhniu for him, or my life tryin'."

The group mulled over Maggie's words silently. Finally, Miach spoke up. "Na that I'd see the mortal dead, but what is Patrick O'Keefe that ye would both bless an' curse him with Fledh Ghoibhnenn?"

Maggie felt all their eyes on her as she attempted to form her answer. *Was it safe to speak aloud of the importance these mortals were to play in the days to come, of their destiny for both mortal and sidhe?* It was ill luck to speak of omens and fate in the shadow of a battle, in the unprotected space of a rooftop. The openness of their surroundings decided her; Maggie drew upon her nobility as Cliodna of the Tuatha de Danaan.

"'Tis an oath Demne asked o' me with his dyin' breath, an' I'll honor it, alone or with ye beside me. The details are between me an' the dead an' are no concern o' yers."

There was a moment of silence while the circle of sidhe considered her words carefully. Then, one by one, they approached her to grip her arm in a silent oath of support. If her heart had not been too numb, she would have been heartened by their willingness to stand beside her.

"Aye, then. We have'na much time," Maggie considered briefly what must be done. "The lot o' ye finish cleanin' up the roof. Away with any signs o' battle." She didn't wait for verbal acknowledgments before moving off in the direction of the desperate music.

She came upon the girl quietly enough not to frighten her, but with sufficient noise to allay the impression of stealth. "Leave off, Kara." The sidhe placed her hand gently on the girl's arm to still the music. "For now, he'll keep."

For a tense moment, Kara looked viciously at Maggie's hand on her arm before slumping hopelessly beneath the immortal's understanding gaze. Even with all the centuries behind her, Maggie had never seen a more demoralized creature. Intuitively, she reached her arm around the girl, sparing a precious moment to offer a comfort most desperately needed.

"Ye've done quite well, *leanbh*, for one untrained," Maggie spoke softly, "but neither yer skill nor mine are enough to finish the job." The sidhe paused as Kara quaked uncontrollably at her words. "But do ye trust me, love? All is'na lost, if ye'll trust me. I'll need ye by me if we're to save him."

There was a glint of madness in Kara's eyes when her head whipped up from Maggie's shoulder. "Aye, the price may be a bit dear," Maggie rushed on, "but there is a way. Will ye trust me?"

"*Please.*" The girl breathed the single word as if she couldn't manage more of a petition. Maggie could not help but be stirred; never had she heard someone communicate so much with a single word. She had to move swiftly though, for

Kara nearly dropped Quicksilver in her effort to clutch Maggie's arm, trying to convey with a viselike grip what it seemed she couldn't put into words.

Quicksilver? How had the girl come by the violin? How in the name of Danu had she gotten past the protections? Moreover, how did she do it without Maggie even being aware of the fact? The sidhe put the thought from her mind. They didn't have time for catching up on details right now. There was a man to save.

"Where is yer mother?" she asked the girl.

"She's at the pub next door," Kara answered, "I found the passage through the caverns, the one that led to the old woman's basement." Maggie was amused that the girl showed no repentance for thwarting her efforts to protect them.

"Through Molly's basement, then? I have'na even thought o' that way out in decades." Maggie called to the others on the roof, "Miach, will ye be watchin' over Patrick a moment? Kara an' I must take care o' a few thin's.

"Do'na worry, lass, Miach has the gift o' healin'. He'll see to yer father 'til we're back. Come along, then."

On an impulse, Kara stooped to lay Quicksilver in her father's arms before she hurried after Maggie. It would only hinder her at the moment, and she hoped that its familiarity might comfort him. "I love you, Papa. I'll pay any price," Kara whispered in his ear. She liked to think his brow smoothed a little from its pained tension.

"Kara, time is dear," Maggie called to her from the door to the stairwell. Kara hurried to join her, praying under her breath that the woman really could help her save Papa.

As they hurried down the stairs, Kara listened to Maggie explain what they were about. "First we must collect yer mother. Once she's with us, we must gather those items here that canna fall into other hands than mine. Some o' them will give us the power we need to see yer father well, the others, 'twould be a danger to leave them to be found."

Kara let the woman talk. She didn't care what went on, as long as Papa would be well afterward. She would follow Maggie and do as she asked; there was no energy for anything more. In fact, Kara was surprised to reach the ground floor on her feet, rather than in a tumbled heap. She never would have thought she had the strength left for an all-out sprint after what she'd already managed today. Adrenaline must have something to do with it, she reasoned, or sheer nerves. It was a good thing too, for Maggie didn't slow down when she reached the side entrance. She leapt across the alley to bang on Molly's door, deftly avoiding the ever-present bowl of cream. As Kara caught up with the sidhe, she was glad she hadn't been sent alone to fetch her mother; the tavern owner answered the door armed with a .22 for protection. Of course, having seen the woman brandish a broom, Kara had to wonder why she would even need the gun.

For a moment, Kara was afraid they were going to have trouble with Molly. Her fear faded away nearly instantly. With no more than a grunt and a cautious glance up and down the alley, Molly pushed open the screen to let them in.

"'Tis over, Molly, but for the cleanin' up an' the healin'," Maggie reported abruptly as she walked into the kitchen. Her eyes darted around until she found what she was looking for. The next second, she was across the room, kneeling beside Kara's mother. "We must speak to ye, now."

Kara's heart ached as she saw her mother's face crumble in anticipation of her worst fear. Madness still hovered in those eyes. "No, Mathair," she supplied hurriedly, joining them. "It isn't as bad as that...yet." Kara gripped her mother's hand when she added that last. There was no softening the situation. It was best out at once.

With a frightened and heavy heart, Kara watched Maggie sit down next to her mother. It occurred to her that the next few minutes would decide the future for all of them, and Kara herself had no idea what Maggie had in mind to save Papa. She had meant it when she'd told him she would pay any price, but she couldn't speak for her mother. *Would Mathair find the strength for whatever Maggie was about to ask of her?* Slumping into the chair beside her mother, Kara waited numbly for Maggie to speak. As faded as she felt, there was little else she could do. She barely found the energy to lift the thick broth Molly placed before her to her mouth.

"Barbara, we've come to tell ye that yer husband has suffered a mortal wound." Maggie's bluntness startled Kara enough that she allowed her mug to thud as she placed it on the table. *Where was the compassion she was used to hearing in the sidhe's voice?* Kara could hardly believe it when Maggie continued her brusque delivery of the facts. "There's no time to be gentle about it if we're to save his life; do ye both understand me?"

"What do you need us to do?" As she spoke, Kara moved her chair even closer to her mother's, and rested her arm protectively over Mathair's shoulders. "What can we possibly do?"

"What about a hospital? Has anyone called an ambulance? Arn's number is on my key ring...." Barbara O'Keefe sounded dazed and anxious and Kara had the feeling that she was reaching for the commonplace to stave off the fantastic reality that she didn't want to acknowledge, regardless of all she had seen already. Maggie shook her head ruefully and Kara watched as the half-hearted hope fell away from her mother's face.

"Ye must both listen closely to what I tell ye." Maggie's unyielding gaze caught and held each of their eyes until Kara had to blink against the intensity. "We've but one chance to save yer Patrick's life, an' 'tis'na an easy one.

"There is a feast held in my land...."

Kara and her mother sat there in stunned silence as Maggie went on to explain the Fledh Ghoibhnenn and how the food and drink of that feast made one immortal. Maggie kept it basic, which suited Kara. Mathair wasn't too up on the legends to begin with, let alone ready to accept them as reality. Kara was familiar with this feast, thanks to Grandda, but she never imagined that would be Maggie's solution. Should they agree, for Maggie couldn't take such action without their agreement, the clouds would carry Patrick away to *Tir na nÓg* to be presented to Goibhniu, the smith god, whose hospitality would include the draught of ale that would keep him from any further ravages of illness, age, and death.

"If ye canna bring yerselves to take the chance I offer, then we'd best be gettin' back to him..." here Maggie paused solemnly, "to say our goodbyes."

The overwhelming chill of those last words gripped Kara as harshly as if she'd plunged into an icy river. She could not bear to think of Papa's death, though the thought of him living forever was a bit frightening in its own right. She had to wonder which he would choose, if he could answer. *Was it a curse to live forever, or the greatest gift imaginable? Even worse, to a good Catholic man, would it be sacrilege? Would he eventually damn them for how they answered for him today?* In the chair beside her, Mathair gasped. Kara could feel the tremors that shook her. One look at her mother's face told her that the same dilemma warred behind those haunted eyes. Their gazes locked and each read clearly in the other's the bald truth: Patrick O'Keefe's life rested in their hands, but did they damn his soul to save him? In the end, neither of them doubted which they chose.

"Will I be left behind?" Her mother's voice was so full of fear and resignation that Kara hugged her even closer, though her eyes never left Maggie's face. She couldn't help but feel a pang of guilt at the awesome flash of agony she briefly saw in the sidhe woman's eyes. How drastically had the events of this day transformed all their lives?

"Do'na believe it, love," Maggie's smile was weary, but kind. "An ye think ye can take it, we'll all o' us ride the clouds tonight, but we must hurry."

Standing on the rooftop, by a pool of blood made ebony by the setting of the moon, one of the few signs that remained of the brutal battle so recently ended, Kara felt stunned at the reality of what she had been too focused to see in the midst of battle. The scenes burned into her memory could have come from any number of news clips from the conflict in Middle East. Thinking back to the raw energy she herself had tossed around, she was horrified to realize that some of the damage had been wrought by her own hand. Her eyes fell to the body of Lucien; he lay in a pool of someone else's blood, drool trailing from his lip and down his chin. Yes, she was directly responsible for some of this damage—all of it, indirectly. Her heart quivered in her chest, thrown off-beat by the reality of this battlefield. She hovered on the brink of guilt and insanity. *What had her life become? What had she become?*

"No, love, no!" Out of nowhere, Maggie hovered next to her, wrapping her in loving, immortal arms. "Do'na think such black thoughts. No fault o' this belongs at yer feet. These men came here to do an evil deed, an' there's no knowin' the whole o' it if they'd managed to get their hands on ye." Maggie squeezed her closer and then stepped back, her hands still gripping Kara's shoulders. "I canna tell ye to let it all go; this night's a part o' ye forever. But, love, be careful what ye choose to learn from tonight's deeds. An' either way, the learnin' 'tis for later; we've still work to do."

At Maggie's gentle rebuke, Kara looked across the rooftop where the others prepared to leave. She watched in amazement as all signs of battle disappeared: blood dried up and blew away on a gently assisted breeze, sidhe bodies faded in a sparkly shimmer of dust (every speck of which was carefully collected in what looked like black velvet bags), and the dead and injured invaders were just suddenly not there.

Kara was so stunned by the events of the past few hours that she didn't even wonder where they were sent; she didn't really care, as long as they were gone. The only evidence of the conflict that had not been banished was Lucien Blank and his henchman, Tony. Apparently something resisted the sidhe's efforts to transport them. She trembled uncontrollably as she turned from the disturbing sight.

Around her, Kara noticed the efficient activity of the Sidhe. In totally focused silence and with economy of motion, they gathered their belongings and prepared to leave. From the looks of the growing pile beside Papa, Yesterday's Dreams had been looted of everything Maggie considered important. There were old books and statues, elaborately carved walking sticks and works of embroidery, even weapons, though Kara had to wonder who in New York City would own, let alone have pawned the ancient-looking sword with the inlayed hilt. The pile could not hold her attention long, though, for now the sidhe readied themselves. Some would join them on their trip to Tir na nÓg—Kara trembled at the mere thought of entering the legendary Land of Youth—the others would return to their own tasks here in the city. Miach, the sidhe with the iridescent hair and a gift for healing, was one of those who would come with them. Right now he was making Papa comfortable for the fantastic journey they were about to take. Beside them, with Quicksilver cradled in her lap where Papa could see it, sat Mathair, anxiously holding his hand. Kara could see the look of love in her father's eyes as he tried his best to hold Mathair's hand in return.

Watching them, Kara knew a moment's peace. She couldn't even begin to imagine what repercussions this night would have, but life definitely wouldn't be the same. Kneeling beside her beloved parents, she kissed each of them and gently extracted Quicksilver from her mother's grasp.

"I'm going to need her for this, Mathair," she said gently.

As she turned away to join Maggie, Kara held the image of them in her mind like a talisman against the despair she would someday have to conquer, but not right now...now was the time to call the clouds.

The darkened rooftop glowed subtly with shimmering light as strands of ethereal music drifted through the air, beckoning the clouds the way one whistled to entice a puckish horse to come closer. Angelic voices sang sweetly, intertwining with the notes while golden mists thickened to shroud the rooftop. Mere heartbeats later, when the clouds lifted, only two broken men remained as testament to the battle.

EPILOGUE

In a fit of inhuman rage, Olcas gathered the remnants of the strength it had hoarded over the last ten years. For a few moments, it paused to relish the feel of mind-numbing power crackling across what could only be called its nerves. The as-yet undirected energy charged the air randomly. Bolts of lightning darted about the sky. Just below the presence of Olcas, Lucien huddled, beaten and completely mad from the girl's attack. Too late, the entity had realized its error in thinking the psychically retarded man below could be anything more than a governed tool, forever doomed to a minimal level of achievement.

Now the boy...he was a totally different matter. Tony huddled on the far side of the rooftop with a vacuous look in his eyes. His physical wounds were nothing; the psychic ones required only time to be healed. Even left to himself, the boy's body and mind would slowly recover from the shock of all he'd experienced that night.

Of course, it was a moot point. Olcas gloated with the complete, pinpoint focus of the obsessed over the opportunity the helpless Tony represented. A flood of pure power would resolve two problems at once.

Using the precision of an adept, Olcas hurled a portion of the crackling energy at the empty shell that had been Lucien. The moment the power connected, the hunched mass arched backward with an insane, half-strangled scream. Current flooded the man's body and incinerated already scorched pathways in the shattered mind. While the black, smoldering husk fell back to the rooftop, still buzzing and twitching with the power that Olcas continued to feed it, its out-flung arm came to rest upon the boy. That one vital connection was all Olcas needed. Ignoring the sizzle as the pure power scorched the boy's leg at the contact point, Olcas carefully transmuted the force, shaping Tony into a most effective tool.

This time, it carefully kept the personality intact. Olcas didn't have ten years to rebuild this creature into something useful. Besides, all its time with Lucien had taught the entity quite a few interesting lessons about control. Next time, the

Áes Sidhe and their bastard children would not stand against him, not with a tool as powerful as this at Olcas' disposal.

As Tony arrogantly walked across the gaping void between the roof of the pub and that of the pawnshop, Olcas claimed a bit of revenge. Without looking back, Tony's hand rose slowly into the air, glowing with a dark, throbbing red light. At a snap of his fingers, the blackened body behind him exploded into crimson-edged flames that rapidly consumed both it and Yesterday's Dreams.

DANIELLE
ACKLEY-McPHAIL

Award-winning author Danielle Ackley-McPhail has worked both sides of the publishing industry for over seventeen years. Currently, she is a project editor and promotions manager for Dark Quest Books.

Her published works include four urban fantasy novels, *Yesterday's Dreams, Tomorrow's Memories*, the upcoming *Today's Promise*, and *The Halfling's Court: A Bad-Ass Faerie Tale*. She is also the author of the non-fiction writers guide, *The Literary Handyman* and is the senior editor of the *Bad-Ass Faeries* anthology series, *Dragon's Lure*, and *In An Iron Cage*. Her work is included in numerous other anthologies and collections, including *Rum and Runestones, Dark Furies, Breach the Hull, So It Begins, By Other Means, No Man's Land, Space Pirates, Space Horrors, Barbarians at the Jumpgate*, and *New Blood*.

She is a member of The Garden State Horror Writers, the New Jersey Authors Network, and Broad Universe, a writer's organization focusing on promoting the works of women authors in the speculative genres.

Danielle lives somewhere in New Jersey with husband and fellow writer, Mike McPhail, mother-in-law Teresa, and three extremely spoiled cats. She can be found on LiveJournal (damcphail, badassfaeries, darkquestbooks, lit_handyman), Facebook (Danielle Ackley-McPhail), and Twitter (DMcPhail). To learn more about her work, visit www.sidhenadaire.com, www.literaryhandyman.com, or www.badassfaeries.com.

GLOSSARY

Áes Sidhe: Irish Gaelic for "the people of the hills". It was one of the names given to the old Irish gods, the Tuatha de Danaan, when they retreated under the hills (*sidhe*) after their defeat by the Milesians.

A ghrá!: Irish Gaelic for "O love!"

A ghrá mo chroí: Irish Gaelic for "Love of my heart."

Beag Scath: A combination of the Irish Gaelic words meaning "little" (*beag*) and "shadow" (*scath*). The name Maggie gave the sprite that became attached to her long ago in Eire.

Bodega: A Spanish word meaning "store" or "grocery store." The term is commonly used in the ethnic neighborhoods of New York.

By the silver hand o' Nuada!: A curse of the author's creation, used by Maggie. It is a reference to Nuada of the Silver Hand, the first ruler of the Dé Danaan, who lost his hand in a battle with the Firbolg (one of the many groups that inhabited Ireland before the Dé Danaan arrived). The injury lost him his throne because no king could rule who was not whole and able to defend his people. He was presented with his silver hand by Dian Cécht, the god of medicine, but it was not enough for him to take up his kingship. Later, Dian Cécht's son, Miach, made him a hand of flesh and blood and Nuada once again ruled the De Danaan. The basic implication of the curse is "Our greatest efforts sometimes fail at great cost."

Calma: Irish Gaelic for valiant. In some accounts, this is also the name of one of the three sons of the Athenian goddess Carmán.

Cara: Irish Gaelic for friend.

Carmán: An Athenian goddess who, with her three sons—Calma (Valiant), Dubh (Black), and Olcas (Evil), terrorized early Ireland. (In some accounts different names are given, usually with similar connotation.) They were eventually defeated by the Tuatha de Danaan. She was bound in chains and made to watch as her three sons were destroyed. It is said Carmán died of grief.

Connemara marble: A type of marble found only in Ireland, noted for its varied range of shades and the fact that it is a true marble.

Cúchulainn (the Hound of Culann): One of the most famous heroes in Irish mythology. Originally called Sétanta, Cúchulainn got his name from defending himself and slaying the hound that defended the fortress of Culann, after which he vowed to defend the fortress himself until a new hound could be found and trained, thus becoming known as the Hound of Culann. Though his achievements are many, he is chiefly known for his single-handed defense of Ulster during the war of the Táin.

Dubh: Irish Gaelic for black. In some accounts, this is also the name of one of the three sons of the Athenian goddess Carmán.

Earl Gerard: See *Gearoidh Iarla*

Eire: The original Celtic name for Ireland.

Falias, Finias, Gorias, and Murias: Four great cities said to be the former home of the Tuatha de Danaan, before they arrived in Ireland. Nothing more specific is mentioned of their original homeland.

Fionn Mac Cumhail (Finn Mac Cool): One of the most celebrated heroes in Irish myth. Born Demna, he gained the name of Fionn (the Fair One) when he burnt his finger on the flesh of the salmon of wisdom, which he was cooking for his master. Sucking his thumb to cool it, he obtained wisdom from the magical fish. He went on to become leader of the Fianna, the royal bodyguard. His wife was the goddess Sadb, who was transformed into a fawn by a spurned druid and whisked away while she was pregnant with Fionn's son. Fionn never found his wife, but his son, whom he named Oisín (fawn), eventually was discovered and came to be with him.

Fledh Ghoibhnenn: The otherworld feast held by the god Goibhniu. Any mortal to take part in the food and drink becomes immortal.

Gearoidh Iarla (Earl Gerard): A great man of the Fitzgeralds, he had a rath (fortress) at Mullaghmast. He was known for standing against injustice and for his abilities to transform himself to any form. It is said that he and his warriors now sleep in a long cavern under the Rath of Mullaghmast. Every seven years the earl rides round the Curagh of Kildare on a steed with silver hooves. At a time when those hooves are worn thin as a cat's ear, the miller's son with six fingers to each hand will blow his trumpet to wake the warriors and Gearoidh Iarla will return to the land of the living. He will defend Ireland against the English, and reign as Ireland's king for two-score years.

The Gentry: A name given to the sidhe by the common folk so that they could be referred to without invoking their name or drawing their uncomfortable attention.

Glamory: A spell to make whatever the caster wishes—himself, an object, or another person—appear other than what it really is.

Goibhniu the Smith: An Irish/Celtic blacksmith god. Son of the goddess Danu. He manufactures swords that always strike true, and he possesses the mead of eternal life. He is also considered the god of healing due to the role of iron in

Celtic life and the magical properties it is said to have. Goibhniu presides over an otherworld feast (*Fledh Ghoibhnenn*) where any mortal to take part becomes immortal, exempt from common death and disease.

Grimoires: ancient, mystical texts, usually full of dark occult knowledge. These texts contain the spells and references that represent painstaking research and experimentation, often of the dark arts, though the term has come to imply any book of spells, be they black or white magic.

Leanbh: Irish Gaelic for child.

Lhiannon: Irish Gaelic for sweetheart.

Mamó: Irish Gaelic for grandma.

Mathair: Irish Gaelic for mother.

The Miller's Son: It is said in the legend of *Gearoidh Iarla*, that the miller's son, who will be born with six fingers on each hand, will blow his trumpet and wake those who sleep beneath the Rath of Mullaghmast.

Olcas: Irish Gaelic for evil. In some accounts, this is also the name of one of the three sons of the Athenian goddess Carmán.

Oisín (little fawn): Son of Fionn Mac Cumhail and the goddess Sadb. Oisín's mother was transformed into a fawn and spirited away from her husband while she was pregnant with him. She bore him as a human child and raised him in her deer shape until he was a young boy. Found by his father, Oisín grew up in the midst of the Fianna and became one of their leading champions.

Pharo! Pharo!: An ancient Celtic battle cry, possibly a corruption of *faire ó!* (look out, ó!)

Rath (fortress): A fortress or earthwork, usually circular, surrounding a chieftain's house. This has also come to mean the hills where the Tuatha de Danaan retreated beneath after their defeat by the Milesians.

Rath o' Mullaghmast: The fortress of *Gearoidh Iarla* (Earl Gerald). This is where legend says the miller's son will blow his trumpet.

The Rom: These are nomadic gypsies, most common in Europe, but found in one form or another around the world.

The Seelie Court: (Holy Court): Comprised of those fae seen as good and kindly toward mankind.

The Sidhe: The fair folk. Otherworldly beings living in Ireland in the time before it was invaded by the Milesans. After their defeat, they were banished underground, living in mounds, also called *sidhe*. They were said to be very long-lived, if not immortal, and possessing mystical powers. (See *Tuatha de Danaan, The Gentry, Áes Sidhe*)

Soul Savior: A part of the author's created mythology, a member of a select warrior group of the Daoine Maith, reborn of the Mother Goddess Danu, who were sent, just after the exodus to Ireland, to the original four cities of the ancestral homeland to destroy the ancient enemy, or *Namhaid*, and free the souls of those of their people held captive as hosts for the spawn of the enemy. The

Soul Saviors were marked as a sign of honor by a tattoo behind their right ear, a spiraling knotwork forming a perfect heart at the center. Also a part of the author's fabrication, the tattoo was later adapted by the Unseelie Court, an elitist branch of the sidhe and other magical creatures that started in Scotland, who view humans as unworthy and prey upon them.

Tir na nÓg (Land of Youth): Part of the Irish Celtic otherworld, this is where Goibhniu presides over the *Fledh Ghoibhnenn*.

Tír Tairnigiri (Land of Promise): Part of the Irish Celtic otherworld, this is where Manannan Mac Lir, the major sea-god, held his seat of power.

Tuatha de Danaan: The Children of Danu, another name for the sidhe, said to be blessed by the goddess Danu, also called Anu or Danaa.

Unseelie Court: Scottish for Unholy Court. In Scottish Celtic myth, the Unseelie Court is made up of elven creatures and other magical beings with a hatred for the human race. Always unfavorable toward mankind, they torment and harm their victims. Their counterpart is the Seelie (or Holy) Court.

Waterkin: a term originating with the author to describe those of mixed blood, with both a sidhe and human parent. It is originally a condescending term referring to the fact that the sidhe blood has been diluted...watered down, thus less than the original, though repeated use has reduced it to merely an identifier.

SOURCES

PRINT RESOURCES:

Ellis, Peter Berresford, *A Dictionary of Irish Mythology* (Santa Barbara, CA: ABC-CLIO, Inc, 1987.)

Ireland: The Complete Guide and Road Atlas, Seventh Edition (Guilford, CT: The Globe Pequot Press, 2002.)

Mac Mathúna, Séamus, and Ailbhe Ó Curráin, *Collins Gem: Irish Dictionary* (New York: HarperCollins Publishers, 1995).

Rolleston, T. W., *Celtic Myths and Legends* (Mineola, NY: Dover, 1990.)

Yeats, W. B., *Irish Fairy & Folk Tales* (New York: Barnes & Noble Books, 1993.)

INTERNET RESOURCES:

http://www.alia.ie/tirnanog/myth1.html
http://www.celticattic.com/olde_world/myths/fairy.htm
http://www.celt.net/Celtic/celtopedia/indices/encycintro.html
http://www.danann.org/library/herb/cup2.html
http://www.deoxy.org/h_mounds.htm
http://www.imbas.org/danubile.htm
http://www.innish.f9.co.uk/Powers/FaeTuath%20De%20Dannon.htm
http://joellessacredgrove.com/Celtic/deitiesg-h-i.html
http://www.ladywoods.org/roots4.htm
http://www.livingmyths.com/Celticmyth.htm
http://magickwell.20m.com/danu.htm
http://myducksoup.com/scotland/fantasy/fairy_oz.html
http://nikki.sitenation.com/celtic/danu.html
http://nikki.sitenation.com/celtic/sidhe.html
http://www.pantheon.org/articles/u/unseelie_court.html
http://www.seanachaidh.com/godcelt.html

Dark Quest Books Brings You
More Dark and Disturbing Fiction

...Great Titles from Dark Quest Books and Danielle Ackley-McPhail

BREACH THE HULL
9780979690198
SO IT BEGINS
9780979690150
BY OTHER MEANS
9780983099352
NO MAN'S LAND
9781937051020
Mike McPhail

DRAGON'S LURE
Danielle Ackley-McPhail
9780982619797

THE HALFLING'S COURT
Danielle Ackley-McPhail
9780979690167

THE LITERARY HANDYMAN
Danielle Ackley-McPhail
9781937051006

The books that put the Dark...

MYSTIC INVESTIGATORS:
9780979690143
BULLETS AND BRIMSTONE
9780982619735
and
FROM THE SHADOWS
Patrick Thomas
(Forthcoming)

DEAR CTHULHU:
HAVE A DARK DAY
9780979690137
and
GOOD ADVICE
FOR BAD PEOPLE
9780982619742
Patrick Thomas

HERE THERE BE MONSTERS
John L. French
9780982619773

WHERE ANGELS FEAR
CJ Henderson
and
Bruce Gewheiler
9780982619711

...into Dark Quest

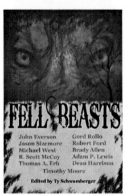

DARK FUTURES
Jason Sizemore
9780982619728

I KNOW NOT
James Daniel Ross
9781937051105

FELL BEASTS
Ty Schwamberger
9780983099376

GET HER BACK!
David Sherman
9780983099345

VAMPIRE CAREER
Phoebe Matthews
9780983099369

STO'S HOUSE PRESENTS...
BEER WITH A MUTANT CHASER
KT Pinto
9781937051297

EARTHDOOM
David Langford
and John Grant
978098309939

Please see our website for further details www.darkquestbooks.com

New Releases...

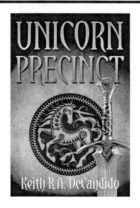

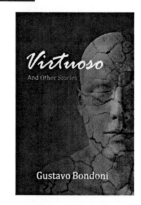

DRAGON PRECINCT
9781937051280
UNICORN PRECINCT
9781937051150
Keith R.A. DeCandido

VIRTUOSO
Gustavo Bondoni
9781937051136

LEGENDS OF LONE WOLF
Joe Dever and John Grant
9780982619704

DEATH, BE NOT PROUD
edited by Thomas A. Erb
9781937051143

IN AN IRON CAGE
Danielle Ackley-McPhail
Elektra Hammond
and Neal Levin
9780982619742

RIVER
edited by Alma Alexander
9781937051235

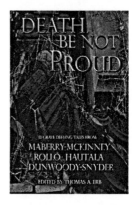